Light from Arcturus

by Mildred Walker

ILLUSTRAT

D1009108

Introduction to the Bison Book Edition
by Mary Swander

University of Nebraska Press
Lincoln and London

⊛ The paper in this book meets the minimum requirements of
American National Standard for Information Sciences—Permanence of
Paper for Printed Library Materials, ANSI Z39.48-1984

First Bison Book printing: 1995
Most recent printing indicated by the last digit below:
10   9   8   7   6   5   4   3   2   1

Library of Congress Cataloging-in-Publication Data
Walker, Mildred, 1905–
Light from Arcturus / by Mildred Walker; illustrated by Frank Peers;
introduction to the Bison Book ed. by Mary Swander.
p.   cm.
ISBN 0-8032-9769-6 (pbk.: alk. paper)
I. Title.
PS3545.A524L5   1995
813'.52—dc20
94-41323   CIP

Reprinted by arrangement with Mildred Walker Schemm.

TO JEANETTE

INTRODUCTION

By Mary Swander

While I was reading Mildred Walker's *Light from Arcturus*, a friend called asking my advice.

"I feel I should be somewhere else. That Iowa City just doesn't have enough opportunities for me. I'm considering moving to Chicago," she said.

My friend, a jazz musician, was longing for more stimulation and sophistication, higher paying gigs, and a better arts "scene." Yet both she and her partner had good jobs in Iowa, and he had family and business ties he didn't want to sever.

"David wouldn't want to leave," my friend said. "He's happy here. He has everything he wants, but I feel restless, like things just aren't happening for me."

Almost sixty years after the publication of Mildred Walker's novel, its basic plot replays itself over and over again. Walker was committed to dramatizing female individualism in the pages of her fiction. Like Julia Hauser, Walker's protagonist in *Light from Arcturus,* my friend registered the same, but most disturbing emotional dilemma that all women experience sometime in their lives. How do we balance our desires for fulfillment with those of our family and/or mate? How do we strike out on our own and achieve our own goals? What compromises are we willing to make for our security? For our freedom? What consequences are we to bear for our decisions?

Light from Arcturus is a midwestern novel of a woman's quest for self-realization, but its reverberations go way beyond the confines of regionalism. The book begins and ends with the constellations. In the opening chapter the light of Arcturus shines down on Julia and her new husband Max leaving Chicago in a Pullman car at the "breathless rate of twenty-five miles per hour" for the 1876 Centennial Fair in Philadelphia. In the closing chapter, Julia and her granddaughter rise up toward those constellations when they fly to California and away from the 1933 Chicago World's Fair. In between those two journeys, we follow the life of a woman as she struggles, both geographically and emotionally, to find a sense of place for herself.

The novel opens with Julia a young bride—a very young bride by today's standards. At seventeen, she innocently marries an older man who is almost a stranger to her but "a good catch" and approved of by her father. In a prescribed way, she leaves the Chicago of her childhood to follow her husband to Halstead, Nebraska, where he has a booming produce business. Her future seems "assured." Then, little by little, we begin to understand her discontent, her restlessness, her longing for more stimulation and sophistication. As Julia bears her children, as she settles in among the families of the other entrepreneurs in this small prairie town, we follow her initiation from innocence to experience.

In the classic *Bildungsroman*, a novel that traces such an initiation, the author follows the path of a sensitive child—usually a male—who grows up in the country or a provincial town and must go to the city to find his mature self. Walker's novel takes a spin on this standard structure. Here, Julia, a polished and well turned-out urbanite whose grandmother had been a lady of the Bohemian court, moves from Chicago to a rural provincial Nebraska town and then back again. On one level, Julia is not innocent at all. She is more worldly than either her husband or any of the other residents of Halstead. Nothing amazes her. She values the cultured life, wants "things to happen," and knows she has the confidence to achieve her goals. On another level, Julia is naive enough to think that she might achieve happiness in the conventional life she has chosen.

So Julia's conflict arises. While she makes her life and raises her family in Nebraska, she holds onto her dream of returning to Chicago. Her quest for fulfillment, her grail, becomes the World's Columbian Exposition of 1893. To herself, she rationalizes that the move will be good for her children, and until her old age, she fights admitting that her need to move to back to the city had more to do with her own betterment than theirs. She does regret the hardship the move placed upon Max and her guilt spills over into her advice to her own daughter to placate her husband. And so the cycle begins again.

For a contemporary reader, why does this story still have such a hold? I found myself galloping through these pages, at once fascinated, frustrated, sympathetic with and repelled by Julia. I was gripped by her dilemma, the societal oppression that even this privileged but fiery and highly intelligent woman suffered. I felt her alienation from her husband, who could only think and talk of making money. I felt her isolation in a small town with a big sense of Manifest Destiny. On the other hand, I wanted to scream at her for playing into that societal structure and placing such a high value on status. I wanted to see her break free of her trap and become actualized, to develop more consciousness of her role as a woman.

In the end, Julia's daughters do have more opportunities for growth than their mother and are seeming more independent women. Still, they all end up questioning their relationships to their partners and we witness each one of them trying to feel out her position in the world. Anne, who had once been the most adventuresome of the children, thinks that her daughter Therese, who has a brilliant musical career, would be better off married. Jennette wonders if she, like her mother in the past, should move from Chicago with her husband to a small midwestern town where he has the chance of a career advancement.

From a current feminist viewpoint, *Light from Arcturus* not only gives us a historical perspective on "trailing spouses" but on women's selfhood. Certainly, since the turn of the century, women have made strides in their sense of self-direction and careers. But don't many still feel they must justify their own steps by seeing them as ultimately for the good of others? Aren't women still socialized to give up the self in the service of family or the larger community? And isn't depression—a feeling of hopelessness, alienation, and isolation—still one of the biggest causes of illness among women?

In this Walker novel, the Midwest becomes a metaphor for Julia's psyche. This book reminds us that the stereotypical view of the happy woman pioneer, facing the hardships of the prairie with fortitude and cheerfulness, her bonnet shielding her eyes from the sun, her children pressed snugly into the folds of her skirt, is not always an accurate one. Many women, like Julia, hated leaving their families, the culture and good taste of the cities farther east, to follow their husbands across the plains in search of better farmland, entrepreneurship, or adventure. Without telephones, radios, televisions and all the communication systems we depend upon today to link us with the world, women could lead lonely lives. The perceived flatness and barrenness of the midwestern landscape could be equated with these women's emotional states.

Julia looked to the 1893 and 1933 World's Fairs to pull her out of her mental depression the same way these expositions helped pull the city of Chicago out of its economic plight. With a total attendance of over twenty-seven million, the 1873 Fair brought dollars, excitement, and a sense of optimism back to that midwestern city, and by extension, much of the rest of the country. In the midst of the Mauve Decade, five years after the outbreak of class violence at Haymarket Square, the White City rose up from the marshlands of the Lake Michigan shore to offer promise and hope. Electricity, then unfamiliar to most Americans, was one of the fair's chief wonders. With the push of a switch, President Grover Cleveland sent a current through the White City and the rest of the country. In his *Memoirs of an American Citizen*, 1905, Robert Herrick described the mood:

> The long lines of white buildings were ablaze with countless lights; the music from the bands scattered over the grounds floated softly out upon the water; all else was silent and dark. In that lovely hour, soft and gentle as was ever a summer night, the toil and trouble of men, the fear that was gripping men's hearts in the markets, fell away from men and in its place came Faith. The people who could dream this vision and make it real, those people. . . . would press onto greater victories than this triumph of beauty—victories greater than the world had yet witnessed.

Both the 1893 and the 1933 Fairs took up the banner of "progress," evolution toward a better standard of living, pride, and courageousness of the human will. Again, in 1933, electricity was seen as the hope for the future of humankind. By means of a photoelectric cell, a beam from Arcturus, which was received in a telescope at Yerkes Observatory, Williams Bay, Wisconsin, turned on the lights at the opening of the Century of Progress Fair.

By 1933, the sparks of Julia's life are beginning to extinguish. The ending of this character's life as well as the book is an enigma. Some will say that this woman realized her goal and that she and her children were better off for it. Other readers will say she only wrought hardship on herself and her husband, forcing herself into a another kind of exile of dependency during his long final illness. Some will say Julia muddled her way through to selfhood in a milieu of feminism unconsciousness. Others will say, that even though she may have reached a glimmer of enlightenment at the close of the book, we are still waiting for her to pull the switch.

"So, what do you think," my friend asked. "If you were me, would you try to drag David to Chicago?"

"What do you want to do?"

"He might end up with a better job there, make a lot more money than here . . . if I could just convince him of that."

"What do you want to do?"

"I don't know. I'm asking you."

I had no answers. I only had a book to offer. "Read this Mildred Walker novel." I told my friend. "It's for you."

CONTENTS

PART ONE   THE FIRE OF SPRING

THE stars burned unseeingly above the flashing, tortuous path of the Baltimore and Ohio's newest Pullman train. First the locked freight cars bearing the mysterious white muslin signs with the legend, "1776 INTERNATIONAL EXHIBITION 1876," had aroused curiosity. Now the endless stream of passenger trains created national excitement. But the stars had already known celebrations in Rome and the great expositions of the Pharaohs thousands of years before.

The darkness thinned into light. The dipper, Orion's belt, the North Star, and even Arcturus paled in the daylight. The passengers awoke and busied themselves with their intensely personal lives. They breakfasted in the amazing dining-car, eating bacon and eggs while the world whirled by at the breathless rate of twenty-five miles an hour. They settled themselves in their seats again.

I

Now it was mid-afternoon. The train would reach the Exposition city by six-thirty if it were on time. The red plush of the seats caught the sun on the left side. The little tassels of the window curtains bobbed together. The curved scrolls of the woodwork held train cinders in their intricate grooves. That was to be expected with the coal-burning engines. Some of the ladies swathed their hats in veils to keep them from the dust. What would our grandmothers have thought to ride like this, they asked each other. It was truly amazing.

But Julia Hauser sitting in the third seat from the end was not amazed. She would never be quite amazed. Her soft brown eyes surveyed the flying world with tranquil expectancy. There was a gentle poise about her head and shoulders born of her spirit rather than any actual experience of her seventeen years. The face turned to the window showed a childlike curve of cheek and chin and a puff of curly hair above a delicate pink ear. There was something: the soft texture of her skin, the extreme delicacy of her profile, or the poise of her slim young figure that was a heritage from the grandmother who had been a lady of the Bohemian court.

Her gaze came back from the moving trees to her new bottle-green dress, the cut-steel buckle, the shirrings on the gored skirt, her gray silk gloves. She took off her gloves for the twentieth time that day and looked again at the wide gold band on the third finger of her left hand. Julia Hauser was on her wedding trip.

Two days ago there had been a wedding-cake, five tiers high, covered with white icing, intricately fluted around the edges. Champagne, sparkling in the treasured goblets of Bohemian glass; quail, quivering in a mound of jelly, and thin bread spread with pâté de foie gras were arranged on the walnut table in the dining-room on Michigan Avenue.

2

Julia had married well. Her father approved of Max Hauser; he was thirty-five and dependable, much safer than someone closer to Julia's age. He had a good business in wholesale farm produce out in the coming town of Halstead, Nebraska. Julia's future seemed assured.

Max had joined a poker game in the smoking salon and disappeared behind the oak door at the end of the car an hour ago. Julia had studied the door a minute after it closed behind him, the three panels, the fret work at the bottom forming two birds and a harp, the heavy iron knob. The whole door looked masculine and somehow secretive just as the door at the other end that was identical, but bore the words "Ladies' Parlor," looked feminine and likewise secretive. The doors were separated by the whole length of red plush seats and the long narrow aisle. Julia wondered if that distance was symbolic of the distance that would always lie between her nature and Max's.

After seeing Max alone only in the cab on the way to a party or in the dim hall after a party, with the family moving around discreetly upstairs, it was queer to be with him all day on a train and have him in the berth across from her at night. He was so much older she had always thought of him with George, her sister's husband, and her father. It was somehow flattering to be grown up enough to marry Max Hauser.

Julia Hauser reached out to all that lay ahead. She wanted things to happen; that was the expectancy in her dark eyes. She had no fear that perhaps she would not be equal to them . . . that confidence was the secret of her poise. Now she was going to the Centennial Exposition on her wedding trip.

The polished door at the end of the car opened. Julia knew almost before she turned her eyes from the window that Max was through with his game. She filled her eyes with him; he was not quite handsome, but his hair was black and curly, his eyes blue. The moody line of his upper lip showed only a brown mustache to the world. Julia saw with pride how his eyes brightened to catch hers, and how his embroidered tie was of rich blue satin, and his coffee-colored trousers looked very fine indeed.

"Well, we're almost there!"

"Oh, Max, I can't wait to see it."

"Those fellows aren't anywhere near as good as my friends in Halstead." He dismissed the poker game and turned to the business of having a bride. "Better get ready, now, Julia."

Julia straightened her small velvet hat. Max held her elegant new tight-fitted coat of ostrich-trimmed velvet for her. She slipped into it and fitted the tiny loops around the two dozen buttons. She pulled on her gloves and took up her bag with the silver top and her serpent-headed parasol.

Max took his new derby hat from the bracket above their seat and blew the accumulated dust from the rim. Then he lifted his coat tails and sat down by Julia.

He reached over and took her hand and held it tightly beneath his hat as the train pulled into the station at Philadelphia. They were facing an eastern city and a great spectacle. He squeezed Julia's arm protectively. She was so young and pretty; he felt older and stronger and better versed in the ways of the world. For just a second when he had looked at her during the minister's words she had seemed a little too exquisite, too removed from him. Her eyes, dark spots in the softly glowing face, had looked back at him as though they expected almost more than he could give. He had been uncomfortable with emotion that he could not express, but now they were going to the Great Exposition on their wedding trip. They would stay at the finest hotel in Philadelphia and see everything. He would build her a fine new house next spring. He would give Julia all she wanted, a carriage of her own when the roads were better. . . .

The train jerked to a sudden stop; the violent expulsion of steam made a tremendous sissing noise. There were calls of the cab drivers and the sharp sound of trotting horses. Max helped his bride down the steps to the station platform. They became part of a procession.

2

IT was raining outside the long station roof, a slow October drizzle. Cabs stood in line the length of the square; the backs of the horses and the tops of the cabs shone wetly in the light from the street lamps. The city was a steel engraving—the black masses of solid objects standing out against the fine gray lines cut by the rain. Under the lights the yellowing poplars and horse-chestnut trees were golden-leaved.

Max Hauser stepped into the cab after his wife, and the horse started down the street at a smart trot. Julia sat forward a little to look out of the window.

"Max, isn't it queer that we're in Philadelphia when only three days ago we were in Chicago?"

Max smiled down at her. She lighted up so over things as though the thing she gazed at were happening just for her. That's what he had noticed first about her, even before her delicate coloring and dark curling hair. She didn't squeal the way some women did when they were excited, either, she just kind of glowed.

"Look, Julia, the driver's pointing over there with his whip. That must be the Fair grounds where those lights are. Do you want to go there tonight after our dinner or shall we wait?"

"I'd rather wait; don't let's see it first in the rain. Oh, Max, see the white steps of the houses and the door-knockers and the straight line of trees. It's a nice, orderly city."

"But it will never grow like Chicago will, Julia," Max pronounced impressively.

The moist fall air made pungent the smell of the horse and the leather and plush of the cab. Mingled with it, too, was the faint odor of Max's hair pomade and the eau de Cologne on his handkerchief. Julia took her lace-edged handkerchief from her bag and there was added another scent, of verbena.

Julia leaned back in the seat. Max put his arm around her gently. "Remember the night on the balcony at the Tremont House, Jule?"

Julia's eyes were bright in the darkness of the cab.

Max Hauser had a flair for knowing the right occasion. He had asked her to marry him in the famous old hotel on Randolph Street. It had been her first public ball. The big gas chandelier suspended in the immense space of the hotel was brilliant with light. The dancers were bright moving figures, all handsome and beautiful, seen from the vantage point of the balcony. She was grown up; no longer Polly's little sister, but old enough to have George's friend, Max Hauser, a business man from the West, bow over her hand and sign his initials opposite every dance. When he asked her to marry him, Julia Stepinka had answered yes simply, not blushing with eyes bent on her dance program or fingers twiddling with her fan, but looking at him with smiling eyes, seeing him a little taller with just a touch more flash in his eyes than was there in truth. And then there had been the wedding and now the trip.

Julia watched the passing street lamps and the gleaming white steps of Chestnut Street. The cab turned a corner. A German band stood around a lamp-post playing *Im Lauterbach*. Max opened the window and threw a silver dollar into the ready cap of the nearest player. The man beamed. Julia leaned her head back to let it rest a second against Max's arm. She caught her breath in a little rapturous sigh. The cab came to a stop before the lighted doorway of the Lafayette House.

3

JULIA lay still in the carved bed of the hotel bedroom. Diffidently she looked through the parted chenille portières over to the alcove. She watched Max shave, much as a child watches some curious operation, wondering if it were not dangerous to scrape that long sharp blade back and forth over the lather on his face. Now he was almost finished. Through half-closed eyelids Julia watched him brush and wax his generous mustache, carefully twisting the ends in his fingers. Then he adjusted his low collar and tied the big knot of his cravat. Men's clothes were queer; she had never thought of them before.

He came across to her side of the bed and bent over to kiss her, such a different kiss from last night's, fragrant with the clean smell of shaving-soap, the cigar in his pocket, the woolen scent of his suit. He was so loving, but somehow clumsy as he bent to kiss her.

"Good morning, my dear, I thought you were still asleep. Well, I'll go down in the lobby and read the paper while you dress."

She smiled back at him, an odd little smile scarcely her own, rather a smile that had come with this new rôle of being married, a wifely smile.

"I'll get right up, Max."

Max saw her as she reached the bottom of the stairway and came across the lobby to meet her. He had bought a boutonnière from the flower-woman at the door, and it gave him a festive air. His smile greeted her admiringly.

"Max, how sweet." Julia pinned the flowers he had brought her into the ribbon that belted her slender waist. She laid her fingers on his arm, and they went into the big hotel dining-room.

The dining-room of the Lafayette House was magnificent. Solid oak paneling reached twenty feet high to a wide plate rail. Above the railing red damask covered the walls between the large oil paintings of game and fish that were inset in the wall. The wide windows were heavily curtained in net and made even wider in effect by the floor-length velvet draperies that crossed above the window in a deep loop.

A waiter with curling mustache and low side-burns pulled out Julia's chair and seated her with a flourish at a table in one of the bow windows. Bright sun poured in on the white tablecloth and silverware and broke into brilliant splinters of light on the cutglass cruet. The sun shone, too, on Max's white shirt-front and his stiff cuffs. A sense of well-being poured from him.

"They serve a later breakfast, I found out; we could have slept a little longer," said Max, smiling.

"Oh, no, Max, you forget we came to see the Centennial."

"I'd have reason enough to forget," Max answered gallantly.

Julia's mouth twitched at the corners, but she looked at him primly over her menu.

"Do you suppose all these people have come just to the Centennial, Max?"

"They say on Pennsylvania Day they had over twenty-five thousand. But I know there was no other bride there as lovely as mine."

Julia's color deepened. Her eyes met his again across the cutglass cruet and dropped to her plate. "Oh, Max," she murmured in a low pleased voice. It was to hear this that the yards and yards of tiny plaiting had been set in laborious scallops around her skirt and the toque bought at Gossage's. Max smiled tenderly if a little complacently as he consulted the menu again.

"Scrapple is a famous dish here, Julia. We'll have to try it."

Max had engaged a victoria to take them to the Fair. He had already obtained a map of the Centennial grounds and their visitors' badges. Julia admired his masterful way of managing everything. He had even gone back for her parasol and reticule. He was perfect.

Life itself was perfect this morning, a spectacle one saw from a stylish victoria with a plush robe tucked around one's knees and gloved fingers tucked in one's husband's a little shyly beneath the robe. Here in the morning light one could forget about having been an actor in that startling, discomfiting drama that went on at night back of the heavy Nottingham curtains. Their horse broke into a trot, his head held high, his hoofs ringing out sharply. All the world was passing by in landaus or broughams or on foot, drawn irresistibly toward one of the thirteen entrances of the Fair.

The carriage crossed the beautiful new Girard Avenue bridge.

"See there, Julia, there're the buildings; that's the Fair."
Max's voice announced it as though he presented it to her
as a gift.

4

THE bright October sun set in bold outline the figures on
Memorial Hall, the great brazen eagles, the fluttering flags,
the tall towers of the gigantic central building. Crowds
streamed in between the buildings; the ladies' parasols
were so many moving toadstools between the high silk
hats and derbies of the men. The excitement of the throngs
of people was contagious.

Max handed his bride down from the carriage. They
stood together under the roof of the guest pavilion. A
slow, satisfied smile spread over Max's face.

"Well, Jule?"

"It's wonderful, Max!" Her eyes danced under the
coquettish tilt of the gray velvet hat.

They stopped before the big desk in the pavilion. Max
signed the register in a flowing hand with shaded capitals
and a fine dash to the downward strokes, "Mr. Max
Hauser and wife, Halstead, Nebraska, October 12, 1876."

"Max, the Nebraska looks so queer." A momentary
shadow fell on her mood. She still thought of herself as
living in Chicago, Illinois. But then they turned and went
out to the Main Building where half the treasures of the
world seemed gathered.

In the building they climbed the stairs of one of the
towers and stood silently in the balcony. The spectacle
below them was dazzling even with broad daylight resting
on the imitation ivory and gold, showing up the props and
framework of the booths. The people were real; people

from everywhere, and gave the glamor of a crowd promenading before the café de la Paix or sauntering through Hyde Park. One man in the aisle below turned his face up toward them, and the light through the colored panes of glass over a doorway dyed his face a deep sea-green.

"Oh, how funny he looks!" Julia giggled and turned toward Max. His expression was one of awe and deepest solemnity.

"I never saw anything so beautiful, Julia!"

Max's complete absorption in the grandeur of the spectacle sobered Julia's giggling. But she couldn't help seeing things like the man with the green face, the woman trying to take the lollypop from the little boy, the fat Chinaman smoking a long pipe in front of the Chinese façade.

On the main floor they lingered before the booth of Cheney silks and the Wedgwood pottery exhibit. Max was interested in wax flowers indistinguishable from real ones and a massive vase of Gorham silver plate. Then Julia saw a malachite mantel from Russia.

"Max, look! We must have one like that in our drawing-room."

"But, Julia, the houses in Halstead don't have drawing-rooms; they just have parlors and most of them just sitting-rooms."

"Why, Max, everybody has a drawing-room; I shall make the parlor into a drawing-room, with chenille portières and Nottingham curtains, and, Max, think how lovely it would look with a mantel like this."

"You better wait till you get to Halstead," said Max patiently.

"I think I'll have a white paper with gold flowers," Julia went on sweetly, going past the bronze "Tauro Farnese" unseeingly.

"There's something I wish we could buy," said Max,

turning toward the display of bicycles. "They say they'll be common in America some day.

"There's that telephone booth I read about in the paper. A man by the name of Bell invented it." Max pointed with his cane, the pleasure of explaining things to a wife was new to him. He shielded Julia with his arm as they pushed into the crowd around the queer little house. Through the glass window they could see the odd contraption.

"You can talk through it and be heard in another house, they say. I read that the Emperor of Brazil tried it out and it worked."

"I'd like to try it a minute," Julia said impulsively.

"Oh, I don't think I would, Julia; my wife's too precious to experiment with." He put his arm around her and led her past the booth. "We've done enough sight-seeing for one morning, Julia. Suppose we have dinner now, and then take a ride through the grounds."

They had dinner in Lauber's German Restaurant, and Max ordered from the German side of the menu without ever looking at the English side.

"We don't have restaurants like this out in Halstead," he remarked wistfully, wiping his mustache with the square yard of napkin. But Julia was watching the people in the restaurant.

They filled the afternoon with a ride around the grounds and more sauntering through the foreign exhibits. At the Scotch end of the English exhibit Max bought her a Paisley shawl.

"I put off buying you a wedding gift, Julia, until we got here; I thought you'd rather have something from the Fair. There, try that one on."

A smiling salesman draped the shawl around her.

"Oh, Max, it's lovely, but it's too heavy. . . ." Julia hesitated. Max seemed to like it so well. . . . Shawls were going out of style, except for older women; Dil said so. She didn't want to hurt his feelings only there were so many other things she would rather have.

"And it costs so much, Max," she said hopefully.

"Never you mind that, my dear, this is your wedding gift."

It was too late; Max was paying the man. Julia looked at the coral earrings in the glass case.

"Thank you, Max," she said slowly.

"I have a feeling of missing things we came to see," Julia said wistfully, walking towards the turnstile gate on their way home that evening.

"We can't see everything in one day, and we've got plenty to talk about when we get home now."

"Max, turn around and look at it again. You can even make out the Horticultural Hall and that big Catholic Abstinence Fountain."

They stood still to look again at the buildings, larger and more unreal in the light from the street lamps. The stained-glass windows of the Art Building were green and blue and blood-red. The flags above the buildings fluttered darkly against a darker sky. Julia thought suddenly, nobody sees them but me. She stole a glance at Max. He was looking at his watch.

5

WHEN Julia came downstairs the next morning, she wore the brown poplin with the yellow pipings.

Max put up his paper and came to meet her. "I met some

13

people from Nebraska, Jule. I said we'd join them after breakfast and go on to the Fair together."

"Oh, Max, I wanted to see the Art Building just with you. It doesn t matter, though, of course."

"I think they'll be good company, my dear, and you and the ladies can visit when you get tired of sight-seeing."

Julia said no more. There would be another day when they could go alone.

Max's new friends waited by the front window of the Ladies' Ordinary.

"Jule, this is Mr. Fleet; he's from Omaha same as my brother, Rudolph, and this is his partner, Mr. Ross."

Julia bowed.

Mr. Fleet admired her openly. "Make you acquainted with Missus Fleet, Missus Ross . . . Missus Hauser." The women rose to greet her with energetic handshaking.

"This is nice to meet someone right at the start," Mrs. Ross began.

"It's such a big Fair, I had no idea; I say you might easily feel kinda lost," Mrs. Fleet explained amiably.

Julia smiled. These women were as old as her mother. Perhaps she and Max could go by themselves after all. She looked over at Max. He had lighted a cigar with Mr. Ross and Mr. Fleet, and they were deep in talk of Nebraska.

"Do you like it in Nebraska?" Julia asked hopelessly.

"Omaha's a nice city," Mrs. Ross told her; "we like it fine."

"I love art," Mrs. Fleet said, as they drove through the Fair grounds toward the Art Building. "I have a sister in Connecticut who does beautiful china painting. I promised to see if there was anything as pretty as hers in the Fair."

Mr. Fleet helped the ladies down. He took Julia's elbow, going up the steps.

"The cat's out of the bag, Mrs. Hauser, we hear you're on your honeymoon!"

Julia looked into his jovial red face.

"Yes," she answered, annoyed at Max.

Once inside the spacious rotunda of Memorial Hall even the men's voices dropped to a whisper. Julia was strangely moved. The high arches of the building, the white figures of the statuary, the rich colors of two great Sèvres vases, gave her an indefinable feeling of quiet. She had even forgotten that she was on her wedding trip. She had caught the feeling she had wanted the Fair to give her. But it was too big a feeling, too diffuse to keep, except in your memory of it. Maybe this was the way Max had felt when he looked down from the balcony with such a solemn expression on his face.

Julia looked around for him. He was looking at a buffalo surmounted by incongruous nymphs. He and Mr. Fleet were laughing at it together. She came up beside him and put her hand timidly on his coat sleeve.

"Look at this, Julia, did you ever hear of nymphs riding on a buffalo?" His eyes twinkled.

Julia walked back to the women, the exalted feeling dimmed a little.

"Mr. Ross says we better go ahead and look at the statues by ourselves." Mrs. Ross gave a knowing smile. "My goodness! look at that one over there!" she whispered with a quick glance back at the men.

The three ladies stood in front of a tall white statue, fleshlike and voluptuous even in marble. A cherubic cupid held both dimpled hands over the eyes of the lovely female figure.

"Love Blinds, Barcaglia," Mrs. Ross read slowly from the bronze title-plate on the base.

15

Mrs. Fleet giggled a little. "I s'pose that's the way with you, Mrs. Hauser?"

Julia smiled politely.

"Look at that; that head is done by a woman. You'd never think a woman could, would you?" Mrs. Fleet asked in awe.

Julia closed her ears to their chatter, filling her eyes with the statues and the paintings. It seemed to her that passion and pride and agony and joy were exaggerated. These were emotions she had scarcely felt. She wondered if Julia Hauser in her brown poplin with the yellow pipings would ever experience so much. The paintings were strangely disturbing; they awed her a little, yet she kept gazing at them with an eager curiosity.

As they left, Julia turned back to look through the archway toward the main rotunda. The cool pilasters, harmonious arches, tall windows, were a rest after the paintings.

6

"YOU see, Julia, they were nice folks." They had said good-by to the Fleets and Rosses.

"Yes, but I'm glad to be by ourselves again, Max. I mean . . ."

"Of course, my dear." Max reached over to pat her hand. "We'll have dinner at that big French restaurant, Le Sudreau, and listen to the concert in the open air pavilion." Max was young tonight. He looked very handsome in Julia's eyes.

"We must stop and have our photographs taken, Julia; everyone does at the Fair."

They walked along the path, her hand on his arm,

holding her skirt up with the other, his cane flashing in and out, very blithe and gay.

In the Photographic Building they took their places in front of the painted forest.

"The gentleman sits down, so; the lady standing." The photographer had a bushy beard, glasses on a ribbon, a flowing tie. His very appearance suggested the artist.

"That is right!" the photographer approved.

"I don't want it that way." Max jumped up from his chair. "I want a separate photograph of each of us."

The photographer looked dismayed. He shrugged his shoulders and lifted his hands in a hopeless gesture.

"Sit down, Jule; take off your hat so I can see your hair." Julia smiled behind her hat as she took it off. Max was so funny when he got excited. His eyes flashed and his voice rumbled. She straightened the gathers of her skirt demurely.

"No, no, not against those trees, against something white, a profile," Max directed. He walked to the back of the studio to see Julia. She stood now against a white sheet, looking out toward the window. Her eyes were wistful, the expression on her face was touchingly youthful.

Julia laughed when it was over. "Did I look awful, Max?" she called back to him.

"A little serious; what were you thinking of, my dear?"

"Oh, lots of things. Now it's your turn."

Max sat in the chair. "I want a front face," he told the photographer. He felt he was handsomer front view. His jaw was not rugged enough from the side. He smiled slightly. But the face caught in the photographer's lens was impassive; the tell-tale line of his upper lip was hidden too well behind his curled mustache.

"They'll be ready tomorrow," the photographer told them.

MAX sat down heavily in his chair at the restaurant.

"It's hard work sight-seeing!"

"Oh, no, Max, I love it." Julia's eyes roved happily over the crowds in the dining-room.

Max turned to the beverage list. He lingered a second over the Rhine wine and lager beer. . . . No, this was his wedding trip.

"Champagne," he told the waiter.

Max had eyes only for his bride. It bothered him that she hadn't liked those folks today. What if she shouldn't like Halstead? He looked at Julia. She was happy now. . . . Well, he was just tired. . . . Her face was all lighted up. Her cheeks were softly pink. He reached over and patted her hand.

The head waiter saw the gesture. He took a rose from one of the tall Haviland vases on the long buffet and gave it to her, bowing stiffly from the waist.

Julia's color heightened. She took the rose with a quick glance at the next table.

"See, you mustn't, Max," she whispered, pulling her hand away. She wished that Max wouldn't, well, wouldn't . . .

"You're so lovely, Julia," Max leaned toward her to say in a low voice.

"Pardon," the waiter murmured discreetly at her elbow, placing their plates before them. He ladled clear bouillon from a silver tureen. Julia's eyes fell on the cupid that formed the handle of the silver cover. She thought of the cupid holding his hands before the woman's eyes in Memorial Hall. Love is blind it meant.

They came out from the restaurant and walked around the lake and the playing fountain. They sat on one of the curved benches. Max smoked his cigar contentedly. Julia looked pensively across the green. She watched a young man on the other side of the circular path. A young woman in a shimmering pink dress was with him. The young man's face showed clearly in the light from the iron lamp back of the bench. His hair was yellow and very wavy. He bent over his companion to hear what she said. Then he put back his head and laughed. The laughter hurt Julia queerly. They were so gay; they were her own age. He couldn't be more than twenty. They must be on their wedding trip. Julia looked back to Max quickly.

"Tired, Jule?"

"Oh, no; yes, I guess I am," she answered slowly.

"I'll hail a victoria and we'll go back to the hotel; it'll be a nice ride with the top back."

The night was hushed in spite of the sharp trot of horses' hoofs coming and going along the river drive. There was a musty smell of dead leaves and a tantalizing hint of wild grapes in the air. The Schuylkill flowed silently below the road. A boat gleamed white and then shot into darkness against the bank.

She wished—only that was it; she couldn't put it into words even for herself—not that she and Max would live happily ever after, that wasn't quite it, it was more than that—that this feeling of living at the very crest of the world would never quite go.

Max threw away his cigar and pulled her closer to him.

"What, love?"

"Max, call me Julia, please; it sounds too silly," Julia answered petulantly.

They rode in silence to the hotel. Julia went swiftly through the wide hall. She climbed the wide rose-carpeted stairs and made her way to their room. She took the heavy key from her reticule and opened the door. The chambermaid had lighted the gas and turned it to a low flame. Julia unpinned her hat and laid it on the bed. She had been rude to Max. Now he would stay downstairs; he would find some friends and play poker or talk business until he had forgotten that she was cross. Men could do that; they could just walk away. Women had to sit in their rooms and feel lonely and a little ashamed.

Julia moved across the room aimlessly. She pulled the spring rocker over to the window and sat down in it. She felt a little abused sitting off up here alone. She rocked back and forth, back and forth. She could see the street below when she rocked forward. There were people coming and going as though in promenade. It was light out there, too. Julia got up with a swift rustle of the brown poplin. She pinned on her hat again with only a quick glance in the shadowy mirror. She picked up her jacket and bag. When she closed the heavy door behind her, the chair still rocked, back and forth, back and forth with a light, protesting squeak.

Julia went quickly down the stairs, not stopping to look over the railing at the landing. She turned discreetly out through the Ladies' Ordinary on to the street. She had never been out on the street alone at night before, never in her life. She felt daring and filled with a strange new excitement.

She walked rapidly down the street of the hotel as though she had a mission in mind. At the corner she turned to the right. It seemed perfectly safe. No one even glanced at her. No one would think of accosting you if you walked right along. It was lovely out on the street tonight. She would take a walk and then get back before Max had even finished his game.

The street was darker here; fewer carriages passed. She

walked more slowly looking through the gratings of garden gates, wondering about the people behind the curtained windows where lights shone softly. She would like a home like that one, with long windows primly curtained, set back from the street in a shadowy garden.

Sharp footsteps cut into her dreaming, and the quick tap of a cane. They startled her. The steps were faster than Max's. They were almost at her heels. She quickened her own gait. She dared not look behind her. The steps were up to her now. She drew over to the inner side of the walk against the garden fence to let the stranger pass. It was just some other person walking down the street at night, she told herself firmly.

"Aren't you going pretty fast?" It was a young man's voice. Julia's heart pounded so loudly she held her hand against her dress to quiet it. The tap of the cane had stopped. This was a judgment on her for going out alone. Julia felt a strong grasp on her arm. She was wheeled violently around under the street lamp. She closed her eyes and squinted tightly. A gloved finger under her chin forced her face up so she felt the light of the street lamp on her eyelids.

"If it isn't Sleeping Beauty, by Jove! Always did want to meet Sleeping Beauty." Julia blinked horrified eyes wide open at the young man's face so close to hers. She tried to think of some defense. The girls at home were always saying what to do if a Strange Man ever insulted them; Polly knew a woman who always carried a box of red pepper in her bag. Julia tried to slip out of his arm.

"And now she wants to go again; well, I should say not!" He wavered a little as he spoke and steadied himself with his cane. Julia sensed with new alarm that he was drunk, almost tipsy. She had never seen anyone really drunk before. She held her face as far from his as she could. She was trembling so that her fingers touched his arm in spite of herself.

"You gave me quite a walk, young lady!" he laughed delightedly.

Somebody must come along the street to help her, Julia thought frantically. Max would worry about her and come to hunt for her even if he were angry. She managed to speak in a small voice that was like someone else's.

"Please, I . . . my husband's waiting for me. . . ."

"That's a likely tale; this isn't any street for ladies so late at night." He shook a long finger mockingly at her.

Suddenly Julia noticed that the face so near hers was a very young face. The young man wore an opera cloak, and his words were bolder than his voice. In the instant she stopped being a little girl in the hands of a villain. She was still trembling, but she reached her free hand out to touch the young man's sleeve.

"Come on," she coaxed, "let's walk a little." Hardly knowing what she wanted to do, she turned him around. He bowed and took his arm from her waist. His cane made a cheerful tap again along the walk. It was easier than she had thought.

Afraid he might demur, she hummed the popular air the band had played at the Fair.

" 'S right, schottische one-two." They took ridiculous fancy steps along the sidewalk. Julia twirled and turned the corner. Down the square she saw the potted palms and the overhanging porch of the Lafayette House. She felt her toque to set it straight.

"Too many people in there," her escort objected querulously as they came to the lighted doorway.

"I'm thirsty; let's just stop and have a glass of wine," Julia said in a voice not her own.

"Or-right, champagne, tha's the idea."

Julia's hand rested lightly on his arm as they went in the entrance of the hotel. She pulled it away now. "Not in the hotel," she whispered. He stepped back to let her go ahead.

In a second Julia crossed the thick velvet carpet to the stairway. She made herself walk up two steps. A man coming down passed by her. Julia gained the wall side of the stairs and was racing up the long flight as though it were the stairs at home. She fled down the broad hall and took the key from her bag with trembling fingers. She knew she heard steps on the stairs. She was inside the room; the door was locked behind her. Max wasn't back yet. Julia threw herself on the bed on top of the lace spread and shams. She let out her breath in a long sigh.

There was a knock at the door, one and then two; Max's knock. She waited to catch her breath before answering.

"Julia, it's Max."

"Coming." Her voice was almost steady now. She slipped off her jacket and toque and went to open the door.

"Up yet?" He kissed her gently. "I thought you'd be asleep. Got into a game and it lasted longer than I thought." He moved across the room, taking out his watch and chain to lay on the dresser. The world returned to normal. Julia slipped out of the full poplin skirt and folded it smoothly on the bed. Then she took it over to put in the tray of the trunk.

Max put his arm around her as she stood over the trunk.

"Were you lonely, Jule? I thought you seemed tired after the Fair." It was his way of apologizing for leaving her alone and for her sharp answer in the cab. It made things right again.

"Oh, Max." Julia laid her cheek against his arm a second.

"What, my dear?"

23

"Oh, nothing," she stopped herself short. "It's been such an exciting day," she finished lamely. She had learned that she could take care of herself.

8

"THIS is a good introduction to Nebraska, Julia." They were walking along the clean-swept aisles of the Agricultural Building the next afternoon. There were glass-topped barrels of sugar and flour and corn; there were shelves of preserved fruits and pickled meats. . . .

"Look there, Julia!" Max pointed with his cane. "That's what I'm going to get for my business in Halstead some day. Yes, sir, before too many years go by."

"What, Max, for pity's sake?" Julia had never seen Max so excited.

"A refrigerator, don't you see?" Julia looked at a queer box-like structure with a glass front. There was a slight peculiar odor from it, and the glass had a sweated look. But back of the glass lay a trout, stiffened against its plate. Underneath a sign proclaimed that the trout had been preserved in perfect condition for three years.

"I wouldn't want to eat it," Julia murmured.

"No, but think how fruits could be kept, and meats. . . . Why, I could get all sorts of things from Chicago and distribute 'em all over Nebraska." Max went up to talk to the demonstrator.

Julia walked slowly along the aisle. She came to wooden tubs marked, "Nebraska soil." Julia took off her glove and picked up a handful. She didn't know anything about soil, whether it was rich or dry or poor, but she wanted to touch it. Across the aisle were tall stalks of corn, nine and ten feet high, labeled "Nebraska corn." Julia fingered them idly. She noticed the papery rustle. It must look as tall as trees, she told herself, and wandered back to Max, who was making notes on the refrigerator.

"Max, does the corn really grow that tall in Halstead? Over there, see."

They went back to the corn exhibit. Max laughed. "Wait'll you see it, Julia! There isn't anything like it when the wind blows in it. We'll be seeing it pretty soon now."

Julia put on her glove again, and they wandered out to the lush-flowering beauty of the Horticultural Building.

"We'll have our last champagne, Julia." They sat at one of the little tables set in French fashion outside the restaurant. They were alone, most of the people preferring to be inside the building.

"It's pretty chilly here," Max remarked.

"Yes, but it's our last night. I want to see the lights come on in the buildings again."

The waiter filled their glasses, handling the bottle wrapped in its napkin with tender care.

"I guess I want to leave before it closes," Julia said, as they walked across the footbridge over the ravine after supper, while it's all lighted up."

"It's been nice, all right," Max said, like a man counting his purchases.

Julia walked silently, her arm in Max's, holding her skirt daintily in one hand. Max's cane struck out its own staccato rhythm. They took a brougham once more, since there would be none of these in Nebraska. The whole evening, it seemed to Julia, had been made up of lovely things they could have no more of: the delicious tingle of champagne reaching way to her toes; oysters in brandy sauce served in an outdoor restaurant; gigantic buildings lighted by myriads of little flames, feeling themselves part of the current of the times; the feeling of people, lovely women, gentlemen talking wittily, saying significant things —they must be, she thought, watching them promenading past, even though she and Max were silent.

When they reached the hotel that night, it seemed almost like home. The man with the foreign-looking beard at the desk bowed to them as they came in.

"I think I'll just stop in and see if Fleet and Ross are around before I come up, Julia. I won't be long."

"Yes, Max." Julia went on upstairs. Now that they had only one more day she hated to think of leaving their big room. She was lonely; she wished Max hadn't stayed downstairs.

Max went through the velvet portières to the bar. He saw no one he knew; he'd have one cigar and see if anyone came in. He ordered a stein of beer, but left it standing in front of him untouched while he watched the crowded room reflected in the great mirror back of the bar. He began his game of guessing the business of different men . . . those men were Yankees, most likely. . . .

"Mr. Hauser, calling Mr. Hauser. . . . Mr. Max Hauser. . . ."

Max shoved his stein away from him on the mahogany bar. He looked up startled. His hand shook as he wiped his mustache. He approached the small boy in uniform.

"That's me, I'm Max Hauser."

"Telegram for you, sir."

Max took the yellow envelope from the tray. Telegrams still unnerved him . . . they usually meant trouble. He put it in his pocket and walked through the lobby to the stairs. He must find Julia before he opened it.

He knocked twice on their door. "Jule?"

Julia opened the door. "Why, Max?" Max looked somehow different.

He sat down in the rocker and took the yellow envelope out of his pocket.

"What is it, Max? What did it say?" The sight of the unusual missive sent a little quiver down her spine.

He handed it to her without answering.

"It's from Gretchen in Omaha. She says, 'Rudolph died suddenly today . . .'" Julia read slowly. "Oh, Max, that was your oldest brother."

Max dropped his head in his hands. He made a queer choking sound in his throat. Julia bent with a swift, instinctive movement.

"Max, dear, don't," she said gently. Max was . . . crying! Julia stood by his chair and pulled his head over against her. She said nothing for a moment, but her stillness quieted him.

"Max," her voice was clear with decision, "you must wire Gretchen that we are leaving tomorrow, that you will go right to Omaha." Julia had taken command of the situation. Max looked up gratefully.

"You must go with me, Julia, you'll know what to do." Max buried his face in his hands again.

"Rudolph was more like a father to me, Jule. Why, he gave me my start in Nebraska!"

"I know, dear," she spoke as she would to a small child. She brought a chair and sat down beside him. He reached over and found her hand.

"Max, you better go down and send the telegram to Gretchen," she said after a while.

Max moved across the room slowly. He felt trembly; a thing like this. . . .

"Wait, Max, I'll write out the message on the back of

this one." She got the pen from the desk and wrote on the back of the yellow paper, even signing it Max. It seemed the natural thing to do.

Max looked at her gratefully as he took the paper. He went silently downstairs with it.

Julia moved the screen in front of the window. She folded down the lace spread and laid the large lace shams carefully over the back of a chair for the night. All her movements had a new direction. She was fixing the room for Max.

"You're good, Julia, not to mind missing our last day at the Fair."

She had minded, but she had liked the way Max had turned to her as though he needed her.

"It's only a few hours' difference, Max; we'd have left this evening, anyway."

They stood by the portmanteau and satchels on the platform of the station looking out at the rain.

"We came in the rain, and we're leaving in the rain; I wish it would stop," Julia said wistfully. Max stood beside her silently. The gray rainy day only deepened his feeling of sadness and loss.

Julia wore a gray cravenette over her bottle-green traveling dress. Max had his macintosh buttoned to his neck. They looked less resplendent than when they had arrived. No one picked them out for newlyweds who saw them standing silently there together.

I. HALSTEAD—1876

BREAKFAST was at six-thirty in the Golden House. In spite of the discomfort of washing in the cold crockery basin on the washstand and dressing hurriedly in clothes that were limp from the night air, Julia felt a kind of excitement at the strangeness of life in this place. Now it was beginning, she felt as she fastened up her dress. Whatever it would be like in all the years was starting now.

Max stood waiting for her by the parlor cooker.

"There, Jule, now when you come back up, just open this draught and you'll be comfortable all morning." Julia wanted to tell him that last night she had been homesick, but now she felt differently. Perhaps he hadn't noticed.

"I'm ready, Max," she said instead.

29

The long dining-room illuminated by a reddish circle of light from each of the big kerosene lamps hanging from the ceiling was full of shadows. A tall, black-bearded man at the end of the long table became a giant on the ceiling. Julia and Max grew too in shadowy stature. For the most part the men at the long table ate silently, blurting out a comment or two, then getting up with a noisy scraping of chairs. Julia refrained from talking, to be less conspicuous as the only woman.

The early hour, the darkness and the cold made her feel as though, in just a moment, they would be starting somewhere. There was nothing settled about the meal or the place like breakfast at home. But to Max it seemed settled enough. He took his hat and started out to the store as soon as he had wiped his mustache and gotten his cigar well started. "Max's Store" it became in Julia's mind.

Julia stood for a minute by the big front window of the hotel watching Max disappear down the street. Two men untied the reins of their horses from the railing of the porch and mounting rode off over the ruts. They were mysterious riding away in the half-gray light. Their horses' hoofs made a dull, pounding sound, different from the smart clop-clop on the streets at home.

A block of two-story wooden buildings faced the Golden House. There was a plaque in the center with "Majestic Block—1875" in gilt letters. Max had pointed it out to her last night as they came up from the station. She read the printing on the windows: Nebraska Land Office, Halstead General Store, First National Bank. . . . On the window above the Land Office neat black letters read, James Dorsett, Attorney-at-Law. Next to it on the corner windows above the Halstead General Store was the name John D. Chapman, M.D., Physician and Surgeon.

A group of men came in from the bar to stand around

the stove. They walked carelessly, boldly into the room. Julia felt suddenly out of place; it was clearly a man's world. She crossed the room and went upstairs, her silk petticoat under her challis dress rustling oddly over the bare wood stairs.

She opened the door into her "parlor." With a fold of her skirt she turned the draught on the stove. How cold it must be here in winter! Then her gaze fell on her trunks with the Wells Fargo Label still on them. They faced her, square-cornered, uncompromising, a sign that she had come to stay, all her belongings with her. Julia walked away from them into the bedroom.

There was the massive walnut suite, complete with dresser, washstand, and large wardrobe, that Max had waiting for her. Julia touched the cold marble top of the dresser. It was nice to know that something in these ugly rooms belonged to her. Then she turned back to the trunks.

She made up the bed with her own linen sheets and the lace spread and shams, the quilt that was made of a thousand bits of silk, featherstitched together, folded on the bottom. She unrolled the delicate Limoges teacups and square plates to match from the many layers of petticoats and set them on the shelf in the wardrobe. There was a brown box of tea and a little jar of special sugared ginger Aunt Dil had given her for her tea table. She wondered who would come to tea here.

The room began to look more homelike with her workbasket under the table, her cherry writing-case on the top and the picture of Mamma and Papa and the girls on the wall. On the dresser she set the pictures they had had taken at the Centennial. Already that seemed long ago.

Julie put on her toque and tucked her hair back into her chignon; she would go down and surprise Max at his store. She straightened her shoulders instinctively. Max's friends must admire the cut of her new bottle-green jacket. It had been made after one from Worth's.

Beyond the Majestic Block a vacant lot let in the open prairie, then the livery stable blocked it off again. She read the names on the windows as she went: Mathorn's Drugstore, Curry's Hardware, a saloon. She was surprised to see two more banks behind impressive wooden fronts. Omaha Street was as wide as Michigan Avenue . . . there! MAX HAUSER—PRODUCE stared at her in bold letters across the side of a large wooden building.

As she neared the store, a horse and wagon drove up in front. A farmer got out and began to unload bulging sacks of potatoes. Then he shouldered a sack and, kicking the door before him, went into Max's store. Julia followed a little shyly.

There was Max in his vest talking to the man with the potatoes. Julia looked around her curiously.

"Hello, Julia." Max came over to her. He was pleased and surprised at her coming. He was proud of her prettiness and her fine figure in the green traveling dress. He led her to the chair in front of the big roll-top desk in the little side office.

"Sit here, Jule, I'll be through in a few minutes."

The light in the store was poor. The man at the front of the long narrow room was a dark figure dumping potato sacks. The big barrels and bins of feed bulked darkly against the wall. The room had a nice smell to it: a dry smell of grain and flour and the dry earth that clung to the potatoes. There were other chairs around the small stove, a cigar stub caught in the lid. Men must come here to see Max. The space around the stove and the desk had a hospitable air. The chairs stood together as though they had hitched closer in the heat of argument.

"They're nice ones all right, Amos. We're all straight then." Julia heard Max's voice, hearty, confident, business-like. Max stuck his pen behind his ear and came back to the desk.

"Well, Julia." The words were complete in themselves. And then, "How do you like the store? I'd have swept out here if I'd known you were coming in." He made a jotting in his big calf-skin ledger and shoved it back on his desk.

"I like it, Max. Didn't you have to pay that man for the potatoes?"

"Oh, these potatoes were for feed he bought from me a year ago, no, a year and eight months it was, when that hail-storm killed things and the snow was so deep. I never jerked him up about it, and he never said a word till today." There was satisfaction in Max's tone. To have his fellow men pay up proved something, something that lay securely at the heart of his world. Max put on his coat and the broad-brimmed black hat that he wore now that he was back West.

Julia felt a sense of security and ownership as Max locked the door behind him then, quickly, a little feeling of superiority to the small store. Max must become something more than a wholesale produce man in a prairie town. The granddaughter of an official at the court at Prague slipped her hand into her muff. Max took her arm and together they went along the frozen ridge of the road that served for sidewalk.

" 'Lo, Max," men called to Max as they passed: a rancher sitting out in front of the blacksmith shop, Aldus Mathorn, who owned the drugstore, the clerk in the bank. He was highly respected in the growing town. Long before Rotaries Max understood the spirit that held men together in a common faith in their town.

"Max, why are there three banks in Halstead?"

"Why, Jule, you've no idea what a lot of money's represented here, money from Boston and New York and Chicago. . . . There're plenty of fortunes going to be made here in our day."

Julia looked wonderingly up the street. She tried to see the bare stretch down to the tracks filled with buildings, handsome buildings like the new Masonic hall at home.

"We'll turn up here, Jule, so you can see our lot. This is all residence section in here."

Some of the houses were like those back home except for the lack of shrubs and trees; some of them were even pretentious.

"Now, Jule!" The tone of Max's voice made Julia stop. "You see up this street? The first block has the courthouse on the corner, then the next block has that big white house, that's Judge Mitchell's, then that's our block."

"Oh," Julia said quietly. It was a little terrifying to be so close to the place where they were going to live.

"That house belongs to Jenks; his wife's a relative of President Grant's, then that's our lot right next. If everything goes all right, Jule, we'll build next spring; a house like Jenks's."

Julia looked at the gray cupola of the Jenkses' house, at the lightning rods on the roof that even on this gray day seemed to draw some special ray of light from the cloudy sky. The house was two stories and a half. It was so tall it seemed to peer over the square blocks between it and Omaha Street.

"And this is ours."

"Oh, Max, how . . . how lovely!" Julia stared at it, at the matted grass. It was treeless with no view but the sky and the wooden church across the street. They would plant

34

trees. . . . Julia started to visualize a house. "I wish we could start right off, Max; I know just how I want it." Julia glowed when she was animated.

"You can talk to Ventner in the spring; he's the carpenter."

"I'll want a drawing-room and a sitting-room and a dining-room. . . ."

"You won't want that drawing-room out here, Jule," Max said as he had before.

"Why, Max, of course we will. Some day Halstead will be a city."

"How do you do, Max." Someone whom Max called Regan bowed over Julia's hand with unusual grace. Julia noticed his gray frock coat. "We will see you at the Withers' reception tonight."

"He's an Irish peer; some say he's a remittance man," Max murmured in an undertone when Regan O'Connor had passed; "he's one of the biggest cattlemen in the country."

They came again to the Golden House. It was beginning to snow. Tiny flakes sifted down on the muddy ruts of the street and the planks of the walk. They fell on the velvet collar of Max's overcoat and on Julia's new green toque. Julia paused a minute on the porch, her skirt held well above the dirty boards.

"Look, Max, whatever is it?" Julia pointed down the street, squinting because the wind blew snow in her face.

"Oh, that's tumble weed. The weeds get dry and break off at the roots, and the wind blows them miles and miles till they get stuck against a fence or something."

"It almost jumps it's going so fast," Julia laughed.

But the big bundle of weeds blowing down through the main street seemed to put to naught the important air of the Majestic Block and make this street part of the open prairie beyond the town. Julia shivered.

"It's getting cold, Jule, let's go in."

In the afternoon Julia had her first caller.

"I know this is an outrageous time to call," her visitor laughed, "but I was just across the street, and I got to thinking how good it would be to see a woman who had just come from Chicago. . . . I come from there, too, and I just couldn't wait. I'm Faith Dorsett; my husband is a friend of your husband's."

"I'm so glad," Julia said. "Come in."

"We haven't been back since we came out here," Faith explained wistfully. "That's four years ago. I can't even think how Chicago must look after that dreadful fire."

"You wouldn't know it; the new buildings are so much bigger. Do you like it here?" Julia asked abruptly.

"Oh," Faith looked down at the toe of her boot, "it's good country for the men. It has a future; perhaps we'll all be rich some day. James and Mr. Hauser and the Senator think so. I'm sure I hope so, but I . . . I paint, and I wish sometimes that I could just see some paintings, real ones, and talk with people about painting again." She raised her eyes to Julia's face. "I believe I hate it here," she finished. Then she laughed quickly. "That was nothing to tell you, was it? Really, some days I like it. And there are a few people here as fine as any in the world. After all we're young." Her words came fast in her embarrassment.

"I wish you could have seen the paintings at the Fair," Julia said impulsively. Her tone cast aside Faith's apology. "The paintings were all together in a big building. What do you paint?"

Faith's eyes lighted with eagerness. Her face was homely except for her eyes.

"Sometimes I paint scenes back home from memory, but it's hard to get them right, it's been so long. Sometimes I paint the cottonwood trees down by Bittersweet Creek and the clouds over the prairie, things like that. Once I even painted the front of the Land Office Building with a prairie schooner in front of it. Did you ever hear of painting a thing like that?" They laughed at the absurdity of it.

"I'm glad you've come here. And forget what I said about the town." Faith stood up to go. "There's one thing about it, the leading people, I mean the ones here that are responsible for it, are mostly young; even the Senator and Mrs. Withers can't be over forty. James says we may have a second Boston here. He comes from there. I tell him I'd rather have a second Chicago!" She laughed again. "I'll see you tonight at the Withers'."

Julia watched her from the window as she crossed the street. Against the vacant lot and light sky her hood was black. Knowing someone walking out there made Julia feel more at home.

2

JULIA waited to put on her best silk petticoat and the black mull dress until after they had come up from supper. But she had on her tightest stays, and her hair was dressed except for the tiny diamond star that had been her grandmother's.

Two round circles of light from the two kerosene lamps shone on the ceiling of their bedroom. One cast a yellowish light on the wardrobe mirror where Max re-tied his satin cravat and waxed his mustache. The other illumined the mirror of the dresser where Julia looked over her shoulder to see the long hooking of her tight bodice.

"There," she turned before him. "Will I do, Max?"

"You're beautiful, Jule."

"We've been looking forward to seeing you ever since Max left for Chicago," Mrs. Withers welcomed Julia. Jessie Withers was a small woman whose hair and eyes and skin seemed all sandy-colored. Back of his wife stood the Senator.

"Well, we had a snow flurry to greet you, didn't we, Mrs. Hauser?" The Senator's deep voice had won him fame in his stump speeches for President Grant.

Julia slipped off her coat and went in through the tasseled portières. Mrs. Withers rustled at her elbow in a stiff dark silk. The room seemed full of people. Max was still in the hall talking to the Senator. She and Mrs. Withers advanced toward the sofa in the corner. There was a lamp on the table back of it. Julia saw the pond lilies painted on it more clearly than the face of the woman on the sofa.

". . . and Mr. Regan O'Connor."

He was the one she had met yesterday. He was very big and dark; his eyes were bright and bold. They admired her. How gracefully he bowed!

They came to Faith Dorsett. She was homely even at night in her green taffeta. Faith squeezed Julia's hand warmly. How tall Mr. Dorsett was. He was the lawyer who had offices in the Majestic Block.

Mrs. Withers was introducing her to someone else. The name was German; she didn't quite get it. She smiled as if she had heard. Oh, Hetzel, that was it. Julia bowed to Mrs. Hetzel, seeing her hair in a stiff pompadour, the pansy earrings in her ears and the amethyst brooch pinned into the lace bertha of her dress. Mr. Hetzel was a little like Max, but older. He spoke with a heavy accent.

"How do you do, Dr. Chapman," Julia murmured after Mrs. Withers' introduction. Then this was the doctor, only he was so young, not like Dr. Barnes at home.

". . . and Miss Eiler, one of our school-teachers." She couldn't be any older than Polly, Julia reflected.

"Now you've all met Max Hauser's bride," finished Mrs. Withers. "My dear, you sit over here by Mrs. Dorsett; you both come from Chicago."

Everyone sat down. Conversation languished for one proper hesitant moment. Max came in with the Senator. He shook hands around. Julia saw how much he liked to be back, how much he liked these people. He hadn't been in such good spirits since the news of his brother's death. Julia leaned back in her chair.

"I hear my wife's been discouraging you already, Mrs. Hauser," Mr. Dorsett bent towards her to say. "You mustn't believe her."

Julia felt a kind of quickness in him. He spoke quickly; he smiled quickly, restlessly. A fleeting remembrance of the tipsy young man in Philadelphia flashed into her mind. She looked back at him twinkling. He seemed younger than Faith.

Faith Dorsett laughed, but her eyes were untouched by the laugh.

Mrs. Withers brought over her chair. "I hope you won't think it's queer asking you here without calling, Mrs. Hauser." But the Senator's going to Washington tomorrow. He wanted to meet you before he left."

"Oh, no," Julia answered. "I didn't think about it at all; I mean except to think how nice of you to have this reception for us."

"I suppose you've been homesick already, Mrs. Hauser."
Miss Eiler moved her chair nearer. "I was the whole first
year."

"Do you like it now?" Julia asked.

"Oh, yes, ever so much. You should see the lovely new
school that was built this year. I'm too busy to think of
Ohio."

Faith Dorsett caught Julia's eye and looked significantly
at Miss Eiler and then at Dr. Chapman. Julia smiled and
nodded.

The little jingling bell sounded through the house.
Senator Withers greeted some late comers. Julia heard the
name Jenks and looked up curiously. Mrs. Jenks was the
relative of President Grant's . . . they owned that house
with the cupola.

Mrs. Withers brought them to meet her. Mrs. Jenks had
yellow curls that fell in a waterfall at the back of her head.
She was as pretty as Martha Wyman at home.

Mr. Jenks chuckled. "This freeze-up will disappoint
Max, Mrs. Hauser; he won't have much excuse for carrying you across the road now the mud's frozen solid!"

"Tell us about the Fair, Mrs. Hauser." Senator Withers
came over to her.

"Oh," said Julia, "it was the most wonderful sight.
Everything you could want to see was there." Julia's face
lighted, her eyes caught some remembered reflection from
the stained-glass windows of Memorial Hall. Her hands
instinctively moved to draw the great spectacle into their
vision.

"Mrs. Hauser, you must have an evening and give those
of us who were less fortunate some of the fruits of your
rich experience," Senator Withers remarked.

Mrs. Withers turned to Dr. Chapman. "Doctor, why
don't you ask Mrs. Hauser to help you raise money for

that operating table you spoke to me about? We could have a benefit lecture."

"Really, I . . ." Julia hesitated, coloring warmly. "I'd love to tell you about it, but I don't believe I could give a regular lecture."

"I wish you would, Mrs. Hauser," Dr. Chapman urged. "We do need an operating table badly." Then he added in another tone, "It doesn't need to be a tremendously serious affair, you know."

"In that case," Julia smiled, "I might try it; I'm not a tremendously serious person."

"I'm not either," Dr. Chapman assured her. "But it would be a treat. There's a terrible dearth of things to see and hear. There's been nothing since Lotta Crabtree came through on her way to the coast two years ago."

"You shouldn't have missed the Fair," Julia said.

Dr. Chapman looked at her for a second before he answered. "You'll be good for Halstead, but I wonder how good Halstead will be for you, Mrs. Hauser."

"I see you two are getting together on that lecture, Mrs. Hauser; you ought to plan on giving it before Christmas," Mrs. Withers told her.

Conversation that had tarried politely around Julia took its natural course. Julia's attention wandered. A few hours before she had never known any of these people, and now she was one of them, even agreeing to give a lecture. The men seemed as old as Max, all but Dr. Chapman and Mr. Dorsett. . . .

"This country is hard to get used to, isn't it?" Mrs. O'Connor broke in on her thoughts. She must be Irish, too, that was why her voice sounded so differently. "When you build you must let me give you some ivy roots to start around your house." Julia wondered what had brought the O'Connors way out here.

"Jessie, what about a little singing?" Senator Withers's resonant voice came from the hall.

"I knew the Senator couldn't wait much longer," Mrs. Withers exclaimed.

"We missed you last time, Max," James Dorsett said, and Julia heard someone else ask him if he'd brought back many new songs from the East.

"Does your wife sing first or second part, Max?" Mrs. Jenks asked.

"She has a high first," Julia was amazed to hear him answering.

"Then you sit right where you are, Mrs. Hauser; the couch and those two chairs can be the first part."

Max and Mr. Hetzel moved forward a melodeon.

"Gracious, you'd think I'd have an organ or piano by now, Mrs. Hauser," apologized Mrs. Withers, "but we brought that with us when we came to Omaha in '70." She touched the satiny surface of the mahogany case lovingly even as she disparaged it, and straightened the candles in the silver sconces by the music rack. She sat down to it and arranged her full skirt carefully around the chair, getting up twice to be sure the gathers fell all around. She lifted her wrists elegantly, keeping her elbows well out from her body.

In a minute without any announcement but the high thin tinkle of the ivoried keys they were all singing.

"Ma-axwelton's braes are bonnie, whe-re early fa's the dew . . ." The volume rose rich and full to the corners of the square ceiling. Julia heard Max's voice, and his warm rounded tenor notes started a trembling inside her black mull bodice. Her own voice was girlish, sweet and without depth, but it blended in with Delia Eiler's, whose voice sometimes wavered too with the uncertainty of youth. It was good to be singing. It was like being in the parlor at home.

They struck into *Oh, Susanna*. Gayety possessed them. Julia looked around in smiling amazement. Mr. Hetzel and Senator Withers looked years younger. Mr. O'Connor and Mr. Dorsett and Max threw back their heads and sang like boys. Max and Mr. O'Connor and Faith Dorsett's husband began the chorus, so they all had to sing it again. The bell jar over the wax flowers rattled against the marble-topped table.

"You sing one, Max; sing, *Long, Long Ago*."

Then while they were all out of breath, Max wiped his mustache elaborately with his handkerchief and began. His voice was tender and the notes came out true and full. Julia looked at him as though he were a stranger. She had never known he could sing. She held her breath, taking the words as if they were sung to her. The haunting refrain made her sad. It hinted of things gone, all her girlhood on Michigan Avenue, as dead as though it had been burned in the fire.

"Long, long ago . . . long ago."

Warm silence held the room when he finished. There was not even the rustle of a skirt or the soft movement of a handkerchief lifted to the nose. For Julia no one else was there. Her face was softly glowing and raised a little toward Max. She had been wooed again. A strange emptiness that had been with her since the Centennial was filled.

Someone clapped. They resettled themselves in their chairs. Max wiped his face in embarrassed pleasure. They sang again. Always Max's voice came through, covering Mrs. Withers' quaverings and Mrs. Hetzel's muffled contralto with its rich tones. Julia sang. Her eyes were dark and sparkling. The music picked her up and carried her along.

43

Mrs. Withers disappeared and Max and Faith Dorsett's husband tried a duet called, *Mush, Mush, tra-la-le-ladie,* but they had to stop for laughing.

Mrs. Withers called from the wide doorway, "Will you all come right in?" She took Julia's arm and led her to the seat of honor at the big round table. In the center of the shining damask cloth was a large hand-painted lamp that shed a yellow radiance on the little wine glasses, on the silver tray of roasted partridge surrounded by rosettes of sweet potato, on hot biscuits and the blancmange molded in the shape of a heart. There was a cake with yellow icing that bore the word "Welcome" superincrusted in white.

"The cake's from Mrs. Hetzel," Mrs. Withers explained quickly.

"Your Matilda certainly knows how to do fancy frosting, Mrs. Hetzel," said Mrs. O'Connor slyly.

"Maids in the old country always like torten," Mrs. Hetzel explained, "but I do think these two I brought back with me this time are unusual. I couldn't stand taking untrained girls from some sod-hut around here, ach!" Impatience with incompetence of any kind was in her face. Mr. Hetzel smiled.

"Mrs. Hetzel doesn't mind living in Nebraska if she can bring German servants with her."

"Ladies and Gentlemen," the Senator began in his most sonorous voice, "we don't have Max home with a new wife every day; I propose a toast to the bride." He took up his wine glass and looked over at Julia. "May she find health, wealth, and great happiness in her new home!"

Julia colored delicately; Max smiled his pleasure as they drank the toast in the Withers' famous cherry bounce.

"Didn't you like them, Jule?" Max asked as they were on their way home, with the wind whipping past them and the flame of their lantern smoking against the chimney.

"Yes, Max. Just at first they were strange, but when they began to sing . . ." She hid her face against his coat as the wind took her breath away. They climbed the steps of the Golden House. There was a solitary light on the counter and the base-burner glowed red. They went up the squeaking stairs to their rooms.

Julia lighted the lamp on the table. The room was chilly. Max threw off his coat. "Here, Jule, you put this around you and I'll start a little fire." He looked big bending by the tiny stove. His shadow loomed even bigger on the wall. Julia pulled the coat around her obediently.

"Max, I never knew you could sing like that." Her warm filled feeling still lingered.

Max laughed his slow, good-natured laugh. "We have to make our own music out here, Jule; that's why folks like my singing, I guess. Music's what I miss out here." It was the first time he had admitted the lack of something in Halstead. He went into the next room and came back with her gown and dressing-gown. "You dress out here by the stove, Jule, where it's warm."

Julia was suddenly tired. It had been a full day. She unhooked the bodice of her dress silently. Always when she reached out to Max she was met by kindness, gentleness. A rare, half-ashamed craving stirred her. She wished Max would hold her tightly so the cold wouldn't matter. She didn't want the fire. She pulled the dressing-gown around her and her fingers fumbled underneath it with the fastenings of her petticoats.

"Thank you, Max," she said quietly.

Max was undressing in the other room. He was winding his watch now. The little metallic sounds fell so reasonably, so methodically, in the room they quieted the excitement in her. He laid the watch on the marble top

45

of the bureau. The chain rattled into a nest of links beside it.

But in the big walnut bed when Max reached out to her, she turned passively to a desire that was a little terrifying in its silence. And she was wistful and quite alone.

3

THE etiquette of calls was as strict in Halstead as in Boston. Julia was duly called upon, and she returned her calls as properly as though she were at home. At three-thirty one afternoon she took her card case and her best gray gloves and the handsome reticule she had "gone away with" and set out for Mrs. Hetzel's.

The Hetzels' house was a story-and-a-half frame building set far back on the lot. Two scraggly cottonwood trees grew on either side of the front steps. Julia liked that. It was an attempt towards the settled look of houses back home. She was disappointed though by the smallness of the house. It scarcely matched the picture Mrs. Hetzel's mention of her German maids had conjured up. But when she pulled the door-pull and the door was opened by a buxom girl in uniform who showed her in without a word, she sensed the dignified air of the house. Nebraska and the raw open country beyond the town were shut securely outside. Julia felt the windows were seldom open; they were muffled in heavy net curtains with side draperies of dark red chenille. Every inch of the floor was hidden by a Brussels carpet; even the furniture and the pictures—one of the Schwarz-wald was framed in carved sticks of wood—were different from the properly American style of Mrs. Withers' or Mrs. Jenks' houses.

Julia sat down on a tufted plush chair with a high-carved back. The scent of a closed room mixed with the hot, sweet smell of fresh bread from the kitchen. Then she heard the rustle of Mrs. Hetzel's stiff black silk skirt.

Mrs. Hetzel was a homely little woman, and yet her pansy earrings with the diamonds in the center, the puffs of shiny black hair and the twisted knot on the top of her head, her small blue eyes, prominent beaked nose and pale thin lips made her striking. Julia could see how Mrs. Hetzel would go back to Germany every two years if she chose. Mrs. Hetzel held out her hand. "Ach! such a windy weather. You must be tired out," she exclaimed. "Make yourself comfortable and Matilda will bring us coffee." She spoke to the maid in German.

Julia felt the order and regularity of this house. Now that she was used to it even the close warm air seemed pleasant. The Golden House slipped out of her mind. This was distinctly another world.

Julia smiled at the quiet fourteen-year-old boy whom Mrs. Hetzel introduced as "Joseph," and the younger girl with pigtails and round blue eyes like her mother's. Mrs. Hetzel admonished them in German and they went obediently upstairs. Like the house, the children were well-ordered.

Mrs. Hetzel plunged into an account of her last trip back to Germany. With her tone of voice she implied that nothing of interest had transpired since and subtly managed to patronize all things American.

"We shall, of course, send Joseph back to Germany next year to be educated."

Julia smiled. "My mother feels a little that way. Her mother was a lady in the Bohemian court at Prague and, of course, she made my mother feel . . ." Julia said it without any attempt to impress. She had just remembered her mother's way of reminding them that in the old country things were different from the new ways in Chicago.

47

Mrs. Hetzel's needles were still for a minute.

"Prague—it's a lovely city." The Hetzels were a merchant family, but not of the court bureaucracy that held court appointments. She was impressed. "You're Bohemian, then."

"My family are," Julia said; "of course, I'm American."

But Mrs. Hetzel deprecated that with a click of her needles.

On the table in the center of the living-room lay a handsome copy of *William Tell*. The gold embossing on the back reminded Julia of some of the big German books on the shelves at home. The crusty top of the fresh coffee cake was mysterious and delectable. Mrs. Hetzel dropped the stocking she was busily knitting to pour another cup of coffee, then she picked it up again while the coffee cooled.

Julia tried to think what had brought them here. Then she remembered; Max said Mr. Hetzel was impatient with the autocratic ideas of the Prussian government. He had come over attracted by a young country. Now he was vice-president of the bank.

How helpless women were, it occurred to her suddenly; they had to go where their husbands went, even this capable woman clicking her needles energetically against each other. But if Mrs. Hetzel lived all the rest of her life in Nebraska, it would never change her.

Julia went down the steps slowly.

Another day she called on Mrs. O'Connor. The O'Connors' house was farther removed from Omaha Street than any of the other houses. It stood three full stories high, straight up with a flat roof. Mrs. Golden had told Julia that one maid who had slept there had nearly frozen with the cold and another was driven out by terror at sleeping up so high.

Julia liked the bareness of the O'Connors' hall, the floor that was always oiled and shining, the branching antlers where Regan O'Connor hung his black felt hat, the queer umbrella stand with a horse's head in brass on it, and the lamp that hung down from the ceiling by iron chains. The windows of the O'Connors' house were wide and longer than any of the other houses of the half-dozen leading citizens. In the dining-room and Regan's den off the hall there were no curtains.

Julia sat on a carved three-cornered chair across from one of the long windows. She had a sense of breathing more deeply, of being farther away from the town even than in Mrs. Hetzel's house. Here the flat snowy wastes, the backside of the buildings on Omaha Street, the few shivering trees, became a picture, remote from this room with the open fireplace in it. It was a restless house, Julia felt. There was none of the snug order of the Hetzels' or the safe comfort of the Withers'. It was built too high to heat easily; it had a fireplace instead of a capable stove in the front parlor, and it was three-quarters of a mile beyond Omaha Street.

Julia looked across at Mrs. O'Connor with her bright, sullen eyes and full red lips that showed petulant little lines at the corners and yet laughed so easily, and felt a recklessness in her, too. She was different from anyone she had ever known.

"Regan's gone buffalo-hunting," she said and laughed. "I'd like to go, but of course he wouldn't take me."

"I haven't seen any buffalo yet; I'm crazy to so I can write back home," said Julia, trying to feel out what it was about this house, the long white windows, this woman, that sent a tingling through her.

"Oh, not around here, my dear; way west a hundred and fifty miles or so. Regan says they're pushing them farther west all the time. You must ride with us sometime out to the ranch. Do you like horses?"

Mrs. O'Connor herself went for tea. She served it with brandy. Julia sipped the sharp hot liquid. It was a new taste. It belonged to this room and this woman. Mrs. O'Connor looked unhappy when she didn't smile. Were all women a little homesick for the place they had come from? Or maybe it was for some happiness they had expected and hadn't found in marriage, Julia thought.

Faith had told her Mrs. O'Connor had had three babies born dead. Maybe that was why her eyes looked so different when her face was quiet. Julia swallowed suddenly; the tea flavored with brandy had gone down the wrong way.

"I hope you'll like it here," Mrs. O'Connor said as Julia left. The conventional words sounded queerly, almost sarcastic, on her lips.

Julia walked rapidly. She hoped the color in the west would last until she got home. It must be colder than when she had come. Next summer Max was going to get a horse and buggy for her. The town looked smaller than it really was from here, somehow insignificant spread out in the middle of so much space. She looked back at the O'Connors' house standing up so square and dark against the east. How could they stand living out so far? It would be different if the country were pretty, but it was so empty and flat. She wondered if Mr. O'Connor was really a remittance man. Max said he was a cattleman. Back home the people you knew were all more alike, or at least you knew all about them.

She came to the courthouse. Judge Mitchell was away. He had gone back East. Faith said she would like the Mitchells. Max said the Judge had done so much for Nebraska. They had the other three-story house, the white one over on the other block. The courthouse was wooden, but somehow managed to be as massive looking as stone.

"We built that, Jule, so it would fit the town ten years from now," Max had said. It had a dome-shaped top and five, six—she counted the steps as she passed—twelve steps up to it.

Imperceptibly the yellows and pinks beyond the courthouse dome faded. The whole sky had gone utterly cold. Abruptly Julia stopped looking at the courthouse, noticing the houses as she passed. She was cold. The cold crept through her high wool-lined overshoes and up the sleeves of her jacket. It seemed so much farther walking back.

Then she saw Max. He must have gotten back to the Golden House and then come out to look for her. She waved her muff. Max waved back. It was nice of him to come to meet her. She shivered a little with the cold. Her limbs had a curious numb feeling. She was like someone else walking along in the crunching snow.

"Jule, I worried about you. It's two below zero." Max came up to her. He wore his velvet ear-muffs under his black hat. It warmed her a little when he held her arm tightly against his coat.

"I am cold," Julia said. She felt like crying.

They didn't try to talk. Suddenly Julia forgot the aching cold. Her mind seemed to slip ahead of her body. Walking over the road that was frozen into sharp outlines of gray, looking on cold fields that were so flat underneath the sky, it was necessary to be clear with one's self. What was she to be to Max? She tried to bring before her the things that she loved about him, but all she could find was Max's gentleness, his coming to meet her like this. She felt in her heart that he could be drawn with simple strokes. He was what he was against the sky; he would never change.

But she was different. It seemed sometimes to her now

51

that she changed from day to day; her face never set constantly in one direction. It turned towards Max and then away. It was drawn to the unflinching sincerity of the dull white sky and flat earth and then repelled by these same things. Her body was making itself into Max's wife, but she had always that feeling of not quite being one with him. It was all mixed up; she couldn't think . . . if only Max could understand how she felt!

But the immensity of the wide white sky made the two of them seem insignificant. She lifted her face from her muff as though in facing the cold she faced her loneliness too. She tried to remember how she had felt at the Fair . . . proud of living, of being herself . . . but that was at the Fair.

They reached the Golden House. Her mind stopped worrying her. She was all body; her hands ached horribly.

"You must never go out so far alone, Jule, when it's this cold," Max was saying.

4

WHAT there was about Dr. Chapman's glance that disturbed her Julia couldn't tell. She thought about it sometimes while he and Max talked about land values or politics. Dr. Chapman ate at the Golden House. Max asked him to sit at their table, but he refused.

"No, you ask me over now and then and I'll come. I'm not good as a steady diet." Then he laughed, and the laugh deprecated himself and at the same time laughed at them.

Even when he was talking to Max and Julia was drinking her coffee, she would look up over her cup and find his eyes on her with a kind of mockery in them. One day she asked Max more about him.

"Don't know much," Max said; "he came out here from England, no, Edinburgh I guess it was, six months before I did. I think he was in some sort of a mix-up, but he's as good as they come."

Once when Max had to go out in the middle of a meal to see a man who had brought a wagon-load of wild turkeys in to sell, Julia frowned quizzically at Dr. Chapman.

"Why are you so amused at me, Dr. Chapman?"

He laughed. "Mrs. Hauser, I'm not amused. I'm baffled. I wonder how you keep your air of eagerness about you in this God-forsaken prairie town; why don't you get settled-looking?"

Julia smiled gravely. It was queer to have a man talk of anything besides the future of the country. It was exciting to talk of things that mattered within yourself. Suddenly it hurt her a little because Max never talked of such things.

The clatter of dishes and tin-ware, the occasional talk of the men at the long table, the red-yellow half-light of the hanging lamp, shut them into a kind of intimacy.

Julia found herself saying, "But isn't it going to be different, Dr. Chapman?"

"I suppose so, but that's all in the future; you're young now."

Julia straightened her knife and lined her spoon beside it. "You're different from Max, Dr. Chapman; you aren't excited about the town at all."

"Oh, yes, I am in spots. Sometimes the wealth of the country goes to my head; sometimes even the idea of building a society out here on this prairie rather excites me, and I don't know of any people better fitted to do it than the Withers and Mitchells and Dorsetts and you and Max, but other times, Mrs. Hauser, I wonder if we aren't utter fools to come away off here, away from civilized living. I get to thinking of places I've known, Princes Street, Edinburgh; Regent Street in London . . . you know." Dr. Chapman's face settled into melancholy lines. His eyes seemed to look through the swing door of the kitchen at other places.

"Oh, I know," she said quickly. "When we got on the train to leave the Fair I felt how awful it was to go off so far."

"By the way, you will give that lecture on the Fair, won't you?" Now he was different again; his face broke into a smile that made him suddenly younger, almost handsome.

Max came back to the table. "Jule, I'm going to give one of those turkeys to Mrs. Golden to cook for us. Chapman, you must eat with us. They're the fattest I've seen this fall."

"Thank you, I'm just persuading your wife to give us that talk on the Fair; quite aside from raising money, you know you owe it to us." He laughed again.

"We should have used the church in the first place," Mrs. Mitchell whispered to Faith Dorsett as she found places for the Terwilliger family.

"But it's so much cheerier here," Faith whispered back.

When the folding doors between the dining-room and sitting-room and between the sitting-room and hall were pushed back, the Mitchells' house could accommodate forty people. Chairs were brought from the Dorsetts' and Withers' and even carried over from the Jenks'. Crowded in with so many people, no one minded the cold December night.

"Do you think I ought to put another lamp in front of Mrs. Hauser?" Mrs. Mitchell asked.

"Judge Mitchell's getting up to speak, I wouldn't now."

"Friends . . ." Judge Mitchell had come from Massachusetts. He had studied law in Harvard and practiced in Boston for fifteen years before a political appointment sent him to Nebraska. He had come with the quiet but firm assertion that in five years there wouldn't be a cattle rustler in central Nebraska.

"Friends, this is a rare privilege for us to hear from the lips of an actual spectator of the glories of the great Centennial Exposition held so recently in that far eastern city of Philadelphia. I am sure we should all be grateful that Mrs. Hauser, even though she is a newcomer among us . . ."

Julia's cold hands were clasped tightly in her lap. She sat very straight against the high-backed chair. "My first memory of the Centennial"—her mind formed the beginning words of her talk though her lips did not move out of their careful smile. The velvet frogs down the front of the wine-red taffeta gave no least sign of the tumultuous trembling within her.

". . . Mrs. Max Hauser," the Judge finished.

Julia stood up, bowing slightly to Judge Mitchell.

"My first memory of the Centennial"—she caught sight of Max beaming proudly, of Dr. Chapman smiling at her. She looked away quickly from him to the young girl back against the sideboard in the dining-room. She was her own age. Perhaps she had come in from one of those sod-huts out on some ranch. She had no idea what the Centennial was like—"was driving from our hotel in a brougham along Belmont Avenue, the great boulevard of the Fair."

Mrs. Kauf, the butcher's wife, sat down in front. She was scrutinizing the cordings of Julia's skirt with her head tipped a little to the side. The woman by the windows was fingering the stuff of Mrs. Mitchell's curtains. Julia made her voice a little louder.

"It was a beautiful day, and it seemed as we drove along

that everybody in the world was driving with us to the Fair. I do hope you can all picture it as I tell you about it." Julia stood very slim and straight in the center of the parlor so she could be seen from both hall and dining-room. Her voice was not quite her own, tinged by the tone of voice she felt a lecturer should have.

"Suppose I take you with us on our first trip through the Fair grounds. . . ." Julia had heard travel lecturers begin that way. It was exhilarating talking to so many people. She had never had quite this feeling. Julia added things she had not written down. She told about the annoyance of the photographer when Max decided to have two separate pictures taken, and Senator Withers laughed so hard she wished she had put in more funny things. She described the newest ideas in house-furnishings for the women and then added mischievously, "Mr. Hauser will have to tell you about Machinery Hall. He pointed out things to me, but I'm sure he felt it was beyond my understanding!" Judge Mitchell clapped Max on the shoulder. A farmer over by the door laughed out loud. The ladies smiled appreciatively. What a big gathering it was, Julia thought as she talked.

The notice in church and the card put up in the store had brought many more than they had expected. Mrs. Mitchell's silver cake basket was full of quarters for Dr. Chapman's operating table. A feeling of success deepened Julia's color.

She passed around the folder of sketches they had brought from the Fair, and the souvenir doily of Irish linen from Belfast. Mrs. O'Connor seized on it eagerly. Two women on the sofa smoothed Julia's Paisley shawl lovingly with hands that were horny from digging potatoes and piling sod.

"As we drove away"—Julia's voice was unconsciously

dramatic—"I looked back at the lighted buildings with the flags blowing from the pinnacles, the people gathered from everywhere, and it seemed to me"—Julia had forsaken her written pages again; she hesitated—"that there were so many glorious things in the world that—why, it made you proud," she ended girlishly. Her voice had a dangerous quaver. She sat down a little confused at her own outburst; that wasn't the ending she had written down.

The room was filled with clapping. Senator Withers reached over and shook her hand as though she had made the finest political speech of a campaign. Judge Mitchell rose to express his gratitude . . . "And that of all of us, I am sure."

Julia knew without looking up from her lap that Max was beaming proudly over by the doorway, that Dr. Chapman was watching her. Her fingers played busily with the fringes of the souvenir doily.

"After the musical selections if you would like to ask Mrs. Hauser any questions I believe she would be glad to answer them," the Judge concluded. There was a stir through the room, then Mr. Kauf, the butcher, played the flute. He had not been asked to feature on the program without due thought on the part of Mrs. Withers, Faith Dorsett, and Mrs. Jenks. All the husbands were consulted.

"It isn't just this one time we must think of, it's establishing a precedent," Mrs. Withers had said. "Of course in the South I never knew anyone who was a butcher."

"Well, in Buffalo, don't think . . ."

"Butchers in Chicago lead the cotillion!" Faith Dorsett remarked dryly with an exaggerated lift of her black eyebrows. "Of course we'll have Mr. Kauf. This is a benefit open to the public. We aren't asking him into our homes for dinner."

Mr. Kauf played a folk song, *Du, du liegst mir im*

Herzen. The rooms were so still when he finished that the light spray of snow drifting against the windows sounded loudly. Max sang *I Dreamt I Dwelt in Marble Halls,* swaying slightly with the song. Julia forgot her confusion as she listened. How could Max sing that way and yet be so . . . so matter-of-fact most of the time?

"Now, friends, we'll have an informal time, and if any of you want to come up and ask questions you just come to Mrs. Hauser, and if she can't answer them, hunt out *Mr.* Hauser!"

Julia was the center of the group of people. The men asked Max about threshing machines and this new-fangled telephone contraption.

"You spoke of the Cheney silk exhibit; were they showing more taffetas or satins?" Mrs. Jenks asked.

"I s'pose it was wonderful the food you got in them restaurants," Mrs. Kauf said wistfully.

The ranch women who were there came up to shake Julia's hand. "I loved what you said about the paintings," one woman told Julia.

"Were they wearing their hair lower? I noticed you have yours in a chignon," Mrs. Livingstone asked.

But all the time that she was answering questions and shaking hands Julia was waiting for Dr. Chapman. While she was telling Mrs. Hetzel about the glass exhibit she knew he was still over by the dining-room door talking to Mr. Dorsett. Then she saw them both coming towards her.

"Mrs. Hauser, you should have been a man and taken to the law; you'd have won over your jury," Mr. Dorsett said.

"I really didn't expect to catch so much of the feeling of the Fair, Mrs. Hauser," Dr. Chapman told her; then in another tone he added, "Did you hear we collected twenty-two dollars?" Mr. Dorsett had turned to speak to Judge Mitchell. "When you were talking there at the end, I wondered . . ."

"Shall we go, Jule?" Max came up. He was still smiling proudly. "Chapman, you'll have a real hospital before long if you get my wife to help you!"

Julia turned away to get her coat. She wondered what Dr. Chapman had been going to say.

Tonight it didn't matter that it was bitter cold, that the snow blew into their faces and stung their eyelids; the sweet feeling of triumph warmed Julia. She could feel Max's pride in her, in the success of the evening. Out here in the bitter cold of the night it seemed a tremendous thing to bring together a crowd where it was warm, to tell them about the Fair, to give them music.

"With you to raise money, Jule, the next thing you know we'll have an opera house here," Max shouted teasingly through the wind.

The Golden House was still brightly lighted when they opened the door. Four men were playing cards by one of the big base-burners. Max nodded briefly. One of the men at the table got up and came towards him,

"Say, Max, there's a stranger here from Texas wants a game; would you join us? I wanted to get Dorsett and Chapman, too; do you know where they are?"

Julia went slowly up the stairs. Max would come up toward morning. She didn't mind except tonight when she wanted to talk it all over and enjoy the evening again. The rooms were cold. Julia opened the stove and found the fire had burned out. She threw her muff and the souvenirs from the Fair over on the bed and took off her gloves and coat. She picked up the coal scuttle and then set it down again. She would go right to bed; she didn't need a fire.

Julia undressed quickly and got into bed in her flannel dressing-gown and slippers. She lay with her knees close to her chin to keep warm. But she wasn't sleepy. The night had been too full. Tonight she even felt some of Max's enthusiasm about the town. Suppose she should raise money for an opera house! How queer it was that she should be here in this funny hotel, halfway to nowhere; Julia Stepinka who was married now and giving an "evening." She must write Mamma about it, and Mamma would tell Aunt Dil when she came to tea. Aunt Dil would say, "I never thought it of Julia."

Through the thin floors she heard the men downstairs. She knew they would be playing at the table near the stove; she could see their faces, very serious, Max chewing his cigar. . . . She had watched one night from the top of the hotel stairs.

Julia listened to the snow blowing against the windows. All the warm triumph of the evening had gone. She was lonely. Suddenly she threw back the covers and got out of bed. She turned up the light and went out to the sitting-room. In the bottom of the trunk was a big book Mamma had given her. Julia got it out and carried it back to bed. She moved a chair by the bed and set the lamp on it. Her hands were icy. She went back and got the Paisley shawl she had thrown on the chair when she came in and wrapped it around her shoulders over her flannel gown. The cold went through everything. It was cold in bed without Max. Then she turned the pages curiously, almost fearfully. The title on the cover in large letters was *The Family Physician*. Her mother had said, "You can't tell about Doctors way out there, Julia, and it's nice to be able

60

to look up about things for yourself. You're a married woman now, and you should know things."

"Thank you, Mamma," Julia had answered, scarcely listening. Her mind had been on the new red taffeta.

With her cold fingers Julia turned the pages. "Signs of Pregnancy," that was what she wanted. She read intently. Once she unbuttoned the high neck of her flannel nightgown and looked at her own white flesh underneath. She cupped her hand around her small warm breast and looked at it critically, at the delicate brown at the center. Then she studied the grossly exaggerated picture in the book. She buttoned her gown again. She turned the page; "a woman in this condition should avoid chills, undue fatigue, excitement, exercise, anything that will cause fear, nervousness, or worry; especially any shocking sights." Julia read through the paragraph marked "Labor." She was very small sitting up in bed, wrapped in the dark Paisley. She closed the heavy book and pushed it under the bed. She spread the Paisley shawl over the bed-covers, put the lamp back on the dresser, and turned down the wick. Then she lay under the blankets with wide eyes watching the white rime sparkle on the window-pane below the shade, and the little aura of red light thrown on the uneven ceiling. There was no fear in her eyes, only a bright curiosity.

5

AS the Nebraska winter settled down on the flat stretches of country, most of the brave attempts at a social life were given up. The houses in Halstead had a curiously sealed appearance. Church services were abandoned for three Sundays in a row because the high-gabled wooden buildings could not be heated. Only the newly organized

Philomathean Literary Society never failed to meet once a month in Julia's "parlor." Faith Dorsett ran over to see Julia every now and then, muttering crossly about the weather that was so cold she had to heat her tubes of paint over the range. Most of the time Julia sat in her front room close to the parlor cooker working on her embroideries, writing letters on her cherry writing-case, looking at the bleak world outside her window.

She busied herself one whole afternoon in February cutting a baby dress out of her finest muslin petticoat. She would have liked to borrow a pattern from Mrs. Withers or Mrs. Hetzel, but she could not bring herself to ask them yet. She cut it as she thought it should be and kept her tell-tale sewing rolled in a fine huck towel in her bottom drawer.

But it was not as isolated living in the Golden House as it would have been in a house of her own. Upstairs in her front parlor she was in touch with the life of the whole community. She could look down Omaha Street through the frosted window and watch the farmers' sleighs going by. She came to know the sound of the bank door that had a different voice altogether from the shrill drop of the latch on the door of the General Store. Whoever came in on the daily trains usually came to the hotel dining-room at meal times. She saw the Methodist evangelist who decided to come back "when the ground was more ripe"; the traveling quack who went from door to door with his cure for consumption, the Catholic priest who was sent out to build a Catholic college in Halstead in the spring, all in the dining-room of the Golden House. When a Mr. Pollard came out to start in the undertaking business in Halstead, Julia took his tearful and bewildered wife up to her sitting-room and saved her sanity by teaching her to do the new Battenberg work. And Mrs. Golden always hurried halfway up the stairs, her head just above the second floor, to tell Julia any news-item before it appeared in the *Halstead Courier*.

Julia was on her way downstairs to press in Mrs. Golden's kitchen. In the lobby she noticed two strangers sitting by the nearer of the two big base-burners, talking over a map they had spread on their knees. They were Easterners from the narrow brims of their hats, their clipped mustaches, the cut of their suits. Julia stopped by the desk as though interested in the big almanac that always lay there.

"You see the Brunswick and Missouri road is going right up through there, and the town'll be right here in the bend of the South Loop River."

The other man pulled at his mustache. "Hard to bet on these towns, Bert."

"I know, but it's the logical place, and that's where the preliminary maps run the road."

"Sure, but the survey stakes aren't down yet."

"You don't have to point that out, do you? There'll be plenty of men ready to buy on the strength of those preliminary maps."

Julia closed the almanac and went on out to the kitchen. All the time she ironed she thought about the town that was still only a point on the map. Once, perhaps, two men had sat over a map and planned Halstead. Then somebody had come—the Withers were among the first—and built a store and a few houses. When eight or ten wooden fronts stood together looking across the prairie they called it a town; that was in '73. She put the ironing board away and went back upstairs slowly, past the men planning a town on the map, past the bar and the great buffalo head on the stairs.

A dreary aimlessness came upon her; the four walls of her parlor bound her world too securely. She looked around wondering whether to work at her embroideries or write Polly, but then there was nothing to write about unless she told her of the baby, and she would wait awhile for that. It came to her that she had never been so much alone before. She wished she could go back home for one night to giggle with the girls after a party when they were undressing at a deliciously late hour. She couldn't remember when she had found anything funny enough to be convulsed with laughter over. Next week if it warmed up any they must go over to the Dorsetts' and have some music. Then the sunset streaking her walls with color caught her. That was one saving thing about this country! Quietly, as if bidden, she pulled the rocker closer to the window, trying to take some feeling of that color to herself.

That night Max lingered after supper to talk downstairs. When he came up he brought with him an air of suppressed excitement; he hadn't yet lighted his cigar; with one hand he brushed back his crisply curling hair.

"Jule, I've been talking to some men connected with the B. and M. Railroad. They've seen maps that show where the road's going over near the South Loop." He said it impressively, drawing in his chin against his collar, looking down at Julia quizzically to see if she understood what that meant. "Where the road goes, the towns go, Jule. A tip like that's worth gambling on. Some of us are talking of buying up some land over there, just to hold it awhile and see what it does. This Western country is full of chances."

Julia looked at him; his face that she had scarcely known last October, she was coming to know so well; her mouth curved a trifle. She dropped her embroidery hoop to her lap. Max was talking half to himself; he scarcely needed any rejoinder.

"Really, Max?" Enthusiasm for this land of opportunity was in her tone. She had had Max spring to the defense of Nebraska before now. "Of course," she added slowly, "I suppose they probably don't want that news to get around too fast either."

"I know that South Loop Valley. I was over there a year or two ago; it's mostly cattle-range now, but it's a good fertile valley and I've always thought when the railroad opens it up there's no telling how fast it'll be settled!"

Julia was shading in a green leaf now. She selected her skein carefully from the thick braid of colored threads in her lap. Her eyes had a twinkle of mischief in them, but her tone was grave. "I suppose it's to their advantage to get people interested out there, they're not just . . ."

"Oh, I think they're interested in the country out there, Jule, and they've got investments in it. They'll handle the land purchases for us," Max explained, taking the first puff of his new cigar.

Julia cut her thread neatly, close to the material. "You've never seen them before, Max. Do you know what their connections are back East?"

Max smoked without answering at once. "I am surprised about the road going over that far, at that; there is no doubt about its going through the South Loop Valley, but Oscar Holtz told me he'd heard when they did take it on west it would be a little farther to the north in case of floods in the spring." His familiar shrewd frown pulled his eyebrows closer together.

Julia put her needle carefully in the emery cushion and folded her work into the bag. No, she wouldn't tell Max that she had overheard the promoters talking. It was fun to have him think her long-headed.

"I think I'll go to bed, Max."

"All right, Jule." Max got up to fill the little stove. The

coal clattered noisily out of the scuttle. "June's early enough to think about buying up land out there, I guess. . . ."

"And building in the spring . . ." Julia murmured. She didn't finish the sentence. It became part of Max's remark.

"Might as well see that done before I make any large land investment." Max wound his heavy gold watch. "I said I'd be down to talk some more with them, but it's ten o'clock now."

6

"I HATE to go back up; it's almost like the country around home down here," said Delia Eiler wistfully, dropping her hands on her work.

"I believe I miss shade most of all. Everything's so glaring," added Faith, her eyes on the filigree of leaves cast on the earth by the twisted cottonwood trees.

"I'm going to have shade by our house when it's built even if I have to spend all my time carrying buckets of water. Max sent way to Illinois for catalpa and maple shoots to plant along the west side of the house, you know." Julia sat on the ground leaning against a tree trunk.

They had come down to Bittersweet Creek to escape the heat of the afternoon. Between the clay banks there was only a tiny trickle of water, scarcely moving, lying like a reptile on the warm mud surface, but trees grew along the banks, twisted cottonwoods, broken and bent by their struggle with the winds.

"Oh, it's good to hear trees rustle instead of that everlasting corn," said Delia.

"I'm going to paint a whole field some day," Faith murmured, her eyes dreamy.

"Don't you see enough of them?" Delia asked incredulously. "I'd like never to hear a cornfield rustle again as long as I live."

"I remember at the Fair," Julia said, "there were some prize stalks from Nebraska and I touched them and asked Max if they really grew that tall."

Delia Eiler and Faith Dorsett laughed. Julia wondered if that had really been only last fall.

"We better start back," Faith said regretfully. Delia helped Julia to her feet. She was big now. Every morning she woke wondering timidly, excitedly, if this would be the day. And whenever she saw Dr. Chapman drive off toward the prairie for some call she worried just a little. She pulled her white Cashmere shawl around her.

"Don't put that on until you get near town, Julia; I'd like to go with only one petticoat, it's so hot." They walked slowly through the dusty buffalo grass toward the tracks.

"The heat seems to get right into your shoes from the ground, doesn't it?" Julia asked. She thought suddenly of the front porch at home and the breeze blowing across Lake Michigan. She could see the cool dark hall at home, the bronze statue of the three warriors on the newel post, and the shining stair-rail curving to the ceiling. How easy it would be to have her baby at home, and Mamma would put her in the spare bedroom and Hannah would wait on her and old Dr. Barnes take care of her.

"The sound of the grasshoppers makes me kind of sick," Faith muttered. "You didn't hear them so loud down by the creek."

"If they eat up everything I wonder what the farmers will do," said Delia. "The children that came in to school this spring from the country were half starved as it was."

"Maybe they'll learn sense then and let the country go back to being a cattle range and not try to make it into farms."

Julia was silent. Her child was going to be born here any day now. Their house was started over near the Jenks'. The framework was up, the catalpa and maple shoots were planted. Halstead was going to be a city in five years' time, Max said so. It was too late to talk of giving it up.

Faith left them at the corner by the Withers' picket fence.

"It looks like a real town here by the Withers', doesn't it?" Delia commented critically. "So many houses have gone up this spring."

"Look, you can see the framework of our house," Julia said happily, looking up the street toward the Jenks' house and the Episcopal Church. "Gracious! there must be twenty horses out in front of the hotel. I hate to go in looking this way." Julia hesitated.

"I'll go with you," Delia volunteered; "just don't look at them."

Together they walked quickly through the crowded lobby. Julia's head was held high, her eyes straight ahead. Delia stole a quick glance around to see if Dr. Chapman could be there. The bar was strangely empty; groups of men talked loudly around the front window.

Upstairs Julia looked down over the stair-railing. "I've never seen such a crowd," she whispered to Delia. "I wonder what it's about."

They heard the front door banging open. More men came in. The murmuring below grew louder.

"I'll tell you one thing you can lay your last dollar to; the sons of bitches'll never see Halstead courthouse while I'm living," a voice yelled above the murmuring.

"You're right, Sandy, they don't need no trial!"

The voices left off murmuring. Anger and violence shrilled into them that carried easily above stairs.

"I'm frightened," Delia whispered; "there're so many of them, and they act so kind of wild."

Julia's heart beat faster. She was glad when Mrs. Golden came up the stairs.

"They're so mad, that pack downstairs, I had to give 'em a dig with my elbows to get through." Mrs. Golden tossed her head indignantly.

"What is it, what do they want, Mrs. Golden?"

"They're bringing in two cattle thieves they caught up in Custer County. They killed the sheriff who went for 'em, and they had to send a posse out from here to get 'em. Now they're bringing 'em in here to the county courthouse to a trial, but these men followed down way from Broken Bow an' Golden says they're fixing to take 'em away from the sheriff." She rolled her eyes to the ceiling. "Golden sent me upstairs. He said it was no place for a woman. I wish they'd get along out of here over to the courthouse," she added nervously; "they're apt as not to have a fight right here." Her anxiety spread to the two girls listening by the stair-rail.

"I wish Max would come," whispered Julia.

"Golden's sent down for Mr. Hauser an' Judge Mitchell, too." She twisted her apron in her hands.

The murmurings downstairs subsided. The girls and Mrs. Golden went into Julia's sitting-room. Julia sat down by the window. She was tired. Maybe she shouldn't have walked so far in the heat. Her ankles were puffy above the straps of her slippers.

"Why don't you lie down for a while," Delia suggested. Julia shook her head.

A queer tense air filled the Golden House and spread along Omaha Street. The sky now at five o'clock was cloudless, impassive. The humans walking on the hot table-land beneath felt anger since that was nearest to heat. Heat pressed on their heads, anger pressed on their brains. There was no chance for mercy on a merciless earth.

The three women sitting in the front sitting-room heard a man running up the steps. "Here they come, boys." His voice had a kind of wild triumph in it. The crowd poured out of the hotel. Julia and Delia Eiler and Mrs. Golden watched from the windows.above. Some of the men sprang on their horses, and the whole body moved restlessly, waiting for the horse and wagon that were just visible down the road. The sound of someone breathing heavily came up to the window. No one spoke. The wagon came nearer. Five men sat in the wagon; handcuffs on two of them flashed in the sun.

"That's the sheriff," whispered Mrs. Golden, "up there in front."

The wagon was even with Julia's window now. Julia could see the gun in the sheriff's hand. Abruptly, almost as though it had been practiced, someone grabbed for the horse's bridle. The sheriff shouted, but his words were drowned in the angry shouts of the crowd. Two men jumped up on the wagon. Julia looking down caught a glimpse of the face of one of the handcuffed men just as he was jerked roughly down over the wheel. It was gray with fear. Delia Eiler saw it, too, and hid her own face in her lap sobbing.

Mrs. Golden bit nervously at her finger nails. "They'll hang 'em sure." Julia could not take her eyes away from that cringing face. The face of the other man was only sullen. It wasn't decent for anyone to be so afraid or for anyone to see him that way.

With no show of resistance from the sheriff the two men were gotten up on horses. They were being led away. The crowd surrounded them, and they moved together down the road across the tracks toward the trees of Bittersweet Creek. Julia caught sight of Max standing with James Dorsett. They had not gone, but neither had they protested.

70

She had never seen Max's face like that. She didn't know him well after all. Ned Jenks joined them. Where was Judge Mitchell? They stood soberly talking together. Julia did not know that the dead sheriff had been a friend of theirs.

"Well, I'm glad they've gone away from the hotel. I'll go down and get a bite of supper an', Mis' Hauser, you stay right where you are and I'll send it up to you. You look plain beat out."

Julia looked around from the window dully. "Really I couldn't eat anything."

Delia Eiler burst into hysterical sobs.

"I'll get her to bed," Julia said; "you send up some brandy. Delia, stop it, dear, they've gone now." Julia put her arm around the girl's shaking shoulders.

"I—I'm going away from here. I can't stand a place like this," choked Delia.

Julia, helping Delia in to lie on her bed, stopped a second. The ache in her back and down her thighs was more than weariness from her walk. Wringing out linen in the lukewarm water at the washstand she wondered how long before the pain would grow worse; whether she ought to send for Dr. Chapman. Anyway she couldn't stop now to look in her book. She pulled the paper shades at the windows and pressed the wet cloths on Delia's head.

Max came upstairs. "Jule, are you all right?" He came over to her anxiously.

"Sh-h, Delia's half sick," she whispered. "Max, did—will they really hang them?"

"It's only justice, Jule; they were cattle thieves, and they shot the first sheriff that went out for them; but it's nothing for you to bother your head about. You just forget it. You mustn't get excited in your condition, Jule."

Julia covered her face in Max's coat. How could you ever

forget the way that man looked? Max felt her shudder.

"Jule, dear," the anxiety in Max's voice comforted Julia, "maybe I better get Chapman."

"Yes, I guess so, but I'm all right, Max, don't worry."

It seemed to Julia lying in the big walnut bed upstairs in the Golden House that dark would never come that night. Outside the narrow windows the sky held light. When she closed her eyes and pressed her lips together against the wrenching pains that came faster and harder, she saw the twisted branches of the cottonwoods by Bittersweet Creek and two figures dangling by a rope. When she turned away from the light into the pillow, she could see that gray haggard face.

And it was light again before Julia could rest. Another cloudless blue sky stretched from one rim of the hot brown earth to the other when her baby was born. Another day of heat and dust and growing corn, but to Julia lying tired and weak but unfrightened it was like no other day. When Max went in to her he was no longer the relentless person he had been yesterday. His hands were damp as he caught hold of hers and his voice broke.

"Jule, I have a present for you." He unrolled a dress pattern of new black satin. "I had Gretchen buy it in Omaha for you, Jule."

"She must be Julia, too," Max said later, looking at the baby.

"No," said Julia, "let's name her Anne, after Mamma."

"I declare, I thought she'd be a marked baby being born after that lynching, but there isn't a mark on her," said Mrs. Golden.

Julia turned her head away from Mrs. Golden's kindly garrulity. The mark of the day before was in her own brain, a mark against this country.

7

THE Hauser place, as it came to be called in Halstead, was finished in September. It stood on the corner two lots above the Jenks' house; they kept the lot between for lawn. It was painted a dark green as Julia had wanted. "So it will be the color of trees and look shady a long way off." Almost as soon as its highest gable pointed due north, it seemed to Julia that the house had always been there.

Julia hadn't been sure about the jig-saw work. Of course a good many of the nicest houses had it back in Chicago, but, "I rather think I like the gables plain, Max," she had said slowly. But Max looked disappointed and a little crestfallen. He had been to such pains to get it, sending all the way to Omaha for it to surprise her. And quickly Julia rallied as she had with the Paisley shawl. . . . "Oh, yes, it does give it a finished look, Max."

Max was reassured. "They told me in Omaha it was the newest trimming." Julia was quiet knowing that inside the house she would be firm about trimmings.

And there was the drawing-room!

"Make out a list of the things you want, Jule," Max had said. "Maybe we can even put in the bathroom next year. One more good year here will send real estate flying. There's a new store at Galleon now that will buy all its produce from me."

Julia had taken out her cherry writing-case and made a list of all the furnishings she needed, listing them under "dining-room, sitting-room, drawing-room. . . ." But Max drew the line at the drawing-room. He had agreed to have four rooms downstairs besides the hall while they were building, but for the present he suggested putting in a roll-top desk and some chairs and using it as a kind of home-office.

Julia was sitting working at her embroideries while Max went over the list. Now she said without looking up, "I think I'd rather not furnish it at all, Max. If we do that we'll never change it. I mean to have a drawing-room, you know." Her tone was low, but a gentle obstinacy underlay it that even she had not been aware of.

Max puffed at his cigar in silence. Then he said, "We'll go over to Omaha and see what we can buy there."

Neither of them had mentioned the drawing-room again, but neither did Max suggest using it as an office. When their furniture was moved in, the room in front of the living-room was left vacant.

Julia had shocked the furniture dealer in Omaha and Max, too, by not wanting to buy suites of furniture.

"Madame, all the best folks buy parlor suites."

Julia, looking sweetly demure, smiled back at him.

"But really I would rather buy separate pieces even though it isn't fashionable, wouldn't you?" And the amazed furniture salesman with his carefully greased curls and waxed mustache found himself agreeing with her and rashly selling a desk with bookcase attached from one suite, a big couch from another, and a piano that was not even in the same color wood.

Julia decided to have oiled floors like the O'Connors. Max was surprised to find her so shrewd in her buying. She bought matting for the bedrooms and avoided the bright-flowered Brussels carpet except for the sitting-room. He had never known she had such decided ideas.

But when Julia hung the big Paisley shawl that he had bought her at the Centennial on the wall in the sitting-room, he was a little worried as to what their friends would think. It looked outlandish hanging from the molding back of the couch, though the pretty colors did show up.

"They'll think we can't afford to buy pictures, Jule, and I bought that for you to wear yourself."

"Let's leave it there for now and see," Julia answered mildly, looking with satisfaction at the effect. It was different, but she liked it.

Life in Halstead was another matter, now that they had left the Golden House for a home of their own. She could entertain properly and run her home by the same conventions that prevailed in Chicago. Julia was dusting down the stairs, her head covered by a white cloth, a ruffled apron over her green challis dress. Of course after today she would have Lena do it. She wondered what Max would say about Lena. Julia sat farther back on the stairs, her hands idle for a moment. She wondered if she had been right to go ahead without consulting him.

But there was no other place for Lena to go. Mrs. Golden had turned her out. And Lena had been so sure Julia would help her. Julia couldn't get out of her mind the broad open face of the girl with her funny buns of braids over each ear, that made her face seem more square. She had cried so much her small blue eyes were only slits, and her mouth kept trembling as she talked. Julia remembered how Lena had looked at her admiringly that first dreadful meal in the Golden House.

One thing Lena had said, choking and blowing her nose between her words, still bothered Julia. "I was bad, Mis' Hauser, but I just couldn't help it, I lov—loved him so terrible." Julia had stood across the kitchen by the cupboards. She had been pitying the big sobbing girl by the door, thinking how dreadful it was, wondering how she could ever bear to look at people again, and then without any warning Lena had said that, and instead of pitying her Julia looked at her curiously, a little shocked. It made her uncomfortable even now, the way Lena's words stayed in her mind. Julia tried to face them frankly, but her thoughts sheared off and then were back again. No nice woman would ever say such a thing or think it. You never thought of such things until you were married, and then there was such a thing as the "married relation" and "your wifely duty," but to love a man so you couldn't help an immoral act! She had almost envied Lena for feeling like that. . . . There, she had faced the truth! She was a little ashamed of feeling that way. "Of course you can come, Lena," her words came out of her with a rush.

Julia's hands began to move again, rubbing the circular grooves of the balustrades. On the rare occasions when Max sang, she felt caught up, almost as though she and Max were together; but he didn't sing very often. Suddenly the thought of Anne came into her mind. Anne was hers, hers and Max's. She was cause enough to bring them together. Wifely duty took on a different light. Of course that was what people had grown to know all these years.

Anne was awake now and lay blinking unseeingly at the red and green light through the colored panes in the top half of the window. Julia thought for one eager moment that the blue eyes met hers. She pulled the shade so the sun didn't touch her.

She stopped to take the dust cloth from her head and pin a black velvet bow at her collar, then she went down to get dinner, enjoying a little the urgency. There was never anything that had to be done, boarding at the Golden House. Her skirts swished gently behind her on the stairs as she hurried.

Julia pushed the swinging door to the kitchen. She felt her house warmly around her after sitting with her own naked thoughts so long. She was conscious in some part of her, of the rub and swing of the door to the kitchen, of the shining whiteness of the boards on the kitchen table, the yellow varnish on the floor and the narrow boards of the cupboard doors. She glimpsed happily, her lovely square Limoges plates behind the glass door of the dish cupboard.

Julia lifted the lid of the coal stove and opened the draught. She glanced up quickly at the big Seth Thomas clock on the wall. Max should be here in five minutes. The days were beginning to slip into a rhythm made up of meals, Max's comings and goings, and the periods that Anne slept or was fed. Time had significance now.

Julia took a mixing bowl from the cupboard, eggs from an earthen jar in the pantry and a steel fork to beat them. Tirelessly her wrist wielded the fork against the glistening whites. Back and forth, back and forth, till the transparent liquid turned to foam and then to white snow and peaked and held in tendrils, filling the big bowl nearly to the brim. It took less time to beat the yolks, piercing the firm spheres of yellow with the prongs of the fork, blending them in and brandishing them until the yellow turned to foam of a lemonish cast.

She took an iron spider from the wall and set it on the outer edge of the range. Then she dropped cold scallops of butter that she had scooped out of the butter tub and let them sizzle gently with a sound no louder than the rustle of leaves. Julia knew too by some secret sixth sense when to let the butter melt noisily on the hot spider until it burned and hissed into a brown liquid. All her movements as she crossed the large kitchen had economy about them and grace as she bent to the low cupboard and reached to the shelf. Meals came from her hands easily, graciously.

She heard Max whistle before his feet sounded on the porch. Then she poured the yolks on the whites and turned them together into the spider where the butter barely bubbled.

"Hello, Max; I'll be ready in a minute."

"Hello, Jule." Max came out to wash his hands.

Julia slipped her flat blade underneath and folded the omelette—high, fluffy, with a tender brown top the color of the crust of new bread. She carried her omelette to the table that was already set and brought plates warm from the top of the range. She went back for the coffeepot and butter, then they sat down opposite each other.

The expanse of shining damask falling in folds almost to the floor lay between them and exercised a restraint upon them, placing them properly at the head and foot of their board. The tall coffeepot, the silver that had been Julia's aunt's, the squat sugar bowl and massive tongs that had come from Max's family, the chairs against the wall, formally arranged and listening to their talk, the plate rail with the hand-painted fruit plates on it, the square proportions of the room—all these things set their talk in grooved ways. Julia sat up straight and poured the coffee with dignity. Max served the omelette.

Max thought, Jule's so pretty when she comes in from the kitchen with pink spots in her cheeks.

Julia thought, Max has had a good morning. I can always tell when he comes out to the kitchen smiling that way.

Max said, "Ralph Chumbly came in this morning to sell me some poultry; said he'd had the best corn yield since he's been out here. He's going to start building a new wood farmhouse this month."

Julia said, "I'll like to see farm houses instead of those low sod-huts." She would wait a minute before she told Max about Lena.

Their talk did not turn to themselves. Subconsciously they felt the listening chairs around them, the expectancy of the shining tablecloth.

78

Max thought, Jule is happy here now. All she needed was a home of her own. That was natural.

Julia thought, if only we talked about something that mattered, something beside the country and the future. Then she remembered, there was Anne.

Max said, "Is Anne asleep?" Their thoughts converged curiously a second.

Julia said, "Yes, she fell asleep just after I came downstairs. She usually sleeps till I'm through the dishes."

Julia took out their dishes and brought the pudding she had made for dessert. "More coffee, Max?"

"Please." Max passed his cup.

"Lena Haas came to see me today," Julia began; "the girl who waited on the table at Goldens'. She . . . she got into trouble and Mrs. Golden's turned her out." Julia's eyes were on the acanthus leaf woven into the linen of the cloth. "She has no place to go, and I told her she could come here." Julia waited.

Max hesitated. His idea of the proper thing for his wife was offended. "Do you think that was wise, Julia? People will kind of wonder about it."

Julia flushed. "She has no place to go. I couldn't tell her no. I think she's a good girl really."

Max disliked complicated situations. He remembered Lena vaguely. Girls like that were always getting into trouble out here. It surprised him that Julia could mention it, and that she could overlook it and say Lena was a good girl. Max liked to think of his home and his wife as separated from any knowledge of those things a man knew.

"I want you to have somebody to help you, Jule, but don't you think someone else . . . ?"

"But, Max, she does need a home. She's going to take her baby to the orphanage at Omaha. She'd love Anne." Julia's voice trembled slightly at the end.

"Well, Jule, I don't like the idea, but if you have already told her . . ." His voice disappeared as he cleared his throat. He folded his napkin clumsily and pulled it through the big silver napkin ring. "I must go, Jule." He came over and kissed her forehead.

"Good-by, Max."

8

THE next June a second dress pattern lay in glistening black satin folds inside its pink paper wrapper, stowed safely away in the bottom drawer of the black walnut dresser. Julia smiled a little, tenderly, when Max brought it in to her and spread it out on the bed.

"Why, Max, my other is as good as new."

"I know, Jule, but I wanted to get it for you."

Julia touched Max's hand gently. Max always gave gifts because he wanted to. He liked to think of Julia dressed in rich black satin. Julia would have preferred a frivolous trinket, a music box that played tinkly little tunes.

"I've sent to Chicago for a silver cup for the baby, Jule, with Christopher on it."

"How lovely, Max!"

"He's the first boy, you know."

Julia looked at Max. He was proud of his children. She hoped there would be another son. This time she had not had curiosity to help her through her labor, but instead a passionate eagerness to see the baby. Now he lay in the bassinet in the bed-sitting-room. Little Anne was in the bedroom next to theirs. Julia's house was filling up.

"I'll just look in at the baby and then I'll go. Good-by, Jule, dear." Max bent down to the low bed a little ponderously to kiss her. He was growing heavier. Julia closed her eyes. She knew beforehand that good wool-and-tobacco and faint whiff of eau de Cologne that was Max's essence. She heard him trying to tiptoe downstairs. He felt it was owing to her illness.

Julia could hear Lena singing in the kitchen and the light click as she fitted the wooden handle into a fresh iron and shoved the cold one back on the stove. Anne was taking her nap. The house was so quiet the noise of the grasshoppers came in at the window and the swift, slipping sound of a scythe in the grass back of the house. A scent of clover came up to her and the acrid smell of dust. Julia lay relaxed. She was still weak and her body rested heavily on the bed. It was good to lie spread out under the sheet. She almost wanted to move her leg to feel the fresh coolness of the sheets, but she was too tired. She had a poured-out feeling as though she had emptied her energy and spirit into the atom of humanity in the bassinet. She would rest a bit, and they would come back to her.

Julia heard Dr. Chapman at the door, and then Lena preceding him heavily up the stairs.

"Here's the Doctor, Mis' Hauser, or would you like to be let alone a minute?" Dr. Chapman was too frail-looking, too studious, to appeal to Lena. She looked now as she came through the door in front of him as though she could pick him up bodily. Dr. Chapman laughed at her.

"You need my professional services, don't you, Mrs. Hauser?"

Julia, who had felt so drained of energy a minute before, smiled back at him gayly. A new color came into her face. Some electricity of spirit always passed between these two.

"Yes, Lena." Lena, shuffling back downstairs in her felt slippers, expressed her disapproval with each heavy thud.

Julia wondered again, looking over at Dr. Chapman's handsome, unhappy features, why he had never married

Delia Eiler. They no longer "went together." Delia still taught school. Julia could not believe that it was because of Dr. Chapman's fondness for poker; why, even Max played poker.

He took the chair by the window. "It's hot out. If it's this way in June, think what July will be like! I just got back from a call across the tracks—Russian woman. Third girl and they're as poor as Job's turkey, but there sits the father playing on an accordion as though it were a Roman holiday. I tell you, these people know how to live." He took out his pipe.

"Does Max know enough to play the accordion for you? No; he leaves you in a dark room to think of your miseries." His laughter was the best thing about Dr. Chapman except when it took on a harsh edge of sarcasm. He was young, thirty-one or two at the most, Julia decided. "If you hadn't given birth to a baby last night at midnight, Mrs. Hauser, I should inveigle Max into taking the train to Omaha to see a play. What's a day's ride for a play? There's a stock company there on their way to Denver." Then the animation in his face died out leaving it discontented. "Why do we live off out here, Mrs. Hauser?"

Julia smoothed the quilt before she answered. "I'm here because it's Max's town, I suppose, but why do you stay?" Julia asked the question in a low voice. She felt herself on the edge of a confidence. She was afraid to say too much for fear of stopping it.

"Because I'm the particular kind of a fool that would hang himself inside of ten days in a city. I'm so lazy that if there were another doctor within reach I wouldn't lift my finger; as there isn't, I'm the hardest-working doctor in the state of Nebraska!" His expression altered. He looked over at her with an admiration in his eyes that made her forget her exhaustion. "But you're meant to live in a city

82

where you could go to balls and concerts and ride in the park. I remember over at the Senator's house the night after you came. You made me think of a gardenia. I wondered how Max had the courage to bring you way out here." He broke off a little confused. "My best bedside manner, Mrs. Hauser!" He bowed. Now his face was different again, sarcastic, apologetic, the apology routed by the twinkle in his eye.

Julia was unaware that her color had heightened, that she was beautiful with the slight shadows accenting the depth of her eyes, her curling hair a little loose in her neck, and the undisguised sweetness of her mouth. But Dr. Chapman was well aware.

"What a success I might make as a fashionable doctor!" He bowed now with mock gallantry. "Here I sit and Mrs. Golden is in bed with shingles!" He laughed again, a young laugh that needed no joke, and was out of the room.

Then the house was quiet once more. Julia turned over on her face. An illusive something in Dr. Chapman's laugh had risen to mock at the middle-aged solemnity of her living. For the moment Julia forgot that she had made her babies the cause and meaning of her life.

9

BY the middle of August of that year the noise of the grasshoppers took on a menacing sound. People left off talking about the heat when they met in the store or bank. Even the Methodist lawn social set for the middle of the week had been given up. There was no rustle of the corn these days, only a dead ominous silence, except when someone cut through the cornfield, going cross-lots, and then there was a crackle like fire. And there was fire. Twice Julia had stood on her porch to watch the red of a prairie fire. The suffocating smell of the smoke crept into the house and permeated every corner. The young catalpa and maple trees along the west side of the house drooped pathetically in the heat, their leaves riddled into paper lace. Only Anne Hauser, patting a wooden spoon against the hot sandy soil along the front walk, did not mind it.

Julia pulled the shades and even hung wet sheets in the baby's room, and rubbed his back and arms and the creases of his neck with meal and orris root to help the heat rash that covered him. She took off his flannel petticoat and let him lie with only two long muslin skirts and bare neck and arms. Finally she carried him downstairs to sleep in the empty drawing-room.

Lena grew a permanent mustache of perspiration across her upper lip and took to muttering prayers or curses in guttural German as she stood over the big coal range.

Julia wilted visibly. The intolerable heat brought the summer before when Anne was born to her mind. Violence was in the parched air that they breathed in their lungs. Even Max lost his cheerfulness and walked up the plank walk to his house a little silently.

Occasionally some wagon creaked past, heavily loaded with household goods—another farmer letting his land go for the mortgage, turning back to Iowa where things were easier. Only those of hardy peasant stock could survive. Once a ragged caravan stopped at evening and asked to sleep in the Hausers' front yard. Max went out to talk to them about the future of the country.

"This is only one year, the next one will be better; you're throwing away hundreds of dollars giving up your claim like that."

Julia, taking out a big pitcher of milk and fresh bread, hunting up clothes for the ragged children, uttered no word of persuasion against their going. Instead, she watched their wagon lumbering on again and heard their thanks with a tinge of envy.

"We'll think of you back in Illinois, Mis' Hauser," one woman called. Julia nodded without answering. The blazing sun on the flat roof of the Lutheran Mission turned fiendishly into ripples like Lake Michigan, but no breeze came from them.

Mortgages lapsed in town. "If there aren't any crops, there can't be any money for payments; it's as simple as A B C," the Judge told Max.

Max stayed late down at the office. No one knew how much he gave away in feed that year. Every desertion of the land hurt him personally. He had staked his faith in Halstead, Nebraska. He had watched every new building go up with a feeling of pride. Now just as it was on the way to becoming a city, the drought fell on it like a paralysis. Everything stood still.

Max and James Dorsett and Regan O'Connor and Ned Jenks left off playing poker to sit in the dim office and talk about the land, about crops, about debts.

"People have lost their nerve. Every man, woman and child has cleaned out of Galleon," muttered Ned Jenks gloomily. "I went up and closed the bank yesterday."

"When you talk about its being farming country and the day of the cattle range being over," said Regan O'Connor, "you're going against nature. You've been talking me into buying up town sites and stock in the wagon factory when I ought to have been buying more grazing land."

The four men sat gloomily around Max's desk. No man wore a coat. Regan O'Connor had his shirt opened at the neck and wore no collar.

"I believe it's hotter inside than out," said Ned Jenks.

With one accord they went out to the front. The town

that was almost a city lay sullen in the close dark. Most of the lights were out in the houses. Above the scattered buildings and ragged leaves of the corn hung the sky, starry, clear, imperturbable.

Suddenly Max threw away his dead cigar. He lifted his head. He walked a few paces out in the road where he could look down the street. Then he came back to the men, his thumbs thrust beneath his suspenders.

"Ned's right; people have lost their nerve, and we've got to give it back to them. This is good land, and we know it. It's the same land year in, year out; it's only the weather that changes. Good weather 'n' good crops'll come again. . . . That's only sense." It was a long speech for Max Hauser.

Regan O'Connor laughed shortly. "Don't heat yourself up, Max." But Max disregarded him.

"We've got to build up confidence; get people buying up land now while it's down; get them counting on the future again. Ned, you talk to Hetzel in the morning, get ahold of Williams over at the Farmers'; the banks ought to start it so the people would have confidence. We've got to turn folks' minds on expansion and get 'em some credit." Max's eloquence ran out. But his sudden energy spread to the occupants of the other chairs. No one spoke for a minute. Ned Jenks walked over to the street and spat loudly. Max sat down in his chair and tipped back against the store window.

"I s'pose you'd say resell these farms that are turned in to the bank?"

"Yes, and not at a dead sacrifice, either," answered Max.

"Max, why don't you start right out tomorrow and undertake to build an opera house worthy of a city like Halstead!" James Dorsett asked jocularly.

"I might," Max answered. "Ned, you talk over what I've said with Hetzel, and I'll drop in to see you tomorrow."

86

They moved their chairs inside the store. Max turned the big key noisily in the lock. Ned Jenks, Regan O'Connor and James Dorsett loitered a minute. Their mood hesitated between joking Max on his optimism and abandonment to their earlier lassitude. Max turned to go, then he faced them.

"I'll play you fellows a hand of poker, showdown. If I lose you can call me a fool. If I win, you've got to put all your money in Halstead; you've got to back any program I lay out." He stopped, abashed at his own outburst. "We'll start with a grain elevator, that'll stir the town up."

Regan gave a thin derisive whistle. He slapped Max on the back. "Get the cards."

They went back into the store. Max got the cards and a lantern. The others pulled their chairs around the table. Dorsett took a pail with a dipper in it and went back to the faucet in the store room. They had forgotten the heat and the flies buzzing through the open door.

Regan shuffled. Dorsett cut the pack with elaborate seriousness and passed it to Max to deal. There was no sound but the cool flop of the cards.

A moth flew inside the lamp chimney and burned with a greasy sizzle that sounded loudly against the silence.

No one spoke until Max finished the third card round. Ned Jenks glanced at Regan with a slow grin. Max looked at each hand, marking them down in his mind; Dorsett was headed for an Ace-high straight, Regan's pair of eights was high, and Ned Jenks had a possible straight; he, himself, had a lone Queen.

"Looks like the weather and the cards are both against you, Max," Regan said. Dorsett hitched his chair closer. Max dealt again.

Regan's pair of eights still held up. The Queen that Max was looking for went to Jenks and left his straight open at both ends. Three Queens had already been dealt. Max must pair his lone Queen to beat even Dorsett's eights.

Max's cigar had gone out. He laid it down on the end of the table, wet his forefinger on his tongue and dealt the fifth and last round.

Three low cards spoiled the two straights and left Regan's eights high. Jenks groaned at his own card.

"Only eights to beat Max, but it takes the Queen!"

"Try and get her with three ladies in sight already!" Regan chuckled.

Max hesitated for a fraction of a second before he turned his card up.

It was the Queen of Spades. He stared at the card. He shook his head. "She did it," he said softly. Then a sheepish smile spread below his mustache.

"Dammit, now we'll all be dragged headlong into this scheme of yours, Max," said James Dorsett, throwing in his hand. Regan laughed; Ned Jenks spread the cards out to look at them again.

"How about both a grain elevator and an opera house, Max, just to start things?" Regan suggested.

It was as though the heat had broken. The tension had gone. Their chairs scraped back from the table jovially. Max put out the light and turned the key in the door for the second time that night. They sauntered along the dark street talking.

Max said good night to Ned Jenks at his gate and went on to his own house. He went in quietly. On the stairs, leaning against the railing, sat Julia. She had been asleep.

"Oh, Max."

"Why, Jule?"

"Chris fretted so I came down here to sit till I was sure he'd be asleep." Her voice was stretched with weariness. Max picked her up and carried her upstairs.

"You're all worn out with this heat, Jule. I'll sit down here with him."

Julia closed her eyes and let her head drop on his shoulder. It was good to be carried upstairs; it was like being a little girl again.

"We're going to have a grain elevator and maybe even an opera house here, Jule," Max said as he laid her down on the bed. "Ned Jenks and Dorsett and Regan—they're all going to back it. Maybe you'll have to give another benefit to help raise money."

"I will," agreed Julia sleepily.

Max had never talked to Julia about his poker, and it didn't occur to him to tell her about the evening's game. He put on his slippers and went back downstairs. He tiptoed in to look at the baby. Then he brought a chair from the sitting-room into Julia's drawing-room. He took off his collar and tie and settled down in the chair for the night.

10

FAITH DORSETT frowned anxiously at herself in the mirror. She held the curling tongs close to her head.

"You're going to singe yourself doing that, Faith," James Dorsett commented, stopping his own dressing operations to watch.

"I will not. You have to get it hot, or it all comes out with the steam from the soup." Faith unrolled her tongs and released a long black tendril of hair. "There!" She took a comb and combed the tendrils into a tight waving frizz. "I get so sick of Alice Jenks and her waterfall of curls!"

"There's Julia, she . . ."

"Julia's hair is naturally curly, James! Go on downstairs till I get through. It makes me nervous to be watched."

James Dorsett laughed. "Vixen! Shrew!" Then he kissed her ear.

"James!" Faith melted. "Oh, James, what would people think!"

"If a man kissed his wife?" Then he went downstairs whistling.

Faith twisted around in her chair, holding the hand-mirror in front of her. She tried smiling at herself.

James was waiting in the hall with her fur-lined gaiters.

"I tell you, Faith, Halstead will be a different place with Regan and Nell gone. Remember that Thanksgiving dinner out there?"

"It's been a week of festivity with all these parties for them: at the Judge's Tuesday night, and the Withers' breakfast, and here Wednesday, and Max and Julia's tonight. It's a pity the Hetzels aren't back from Germany. . . ."

"Mr. and Mrs. Max Hauser entertained at dinner in honor of Mr. and Mrs. Regan O'Connor, who are leaving our city for Wyoming. Covers were set for fourteen. . . ." The *Halstead Courier* read the next day in its Social Column. "Green ferns formed the graceful centerpiece, surrounded by tall white candles in silver candlesticks with white fringed shades. The guests were: Mr. and Mrs. Regan O'Connor, Judge and Mrs. Mitchell, Senator and Mrs. Withers, Miss Delia Eiler, Mr. and Mrs. James Dorsett, Mr. and Mrs. Ned Jenks, Dr. Chapman."

Julia, helping herself to the frozen punch, shook her head at Regan O'Connor on her right.

"But why Wyoming, Mr. O'Connor. I'm just getting over feeling that Nebraska is 'wild west.'"

With the other part of her mind she was grateful that Lena had remembered to serve the punch between the joint of beef and the quail. The dinner was going well. She looked down the shining table. Mrs. Mitchell was talking heatedly to James Dorsett. Max did love giving big dinners.

Lena came solemnly to take the punch glasses. The quails in the nests of purée of chestnuts looked exactly right.

"Oh, yes, I am liking it. I think I liked it from that first night at the Withers'," Julia said, answering Regan O'Connor. "Our friends, though, never the country."

The truth of her own words grew upon her. After all, it might easily be a dinner at home, she thought with pride, looking at her guests, at the table. Julia wore the diamond star in her hair tonight and the black mull with the gold thread, made a little larger because she had never been quite so slim since her second baby. The shadows in her neck had filled. What had been grace of body before was now graciousness. Pride touched Max's expression when he looked down the table at his wife.

"I don't care what you say, I believe our daughters should go to college as well as our sons!"

"Oh, Gertrude," Mrs. Withers protested.

Mrs. Mitchell's color rose. Everybody knew that she did some of the Judge's secretarial work. She was forty-five and very plain. Alice Jenks shook her curls.

"You make us all feel very ignorant." She pouted a little coquettishly at the Senator. "What do you think, Senator Withers?"

"I am sure that you could not be improved upon, my dear," the Senator said gallantly.

"I believe in higher education for women," Faith Dorsett

declared earnestly. "Why should women know nothing but fancywork and housekeeping and child-raising?"

"How about you, Mrs. Hauser? You're being very discreet," Regan O'Connor asked.

"I believe in it, too," Julia said quietly. "I have ever since I saw the Centennial and felt how small an idea of the world I had."

Lena set the Nesselrode pudding in front of Julia with the monogrammed silver server and the square Limoges plates.

"You know," Dr. Chapman frowned seriously, "I believe this higher education might be a good idea. It would keep some of the gentler sex from being so intent on getting married." Everyone laughed, even Delia Eiler who blushed at the same time.

"Well, at least we can be thankful that they are not discussing having them go to the same colleges as men," Alice Jenks remarked.

"You know what Ruskin says," Judge Mitchell said and quoted sonorously, "'We are foolish, and without excuse foolish, in speaking of the superiority of one sex to the other as if they could be compared in similar things. . . . They are in nothing alike, and the happiness and perfection of both depends on each asking and receiving from the other what the other only can give.'"

"Capital!" Dr. Chapman's eyes twinkled at the oracular delivery of the quotation.

Alice Jenks' bright interest dulled before the long quotation. Max twisted his mustache and frowned at this interruption of good talk.

"Ah, Judge Mitchell, that is exactly what I tell my wife," Regan O'Connor murmured slyly.

Julia ate her pudding very slowly so she would not finish before the Judge.

"The ladies are leaving us for the realms of higher education." James Dorsett bowed low in mock reverence. Julia and Mrs. O'Connor led the way through the folding doors. Julia felt the success of her dinner pleasantly, the warmth and light of her rooms. How lovely it would be if they could go on through to the drawing-room instead of stopping in the sitting-room.

"I must go upstairs; I laced my stays so tight I can just barely breathe," Alice Jenks whispered to Julia.

"Such a delicious dinner, my dear," Mrs. Withers murmured to Julia.

"Oh, thank you," Julia replied, as though she and Lena had not been working for two days to achieve it.

"Nell, why do you have to leave and go off to Wyoming?" Faith Dorsett burst out. "I loathe having things stop."

"I know." Nell O'Connor's face was almost pretty, Julia thought, when she looked so pensive. The sharp nose and prominent cheek bones had a certain distinction. "But Regan says the day for cattle is over here in Nebraska. He hates living anywhere where it's so settled. He even hates to see people building in that new subdivision near us. We thought we were almost on the range when we built there," she laughed.

Lena brought the coffee tray. "Don't forget the coffee for the gentlemen, Lena."

"Except for leaving here," Mrs. O'Connor continued, "I think I'll like it. I like wild country, too, and I do despise the betwixt and between thing. I'd rather live right in Dublin or London or New York or way off on the range."

"Not for me, thank you," Delia Eiler declared emphatically. "I'm not made for pioneering."

Julia poured the coffee into her own cup. Something

93

had gone from her pleasure in the evening because the O'Connors were leaving. She felt suddenly depressed.

Max passed cigars around the table and brought the silver decanter of his best wine from the sideboard. The wine glasses had been a wedding gift from Julia's aunt in Prague.

Ned Jenks settled back in his chair. "I had a letter from a banker in Chicago today, Max."

"What did he say about the strikes?"

"That a lot of railroad property was destroyed, but the troops were called out in time to save too serious damage."

"Well, I heard from a man in Cleveland saying that a lot of stuff he'd ordered is spoiling at the depot because the freight man wouldn't let him have his goods," Max added.

Senator Withers gave a snort. "Why, sir, there's a mob in every city ready to join with the strikers, and we have no way of enforcing law in the case of a sudden attack. The army has been destroyed by dirty politicians!"

Regan refilled his glass. "You talk like capitalists from the East instead of Westerners!"

"Well, I'll tell you, the East is a troubled place these days. There's some satisfaction in living out here in a new country," Senator Withers continued.

Dr. Chapman offered no comment. He listened, his mouth curved sarcastically. Regan was right, it came to him. These men were Eastern still in their convictions. Nebraska had done nothing to them. They were as much conservative reactionaries as though they lived in New York City. Dr. Chapman looked at O'Connor just as he laid down his cigar and said in his Irish voice:

"Of course, I'm a cattleman, but I'll tell you what's wrong down there in Washington. . . ."

Dr. Chapman didn't listen. He was looking at Regan's

black head, thrust forward now, at the English line of his coat, the brown-red color of his skin that was as dark as a cowboy's. When he went away, something would go with him that would never be replaced here. . . .

"Regan, why do you have to pull up and leave?" he asked aloud. "Three years ago you thought there was no place in the country that had the possibilities . . ."

"Three years ago," Regan cut in on him, "the range wasn't all cut up into farms. Nebraska's changing, John."

The conversation dropped off. Silence hung over them a single, uncomfortable instant.

"Shall we join the ladies?" Max asked shoving back his chair, trying with the heartiness of his voice to wipe out that silence.

II. 1882

"FIVE years mean a lot to a cottonwood tree, Mis' Hauser, but they don't tell much on these maples an' catalpas, didn't you say they was?" Otto Herman pushed his felt hat back on his head and scratched the few hairs on his scalp with something of the fervor he put into raking. "No, ma'am, what ain't natcheral to the soil ain't going to do well, but I'll put manure round 'em if you say so. If you'd 'a' had cottonwoods put in here, now . . ." He shoved his hat forward again over his sweaty brow. He took up his shovel and went around the house to the barn.

Julia Hauser sat on the top step of the porch where the sun was warm on the boards. It was true as old Otto said, the young saplings that Max had imported from Illinois were still frail-looking and gangly. Down the street in the Jenks' yard and below them in the vacant lot the gray trunks were thick as porch posts. Dry years and wet alike they put forth fat buds the color of molasses and filled the air with the flying cottony web of seeds. Soon they would be full-leaved again, and Alice Jenks's walk would have green shade. It had been foolish to try to raise trees that grew so slowly after all. But this year they did look healthier. They came above the sill of the sitting-room windows. Maybe they were really going to grow.

Julia's gaze drifted down the street. Anne was jumping rope with Lucy Jenks. Her fair hair flew out from her shoulders every time she jumped. Julia came halfway down the steps. Then she smiled to see Christopher, as usual, intent on work of his own. He sat flat on the ground, his fat legs straight out in front of him, pounding something—it looked like a spike—into a wooden box.

The children had grown a little pale during the winter. It was good for them to be out in the sun. It was good to be out herself. She grew tired of the long winters. And this winter had seemed so long, perhaps because of the baby. She had almost forgotten how she had felt before Chris was born. Five years was a long time between babies. The baby would be born this month. He would have time to get a good start before the winter began. And in the spring . . . Surely, she could make the trip back home this year.

Julia leaned against the railing of the steps, curiously reposed for a woman in the middle of the morning. In her white muslin dress made very full in the belt with high neck and long sleeves, she was a gracious figure, still giving a sense of smallness, even fragility. She sat in the sun bareheaded, her hair curling up to the new high knot she made on the top of her head.

In the five years the town had grown along with the cottonwoods. It was spoken of as one of the strong towns of Nebraska. There were three banks, two hotels, three blocks of stores, not counting saloons and billiard rooms down near the tracks. A new brick building housed the *Halstead Courier* and a rival newspaper was just down the block in the old Land Office. The Opera House had been built three years. The town was possessed of all the conveniences of city life, gas, a water-works, and a new county jail. There were three drug stores; James Dorsett was the head of a law-firm in handsome new offices in the Withers Block. There were four dentists, two more doctors, a home for the insane, and three more churches. The town had shot up over night, it seemed to Max, but to Julia it seemed to have grown with the slow rhythm of a nine long months of pregnancy. It had been a duration not to be measured in terms of time but of nostalgia, of growing doubts and enthusiasm that yielded often to disappointment. It had been all physical development. It had not grown either socially or culturally, she felt within herself.

And the country was the same. Halstead was still set down in the midst of a flat plain, remote from everywhere. The cornfields were larger, that was all. The cattle range was almost entirely fenced in and being made to produce. Farmers jogged into town on wagons now; the cowboys on their way up from Texas who used to clatter up to the Golden House bar were only a memory. Sometimes Julia wondered if the town had found its natural limits. Max and Dorsett and Ned Jenks had given over thinking it might ever equal Omaha. But it was a good lively town; the center of a wide agricultural territory, they told each other and themselves.

But it must be more than a "good lively town," and Julia would go over to Mrs. Mitchell's to plan the new program for the Literary Club, or send to Chicago for the latest fashion plates. The town had grown, but its isolation was as great as ever.

The people were changing, she felt sometimes; there had never been anyone to take the O'Connors' place, no one who brought with them a sense of larger places. And that mattered so. Once after they had gone to dinner at the McCartneys'—Mr. McCartney owned the handsome jewelry store on Omaha Street—she had come home feeling so dulled by the contact with people who had so little to say, who ate so vulgarly, that she had talked to Max about leaving Halstead. But Max had pushed the subject away. He hated to be made uncomfortable. He was so content and so proud of the way the town had pulled itself up after that dreadful drought year and gone on growing. He was well-to-do; one of Halstead's leading citizens. Her mind curled disdainfully away from the thought. He put the money back into the business as fast as he got it out. Perhaps there was nothing to do but improve the town, keep up one's own standards.

Once Max had said affectionately, contentedly, "I believe you like it here as much as I do, Jule." She had tried to look right at him so he could see how much there was that she hated, but she couldn't hurt him. Instead she had retied Anne's hair ribbon and only said:

"Not that much, Max."

The bold adventurous air that had been around the town in the beginning had been lost in its new stolid growth. Halstead had grown, but in littleness, too. It was still as hot in summer, or very nearly, and bitter cold in winter. There was no view for the eyes or for the soul except the cornfields, or was she just growing older? Soon she must think of the children more than Max. She didn't want their knowledge of life to be only this.

Julia got up from the porch steps and went into the house. Her house had not changed greatly in these few years. The front room on the right of the hall was still unfurnished. The children used it as a playroom. There were grotesque paper horses Anne had cut from some old newspapers lying on the floor, and a rag doll of Anne's drooped in abject shame in the corner. Still there was no formal furniture and no curtains at the windows, only shades. Even Halstead was used to it now, although no one had ever heard a proper explanation for it, and it was held as a queer thing about Max Hauser's wife.

It was close to noon. Lena was setting the table in the dining-room, humming as she moved around the room.

"Lunch is ready for the children, Mis' Hauser."

Julia went back to call them. Anne came quickly, ready to leave her game at the drop of the hat. Christopher frowned over his pounding and went on until he was called again. Julia's children minded. Mrs. Jenks often wondered why.

"She's so kind of gentle with them all the time."

But there was no lack of firmness in Julia Hauser.

Julia watched them coming up the street. She knew everything about them so well she could shut her eyes and see them as clearly as when she looked: the looseness of the tops of Anne's shoes around her ankles, the new slender look she was getting now as she grew out of babyhood, her fleetness as she ran. Chris was only ten months younger and yet he was still a baby; his face had fat curves. His hair that was growing darker curled over his forehead. He never quite caught up with Anne. He still hung on to his hammer and spike. He climbed the steps laboriously, planting two feet on each step. Anne made a dance of it and was on the porch.

Julia looked at them, a pride on her lips that didn't show in her words.

"Go wash your hands and then have lunch." She watched

them down the hall toward the kitchen. Julia Hauser had queer ideas for a woman living in Halstead. Her children still ate by themselves at the table in the sunny kitchen. She put a distance as wide as the space from the swinging door of the kitchen to the edge of the dining-room rug between her children and herself. Max liked to talk of business plans at the table, talk that was too old for children.

She snipped off the brown tips of the fern in the dining-room window. She could hear their spoons clattering against their bowls. Anne's high voice came clearly out to her as Lena came in with the water pitcher.

"You spilled; you spilled your milk, Chris!"

The day was interrupted as all the days through the past six years had been by Max's coming home at noon and in the evening. Regularity was one of the cords of Max's being, and he never chafed against that regularity. His days were full, vivid, engrossing. The daily callers at the store brought color and excitement. He had a deep feeling of content in his life. Part of it he drew from Julia's presence, from his children. He had no least idea that Julia craved excitement and outrageous fun that had no place in the solid living of Halstead.

Max had grown heavier; his curly brown hair that was so like Chris's had gray in it. He still smoked his big black cigars. He had a cough that had come to be almost a mannerism with him. He held his cigar between two fingers of his left hand and coughed a deep loose cough. It gave emphasis when he talked, though it got in the way of his singing so he didn't sing much any more. Max had prospered with Halstead more even than Julia knew. He was known in the neighboring states. Many of the wholesale houses on South Water Street in Chicago had the name of Max Hauser on their books.

Today he came into the dining-room beaming.

"Well, Jule, it came!"

"Oh, Max, how fine!"

They sat down across the table from each other where they had talked about so many things cryptically, with a formality that fitted the dignity of the room.

"Oscar and John helped load it, and it's all ready to be set up. Ventner is working on the storage room now. It's worth what it cost, Jule. You come down this afternoon and see it."

"Think of your having the first cold-storage plant west of the Mississippi, Max!" Julia was stirred as always by the drama of the event. It satisfied her desire that significance be attached to their living and doing.

"It's greatly improved, Jule, over the one we saw at the Fair, remember?"

Julia laughed and looked across the table. "All I remember about that refrigerator is the way the fish looked that had been preserved for three years!"

Max brushed aside her remark. "You know this is an ammonium plant, and you can keep food. . . . Why, I'm going to be able to buy meats and poultry months ahead. You wait, Jule, I'll be getting fruits from the coast one of these days!" Max's eyes sparkled. "Jule, you won't be sorry we had to put off furnishing your drawing-room awhile or that trip back East."

Julia was silent, buttering her bread.

"Come down around three o'clock, Jule; it ought to be all installed by then."

Max hurried back after his dinner without even waiting to smoke a cigar. The excitement that possessed him showed in his quick step down Second Street, the way he wore his hat. In his coat pocket was the copy of the *Halstead Courier,* folded at the account of "Max Hauser buys elaborate new equipment . . . first in Nebraska."

In the afternoon Otto harnessed the horse Max had bought for Julia and brought her around to the hitching post.

"Mis' Hauser, she sure fought me today when I give her the bit." Otto distrusted the horse that had once been a racer. "Sure you don't want me to drive her down for you?"

"Oh, no, Otto, thank you; she's really gentle."

Julia climbed in the shiny black buggy and took the reins. Otto lifted Christopher and Anne up beside her, but he shook his head doubtfully at Mrs. Hauser driving out in her condition. He chewed at the inside of his cheek and went on back to speak his mind to Lena.

Julia liked to drive. She had seen this horse at Regan's ranch, and when the O'Connors came to leave, she had asked Max for it. The horse's name was January.

Julia hadn't been driving much this spring. The roads had been bad, and she had stayed at home a great deal on account of her condition. But today she had acted on a sudden dramatic impulse to drive down to Max's store to see his new cold-storage plant. Christopher wore his best suit, Anne's hair was brushed till it shone, and she wore her flower-sprigged lawn. Julia wore her best black satin that Max had given her when Chris was born. She had only had it made up last year. Over her dress she wore a cape that fell in properly concealing folds. Julia sat up very straight, the reins held out in front of her, a child on each side.

"Mamma, are we only driving down to Papa's store?" Christopher knit his brows and tried to puzzle it out. He was very like Max. Anne smiled happily. The horse was a pacer, and her hoofs sounded smartly. The buggy whirled onto Omaha Street, flashing past the Majestic Block, the new bank, the Withers Building and drew up before Max Hauser's.

"Mamma, what are we going to do?" Anne asked. She could feel that it was a special occasion from Mamma's best black satin dress, the way she drove, something in Mamma's face that made her look extra smiling.

Ned Jenks saw her and hurried out to tie the horse and help them all down from the buggy.

"Max is sure a hustler, Julia; we're proud of him. There's been a crowd of people in all afternoon to see the refrigerator. It's like a reception."

Julia smiled. "I'm glad. He wanted to buy it long ago, but we've had so many poor years. Here, children." Anne and Christopher went in ahead of her.

Max's store always had an effect of darkness after the bright sun on the street. It still smelled of grain and earth and spices, but Max had enlarged his space greatly. He had built on in back, and he owned a big barn across the tracks that had painted across one side where passengers on the B. and M. all saw it as they came into Halstead, "Max Hauser, Warehouse."

Max had suspended business for the day and given himself up to the delight of explaining and demonstrating the new cold-storage plant to twenty or more admiring spectators.

"Can I see it, Papa?" Chris called out plaintively. They had come up to the crowd, and the grown-ups were too tall for him to see the center of the excitement.

Max laughed with pleasure. "Here, Chris; the future partner of the firm ought to look it over!" He lifted him up on his shoulder to see and smiled over at Julia. He was pleased that she had come.

Some of the group were strangers to Julia. Some were

farmers from outside the town; everybody knew Max. Mrs. Mitchell was there with the Judge.

"Julia, it is wonderful!" She came over to Julia. "I've never seen one before. Think what a metropolis Halstead is to have a cold-storage plant! How are you feeling?" she dropped her voice to ask. Max had turned back to his new possession.

"Just walk right in, it's large enough, and see for yourselves how cold it is. We ought to be able to keep all the milk you get on your place next summer, Haseloff," he joked. Then Max closed the refrigerator door with satisfaction in the heavy squishing sound of the weather-stripping and the clang of the big clamps that barred it. He passed out cigars like a man at a wedding-feast or an election.

"Max, you'll want to take out some insurance on that." Arthur Dalton was a newcomer to Halstead who had opened an insurance office in the Stone Block.

"Are you going to pack away any beer in there, Max?" another farmer joked. But the town was proud of Max Hauser.

Julia stayed until most of the crowd had gone. She talked to Mrs. Mitchell and Mrs. Withers. Chris got down from his father's shoulder and played Follow the Leader with Anne all around the store, touching the barrels, hopping on one foot in front of the potato sacks, walking backwards towards the front window.

When everyone had gone, Max came over to Julia. "Let me show it to you, Jule." He opened the door for her and pointed out the guarantee printed right in the zinc lining of the door. "Then see here, Jule." Julia's thoughts flashed back irrelevantly to the Fair. Something in Max's voice, explaining, pointing out things to her, had brought it all back. She touched the coiled pipes coated with frost and pulled her finger-tips away with an amazed little squeal.

"Come, dear, you mustn't get chilled." Max led her out of the storage room a little regretfully.

Max put the children in the buggy and helped Julia in.

"Can't you come home now, Max?" Julia asked.

"Not quite yet, dear; someone else may drop in and want to see it." Max couldn't leave his new possession yet or miss explaining it and hearing the comments. "I'll be along. Drive slowly, Jule." He waved to her as she turned around and drove off down the street.

"Can't we go for a ride, Mamma?"

"Just a little tiny ways, Mamma, out past the grain elevator and back?"

"A little ways," said Julia. She drove slowly, letting the reins lie loosely in her gloved hands. The children chattered without her listening. She looked over toward Bittersweet Creek where the trees made a faint haze of green against the sky. A man was plowing in the field near the river. She liked the fields best now when they lay black and hummocky and gave up a moist smell of loam, before they turned into the monotony of endless cornfields. Sometimes it seemed to Julia as if those rustling cornfields, rising green and tasseling into yellow at the top and finally fading to a dusty colorlessness from leaf to stalk, brought down the blasting heat of a Nebraska summer. When it was most stifling, Max always said, "This is good growing weather for the corn." But the country still had an unfamiliarity about it; she would never come close to it as to the lake at home.

The road looked muddy ahead past the Martins' place. The Martins never took time from their fields to work the road. Julia turned around and drove back home.

"It is not."

105

"Well, it could if Papa wanted it to."

"Could not."

Julia roused from her own idle gazing to hear Anne and Chris arguing shrilly.

"Children! Anne! What is it?"

"Oh, Mamma, Chris said the new refrigerator made quarts and quarts of ice cream."

"I didn't; I said it could if Papa wanted it to."

Julia smiled. "No, I don't think it could make ice cream, but it could keep it from melting quite awhile."

"Chris said it could," Anne continued, hating to give up the argument.

"I bet Papa could make it if he wanted to," Chris muttered, giving elaborate attention to the whipstock.

As they turned back, the spring wind blew dirt in their faces. Anne hid her face against Julia. Christopher sat up like a man and shielded his face with his hat.

"I don't like the smell of the dirt, Mamma," Anne whimpered. Julia shut her teeth on gritty particles that blew into her mouth.

"Some day when the streets are all paved with cedar blocks and there are more trees, there won't be these dirt storms, children," Julia encouraged them as Max had encouraged her, "or maybe we'll all move back to Chicago." Julia stopped short in her thinking. Why had she said that? She had never put it into words before.

"Where's Chicago, Mamma?" Chris asked. But Julia spoke to the horse instead of answering. She drove around to the barn whose big door opened on a grassy alley-way. Otto left digging by the pie-plant bed to come over to take the horse.

"Some dirty to be out, ain't it, Mis' Hauser? An' it ain't a good sign to have the wind blow so in April, neither."

Julia shook the dust out of her skirts. The black satin

had a dull look to it. She went into the house and upstairs to lie down on the big walnut bed to rest. It had tired her more than she thought; a different kind of tiredness than she remembered before. Perhaps the baby would be born this week. But Max had been pleased to have her go down to see the refrigerator. He had wanted it for so long. Now he had gotten it. It was a kind of milestone.

Lying so still in her familiar room that Lena looked in and then tiptoed downstairs to shush the children, Julia wondered what she had really wanted that she had gotten, except the children. Not the drawing-room; but that didn't matter any more, it made a good play-room for the children. Once she had wanted Max to be different, but he never would be. He would never want the same things she did nor ever feel the same way. It was queer how easy it was, after all, to get used to a kind of loneliness. She had always told herself that after a bit she would change things: the town, the house, even Max's ideas; she had always had a secret confidence that everything would come out right in the end, of being able to make it, but today, lately, she wasn't sure. Perhaps nothing would ever happen except that year by year she would grow older, and Max would grow older even more rapidly.

Jeanette was born on Palm Sunday, just after Max had bought the refrigerator.

"Seems like there's too much excitement all at once in this here family," Lena told the children as she dished out their oatmeal. "Your pa's got a new ice-box, and your ma's got a new baby, an' it's Palm Sunday at the same time!"

Anne and Christopher talked the baby over, sitting out on the porch steps that morning.

"Mamma says the baby comes just like the crocuses out by the fence," Anne announced conclusively.

"Flowers aren't babies," stubbornly objected Chris, shaking his big curly head.

"Anyway, Mamma said so," Anne answered witheringly. Anne sat still, drawing the end of her hair through her lips because Lucy Jenks told her it would curl if she kept it wet all the time. A kind of mystery, greater than the weekly one of Sunday, hung over the house. It reached even out to the step of the front porch, a feeling half-way between a surprise and a birthday. Anne sucked her hair with secret pleasure.

"I wish it wouldn't be Sunday so I could hammer." Chris rested his fat little chin on his fists and glowered darkly down the walk.

Suddenly Anne darted down the steps and ran around the house. She came back drawing in her breath with a sharp excitement. Christopher looked up suspiciously.

"I didn't do anything," he muttered in quick defense.

"I've got to tell Mamma something," Anne said importantly. She hurried in the house, Christopher after her in swift pursuit.

"You mustn't bother or the baby'll die; Lena said so," Christopher whispered loudly, panting up the stairs behind her.

Anne flung the door of Julia's bedroom open with sudden daring. She saw at a glance that Dr. Chapman had come back, that Papa was there, and Mamma still had the little baby in bed.

"Mamma," she began, then her daring gave out.

"What is it, Anne?" Julia stretched out her hand.

"Oh, Mamma, the trees; they're all cut off, the branches, I mean; there isn't any green left on them." Christopher pushed the door open timidly and came in to hear the last of Anne's news.

"Why, Max, what happened?"

Max had been explaining the principle of the cold-storage plant to Dr. Chapman who had been listening politely, wondering how a man whom Julia Hauser loved could be interested in refrigerators. Max got up and hurried downstairs. "I don't know, Jule, I'll go see."

"I'll bring you advance news, Julia." Dr. Chapman followed. Julia strained to hear Anne's shrill little voice down in the hall.

"Here, Papa, I'll show you!"

"Me too," shrieked Christopher, his copper-toed boots clumping down the stairs.

Julia looked at the sleeping baby beside her. She was a pretty baby as Anne and Chris had been. Julia pulled the bundle a little closer with a rich sense of possession. This baby would be Jeanette.

There was Lena on the stairs with her tray; the top of the sugar bowl, that was always a little loose, clinked against the edge of the bowl. Lena came in beaming. She was pleased over the new baby. She set the tray on the dresser to take the baby back to its bed.

"Lena, Anne says someone's cut all the branches of the trees. Do you know what she's talking about?"

"Ach, Mis' Hauser, Ma'am, I thought you wouldn't mind, and I thought how lucky they was all leafed out, an' I cut 'em off to take to Mass for Palm Sunday—you know, place of palms."

"Oh, Lena! Mr. Hauser sent way back to Illinois for those trees, and we've had such a time growing them," Julia finished weakly and burst into laughter. "Oh, Lena!" she gasped through her laughter.

Max and Dr. Chapman and the children, who were

round-eyed with excitement, came back upstairs like a baffled scouting expedition. Julia choked trying to get her face straight.

"Oh, Max, Lena cut them all off for Palm Sunday, to take to church!"

Max's face was bewildered. "You cut them off, Lena?"

Dr. Chapman gave a shout and clapped his knee loudly so that Chris laughed too. And Julia burst out again. Lena left the tray and stalked out of the room haughtily, mumbling, "It was for the church, sir."

Max looked a little hurt. "I don't see," he began, "exactly what's funny. They'll never be the same."

"Oh, Max, it's a shame, but it is funny," Julia said gently, smiling at him, understanding him. The children stood looking from Max to Julia. Dr. Chapman looked at Max's expression, and his own face reddened. Then he picked both children up on his back and carried them whooping downstairs on his way out.

12

JULIA HAUSER was standing in the bed-sitting-room "being fitted." Wiry little Miss Morey was down on her knees taking the hem. Her words which came almost continuously had to trickle through the barrage of pins protruding from her lips.

"I'm glad you could give me the first two weeks of September, Miss Morey."

"Oh, Mrs. Hauser, I wouldn't give 'em to nobody else. Mrs. Dalton wanted me because she's going back to Iowa to her sister's wedding, but I told her I had to take care of my old families first."

Julia was startled to hear herself classed as one of the

"old families," but in a town that was only nine years old, perhaps the title was fitting.

"I always like that first black satin I made you, Mrs. Hauser. I remember it was just after your first baby, that was Anne, was born. You had the waist made like the green dress you brought with you from Chicago. There, now, just walk over to the door." Miss Morey sat back on her heels with her small head tipped to one side to survey the hem.

"But I liked that blue challis you had made when you were—before Jeanette was born, even if I do say it. . . . Nope, it goes up just a mite on the back gore." Julia walked back to Miss Morey.

Are children the milestones in every woman's life? Julia wondered. All her living since her wedding had been "before Anne," "before Chris," "when Jeanette was born." The greatest reach of memory was summed up in the words, "before the children were born." If a woman had this higher education would her life have different terms?

"Now I don't say that Mrs. Dalton isn't a lady, and I don't say she is. I'm not one to run around talking, or I wouldn't be sewing in the best homes in town, but she don't care a snap what quality goes into the lining. I told her the last time I sewed for her that you can tell a lady by the inside of her dress. Mrs. Hauser, you're getting just a bit heavier. My! you were a slip of a girl when you come here, and such a young thing. But a little more flesh gives you a better figure. Do you want I should pad it here over the hips? You're a mite flat, you know."

Julia stepped out of the new wine-red poplin.

"Woops! it's just pinned. There!"

Miss Morey wearied her. Having clothes made was such an undertaking, something you had to do fall and spring, like house-cleaning. The red silk was going to be lovely, though. She had planned to have it as soon as Jeanette was born. It was almost exactly the shade of that dress in her trousseau, only it was poplin instead of taffeta.

"Did you get this dress patte'n here, or did you send East?"

"Here," Julia answered. "I bought it at Naughton-McNary's."

"Oh, the new store!"

"Yes, Bush's didn't have this shade."

"Have you been into Stevens's? That's a good place, 'specially for shoes. I've never seen a place grow like Halstead—two shoe stores in one year!"

Julia escaped to care for Jeanette. She lingered purposely over her bathing. When she was dressed, Julia pulled the shades and sat down in the low rocking-chair to nurse her. Jeanette was three months old. Julia set the chair to rocking gently and gave herself up to her own thoughts. The baby's fist lay against her breast so she could feel the tiny nails.

It was queer, the energy that seemed to flood back in you after every childbirth. When you were carrying the child you were taken up with that and with the things of your own home. Max was always so solicitous and undemanding. The last few months he had gone to sleep in the back bedroom. It had been restful lying alone in the big bed, being alone. But now that the baby was born, she wanted to take up living again. That was why she had bought a red poplin instead of a blue or dark brown. The Literary Club would start next month. She must have the Withers and the Dorsetts in for dinner. There would be church; perhaps there would be a stock company here this winter. . . . Julia rocked silently. They would finish up the sewing, and there would be canning and house cleaning. She would keep busy, but it would be so like last year. She wished she were more like Max; he liked things to be the same year in, year out.

Julia put the baby back in the bassinet that was freshly lined again. She pushed the window up. Surely air and sun couldn't hurt her. It was like Indian summer. Then she got her thimble and sewing apron and went back to Miss Morey.

Miss Morey was a tartar in her way.

"Now, Mrs. Hauser, if you'll just baste along there where I've got it pinned, I'll get the sleeves stitched up."

"Miss Morey, I thought we'd do Anne's sewing next week, and then I've got some waists and little pants for Christopher."

Miss Morey nodded. The machine made too loud a noise for comfortable conversation.

"There!" Miss Morey sat back against her chair. "I was to Mrs. McCartney's house last month. You know, he's the head of that jewelry store on Omaha Street. Well, I'll say this, I've never seen more cut glass on any sideboard in this town." Miss Morey laid her shears down impressively. "And she wore a diamond ring as big as the end of this emery bag, but do you know, I don't believe her husband lets her call a cent her own. She wanted a dress made up with ten gores, and when I said you couldn't get that out of six yards, not with big sleeves and all, she said her husband thought she should do it on six, and she didn't like to ask for more!"

Julia broke off her thread. "I thought I'd have some wool dresses made for Anne this winter. Mrs. Jenks said I could borrow her pattern."

"My, it seems to me Mrs. Jenks looks twice as old with those curls she used to wear tucked in that way. There's folks in this town think she's kind of stand-offish. I know one of the school-teachers I sewed for last May said that, but I thought to myself, why shouldn't she be? Her husband was president of the first bank in town, and she came out here from the East; Buffalo, wasn't it? And she knows how things ought to be done; you know how that is yourself, Mrs. Hauser. The new folks that are coming to town, like those Rollinses that used to have a farm, they aren't in the same class with the rest of you. There's nobody knows a lady better than her dressmaker." Miss Morey bit her thread off close to the cloth.

Julia sewed silently. Once she rapped on the window with her thimble to tell Chris to get down from the grape arbor.

"There's plenty that feel that way. Mrs. Edwards, the new dentist's wife, told me she'd never seen a town where society was so tight, and though I wouldn't want her to hear it, she did mention you and Mrs. Mitchell and Mrs. Dorsett. Well, I told her, it's just unconscious, 'cause they're as fine ladies as you ever knew."

"I'm sorry she feels that way," Julia murmured. "I think I called when she first moved here. I have to go down to speak to Lena." Julia laid her thimble on the sewing-table and fled out of hearing of Miss Morey's tongue.

She hurried downstairs into the sitting-room. Miss Morey's gossip was harmless enough, but it made the town seem so hopelessly little. It put into words the fear that sometimes grew in her own mind: that the new people who were moving into Halstead, who were even in the Literary Club and on the School Committee—people she had to live with—had no traditions, no feeling for the larger ways of living. Even Max said one day that the town was changing. "It isn't like the old days when a man could raise five hundred dollars on his word." And James Dorsett talked sometimes about the West going out of it. She had a sense of foreboding, of looking back to those first years as the best time. Halstead was just becoming large enough, so there weren't so many physical limitations, and now there were to be other limitations.

When Julia went upstairs for another fitting, Miss Morey said brightly, "Well, I was just sitting here sewing, Mrs. Hauser, and I looked over at that pile of things for Anne, and I said to myself, one of these days I'll be making her wedding dress." Miss Morey leaned back on her heels and then forward while she gave a giggle that was scarcely more than a squeak and to Julia seemed a little lewd.

Sudden anger flashed a second in Julia's eyes, then she smiled meaninglessly as she tried on the half-finished dress. Anne, growing up here in this world of Miss Morey and the women she sewed for! Anne, knowing nothing of life that concerned itself with the larger world! No, Julia felt within herself, Miss Morey would not be making Anne's wedding dress. But it was not a sudden knowledge. It was as though she had known it before. Only Max . . . But Max must see when the time came, she thought vaguely. She wished she could go home for a visit, away from Halstead for a bit.

13. 1885

THE new hospital still smelled of fresh plaster and paint. The inscription cut in the stone over the arch of the front door read proudly, "Halstead Hospital, October, 1885." Inside the front vestibule was a tablet on the wall which read, "Through the kindness of," and there followed a list of the donors. Senator Withers' name headed the list; Judge Mitchell, Ned Jenks, Max Hauser, John Chapman, Thomas Hetzel . . . the list ran to twenty names. Across on the other wall was a tablet listing the first board of directors.

"I like its being a community project, neither Catholic nor Protestant," Julia said to Alice Jenks at the first board meeting.

Julia liked, too, being on the board. When she was elected head of the board she accepted the position without any show of pride, but inwardly she felt it was quite fitting. After all, she had raised the first money way back in that first winter. She liked feeling that she could manage the other members of the board sitting around the long oak table in the board room. It was not so different, after all, from helping Max to arrive at a decision. She knew them so well; how Alice Jenks would do a good deal if her name appeared with it, how it had to be pointed out to Mr. Hetzel that if the hospital flourished it might become one of the important depositors at the bank. Julia knew that it would pay to have that new Mr. Dalton on the board even if he was a little crude because he understood so well about the best insurance. And then John Narberth gave the sheets and pillowcases at one-third the regular price because he was a board member.

Julia Hauser managed with equal adroitness to have Dr. Chapman made head of staff rather than the new doctor who owned a microscope and could tell all about germs. She had discovered that Dr. Chapman was fiercely sensitive for all his sarcastic way of laughing at things.

But Julia Hauser sitting at the head of the board table in her best black satin showed no signs of her managerial ability. Above the white piping at the high neck her face was softly feminine. The brown hair curled around her ear and up to the velvet bow twisted in her knot. More color than usual glowed through her white skin because of the pleasant excitement of sitting here as head. She looked very solemnly over the little pile of by-laws lying in front of her, then her eyes crinkled.

"I wonder if it wouldn't add distinction to this board room to have one of Mrs. Dorsett's paintings. Perhaps she might even be willing to donate one."

Faith Dorsett had not been included on the board. She had flashed her sullen black eyes and said, "Oh, well, I can live without it." Now she would feel better. Someone made a motion. It was duly seconded.

"All in favor?" Julia asked sweetly. The motion was passed. Julia turned again to the by-laws, written in a flowing Palmer Method hand by the new teacher of penmanship in the high school.

"We will not meet again until January unless a special meeting is called. I shall be away for two months, and in my absence Mr. Hetzel will be the head of the board." Julia looked down the surface of the oak table, seeing the glass ink-bottle happily. She was going back to Chicago next week!

She had planned to go before this, but there had been that bad summer, then Max had lost so much bringing fruit from California at first, then Anne had had diphtheria, but now she was going. It was her last chance; Mamma and Papa would be back in Prague next year.

Max hadn't said definitely. Perhaps he would meet her in Chicago. Perhaps he would see then how small Halstead had grown for all its prosperity. She asked for a motion of adjournment. It was seconded. Halstead Hospital was an institution to be proud of, the board members felt, as they left and went to their homes. It gave them all a feeling of importance.

Julia got into her buggy and drove along Omaha Street. She would stop at Max's store for the mail. It came in at two o'clock, and Max would have sent over for it.

The buggy top was down, and Julia leaned back against the tufted seat to see the whole warm blue sky and the fall haze on the farthest field of corn shocks. The fringe of trees over by the creek and the scattered cottonwoods of the town made a brave show of gold leaves, but in between, every building and wagon and animal stood out sharply against the flatness. The new grain-storage elevator was the ugliest. The only mystery of the whole country was in the rich fall smell of leaves and over-ripe pumpkins and weed fires and the shadows of the clouds on the dirt roads beneath.

Julia drove up past the Golden House. It was as square and abrupt as nine years ago. The rooms were "redecorated" now, and there was an elaborate sign across the front of the hotel. Mrs. Golden had joined the Literary Club. Julia looked at the Golden House with a carefully calculated feeling of unfamiliarity and sharp distaste. Then she pulled on the reins, and the buggy wheels, black with yellow lines, flashed in the soft dust. January arched her neck and lifted her hoofs lightly. Julia had a sense of swiftness and well-being, driving smartly in the new buggy. Everything took on new color because she was going back to Chicago. Nine years was a long time to wait, but now she was going. She pulled up in front of Max's store and waited until John Sorenson saw her and told Max.

"There was a letter for you, Jule, and the fruit car came. I have some fresh pineapples straight from California, and the rest of the car was oranges; I'm going to repack them in boxes and send them in to Omaha."

Max was proud of having California fruits. It meant achievement in a tangible form. With his cold-storage plant he could buy up a whole carload and store the fruit in his own warehouse until he could sell it, even if it took a couple of weeks. Whenever a car with the bill of lading addressed to him arrived in the station yard, he was always there waiting, as excited as any merchant watching in a ship from the Indies.

He came back out with the pineapples for Julia to try. "You won't get any better in Chicago, Jule."

Julia smiled at him affectionately and drove up the street. She would wait to read the letter when she got home. It was from Mamma. The feeling of it in her lap meant her trip next month. She hadn't told Mamma this time; it was to be a surprise. She had written her so many times before that she was planning a visit and then been disappointed.

"Mamma, Mamma's back, Chris; I'll beat you!" Anne had seen the buggy from the side of the house where she was cutting out paper dolls, and came running across the yard. Julia pulled the horse to a standstill. Anne was still quicker than Chris. She gained the carriage and climbed up beside Julia. Chris climbed up in back.

"Drive fast, Mamma, back to the barn; make January gallop," Chris urged.

Julia laughed and touched January with the tasseled end of the whip. She felt as gay as the children today.

"There, children, now climb out." Anne slid down over the wheel. Chris jumped out of the back and walked up to the house with Julia.

Julia noticed how well the grass had come through the hot summer. It was like a real lawn. They could have a croquet set there. She'd buy one in Chicago. Jeanette was on the back porch playing with a tin cup. A rich sense of pleasure came to Julia as she went up the steps.

"Hello, Lena." She went on through the kitchen to the dining-room and sat down by the table to read her letter.

As she read, the pleasure changed to excitement. Julia turned back hastily and read again to the end. Automatically she straightened the cut-glass stopper of the vinegar cruet. She folded the letter, slipped it slowly back in its envelope and hurried out to the back door.

"Chris," she called in a queer high voice, "run down and tell Papa we'll have to leave for Chicago tomorrow. See if he can come home now."

"Oh, Mamma, are we?" Christopher's round boy's face glowed.

"Never mind, Chris, do as I tell you; go tell Papa."

"Lena, remember to take care of Mr. Hauser; I'm going sooner than I thought."

Lena set down her bowl heavily. "For goodness' sakes, Mis' Hauser, is it bad news?"

"No, not exactly, Lena." Julia went upstairs abstractedly. Upstairs she put on her dressing-gown and set about laying out clothes on the bed. Suddenly, as she planned what to take, excitement possessed her and lightness of spirit. They were going home! They would cross the Mississippi; they would be back in Chicago. Julia laughed out loud. There was a half-sob of excitement in the laugh.

Would she need to take the children's red flannels? She couldn't think; she put her head down on the pile of red petticoats in her arms because she couldn't bear the excitement. Mamma and Papa and Dil . . . The children would play in the big yard under the poplar trees and ride downtown on the horse-cars. She would take them to Field and Leiter's and to the theater. . . .

"Jule?" Max was back. He had come at once with Chris.

"Oh, Max," Julia's voice sang. She went to the head of the stairs to meet him. "Max, Mamma wrote . . . Here's the letter. She and Papa are going back to Prague this month. They've got to go the twenty-second so they can go with Uncle Charles. I've got to leave tomorrow or I'll miss them. Mamma says"—she was reading now—"'I feel as though I couldn't leave without seeing you and my grandchildren. It's been so long, Julia, and Papa and I are getting old. The trip is too much for us alone, and we must go with Charles. Dil is going with us to the boat, as she is moving to New York to be near Polly. . . .' Oh, Max, Mamma will be so happy. She won't be able to believe it."

Max leaned against the railing of the stairs reading the letter while Julia talked. He had never seen her so excited. She was always calm, always planning things out carefully. He scarcely knew her like this. He frowned.

"Jule, I don't believe you could make it in time," he said slowly. "Your mother writes, 'We will sail the 22nd.' You see, they'll have to go to New York to sail, that will take them almost three days. If you left here tomorrow, you might go over to Omaha and then change, but . . . I wish you hadn't planned to surprise them; they would have waited. But you see, Jule, today's the eighteenth."

Julia sat down on the stair. All the color bleached out of her face. Her eyes looked red-rimmed as though she had been crying.

"You see, Jule, it takes . . ." Max started to explain gently.

"I see," Julia cut in in a dull tone. All the spirit had gone from her. Her voice stopped Max.

"Jule, dear, I'm sorry. You should have gone last year when we talked of it."

Julia didn't answer. As if being sorry helped any. He didn't know how much she had counted on this.

"Jule, we could send a telegram to Chicago. . . ."

"It's too late, Max. Today's the eighteenth. They'll have

left." Julia could see clearly now: the long narrow hall, the varnished balustrades, Max standing there, kind and sorry. She looked down the stairs and saw Anne and Chris sitting silently, trouble and fear in their little faces that were white in the dark hall. She stood up. Her voice was brisk and natural. "Run on outdoors until supper, children. Never mind, we'll go some other time."

"Jule," Max wasn't deceived by her tone of voice, "you could go anyway, just for the trip."

"There's not any point in that unless we were going to move there." Now that the children were gone, she let the bitterness come back in her voice. Then she walked away from Max into the bedroom and laid the red flannel petticoats back in the drawer. She was aware of Max hesitating in the hall. She knew he felt badly about her missing her trip, but just now she wanted to feel in some way that he was responsible. It was true. She would have gone last year if it hadn't been for the losses Max had had in the first carloads of fruit. She could have gone before that except for buying the cold-storage plant. But Max, standing out there hesitant and sorry for her, was all kindness and goodness. She couldn't blame him. She pushed the bureau drawer shut with nice precision. She heard Max going downstairs. Why hadn't he come in? But she knew that he wanted to and hesitated because he felt she wanted to be alone. Max was coming to understand a little, they had lived together so long.

She looked in the mirror and saw her face. Her eyes burned out of it angrily. In her hurry to pack she had not smoothed her hair since her ride. No wonder the children stared up at her so silently. Poor children, they mustn't know how she felt. Mechanically she smoothed her hair as if by so doing she could compose her spirits. But she had been counting so on this.

The front gate clicked sharply. She crossed to the window and looked out. There was Max taking the children down to the store with him. He had one by each hand. She watched him, knowing that he wanted to keep them from bothering her. He didn't need to.

She sat down at the front window. Across the street in the yard of the Episcopal church they were stringing Japanese lanterns for the last lawn social of the year. The lanterns bobbed pathetically on the wires, such an obvious attempt at gayety. Julia watched without interest. On her bed were spread the piles of clothes ready to be packed. She had no energy to put them away.

At home the house on Michigan Avenue was closed now; perhaps they had even sold it. If she got there day after tomorrow there would be no one to meet her at the station. She had been counting on that drive up from the station, showing the children everything. Papa would fling open the door, Mamma would exclaim about the children. Mamma, who was so slender and carried her head so high. She would be wearing her coral brooch. Julia forgot that now she would not go; she was already there, standing in the front hall, seeing the warriors on the newel post, the curving stair.

Then she remembered again. Her bitterness turned against her own family, Papa and Mamma, who took for granted that she would go on living "way out in Nebraska." How easily everybody else accepted your life! Julia leaned back in the chair, closing her eyes, feeling a moment of self-pity. Disappointment and loneliness were easier to stand, dramatizing herself.

A little breeze stirred the Japanese lanterns on the wires across the street and came through the bedroom window. Smoke from the yard below where Otto was burning old vines came with it. The sharp scent stung in her nostrils.

A red leaf blew noisily against the screen from the wood-bine that climbed the pillar of the porch. Julia opened her eyes. The leaf rattled there for a second, slid to the sill, danced against the ledge an instant and then was blown down again to the lawn. Julia sat straight in her chair, the laxness gone out of her. Something in her mind vibrated to a fall scent years ago along a river in the Fair grounds; there was something left of an eagerness she had felt then. Without knowing why, her nerves had tightened as though in suspense. She breathed in the restless smell of the smoke again, leaning close to the screen. Max and the children were coming back up the walk.

"Hello, Max, Anne, Chris, look up here," Julia called out. Max looked up, surprised at her voice, relieved, re-assured. She could see it in the way he lifted his head.

She stopped to take a fresh handkerchief from the pile already laid out on the bed for packing, scented it with verbena water; then she went downstairs. She was sud-denly in a hurry, yet waiting.

14

BY 1888 the Hausers' dining-room table no longer had long spaces of white damask between Max's place and Julia's. On each side now there were two children: Chris and Jeanette on Julia's right, Anne and the baby on her left. On Sunday noons they all had dinner in the dining-room. Anne was eleven and Chris ten, old enough now to sit with grown-ups; and so, having the two children, they might just as well have Jeanette and the baby, too. Max liked to see his family all around him. He sat in the big chair at the head of the table sharpening the carving knife and beaming on them.

"And two were light and two were dark!" he teased them, smilingly looking at Anne and the baby and Jeanette and Chris. "The dark get dark meat and the light get white." Max brandished his carving knife and fork over the roast chicken on the platter in front of him.

"No, Papa."

"Papa, you're teasing; you know how I hate dark meat," stormed Jeanette and Chris together.

Anne smiled sweetly. "They shouldn't talk about food at the table, didn't you say so, Mamma?"

Julia nodded her head. "Papa's only teasing, Chris." Chris was hurt so easily and was so slow to detect teasing. Julia could always see the puzzled frown that came on his forehead. He was all like Max with none of Julia's quick comprehension. Jeanette was only five and followed Chris's lead. Chris still pouted as he watched Max lower a slice of dark meat on his plate first. Max made a pretense of passing the plate.

"Oh, let's see here, I guess I'm forgetting something!" Max took the plate back and added a slice of white meat.

Anne, across the table, formed the word B A B Y silently with her lips. Chris's pout that had disappeared when he saw the white meat returned.

"Children," rebuked Julia gently.

Lena, grown heavier and more stolid, came in bearing a high-piled dish of mashed potatoes, molded with the tines of a fork into a grooved pyramid. Always to the Hauser children mashed potatoes were to lose a little in their eyes because they were not molded as Lena fixed them. Lena returned with the corn. Hot steam rose from it as she placed it on the table.

"Why does the corn have to be hot, Mamma?" Jeanette asked.

"Because it tastes best hot," Julia answered. She always

answered the children's questions, even Jeanette's who wanted to know everything and at once.

"Did you ever see corn that made smoke rings?" Max asked her, his eyes twinkling with amusement. Anne laughed quickly. Little Jeanette was all attention, trying to understand the turns of the conversation. Chris suspended his fork in mid-air a minute.

"Oh, Papa!" And then Chris laughed, now that he was sure it was a joke. His slowness bothered Julia just a little.

Julia turned to the baby in her carved oak high-chair. She could never look at little Louise without a touch of wonder. She was the fairest baby of all—blue-eyed with short curls the color of corn. She was ten months old now.

"Mamma, I do think I could wear two bows on Sundays anyway!" Anne's face had never rounded again. It had a delicate look. Julia glanced at Anne's shining yellow braid and said:

"I like to see children plainly dressed, Anne, even if Carrie Jeffreys does wear two." Anne flushed quickly that Mamma knew then that it was because Carrie had two bows on her hair that she wanted them.

"Carrie Jeffreys's nothing but a tattletale," burst out Chris, shaken out of his slowness by conviction.

"She is not; just because you boys were caught is no reason."

"Carrie's a tattletale, a tattle . . ." sang out Jeanette, championing Chris strongly.

Max's benevolent expression disappeared before the din. Julia, pouring coffee, saw it go and knew beforehand what would come. She saved her discipline for graver matters. Max flourished his snowy napkin in one hand and brought his fist down on the table with a crash.

126

"Fly from the table!" he brought out with a deep bass roll to the words. The edict startled the four into instant silence. Anne slipped sulkily out of her chair.

"Excuse me, Mamma."

" 'Scuse me," mumbled Chris in embarrassment.

"Won't we have any dessert?" Jeanette came around to whisper to Julia. And Julia whispered back:

"In the kitchen. Lena will give it to you."

"Mamma, can I take the baby out on the porch?" Anne asked from the doorway.

"Yes." Julia smiled at Anne's ingratiating request. "Put her in the carriage."

Max sighed his relief. "Those children!" he grumbled affectionately. "I do think, Jule, you should teach them to keep quiet at the table."

Julia laughed at him, her warm-throated, gentle laugh. "Max, they just get started; they're good children."

"Well," Max agreed indulgently. "I wonder if they did have enough to eat?" He began to worry.

"Lena will see to that," Julia assured him, thinking how like Max it was. A kind of understanding had grown between these two. The space that had been between them at first was filled by the children. To Max they were his children whom he was proud of. To Julia they were superior individuals, apart from this place, born for a larger world.

Max and Julia finished their pie alone in the sunny peace of the dining-room. The ferns had grown so high in the south window that the light streaming in took on a vivid green-gold tinge that fell on the carpet in a design more delicate than the woven pattern of the rug. Julia looked above the leaves of the Star of Bethlehem at the yellow leaves of the catalpas outside. They had never grown into trees and seemed still like thick-stemmed shrubs. Always she looked at them with conscious humorous pity.

"It does seem like fall today, doesn't it, Max?"

"Yes; I'm glad, too, a drought year like this, the sooner done the better. The Daltons are going to move into Omaha to have a bigger city."

Julia looked at Max and knew how he hated to have them go. He always hated to have people leave Halstead; it was almost as though he thought they were disloyal.

As always, pleasant Sundays after dinner they would sit on the porch awhile. Julia noticed as she went through the sitting-room that there was no dust on the edges of the table, that the backs of the *Famous Author Series* were even against the glass of the bookcase. The sitting-room was as she had first arranged it except that there was a new sepia print of the Raphael Madonna over the bookcase. The Paisley shawl still hung on the wall back of the couch. Julia straightened the lace-edged window shade before she followed Max. Then she, too, turned the cushion in the rocking-chair to shake the dust and sat down. The yellowing vines shaded the porch, yet you could look obliquely down the steps and see who passed.

Anne came around from the back of the house with the new volume of Tennyson and sat on the steps. Chris appeared with a pinwheel he was whirling. Jeanette and the baby were still in the kitchen with Lena.

Julia's chair fell into the rhythm of Max's. His after-dinner cigar settled on the October air like heavy incense. Max was frowning a little. His mind was on the corner lots he and Dorsett had bought awhile back. Values had dropped. He was embarrassed this year to keep up taxes. "Land poor, that's what we are, Max," James Dorsett had stormed angrily, but Max had shrunk a little from putting a painful fact he knew well enough into words.

"Times will turn, James; we've got to expect bad ones once in a while. Remember back in '78. You've never been sorry we put our money into it then, have you?"

"Oh, I don't know," James Dorsett had answered. "I was thinking I'd like to try the West where Regan's gone. There's the country with a future!"

Max had listened silently. Flighty talk, he called it to himself, but it bothered him. He had expanded a trifle too much, maybe. The town was settling a little. There were close to fifteen thousand people here now, and a new water-works and street-cars just this last year . . . but would it keep on growing?

Max shifted in his chair and refused to be worried by his own thoughts. Dorsett had been talking to him too much, that was all. The law business and the wholesale produce business were two different things. There was no falling off in his shipments. Max pulled his chair nearer to the railing so he could support his legs comfortably. He settled his head against the cushion and closed his eyes placidly.

"Guess I'll take forty winks, Jule."

"Anne, don't sprawl that way; pull your dress down over your knees," Julia said mildly, thinking with the outer edge of her mind. She sat on the vine-covered porch and rocked gently. Her expression was one of tranquil expectancy.

Julia saw a movement of white on the Jenks' porch across the vacant lot. The Jenks had come out to sit on their porch. It was a Sunday custom in Halstead. After a while Ned would come over to talk politics with Max. Perhaps Alice would come over, too. Julia knew Alice's mind as well as her own bureau drawers. She always went on with her own thoughts while she listened to Alice tell how she had let down Lucy's dresses two whole inches and was going to let her grow into them this time.

Julia saw Doris Livingstone come up the street and go into the Episcopal church with Hillary Flack, the church organist. Doris carried a roll of music to proclaim to any who should see her that she was going to practice her solo for evening service. Julia noticed it; noticed, too, the way she blushed and giggled nervously, the sly, devil-may-care look of Hillary and drew her own conclusions but without malice or secret delight. Alice would see the couple and come over to whisper about them, but Julia would only seem to hear.

Julia no longer had that bewilderment about human beings that she had had in the lace-curtained room at the Lafayette House. She would not sit on the stairs with troubling doubts in her mind if Lena should come sobbing to her today. She understood Max and herself so much better now. She had looked to him at first as she had to the wide endless stretches of cornfields and sky, wanting to be drawn to him. Neither quite satisfied her. She realized now Max's limitations and her own needs. She gave to him understanding and sympathy. Her body was gracious, but all the love of her spirit was piling up in her to be lavished some day on the children when they were ready.

She had no way of knowing that she was still young, whether twenty-nine was young or old. She had four children. She had been a child herself when she came here, and overnight she had taken up her living in this town. Little by little the new people had moved in, people who were sober, dull, their minds intent on money-making. Adventure had gone out of the town. She dressed and acted much as the women of the town did except for the rare outbursts of gayety when she drove January full-gallop out over the flat country. Then her eyes shone, the wild blood flowed under her skin, and she felt power and the holy joy of unchecked speed. Or sometimes when Dr. Chapman laughed at her in such a way, something unreconciled rose in her; some faint uncomfortable memory of the loneliness of a night years ago at the Fair, watching two young people laugh together on the other side of the fountain.

Lena came around the sidewalk. "Mis' Hauser, I put the baby to bed, and if it's all the same to you, I'm taking Jeanette with me to walk." Lena was resplendent in her Sunday plaid silk. She wore a chip straw pinned at a dangerous angle on the top of her head, a turkey wing pointing rakishly to the side. Jeanette's fat legs appeared absurdly stolid in black stockings and buttoned shoes under the lace ruffle of her Sunday dress.

"Can I go, Mamma?" The longing for adventure that shadowed and glowed in Julia's eyes was in the child's round brown eyes.

Julia nodded. "Be careful of her, Lena; don't take her too far."

Then Lena went proudly down the walk and out the gate to show off Jeanette on her call across the tracks. Lena was as proud of the Hauser children, of Jeanette in particular, as she could be of any child of her own, and Julia understood.

Chris wandered off to the hammock swung between the corner of the house and the post of the grape arbor. Julia watched him go, a solid, stocky boy who hated school. She wondered abruptly if he would get over it.

"I'm going in to practice, Mamma, can I?" Anne picked up Tennyson. She stood against the screen door a minute. The darkness of the doorway accentuated the extreme thinness of her body, the pale clearness of her face. She was all eagerness and restlessness. "I got a new piece yesterday."

"Softly then, Anne, and close the double doors."

Max still dozed. Julia sat alone on the porch in the next rocker. She closed her eyes, but she was not sleepy. She was tired of the sight of the bold angles of the church across the street, of the dusty road between. She wished there would be a frost or a heavy rain to set the dust. Now again in the fall as in the early spring the land gave her a feeling of waiting.

Julia held her rocker quiet against the balustrades. From behind the closed doors of the sitting-room came slowly, broken by a false chord, then a pause, then beginning again, the uncertain whine of a bow across the strings of a violin. Anne was working with eager moist hands at one of Schumann's Lieder. Some hint of beauty and promise clung to the bow. The restlessness of the fall, the wanting in herself, had a voice in the thin melody inside the house. It answered a kind of anguish in Julia's mind, haunting, unbearable, hanging in mid-air. Slowly it released the tension of her body and mind. Her hands opened loosely on the arms of the chair. Her foot set the chair to rocking once more.

15. CHRIS

CHRIS HAUSER sat in the fifth grade schoolroom. He sat at the back bent over his desk. His round face was solemn. He was squinting at the paper in front of him as he wrote.

"April 4, 1890, Halstead, Nebraska."

The letters were badly formed and straggled uphill to the corner of the page.

Then he rested his chin on his elbow and looked moodily across the schoolroom, watching the way the stovepipe turned twice and traversed the length of the ceiling. His eyes bothered him. He couldn't think of anything to say. He saw funny wiggling specks against the stovepipe.

"Christopher!"

"Yes, Ma'am," Chris blurted out thickly. Mamma didn't like "ma'am," and it felt queer on his lips, but the other children said it. He wanted with all the intensity of his twelve years to be like the other children.

"Why aren't you writing your letter? Why were you sitting there making faces?"

Chris looked around at all the other children's faces turned toward him. He discovered that he couldn't see the faces on the left half of the room. He moved his head. Still half the room was blocked off.

"I wasn't making faces."

"Now get to work! If I see any more wasting time or making faces, I shall punish you so you won't forget it."

Chris raised his eyes timidly. Everyone had turned around now. Miss Hawkins was looking down at her own desk. Sudden courage descended on him. He dipped his pen in the ink and wrote:

"I do not like school very much at all. I like business. [Then he counted the lines of the page. There were eight more. What more was there to say?] But numbers are better than history, spelling or compositions. [He stopped and counted his lines again.] I am going in my papa's business as soon as he will let me. [There were still three-and-a-half lines to go. He couldn't write any more. Then he thought triumphantly that it was a letter. He dipped his pen in the ink and wrote with ample spacing],

"Your loving son,

Chris."

He looked at his paper with satisfaction. It hadn't been so bad as he had feared. Two seats in front of him Clara Murphy turned her sheet and started on the other side. Chris sank back in discouragement.

When the class was excused, Chris was the first one out. He slipped out through the cloakroom door and took his cap from the hook on the way. He wouldn't wait for anyone today. He would go home all by himself, the long way, along Omaha Street. His fingers in his pocket came on the sling-shot he had made yesterday. He hesitated a minute, then he decided not to stop even to show Bill Holtz how good a shot he was.

At the corner of Omaha Street and Fifth he stood still, held by the brilliant red liquid in the bottle in the window. He read to himself the wonderful legend on the sign that hung out over the street:

MATHORN DRUGS

Chris walked along the window scrutinizing the package of cornplasters, the bottle of bromo-seltzer, the paper almanac, the cough-syrup. The sun caught the red liquid in the big glass and made it more wonderful than before. There was a pasteboard lady just under the bottle sipping at a straw. Straws were just new in Halstead. Mr. Mathorn's was the only drug store that had them.

Chris had no money in his pocket. He thought of going on down to Papa's and asking him for a nickel, but he had asked him yesterday. Papa would want him to earn it this time.

134

Then a new idea occurred to him. It was more than an idea. It was an inspiration. He was in an agony of fear and hope. Still he was big for his age, bigger than lots of kids he knew. He pulled open the screen door. Mr. Mathorn was the most up and coming druggist in town; everybody said that. Of course he'd have his screen door on even in April.

Inside Mathorn's store a faint smell of chocolate sodas hung on the air. Chris looked at the new soda fountain of gleaming white marble with reverence. The medicine bottles on the shelves on the other side inspired him with awe. They had real Latin names written in purple ink on the white paper labels. Mr. Mathorn was in back where there was a kind of saloon door that only came down half-way. Chris stood still squinting at the nearest bottle. He read its name laboriously. Cinchona Co. A little shiver of delight and embarrassment made him rub the back of his head against his coat collar. In summers he could be here all day if Mr. Mathorn wanted. And it would be cool here, cool and kind of shady. It wouldn't be like helping Otto mow the lawn or pile baskets of stuff down at Papa's warehouse. Maybe Mr. Mathorn would let him have a soda free sometimes. Anne and Jeanette and the other kids would come in and see him back of the beautiful white marble altar. Chris shoved his hands into his pockets for greater confidence. The fingers of one hand closed on the sling-shot. The other hand was on the bait box he had forgotten was in there. Just then the half-doors at the back swung open. Mr. Mathorn came through.

"H'lo, Chris, what'll you have?" Mr. Mathorn had a kind of tic, a way of twisting his mouth into a half-smile between every few words. Chris couldn't talk for watching it. He looked away a second. The sight of the big bottle of castor oil on the shelf bolstered him up.

"Mr. Mathorn, I wondered if you don't need a boy to help you here after school and summers. I mean I'm looking for a job, and I'm bigger than I look, and I've had experience in stores—down at Papa's." Chris was a different person when he was getting his ideas across. His round eyes became wells of sincerity.

Mr. Mathorn's mouth slid into a grimace and then he laughed. The kindliness of his nature was in the smile that followed the grimace.

"Well, I hadn't felt the need of any help just yet. 'Course with summer coming on folks are going to need lots of sodys."

"That's what I was thinking," Chris said, his eyes on Mr. Mathorn.

"I'd need a boy that was real neat and didn't mind washing the sody glasses."

" 'Course, I supposed you would," said Chris. "I've helped Lena sometimes."

"How much would you think of asking for your services?"

Chris hadn't thought of the money. He did now quickly. "Of course when I was working for you all the time in the summer I'd need more than just now."

"Yes, I s'pose you would," agreed Mr. Mathorn.

"But now, just afternoons, I guess I could afford to do it for . . . would you want me all day on Saturday?"

"Boys need Saturday mornings I guess to play ball in. I guess afternoons would be all right."

"Well," said Chris slowly, "I guess a dollar and a quarter a week would do." He watched Mr. Mathorn anxiously. With that funny way his mouth twisted, it was hard to tell.

"Done," said Mr. Mathorn. "I believe you'll be quite a business man when you grow up, like your pop, Chris.

136

What do you say we have a sody to clinch the bargain on?"

"Yes, sir," said Chris. He could feel the perspiration on his body now that he was hired. "Would you want me to begin today?"

"Oh, I guess tomorrow'll do, Chris." Mr. Mathorn went behind the marble counter. He held a glass under one of the faucets. Chris watched with eager interest. It was wonderful the way the bubbles sissed into the glass. Mr. Mathorn took a long spoon and stirred the liquid vigorously. It made a special sound.

"Here, Chris, do you want to stir this one? You might as well start learning." Chris dipped in a long spoon and made the same noise. It gave him a feeling of power.

"That's the way," said Mr. Mathorn. Then they both drank. Chris wanted to use a straw, but Mr. Mathorn didn't. It was exciting. Chris had never had a soda in April, before it was even hot.

"You know, Chris, this is going to be a good corn year. Business ought to be pretty good." He winked at the same time his mouth twitched.

Chris was a little embarrassed, but he felt important. He made his voice as much like Papa's as he could. "We've had plenty of rain," he said. The soda left a ring of chocolate around his mouth. It contrasted oddly with the grave expression on his face. He finished the soda in three gulps. He wanted to get home to tell Mamma and Anne and Jeanette. "Do you think we ought to have a contract, Mr. Mathorn?" he asked suddenly.

Mr. Mathorn pursed his lips. "Well, that's always a good idea, son, but long as it's between friends, I guess we can trust each other."

"Sure," said Chris. "Well, I'll see you tomorrow night

after school, Mr. Mathorn." He offered his hand solemnly. Mr. Mathorn shook it.

Chris walked out of the drug store feeling a little light-headed. He looked up at the red liquid in the glass happily. He tried twisting his mouth the way Mr. Mathorn did. It made him feel more grown-up. Now if only Mamma wouldn't object. But then they'd made an agreement, he and Mr. Mathorn. He'd have to keep it. Chris walked along without playing with the sling-shot or the bait box. He was in business. Maybe he'd be so good Mr. Mathorn would ask to have him stop school next fall. Chris looked out behind the Jenks' garden where the little wisps of corn would soon show green along the black rows. Yes, sir, this was going to be a good corn year!

16. ANNE

"I DON'T think Mamma would mind at least if we were back by eight o'clock," Anne Hauser said slowly. She was just past thirteen this summer.

"You could wear two bows of mine," Carrie Jeffreys urged. "We'll ride on the merry-go-round once and have ice cream; sure you can, and Mamma'll be there. She and Papa always walk down on Saturday nights."

Anne weakened visibly. She was sitting on the Jeffreys' front porch. She had been with Carrie all afternoon and stayed for supper. She knew secretly that Mamma thought she was at Hetzels', but Carrie Jeffreys was more interesting than Bessie Hetzel, and if Mamma only knew the Jeffreys more she would like them. Mr. Jeffreys owned the new laundry in town, and they were "wealthy." Besides she had never been to the park after dark.

Still the July air was soft with a wistful promise of

moisture about it. It was only just dark. The syringa bush in the round plot in the middle of the Jeffreys' yard gave up a scent so heavy-sweet it made her sad, like the piece she had on the violin now. Somebody drove by in a carriage, and the horses' hoofs clip-clopped dully on the dusty road. They were sad, too. Anne shivered in a sudden ecstasy.

"I think Gilbert Withers'll maybe be there," Carrie giggled in embarrassment.

Anne bit her finger nails without answering. Then she remembered how they would look and stopped. Mamma said a lady always had nice hands. Lena's were red and checked with black, but Mamma's were little and pink and always smelled faintly of verbena water. She wondered if Gilbert Withers noticed hands. Gilbert was nineteen and home from college. Gilbert was wonderful only he didn't notice her very much. Once he had spoken to Carrie.

Anne asked, "Can I wear your blue hair ribbons?"

"Sure you can," Carrie promised eagerly. The two girls ran upstairs to Carrie's room. Carrie scratched a match on the pad by the dresser and lighted the gas.

"Can I borrow your brush?"

Both girls took off their hair ribbons. Carrie's hair curled tightly. Anne's fell in a heavy weight of fine yellow strands. She bent over so the hair was a torrent in front of her face and brushed vigorously. When she tossed the yellow waterfall back, her face was flushed to the roots of her hair.

"My, it shines in the light." Carrie admired it openly. Anne was busy tying the first bow at the back of her hair.

"But it's so heavy Lena says it takes all my strength," she deprecated mournfully.

"Do you remember that story we read in Lena's *Fire-
side Companion;* how Lord Abercrome loved Marabelle for
the 'golden hair that is more beautiful than a crown'?"
Carrie quoted rapturously. Anne nodded, pitying Carrie
a little. They tied each other's bows and turned out the
light.

Mr. Jeffreys was on the porch when they came out. He
took two dimes from the pocket of his white vest that
gleamed broadly in the dusk. "Here, Carrie, you and Anne
buy a dish of ice cream and have a ride on the merry-go-
round." Anne felt better about going. Mr. Jeffreys even
gave them money. She felt almost all right. She and
Carrie walked down the street slowly, arms twined around
each other.

"I wish we had bicycles," Carrie said.

"Think of riding in a tandem with Gilbert Withers,"
Anne said slowly. She could almost see herself. Carrie
sighed dramatically.

Halstead was festive on Saturday night. As they walked
along, they could see people rocking on the porches they
passed. The sound of voices drifted out to the sidewalk.
Lights from inside the houses shone out through the
screen doors. On Mrs. Dorsett's porch a slight breeze blew
the prism glasses into a musical tinkle.

"Mamma says Mrs. Dorsett's almost always alone evenings," Carrie confided in a significant voice.

Anne puzzled over this statement in silence. Carrie
heard so much. Mamma never talked about anything before her. Mamma treated her as though she were only
Jeanette's age.

"Look, there she is now; I bet she's lonesome."

There was a patch of light behind the balustrades of
the Dorsetts' porch that they knew was Mrs. Dorsett's
dress. It moved as she rocked.

"Good evening, Mrs. Dorsett," Anne called out without knowing she was going to do it beforehand. "It's Anne Hauser," she added.

"Good evening, Anne," a voice called back. To Anne the voice was sad. A feeling of sympathy caught her sharply and grew in her until she could scarcely bear it. Instinctively she tightened her arm around Carrie's waist. It was comfortably plump. She knew now what Carrie meant about Mrs. Dorsett.

"Carrie, she's going to give me china-painting lessons; Mamma said I could take them." Anne was stirred by art for Mrs. Dorsett's sake. She walked on with Carrie thinking how big and dark Mrs. Dorsett's eyes were. The sadness still filled her, but pleasantly now.

A screen door down the street banged sharply. From the Freehahns' house the sound of an ice-chest door shutting came out to them with odd distinctness. Then they turned the corner around Mathorn's drug store.

"I wish Chris worked evenings at the drug store," Anne said importantly.

The stores were all open on Saturday night. They were different places altogether. Even the rakes and hoes and lawnmowers in the window of the hardware store became interesting. Anne wondered for one anxious moment whether Papa were downtown. Two blocks before they got to the park they could see the lights of the merry-go-round and the pavilion and hear the music.

"We can watch the dancing a minute, too," Carrie anticipated happily.

"I'd just as soon divide my dish of ice cream if you want to use one nickel for pop corn," offered Anne.

They bought a bag at the open booth at the corner entrance to the park. The tiny colored stripes on the bag like stick candy were satisfying some way, and there were shiny spots where the butter leaked through. A foreigner from across the tracks ran the stand. He grinned at them with a wide gleam of white teeth under his black mustache. It was queer how clean his teeth looked because his face and his shirt were dirty, Anne thought. Then she saw the merry-go-round.

It was the most wonderful sight at the park. It was all scarlet and gold and bright blue. The horses rode up and down, and their manes seemed to blow out in the breeze. All the time there was music. *Little Annie Rooney* it was playing now. Carrie could sing some of the words. Anne listened and hummed it with her.

The park was crowded tonight. Some people brought their supper in picnic baskets and stayed right on till the park closed. A baby was asleep on top of one of the big picnic tables, covered over with a folded red tablecloth. Anne and Carrie could see Muehler's Beer Garden with people sitting at the little round tables. Anne wrinkled her nose at the sour smell. The music from the dance pavilion drifted through the trees, rising somehow above the music of the merry-go-round.

"Look, there's a tipsy!" Carrie whispered. "Why, it's Mr. Holtz." Anne looked. She had never seen anyone really tipsy before. She watched him weave around a bench and sit down heavily. All her misgivings about going to the park came back upon her full force. The pop corn seemed to lose its salty flavor.

"Let's go over to the merry-go-round," she urged, but all the time she couldn't take her eyes away from Mr. Holtz. "It's going to start again!"

They ran, jumping on the circular platform just as it began to revolve. They disdained the leather upholstered carriages. Carriages were for children like Jeanette. Anne left Carrie on a reindeer and chose a white horse that pranced as high as any, way over on the other side. She arranged her skirt carefully in the side-saddle and held the reins in one hand. Her hair blew out from her shoulder. She was exhilarated. It was nothing like this in the daytime. Then you could see all the time that it was just Burns Park. Now outside of the lights it was dark. There were crowds of people, not just children, and the lights made it gay.

The music stopped and nobody came for her ticket. She must have missed the man. People got off but Anne sat still. She'd let Carrie come to find her. She was somebody else sitting on the white horse, the lady in Tennyson's *Idylls of the King,* riding through the woods ahead of Sir Gareth. The music started again. There was Carrie over by the entrance. Anne waved her ticket at her triumphantly. It was glorious. Then she saw Gilbert Withers.

He was as handsome as ever, more handsome, in light gray trousers and a plaid coat. He wore a wing collar and a straw hat. He was helping the Withers' hired girl into the carriage in front of Anne's white steed. The girl, Anne remembered her name was Thelma, looked up at him in a funny bold way. Anne's hand on the reins was suddenly cold. The hilarious music blaring from the center of the merry-go-round faded into a mere din. Anne rose in the air on her white horse so she could look down into the carriage in front of her where Gilbert Withers was holding Thelma's hand, squeezing her fingers.

Anne's horse descended again with a flushed rider upon it. Anne no longer felt like the lady in the *Idylls of the King.* Something was damaged for her. Thelma looked as if . . . she did have color on her cheeks, paint. Carrie said some people did that. And Gilbert Withers was holding her hand! Anne tried not to look when she rose again, but her eyes were drawn irresistibly to the couple in front of her. She hoped no one else could see them. She was glad Carrie couldn't. No one should know that their idol, Gilbert Withers, had feet of clay; there was a poem about that. She tried to look at other people on the merry-go-round. In the daytime on Saturday afternoons there were mostly children that you knew and could call to; tonight she didn't seem to know anyone. There was a couple on the horse on the other side. They were riding together, and the man had his arm around the girl. Anne could see them when their horse rose on its pole, holding tightly to each other in sight of everyone. They were foreigners from across the tracks.

She wished she hadn't come. Mamma would hate her being there. She hated it herself. She held her head high and looked straight ahead, above the top of Gilbert Withers' straw hat. Her cheeks had flaming spots of color. She was Julia Hauser's daughter as she rode there scorning her surroundings. When the music of the steam pipes stopped, she was glad for the first time in her life. She slid down from her horse and hurried toward Carrie by the ticket box.

"You were lucky. You got two rides around," said Carrie.

"Mmm-hmm. I think I better go now, Carrie, really," Anne answered.

Carrie grabbed her arm. "Look, isn't that Gilbert Withers ahead with the gray trousers? Let's walk fast and see who he's with."

"No," lied Anne Hauser scornfully, "that's somebody else. Let's go this way. I don't want to see the dancing anyway." She was almost running now.

The park had lost its glamor. Anne saw with the naked and unhappy eyes of disillusion the litter of papers, an empty bottle, a trail of orange peel, a half-eaten sandwich.

A colicky baby's crying rose above the waltz over in the dance pavilion. The music of the merry-go-round, *Little Annie Rooney,* had a tinny sound as though ground out by the turn of a crank.

"What's your hurry? We haven't had our ice cream yet," Carrie complained bitterly.

"I don't care, I can't wait. I've got to go home. You stay if you want to."

The glamor of the dark porches and the dim lights through the screen doors was gone, too. Anne hurried too fast to listen for the tinkle of Mrs. Dorsett's glass prisms. She paid no attention to Carrie's exasperated exclamations. She walked swiftly ahead, her body held straight as a ramrod. At the Jeffreys' gate she paused for only a second.

"Listen, Anne, maybe Mamma and Papa have gone down to have some beer. Let's go over and ask your mamma if you can sleep with me tonight."

"No, thank you, I don't want to," answered Anne tersely. "Here's your hair ribbons." She jerked them off and held them out to the tried but loyal Carrie. Then she was gone, running across the Jenks' lawn, her hair falling down on her shoulders like a veil. She could see Mamma on the front porch with Papa. She tiptoed around to the back and slipped quietly through the door and up the back stairs.

She needed no light; the street-lamps shone through her end window. She undressed quickly, dropping her clothes in a heap at her feet until she stood naked in the half dark. She hung her clothes on the chair without sorting them and crossed over to get her nightgown. It hung limply on the first hook. She slipped it over her head, and the feeling of the soft muslin falling around her was comforting. She tiptoed into the bathroom with bare feet and washed her face vigorously from the cold water tap, splashing the water with her hands way up to her hair.

She hated Halstead, she told herself, and Gilbert Withers. She closed her mind deliberately on the picture of him squeezing that Thelma's hand. She took the cake of soap out of the dish and rubbed it on her face and hands. Then she splashed more cold water on her face and dried it. Her skin felt shiny and clean.

At the head of the stairs she hesitated.

"Good night, Mamma and Papa," she called down.

"Oh, Papa was just going to walk down to Hetzels' for you, Anne, good night."

Mamma's voice reassured her. It had a calmness that removed from her the sound of the merry-go-round and Carrie's excited whisperings about Mrs. Dorsett, but it couldn't quite take from her the sadness that stayed in her mind, like the unhungry feeling after a stomach ache. She turned restlessly in her bed. Tomorrow she would practice two hours instead of just one, and she would join Miss Ollie's confirmation class next year. She would never think of Gilbert Withers or boys any more. But her cheeks were hot again as she turned against the cool pillow.

17. JEANETTE

JEANETTE had been pretending in front of the statuary group on Mrs. Withers' parlor table while Mamma and the Senator and Mrs. Withers were talking in the dining-room. It was cold in the parlor, but Jeanette liked to look at the little baby on his mother's lap; it looked so real. She could even get her little finger into the hollow of the fat bronze hand, and she was always surprised that the twisted curls on the baby's head weren't soft when she

146

touched them. The big dog by the mother's knee had a chain with honest-to-goodness links fastened into his collar. It wasn't really like statuary, more like dolls.

Jeanette was seven.

"Come, Jeanette," Mamma called from the dining-room. Jeanette left the bronze baby and the dog and went into the dining-room. She liked to go to the Withers'. Mrs. Withers always got out the toys the boys had when they were little. Jeanette knew the Withers' house almost as well as their own. Sometimes Mrs. Withers let her play the tinkly keys of the old melodeon.

Almost without having to look she could see the bright red roses in the carpet and the place where the roses were worn light under the Senator's armchair. Jeanette thought it was a very fine house since it had statuary and a bright patterned carpet in every room, even upstairs. Mamma had matting in their rooms.

Jeanette looked at the big ferns and the bird in its cage and the china twins, that were really salt and pepper shakers, without listening to what the grown-ups were saying. The Withers had a kind of sitting-room place at the end of the dining-room near the bow window.

"Come here, Jeanette," the Senator said. The Senator had a habit of carrying horehound drops in his pocket. Jeanette went over to him. "This one's the most like you of any of the children, Julia." The Senator put one finger under her chin and cocked it up toward the light. Jeanette wondered abruptly if the whiskers on his cheeks didn't bother him when he slept.

"She has your eyes, Julia," Mrs. Withers added in confirmation.

Jeanette moved her head away from the Senator's finger and regarded her mother in a new way to see if she really did look like her. She hoped so. Then she saw how different Mamma looked. She couldn't remember ever having seen her like that. She sat forward a little, her cheeks were very pink, and her eyes were all sparkly. Jeanette couldn't take her eyes away from her. And Mamma's voice when she talked had a new sound in it as though in a few more words it would burst into laughing or maybe even crying.

"And, Senator, the bill really passed?"

"Oh, yes; it's on the minutes down there in Washington, and the World's Fair's going to be in Chicago. Chicago pledged ten million dollars and no other city could beat that. It made the East sit up."

Even the way the Senator said ten million so it sent little shivers down Jeanette's back didn't make her take her eyes away from Julia. Mamma was so exciting to look at. She clasped her gloved fingers together and for a minute Jeanette thought she was going to clap her hands. Then she said in the quietest kind of a voice and yet it stirred shivers in you more than the Senator's:

"I shall go and take the children."

Then Mamma was putting on her heavy coat with the fur collar around the shoulders and saying good-by to the Withers. Senator Withers did give Jeanette a horehound drop after all, but Jeanette put it in her mouth without really tasting it because she was so busy wondering where Mamma was going to take them. The Senator put on his cap to go out with them and unhitch the horse.

"You've got your buffalo robe out already!"

"Yes, I always feel the cold in November here as much as at any time."

Jeanette loved the funny smell of camphor in the buffalo robe just like their winter flannels when they first put them on. The fur on the outside of the robe was long enough to hide your fingers in. It was more exciting to ride with Mamma than with Papa. Mamma seemed almost to be trotting with the horses, she held herself so sort of springy.

"Good-by." Mamma touched January with the tasseled end of the whip so she sprang away down the street over the frozen ruts as though she were glad to be moving. Jeanette sat close to Mamma.

"Why, Mamma, we're driving the wrong way!"

A funny little smile was on Mamma's lips and that excited sort of sparkle in her eyes. "A ways; I want to think a little. You just sit still awhile."

So Jeanette sat still. It was easy to mind when you were sitting so close to Mamma; you could almost feel her being excited. Only Jeanette wished she could ask her where they were going, where there were ten million dollars. Maybe it was Chicago. Sometimes Mamma told them about Chicago—where she lived when she was little. Anne told them more, though. Mamma hadn't talked about Chicago very much lately.

"If Max could only get an appointment of some kind as delegate from Nebraska!" Mamma said out loud, but that didn't help much. Jeanette turned the words over but couldn't get any meaning to them.

It was lots colder. The cold crept in under the edges of the buffalo robe. The sulphur that Jeanette wore inside her shoes to keep from taking cold didn't help much. She wished they had driven out toward Bittersweet Creek where there were trees. It was so bare this way.

"Mamma, don't the corn shocks look cold?" Jeanette asked without thinking.

"Horrible," Mamma answered so quickly Jeanette was surprised.

The wind seemed to blow more out here where there were only frozen corn shocks. Jeanette gritted her teeth together to keep them from chattering. She didn't want Mamma to turn back yet. She pulled the buffalo robe up to her chin and put her cold face down so she could feel the fur.

Suddenly the carriage jerked so it seemed to be almost tipping over. The trotting sound of January's hoofs broke off sharply; the carriage went forward faster than ever but with a queer swaying. She felt Mamma pulling hard on the reins. Jeanette raised her head.

"Slide down in the bottom, Jeanette, and hold onto the dashboard," Mamma said sharply. Jeanette obeyed, but she had time to see how fast they were going, almost like flying. January seemed to be trying to get away from the carriage; her ears were laid back on her head. Jeanette clung to the dashboard with cold hands. She didn't dare look any more. Mamma put her feet against the dashboard and braced herself. Jeanette could feel how strong Mamma was.

Mamma didn't speak. They were going too fast for January to hear. Jeanette looked out around the dashboard. There was a fence way over across a ditch. She wondered if they would be thrown against it. She didn't believe she could hang on much longer. She looked down, and the flying road and the turning wheels made her dizzy. She felt she was going to be sick. She had to look up in Mamma's face. She took a tighter hold on each side of the dashboard and screwed her head around till she could see Mamma.

Mamma's face was white. Her teeth were biting into her lower lip; her eyes looked almost black. Jeanette could see her chin held up above the fur collar. Mamma was scared, but she wouldn't let them be killed.

There was a terrific lurch. Jeanette's head struck something, and she crumpled into a heap on the bottom of the buggy.

It was pitch dark when Jeanette came to consciousness. She was cold and cramped. She couldn't think where she was. Then she knew; Otto was lifting her out of the carriage.

"Take her up and put her on my bed, Otto." Mamma's voice was as calm as ever, but kind of proud, too.

"If you was to ask me, ma'am, I'd tell you to get rid of that beast. She ain't never been what you'd call broken proper."

"Oh, no, Otto. A white rabbit jumped out of the ditch and scared her. She went five miles before I could turn her around. Hurry in with the child."

Jeanette closed her eyes again. She remembered now; January ran away.

Lena opened the door of the house. It was so warm and had a nice smell. Maybe they'd had gingerbread for supper. Chris and Anne were on the stairs in their nightgowns. Jeanette felt sleepily important.

"Poor child, I'll take her some hot milk," Lena said. Jeanette wanted to say she didn't want hot milk, but she was too tired. She laid her head back again limply on Otto's shoulder.

"Where's Max?" she heard Mamma asking.

"He didn't get back yet from some ranch he went to," Otto said.

Mamma's bed seemed broader than any she'd ever seen. Lena folded the shams and laid the pillows flat. Somebody, oh, it was Anne, was taking off her shoes.

From way off Lena's voice said, "Better let her sleep first. You better look at the baby, ma'am; she has the croup again. I'm afraid you'll be up most the night with her."

Jeanette woke suddenly.

"Jule, dear, I couldn't get back any sooner." It was Papa; Mamma was downstairs. Papa bent over and kissed her. It was a queer kind of kiss on the mouth with his lips.

"Oh, it's Jeanette!" He seemed surprised. He stood up again and went softly down the hall.

Jeanette was all awake now. But she lay very still trying to think what had happened; why, she could still feel Papa's kiss. Then she knew; Papa thought she was Mamma. Something shiny, like the light through the doorway from the kitchen before you could really see the birthday cake, was in the room, yet it was still quite dark. There was a happy feeling inside of her. It was as though she had stayed downstairs with Mamma and Papa, and the other children had gone upstairs to bed.

Two scraps of the day: "I shall go and take the children . . ." "Oh, it's Jeanette!" hung in her mind like packages on a Christmas tree, mysterious, exciting, secret.

Jeanette could hear Mamma's and Papa's voices now, very low as they came upstairs. Papa tiptoed heavily in and opened the wardrobe door. Then he went out again. Jeanette tried to stay awake. Maybe in the morning the special feeling would be gone. Still she had something like a string tied around her finger to remember by.

"I shall go and take the children . . ." "Oh, it's Jeanette!" She wondered if Mamma weren't even scared when January ran away.

18. LOUISE

THE room was very still. Anne and Chris and Jeanette were all in school. Louise was sleeping upstairs. The stillness took on a deeper edge of quiet that seemed to rise and fall ever so softly as though with the baby's breathing. A house with a child sleeping has a different feeling from any other. Julia wound the thread twice around her needle for a French knot. This time in the afternoon was always like a piece out of time. It was more really hers than any other time in the day. Queer, she thought, how time had no separate value at first in those days in the Golden House; each day only an empty space, but now, with things to do and the children, each part of the day had its own value. Now even these winter days were short. Julia looked up from her embroidery.

There was the Paisley shawl. How typical of her life with Max! He was so generous at heart and yet just missed understanding the things she wanted. She glanced across the backyard to the fence.

The hollyhocks were pitiable standing with their heads down, frozen stiff in their dejection. Beyond the barn were frozen corn shocks. Always the world seemed more empty when the rustling vagrant life of the corn was over. All the attempts at shade and color that she and Otto managed in the summer were futile in the winter. There was the sky meeting the flat earth, one sharp edge against another, without any least blurring or welding of the two. But now, for all of this month, the freezing world had not mattered so much. The drearier and more empty it was the more fiercely glad she felt. She was already removed from it.

This removal of spirit had begun when the Senator first told her about the new World's Fair. Excitement had possessed her ever since. And she had almost forgotten what that was like. This was no country for inner excitement. The bitter winter pressed you in and in until there was no room left for it. The summer drained it out of you. Only a few weeks in the spring and again in the fall there was room, but she hadn't felt excitement then, only the haunting lack of it. But now Julia let her embroidery lie on her knee. The excitement within her was so great she had to look out again to the frozen yard as one looks away from the fire to cool the eyes and face. This Fair was what she had been waiting for.

They must go and take the children, she had been saying over to herself ever since. Not just for a few days— that had been too short a time at the Centennial—a month, anyway, unless they could go and stay even longer! It would be too wonderful to miss. After living out here away from everything, to be suddenly in the midst of things, seeing all the glories of the world spread out! She began to mix the new Fair up with that other one in Philadelphia.

Getting off the train in the station. It was raining. She remembered it so well: the way the cab smelled horsy and the cobblestone streets glittered in the wet. They stayed at the Lafayette House; that beautiful dining-room, the people, the feeling that the world was at its height and she was in time for it. The streets in the morning sunshine filled with cabs and people on foot all going in the same direction, the big buildings and the flags!

A cry, fussy, protesting the outrage of being left alone in a dark room came from above. Julia hurried upstairs. She would bring the baby down and dress her by the stove; it was too chilly in the bedroom.

Julia held her fourth child in her lap and looked at her with a certain proud wonder. Louise was the prettiest;

she was so fair, her eyes were a deeper blue than Anne's. Her hair was curly like Jeanette's. It was incredible that she was really two. If the Fair were held in '93 she would be five then, old enough to remember it.

The Fair was coming just the right time for the children, Julia thought, pulling up Louise's long black stockings. Chris talked as though there were no other place in the world but Halstead, Nebraska. She must get him away from Mathorn's soon; he was beginning to grimace sometimes between his words the way Mr. Mathorn did.

Anne was the other way. She was strangely aloof from Halstead. She mooned around by herself so much. Once she had said, "I think Carrie Jeffreys is so ordinary, Mamma." Julia had told her it was more ordinary to hurt people's feelings, but secretly she had wondered if she could send Anne to Polly or Dil for a winter.

Julia slipped the red flannel petticoat that flared out so saucily from its feather-stitched band over the baby's head.

And Jeanette; what had Halstead to offer her? Sometimes she would catch the child looking up with her round brown eyes and know that she understood more than the older children. And she had a gift for acting and reciting that it would be a pity to waste.

Julia twisted the yellow hair around her finger. What little things women lived by—like curling the baby's hair. If she lived to be a hundred, she would still remember the feeling of Jeanette's wavy curls or Louise's soft clinging hair with the wet bristles of the brush going around and around over her finger.

"Burn?" asked Louise suddenly pointing at the baseburner. "Yes, mustn't touch," answered Julia, shaking her head and looking grave. Julia picked up her embroidery again.

The Fair would make such a difference to all the children. They would have a taste of the world. She looked out the window and saw there her fourteen years running along in a sober line. She didn't want her children to live here. They were to count in the world. . . .

"Mamma, I'm going to Omaha with Papa." Jeanette came running in from school, her face above the green coat was eager, her eyes danced. "We're going to stay two nights, Papa says. And, Mamma, if they ask me to speak my *Sheridan's Ride,* can I?"

When Jeanette had gone, clinging to Max's hand, Julia went back once more to her embroidery. Louise trotted over to her and then sat down heavily with her fat little legs out in front of her, just as Chris used to do. Julia watched her a moment.

If Max could only move his business to Chicago—he had made enough here—and if he invested wisely in the city, Louise would never even remember Halstead. Julia hid the idea deep under sensible thoughts that could bear looking at. She must tell Lena that Mr. Hauser and Jeanette wouldn't be back for supper. It was time for Anne to practice her violin lesson.

19. 1890

JULIA and Faith Dorsett were on their way to the meeting of the Literary Club at Mrs. Edwards's.

"Julia, you didn't wear brown!"

"I know, but it seemed so silly."

"Did you ever see such funny invitations? 'Since our subject this month will be on the poet Browning, the hostess requests that each of the members try to come dressed in brown.'" Faith repeated the invitation in a falsetto tone. "But I wouldn't miss it for a good deal!"

Faith's eyes held a malicious gleam in them. "Remember, Julia, the first meeting we ever had of the Literary Society?"

"I should say; we started with only seven, at our house, and we read *The Merchant of Venice*. There are thirty-five now, aren't there?"

"Julia, I wish we'd kept the number small. I liked it better then."

"I did too, but the idea of having a literary club in the first place was to keep the women of the town interested in something outside of their own homes." Julia was very serious.

They turned up the newly shoveled walk to Mrs. Edwards.

"Julia, there's Mrs. Jeffreys; she's got a brown cape on," Faith whispered.

"How do you do, Mrs. Hauser and Mrs. Dorsett; come right in," Mrs. Edwards greeted them at the door. "Well, some of 'em are leaving off their overshoes in the storm shed, but I say the floor will wash. My goodness! that's what I keep a maid for!" Mrs. Edwards's laugh was a little loud. Julia always found herself speaking even more quietly than usual when she was with her. Mrs. Edwards wore a brown mohair dress and a brown bow in her hair.

The front parlor was filled. Women sat along the wall in the dining-room. The dining-room table was pushed back against the end wall to make room for the speaker's table. The base-burner in the sitting-room made the two rooms a little stuffy. A slight smell of camphor that never got quite out of clothes stored away so many summers, of the flannel soaked in linament that Mrs. Jeffreys wore around her neck, mingled.

There was a little stir as Julia and Faith came in, quick nods of many heads. Mrs. Jackson and Mrs. Drury were poring over a volume of Browning to find their quotations at the last minute. Mrs. Livingstone was president. She had already taken her place.

"The meeting of the Philomathean Literary Society is called to order!" The whispering and rustling subsided. The room was very still except for the sound of a spoon beating against a bowl in the kitchen. Mrs. Edwards sat in the doorway smiling, oblivious, as one who has no need to be bothered by the cares of the kitchen.

"Mrs. Edwards, our hostess for today, tells me that the program is long, so we shall just have the roll call and postpone the business until after the literary program; the needs of the spirit come first." Mrs. Livingstone had a firm way of speaking that did away with objections. Mrs. Bush rose to call the roll.

"Mrs. Dalton?"

Mrs. Dalton was heavy-set. The words came queerly out of her lips:

> " 'My times be in thy hand!
> Perfect the cup as planned.' "

Mrs. Dalton settled back with a satisfied smile. She wore a brown silk apron over her dress.

"Mrs. Dorsett?" Faith answered with solemn face.

> " 'This hour has been an hour!' "

Julia looked quickly at Faith and then away. Faith took a sharp pleasure in startling the members of the club. Mrs. Livingstone frowned. The secretary continued:

"Mrs. Foster? . . . Mrs. Hauser?"

> " 'Ah, but a man's reach should exceed his grasp,
> Or what's a heaven for?' "

Julia spoke the words so quietly Mrs. Edwards had to lean forward to hear.

"Mrs. Jenks, Mrs. Jackson, Mrs. McNary?"

Mrs. McNary spoke with a rich Irish brogue:

> " 'Open my heart and you will see
> Graved inside of it, "Italy." ' "

Julia caught the smile on Mrs. Withers' lips and looked fixedly at the antimacassar back of Mrs. Livingstone's head.

"Would anyone like to challenge any of the quotations?" Mrs. Livingstone asked as the roll call was ended. "Mrs. Dorsett's seemed a little unusual, but quotations sometimes do when taken out of their context. I shall now turn the meeting over to Mrs. Edwards."

Mrs. Edwards and Mrs. Livingstone changed places. Mrs. Edwards settled her books, bristling with paper markers, on the table. Beside them she laid the pages of her "paper."

"First I want to thank all of you who complied with my request that you wear brown." Mrs. Edwards was an energetic woman of forty who prided herself that whatever she did she went into "tooth and nail." Now that it was her turn at the Literary Club she meant to make it stand out. She had thought of the idea of having as many attributes of the meeting brown as possible, one night after she had gone to bed and woke her husband to tell him.

"I am sure we should turn with pleasure this snowy day to a study of Robert Browning, the poet who has inspired so many of us and helped so many through the trials of this life, even the death of beloved ones." She cleared her throat. "Most of us were first attracted to Browning as girls; I know I was, by the romantic story of his love affair and marriage to Miss Barrett, a poetess. [Mrs. Edwards added the word marriage as though it were so natural a sequence of a love affair as to be unimportant.] It is so seldom that you read of two poets falling in love." Mrs. Edwards turned the page with a loud rustle of paper. As the pages fell away from her fingers, many of the club counted the edges. Her talk was barely started.

Mrs. Edwards finished with the life of Browning and turned to the poetry itself. "We observe first that Browning, unlike certain other poets"—she paused significantly so that Mrs. McNary formed the word "Byron" to Mrs. Rollins who had been absent last time—"is a moralist of the highest kind. Nearly every poem exalts some virtue or deplores some vice." Mrs. Edwards's voice grew dramatic over vice.

The noise of the school-children coming from school penetrated the heavily curtained silence of the parlor. Then Jerome Edwards, Mrs. Edwards's oldest boy, came tiptoeing in on squeaking boots with a scuttle of coal. Mrs. Edwards paused.

"Yes, Jerome."

The coal clattered into the top of the burner. Jerome tiptoed out and Mrs. Edwards continued:

"He is a poet whose meanings we must ponder. He is not a poet for the uneducated man in the street but for the serious student of culture. . . ."

Julia rested her chin on her hand. This was not the way they had meant the Literary Club to be. Her own thoughts blocked off Mrs. Edwards's affected lecture voice. She glanced at Mrs. Mitchell in her black satin, oblivious of the brown band Mrs. Kauf had on her sleeve, of Mrs. McNary's brown striped bombazine. Mrs. Mitchell had brought her own copy of Browning. She followed Mrs. Edwards's quotations; sometimes she read a little after Mrs. Edwards had returned to her own remarks. Julia glanced around the room.

Mrs. Rollins was dozing back of the stove. Mrs. Dalton sat stolidly back of Mrs. Rollins; Mrs. McNary, Mrs. Jackson, Mrs. Jeffreys—they had all come in the last ten years. And she knew none of them any better than when she had first met them. They lived so differently in houses like this, the parlor and dining-room filled with signs of prosperity set aside for show. She had called; she had even had Mrs. Bush and Mrs. Jackson and Mrs. Edwards to dinner and had gone in turn to their homes, but there had been an end of it. She had heard afterwards that Mrs. Bush had been shocked by the picture of the Madonna over her bookcase. This Literary Club was important to them only because it seemed a sign of leisure.

A feeling of bewilderment came to Julia. She looked over at Mrs. Hetzel. Mrs. Hetzel had kept her home a replica of the best in German living all these years, but she had not influenced one person beyond it. Her children went with Mrs. Jeffreys' children and Mrs. Edwards's and Mrs. Kauf's. They were ashamed of the differences in their own home. Bessie Hetzel hadn't wanted to go back to Germany last year.

Mrs. Edwards was ending her paper. The smell of coffee came through the rooms from the kitchen. There was a sound of greater activity behind the swing door.

"Now we've covered all the poems except a very long one called the *Ring and the Book* that I don't believe would be very interesting. I wonder if anyone here has read it?" The women surveyed each other with disinterested gaze. When Mrs. Mitchell lifted her hand slightly from her book, the woman next to Julia whispered to Mrs. Kauf that Mrs. Mitchell thought she was better than the rest. "Perhaps at a later meeting Mrs. Mitchell will give us the benefit of her wider reading," Mrs. Edwards suggested. "I am afraid we shall have to stop our perusal of this inspiring poet's works for the refreshments." She sat down arranging her papers in place, the glow of a task well-performed showing through her expression.

The women clapped. Mrs. Livingstone asked if anyone would like to express her appreciation in the form of a standing motion.

"Now just move your chairs around sociable like so you can be comfortable." Mrs. Edwards's voice returned to normal. The women relaxed.

"My, you were in a brown study!" Faith murmured in Julia's ear.

Julia didn't answer. She realized that she and Mrs. Hetzel and Mrs. Mitchell and Mrs. Withers and Faith had grouped together, just as they always did, walled in between the piano and the claw-foot table. Alice Jenks joined them. The newer members had gathered in their own groups. They were definitely the older members.

Mrs. Edwards came to the doorway. "If you'll all come in the dining-room, we're going to have a buffet lunch, and I hope you'll notice the significance of the menu!"

They trooped out, protesting a little at being the first.

"Dear me! I don't want to seem a pig," Mrs. Kauf giggled.

"You're always in on the eats, aren't you, Laura?" Mrs. Rollins called to Mrs. Jackson.

"Why, Mrs. Edwards, you're just as clever as you can be! You've got everything brown!"

A large brown bake dish held baked beans. A towering pile of brown bread rested on a large brown plate. There was brown sugar instead of white for coffee and a brown cake with brown frosting.

Faith's face grew very red. She blew her nose violently.

"Faith," Julia murmured, "don't; it isn't funny." She wanted to leave these stuffy rooms filled with women who had no larger conception of their old Literary Club than this. It was simply a field for displaying Mrs. Edwards's ingenuity. Only her eyes showed her contempt. She took a slice of brown bread and coffee and carried it back to the chair by the piano.

Mrs. Mitchell was talking to Mrs. Withers and Mrs. Hetzel. "I don't think Browning has the smoothness of Tennyson, but I do like his ideas and his spirit better."

"He seems more like the German poets to me," Mrs. Hetzel remarked thoughtfully.

"Julia, did you ever in your life?" Alice Jenks brought her chair a little closer.

"No," said Julia. She couldn't join in with Mrs. Mitchell; Browning was too remote. She watched the women eating, chattering, almost hilarious now that the program was over. She saw them clearly as they were. They didn't want to have their interests widened. They warped even Browning to their own petty uses.

"I must go," Julia said, standing up.

"I'm ready, too." Faith pulled on her gloves.

They found Mrs. Edwards and took their leave.

"Thank you," Julia said simply.

"Mrs. Edwards, I've never heard such unique treatment of Browning," Faith told her in a bland voice.

"Now we can laugh," Faith declared when they had reached Fourth Street.

"I know," Julia said solemnly, "but, Faith, when you think what we set out to make it; remember, we used to talk about building up the town, making it a center of culture?"

"A second Boston." Faith's mouth twisted. "We were young then, Julia; you weren't twenty, and I was only twenty-two."

"Faith, I can't stand this town. I'm going to get to that Fair in Chicago if it's the last thing I do."

"But you'll have to come back here. Max and James and Senator Withers, why, they couldn't get out if they had to; you couldn't make them," Faith answered bitterly.

20. 1891

JULIA wrote Dil and Polly about the Fair, but they had moved away from Chicago and only wrote back that it seemed a pity the Fair was to be held in Chicago instead of New York City.

Julia talked again to Senator Withers and to Ned Jenks, but theirs was the careful attitude of spectators waiting to see.

"'Tisn't slated till '93, Mrs. Hauser," Ned Jenks reminded her. "But we'll be hearing more about it all the time."

Julia heard them impatiently and cherished the feverish excitement within herself. She mentioned the Fair to Max now and then, but always with guarded casualness.

"I wonder where they'll put the Fair buildings, don't you, Max?" she asked one time at dinner.

"Oh, in one of the parks I suppose. Chicago's got plenty of them." And then his interest came back to Halstead like the bubble in a carpenter's level. "You know Burns Park is a pretty fine one for a small town." And Julia turned to pouring coffee.

One night she woke up in a panic of fear. She sat up in bed looking at the calm familiarity of the room, trying to think what she had been dreaming. Then it came back to her; someone was home from the Fair and telling her about it. She had been so eager, so excited. "We're going, too," she kept repeating until the person said:

"But you can't; it's all over. It ended last week."

Julia put her cold hands under the pillow and lay down again. But it was a warning. The Fair could go on and be over while she went on as usual.

But she had to go on as usual, even with the secret excitement in her. She attended the meetings of the Literary Club and the Hospital Board. She even became a member of the School Board and outraged the firm advocates of the three "R's" by proposing that music be taught in the elementary schools.

She helped Miss Morey on her annual visitation, letting down the girls' skirts to keep up with their legs, and making shirts with broader shoulder-pieces for Chris. She admired the silver spoon Chris got for selling baker powder, watched Louise learn to dress herself, and transplanted the honeysuckle to the other side of the porch, while in herself she wondered how she could ever persuade Max, how she could ever make him willing to leave . . . around and around. One thing was fixed. She would go to the Fair.

They heard little in Halstead about the progress of the Fair buildings. Julia had to imagine to herself how they must be. In her eagerness she could almost see them.

It was 1891. Max brought a new calendar home advertising one of the Chicago produce houses. Julia had always relegated the violently painted calendars of other years to Max's store, but this one she kept, hanging it by the east side of the bow window.

At spring house-cleaning time the house reproached her for her scheming. It stood for all that was held in highest repute in Halstead, and she loved it even while she planned to leave it. She was watching Otto polish the outside of the windows of the sitting-room.

"Now the drawing-room," she said, shaping the words plainly with her lips so Otto could understand through the window. Otto moved the stepladder to the front room windows and Julia followed through the double doors. She looked around the room. Anyway the drawing-room would be easy to leave. There it was as bare as the day it was built except for the children's toys. It was almost a symbol. Julia's lips curved into a small smile of satisfaction. It mattered suddenly that she had held out for a scale of living that was larger and more gracious than Halstead's. Max had never understood why it had to be furnished just so; he had never liked it.

Faith Dorsett came in through the back door. "Julia, I just got a new magazine, and it has an account of the Fair in it. I thought you'd like to see it."

Julia turned the pages slowly, smelling the fresh print, stopping over an illustration, then leafing over the pages again.

"Oh, Faith!"

Faith kicked the sateen flounce of her dress. "My, you get excited over it. Do you really think you'll go and take the children?"

"I'm sure I will, Faith. Why, I think it would be terrible to miss it. Think of it; there may never be another one in our lives, all countries will have representatives. . . . It'll be as good as going to Europe!"

"After twenty years of missing things you get into the habit," Faith said with a smoldering of her sullen eyes.

"But, Faith, it isn't as if I were alone. I have the children, and I want them to go. It will make a difference all their lives."

Faith still sat moodily. Julia had a quick flashing back to the first time she saw Faith; how she had talked of painting so breathlessly. Now she only painted china. In the strong light from the window Faith's homely face looked older.

"And you have only James to think of, of course," Julia added slowly. "The men would rather stay home."

Faith's eyes narrowed slightly. "Yes," she answered without inflection. Then she burst out suddenly, "I'm glad there'll be a play here next week. The bills are posted up downtown. They're going to give *The Mountebank*. Lissa Monteroy and Arthur Blackmore; remember, he played here the year the Opera House opened?"

Play nights were different from any others in Halstead. The town itself was divided roughly into the element that attended the one-night stands of stock companies on their way out to the coast and that which lived for the spring and fall revival meetings held in the churches. It was hard to say whether more feminine hearts languished over the dramatic figure of the evangelist or the hero of the stock company. Both brought to the bare life of Halstead a disturbing and delicious excitement. Tears, whether for one's own sins or the sorrows of another, coursed luxuriously down cheeks that were unused to them, and the tears were as precious to the emotions as moisture to the un-irrigated soil.

The Hausers were followers of the theater. Chris haunted the ticket office of the Opera House until he was given the job of stage-hand. For those two days before and after the play even the job at Mathorn's was insignificant. Anne teased Julia into letting down her blue striped muslin even though March was early for it. Julia herself felt exhilarated at the prospect of an entertainment.

Troops of children watched the train come in and picked out the probable villain, the hero, the comedy actor and decided which of the two women was the lovely Lissa Monteroy. They watched from their vantage point on the baggage cart while the cast got into the one cab of the Golden House.

"I'm glad she's dark," sighed Minnie Yerkes rapturously, braiding and unbraiding the end of her own blonde pigtail.

"I bet the one with the mustache can fight good," declared William Jenks.

"Don't say bet, Willie," rebuked his sister.

"Come on, if we run fast we can watch 'em go into the hotel," Chris suggested. Like a streak the children tore across the tracks and up back of the new stone block. "I'll get to know them all," Chris reminded the others with pardonable pride. "I'll interduce 'em to you."

Jeanette Hauser stood silently at the corner of the barber shop. She was breathing fast after the dash up from the station, but they were in time. She had eyes only for the heroine. Could anything be more wonderful than being the star of a traveling theatrical company? Maybe, Jeanette told herself, maybe she would be an actress and be as famous as Lotta Crabtree and have people give her bags of gold.

And then came the crowning thrill for the town of Halstead. The cast needed a child in the play. What more natural than that they should ask for Jeanette who was the acknowledged star among the town's children.

Julia hesitated at first and then agreed. Above all things she wanted color and experiences for her children. Perhaps Jeanette would go on the stage; this would be a romantic beginning. If many of the good women of the town raised their eyebrows, Julia Hauser cared not at all.

Anne took Jeanette down to the Golden House. They went importantly up to the front bedroom, forgetting if they had ever heard that Papa and Mamma had once lived there, that Anne had been born there. But the room was different now with the new bright wallpaper and gas lights and a "register" instead of the little parlor cooker.

There was a brass bed, too, that was the Golden's pride. Anne knocked at the door, holding Jeanette by the hand.

The door opened swiftly. Anne knew in an instant that the young woman standing there was Lissa Monteroy from Melbourne, Australia.

"Oh, come in," the wonderful being laughed. "Curt, tell Art the kid for the child part is here," she called into the next room. Anne and Jeanette were both aware of the "kid," but in Lissa Monteroy's laughing voice it became proper, even refined. They were busy looking at the blue dressing-gown trimmed with four rows of lace-edged ruffles, the dark hair piled in little puff things all over her head. The blue eyes were a disappointment because a proper brunette should have dark eyes. And she did have paint on her lips and maybe on her cheeks. Anne couldn't help but catch her lower lip in her teeth for an instant's shocked disapproval, but of course actresses were different.

Miss Monteroy sat down on the bed. "You children sit down, and Mr. Blackmore'll call you in a minute. What's your name, dearie?"

"I'm Anne Hauser, and this is my sister, Jeanette." Anne made the introductions in a tone copied from Julia's.

"Curt, come here and see some cute kids," Lissa Monteroy called in to the next room.

"Curt" had reddish curls that were awfully unreal-looking, Anne told Julia critically.

"Come on in my room, you kids; Lissa is half sick."

They followed her in, seeing all that made this room so different from Mamma's: the sweet smell of perfumery, the little jars on the dresser, clothes thrown over the foot of the bed, a curling iron balanced across the gas jet, and a pair of shoes lying apart from each other, not side by side, as though their owner had just stepped out of them.

169

"Have some candy? My name's Julia Curtis, but you can call me Curt."

Anne didn't like it that her name was the same as Mamma's. She was glad that she wasn't called that. Both Anne and Jeanette called her *Miss* Curtis. It didn't seem right to call her by just one name. The chocolate creams were good.

"What's yours?" Anne asked before she thought. They always compared fillings at home.

"Raspberry," answered Jeanette promptly. "Oh, yours is just plain white."

Miss Curtis laughed at this, and Anne blushed in embarrassment.

"Do you think you'd like to be an actress?" she asked Jeanette.

"I'd love to," Jeanette replied ardently.

"You want to be strong then, like me. This traveling around's hard work. That's what's the matter with Lissa. Say, who's your doctor?"

"Doctor Chapman," both children chorused.

"I'll tell you, I wish you'd stop in on your way home and ask him to drop in here." Her voice had sunk to a whisper. They were proud to have her talk to them so confidentially.

Then Mr. Blackmore came in. Anne noticed the way he flung open the door without even knocking. He had curly hair, too, and side-burns and a mustache that was stiff at the ends.

"Here you are; yes, the little one should do; how old are you?"

"Nine," answered Jeanette.

"Isn't she a doll?" Miss Curtis put in. "Look at those eyes."

"Sure you won't get stage fright?"

"She never gets afraid speaking pieces," Anne assured him in an older sister, proprietary way. Miss Curtis laughed loudly at this. Why, neither Anne nor Jeanette could make out.

"Here's your lines," Mr. Blackmore said, handing Jeanette a whole sheet covered with pale, purple writing. "You learn them and come down at five o'clock tonight to say them for me. I'll give you the action. How's Lissa?" He turned away from them to ask. Anne waited a moment then pulled Jeanette's hand.

"Good-by," she offered tentatively at the door. "Good-by," Jeanette added.

"Oh, good-by, see you tonight, and don't forget what you're going to do for me." Miss Curtis winked at Anne.

"No, I won't," Anne promised, and closed the door behind them. "Walk downstairs," she whispered to Jeanette. "Don't run till we get outside; Mamma wouldn't like us to."

With due decorum and dignity they walked down the red-carpeted stairs and through the lobby. Anne looked straight ahead, but Jeanette looked around at the traveling men, at Mr. Fleischer and Mr. Golden. This wasn't really as nice as the hotel where she and Papa stayed in Omaha, she reflected silently. Once outside they ran all the way home, except that Jeanette stopped to read the first line.

" 'Where is my mother' "—fear in the voice—" 'I want my mother.' See, Anne, I know the first line already." Jeanette's exultation over having a real part in a real play was in her voice instead of the fear.

The G. W. Edwards Stock Company featuring Miss Lissa Monteroy of Melbourne, Australia, and others, played to a full house. People climbed the three steep flights to

171

the second balcony eagerly. Julia Hauser and Louise occupied a box as the family of one of the actresses. Max had had to go to Burlington at the last minute. He was sorry. Nothing gave Max Hauser greater pleasure than to watch his family perform. He would sit in the audience holding Louise on his knee and beam proudly.

Julia was there early in her best black satin with the real lace collar and cuffs. Louise was a picture child in a white dress with blue ribbons, a blue ribbon around her hair and wearing her eight-strap black leather slippers. Anne had been asked to play the violin before the curtain went up and in the intermissions. Gilbert Withers was to play the piano. Julia looked down over the gilt railing of the box at Anne. She had eaten no supper, only sat at the table in an agony of nervousness.

"What if I should make a mistake, Mamma?" Anne had wailed hopelessly.

"No one would notice; just don't stop, go right ahead."

"But he'd know, Mamma."

Julia divined that "he" was Gilbert Withers. "That won't matter if he does."

Julia had stood on the porch and watched Anne and Jeanette go down the street together. They were so different: Anne, cold with fear that she would forget her piece, that she would fail in some way, terrified in front of all those people; Julia yearned over her. And there was Jeanette without a thought of self-consciousness, tingling with excitement, gloating at the thought of having a speaking part.

Gilbert Withers turned to speak to Anne. Julia could see Anne's pink ribbon bobbing vigorously. Julia smiled to herself, participating wholly in Anne's feeling of pleased shyness.

Now they were going to play. The gas footlights were

on. Anne looked very small down there. The bow seemed to draw assurance; the notes came more roundly. Anne would walk on air tonight. Anne, Jeanette, Chris, Louise: life was many-sided.

Jeanette sat on a camp stool in the wings. Her sheet of lines was folded into a tiny size and hidden underneath her sash. She had even stopped saying them over and over to herself, she was so occupied watching Lissa Monteroy. It was plain even to Jeanette that Lissa was sick. Miss Curtis had given her something to drink from a little glass and said, "Brace up, Lissa. Get through tonight, and you'll have three days on the train to rest up in. That country doctor don't know everything. Here, let me give you more color, dear."

Lissa looked all tired out standing there under the gas-light, but when the bell rang she picked up her skirts and ran out on the stage. For the minute Jeanette forgot to think about when she grew up to be an actress. Adoration filled her.

Now she couldn't see her; she was over too far. Jeanette leaned as far forward as she dared. Then Lissa laughed. The laugh sounded almost real but not quite. The queer sound in the laugh as though she were pretending started a shiver in Jeanette's knees that ran down her legs and made her swallow suddenly. Lissa didn't feel like laughing; she was only making the laugh. She must be awfully sick. Jeanette tiptoed over to Miss Curtis who held the prompt book.

"How long before I go on the stage?" she whispered.

With a frown of annoyance Miss Curtis looked ahead. "Six pages. You'll have to hurry; the toilet's way down in the basement."

Jeanette didn't even bother to tell her that she wasn't a

baby. She hurried down the steep back stairs that were built on the outside of the Opera House and were slippery on the outer edge. Breathlessly she ran around to the front door of the theater and in through the lobby. Mr. Flinters stood inside the curtained doors of the theater watching the play while he stood guard.

"I'm one of the actresses," she told Mr. Flinters in an important whisper and squeezed by him. The stage was unreal, brilliantly lighted, not like it was from the wings. Miss Monteroy didn't look sick from here. She looked beautiful! Jeanette hurried soundlessly along the side of the room to the box. She stooped down between Mamma's chair and the doorway.

"Mamma!" Julia looked up startled.

"Mamma, quick; I've got to get back in a minute, but Miss Monteroy, she's sick, Mamma, awful sick. She's only pretending to laugh. And they've got to go on the train tonight and travel three whole days. Mamma, please can we take her home and put her in Anne's room and have Dr. Chapman take care of her?"

Julia hesitated.

"Quick, Mamma, please, I have to get back."

Stage folk were definitely stage folk and yet . . .

"Mamma, she's really sick. You know, she had to have Dr. Chapman, and he told her to get to bed and stay there. . . ."

Julia looked down at the flushed face, the round brown eyes. This might be a contact for Jeanette, who knew? "You can ask her, Jeanette; I'll come around after the play."

Then Jeanette was gone, running softly along the wall and past Mr. Flinters. Outdoors the cold March air smelled good and clean after the hot air of the dressing-room with its grease-paint and gaslight and that other unpleasant smell from the old costumes. What if they had come to the place where she came in and she wasn't there! She clambered up the icy fire-escape steps holding tight to the railing. Once she stumbled and scratched her knee. She was out of breath when she opened the door of the dressing-room.

"Here she is; quick, child!" Miss Curtis pushed her on the stage. Jeanette swallowed hard. They might be cross if they knew she was going to keep Lissa Monteroy here. They mustn't know she had been out. She opened her mouth to speak. Her words sounded strangely loud, not like her own words at all. The lights along the front of the stage were like a curtain between herself and everybody out there in the seats. Jeanette threw herself into the part.

In the intermission Jeanette found Chris out on the stage.

"Basket!" The basket wasn't on the table for Act IV. Chris produced the basket. He was profoundly happy in his important position. "Umbrella for Mr. Blackmore," he muttered.

"Chris!" Jeanette came up to him.

"Look out, Jeanette, can't you see I've got to get everything ready here?"

"Listen, Chris," Jeanette came close now, "Mamma's going to take Miss Monteroy home with us after the play because she's so sick."

Chris stood still. "In our house?" Naturally conventional, this offended his sense of the proper. "I don't believe it!"

Jeanette nodded her head triumphantly and ran off to keep an eye on Miss Monteroy. Already she was as much at home around the stage as at Papa's store. She slipped through into Miss Monteroy's dressing-room.

"I'm all right now, Curt, only dizzy and kind of chilly." Miss Monteroy didn't look beautiful here. Her hair was mussed from lying down; her eyes were somehow too big. She had her real coat around her instead of the lovely cape she wore on the stage. Jeanette stood by the couch.

"Mamma's going to take you home after the play, Miss Monteroy, an' you can stay till you get all well."

Miss Curtis looked at Jeanette sharply. "You run along, Doll, she'll be all right."

"Oh, Curt, I can't even think of my lines, my head aches so."

"Sure you can. Don't think about them. Just open your mouth and the right ones'll come. Sit up now and I'll do your hair over."

After the play the audience clapped and stamped and cheered at each new curtain call. Still Miss Monteroy didn't appear. At last the crowd gave up good-naturedly and trooped out, talking to each other, jovial and smiling after the emotional debauch. They got into their familiar wraps, amazed to find them still the same ones. Glamor stayed with them for a bit.

"Pretty good," they said to each other; "yes, sir, you couldn't beat that much."

Back of the wings Julia and Dr. Chapman were in Miss Monteroy's dressing-room. Miss Monteroy lay on the couch with a coat over her.

"I'm all right. I just have a chill, I guess," Miss Monteroy said weakly.

"You've got a high fever," said Dr. Chapman brusquely, "and you'll take your life in your hands to go on any train tonight."

Julia looked at Miss Monteroy. "My dear, we'll be glad to have you," she said gently. "You can catch up with your company in a couple of days." Now that she had yielded

176

to Jeanette's begging she was uncertain how wise she had been. What would Max say? Dr. Chapman drew her aside:

"I can take her over to the hospital, Julia. That's the place for her."

"No," said Julia firmly, "she can come home with us just as well as not. She's only a young girl, not more than twenty, and I don't suppose she has any money to spare for hospitals."

In the end Chris went running home for Otto and the buggy. Lena in high displeasure heated a soapstone and made up the bed clean. "Don't know what your mamma's thinking of, bringing an actress home here," she snorted to Louise who was already asleep.

Jeanette hovered close by, watching, taking in with her round brown eyes that Mr. Blackmore was cross about their taking Lissa Monteroy home, that Miss Curtis felt bad, but that Miss Lissa Monteroy herself seemed too sick to care. Jeanette tied the silver dollar that Mr. Blackmore gave her for acting, tightly in her handkerchief.

"We ought to carry you along with us to take Lissa's place," he said, and the deep glow that spread through her was still with her. Maybe she would tell Anne tonight, maybe she would keep it all to herself.

21

MAX heard about Miss Lissa Monteroy before he reached home. Oscar Holtz, the station manager, hailed him as he got off.

"Hear ye got an actress at your house, Max!"

"What's that?" Max asked.

"Sure, the star of the show Saturday night took sick

and Missus Hauser took her home. Say, she's a good-looker, too!"

Max decided to go home before stopping in at the store. When he opened the door of his house, he saw Dr. Chapman's hat and bag on the hat rack. Lena came out to see him and rolled her eyes expressively. Then Anne heard him from the sitting-room.

"Hello, Papa."

"Hello, my dear." Max was too disturbed to take pleasure even in the sight of his eldest daughter. "Where's Mamma, Anne?"

"She's upstairs; Miss Monteroy, the actress in the play you know, is awful sick, Papa."

Max met Julia in the upstairs hall. "I do think, Julia," he began irritably.

"Shh!" Julia put her finger to her lips. "Max, I know it was impulsive, but if you could see the poor little thing, and it's so lonely to be alone in one of these towns. Dr. Chapman thinks she's a little bit better today. She's been out of her head for two days."

Max wrinkled his forehead. He disliked having the house upset. Even now a medicinal odor came out to him from the bedroom. Dr. Chapman opened the door.

"Good morning, Max." Dr. Chapman looked tired out. He had stayed at the house all the night before. "Your wife's the most generous woman I know, Max."

"Yes," answered Max shortly.

Anne came upstairs carrying a cup of bouillon. An anxious feeling, something Max couldn't put his finger on, hung in the air. It was disturbing for a man to come home and find the whole house dancing attendance on some actress.

"Well, I must get down to the store," Max announced in a bewildered tone. But it was against his code to find any fault with his wife's management beyond his expression of distaste. "I hope the children don't come down sick next," he added grimly.

Downstairs with the chair drawn into a corner sat Jeanette, hands in her ears to shut out the household. She was committing to memory a new piece to recite when Miss Monteroy got well. It was from *Romeo and Juliet*.

"She speaks, she speaks, yet she says nothing," Jeanette mumbled to herself. "What of that? . . . I will answer her. . . ."

Anne was practicing a new piece of music to play for Miss Monteroy, but she had to take her violin down to Hetzels' lest Miss Monteroy be disturbed. Chris had discussed with Mamma plans for making a back-rest for the bed, but Julia discouraged him, saying she thought the pillows would be softer.

Even the town shared in the feeling of excitement. People went out of their way to walk up by the Hausers'. Mr. Wentz, who ran the post-office, had to give out the latest information with the mail. "Chris Hauser says the Doctor says she'll pull through," he announced one day. It was romantic to have the star of the stock company sick abed right in their own town. Some of the glamor of the play spread to the town and rested on each individual.

To Julia, on whom most of the nursing fell, Miss Monteroy was first pathetic and very sick, then overnight she became again the star of the stock company. In ten days she was sitting up and having her meals in the little bed-sitting-room. Julia had the blue negligee carefully laundered. Whether Lissa noticed it or not was hard to tell. She wore it with undeniable charm, looking very pale with the rouge gone from her cheeks. It amused Julia to see the children such willing slaves. They hurried up to see her the minute they were home from school, behaving much the same as they had a year before with a new litter of kittens.

Sometimes a friend from school came tiptoeing up the stairs with them and was introduced with a condescending air of ownership toward "the actress." Lissa Monteroy never lacked for entertainers. One day Chris brought home a little bottle of perfume from the drug store which he proffered shyly. But it baffled Julia that now at the end of two weeks she knew her scarcely better than before.

Lissa Monteroy was always sweet, always smiling her appreciation of anything that was done, offering no least information about herself. One day she asked if there were any mail, but there was none. Julia explained that Dr. Chapman had sent a wire to the manager of the company saying that she was too ill to move. Lissa said nothing herself as to whether she would rather go or stay.

At the end of the second week Lissa moved downstairs, and one mild April day even sat on the sunny end of the porch wrapped in an afghan. "I'll surprise the children when they come home from school," she said, smiling. "I feel so much better today. I think I can be leaving in a few days."

She had her meals downstairs now and sat in the sitting-room after dinner. Julia invited a few people in one night, just the oldest friends: the Withers and the Jenks, Faith and James Dorsett, and the Hetzels and Dr. Chapman. Jeanette would recite, Anne would play, she would serve raspberry wine and cookies.

Coming back from the kitchen with the tray of little glasses Julia stood in the doorway a minute seeing the room as a whole. Everyone was trying in some way to shine, to be a little more than reality. There was Anne, pretending not to be nervous, playing without her music; Mrs. Withers, who only half approved of Lissa Monteroy, telling Alice Jenks under cover of the music about when she saw *Uncle Tom's Cabin.* Max remembered seeing Lotta Crabtree in Denver one time when he was just a youngster. Tonight the men hadn't drifted to one end of the room to talk about "conditions" the way they usually did. Even Max and the Senator were listening to what Lissa Monteroy said. Then it came to Julia: it was because of Lissa Monteroy.

Lissa was pretty in that dark blue satin dress with the cherry ribbons around the neck and sleeves. It was just a little lower than need be. Everything about Lissa suggested faintly that she had seen many places. She wasn't strong yet; her very fragility gave her charm. When she laughed, she put back her head so her curls fell over the back of the chair. She had painted her face a little tonight and wore long jet earrings.

James Dorsett bowed over her to fix the pillow behind her back. He was talking to her now. She looked up at him and then dropped her eyes and played with the bow at her wrist. It was a silly coquetry; it belonged rather to the stage. Julia looked quickly down at her tray. Lena had laid out the second-best tea napkins. In spite of a reluctance in herself Julia went over to the sideboard and got instead her best damask squares embroidered in Dresden.

"Here, Anne, you and Jeanette may pass." Julia saw Jeanette curtsey as she gave Lissa her glass. Lissa had been teaching her how. Julia sipped her raspberry wine and nibbled at the thin sugar cookies.

"Anne, Chris," Julia said in a low voice, "it's past your bedtime now. Take Jeanette and go on upstairs." Somehow she didn't want them down here any longer watching

Lissa Monteroy. This wine was too sour. Some friend of Max's had made it and brought it to him at Christmas time. He usually made such good wine. James Dorsett was still sitting by Lissa. Max and Dr. Chapman were listening to Lissa, too. She was more talkative tonight than Julia had ever seen her. She was the center of attention. The women were looking at her dress as they had studied her own black mull once, Julia thought, but she doubted whether Lissa felt their gaze.

"After the show we went to Delmonico's," Lissa was saying, "and there's no place in the world like it! You should taste their lobster; I don't suppose you ever get it out here. . . ."

Julia glanced across the room at Faith. Faith was looking out the window at the darkness. Why did she wear that brown moiré; it was so unbecoming. Dr. Chapman came over to say good night.

"I regret that I have to leave, Julia; our little patient is outdoing herself to be entertaining." Dr. Chapman was talking in that sarcastic tone he had. Julia looked at him quickly.

"It's a little pathetic, you know; out here there is nothing, so we give ourselves to anything that has glitter. You should have seen Mrs. Livingstone in hysterics after the last revival!" He twisted his mouth. Julia went with him into the hall.

"Now we are all licking our chops over the thought of lobster at Delmonico's, freshly boiled, dripping with butter, and a bottle of champagne, ice-cold. Lobster's as good a symbol as any, eh, Julia?"

"Don't, Dr. Chapman." The tone of his voice hurt her. Why did he talk like that; he hurt himself so.

"Don't let any of my good friends elope with the lovely Lissa!" He pulled open the door. "Damn it, it's raining."

"Here, take an umbrella," she called, getting Max's big green one from the stand in the hall. But when she came back to the porch, he was already down the street, his felt hat pulled down all around and his coat collar turned up, striding recklessly through the puddles. Julia watched him go. He had disturbed her as he always could. Lobster, Delmonico's . . . Just his foolish talk, but he was right, too; there was so little here, and so often you could tell it even on the people's faces. She didn't want her children hanging on the words of some stock-company actress twenty years from now.

As Julia went back into the sitting-room, she heard Lissa saying, "You must excuse me; I'm still something of an invalid." She smiled back at them archly.

She needed an audience to bring her out, Julia thought in a quick guilty instant. Tomorrow she would be quiet again. Julia wondered impatiently how long she planned to stay. After all, Jeanette would learn nothing from her. Lissa was not a symbol of the theater as she had imagined to herself. She should know by now the real Arts did not come to Halstead.

22

JEANETTE sat on a barrel watching John Sorenson taking grapes out of their sawdust bed. He handled them as carefully as though each cluster were a new live baby chick. It was cool in Papa's store; the dingy windows in front kept most of the light out. The poster announcing Lissa Monteroy that had been there all spring was covered over with the circus poster. The one gas jet hanging from the ceiling only seemed to intensify the dark. Back of the board wall at the end was the cold-storage room. The knowledge of its cool darkness made her feel cooler now.

Louise was playing with some empty boxes. It was easy "to entertain" her down here, lots easier than walking along Omaha Street in the hot sun. And it was more exciting than being home. Mamma wouldn't let her go down to the Golden House to visit Miss Monteroy any more. She had moved away from their house over a month ago.

John had finished now with the grapes. He opened the office door and called in, "48 2-quart baskets a grapes, Joe." Joe stuck his pen back of his ear and made a mark with a pencil on a yellow paper. "Telephone the store they can have 'em any time they want, but it better be today, Joe."

Jeanette was proud of the telephone hanging on the wall in the office. There were only ten in Halstead, and Papa's had been the second one. Joe turned the crank on the side to ring the number. John began ripping apart orange crates, and Joe kicked the office door shut on the agonizing shriek the nails made as they let go.

"Here's the first one for you," John said. That was really what she had been waiting for. Jeanette caught the orange John threw over to her. "Here's one for the little tike."

"I'll have to peel it for her." Jeanette peeled it into sections for Louise, but she sucked her own. It made your lips smart a little, but it was deliciously sweet and cold. She pulled her knees up under her chin and tucked her full plaid skirt all around them. Papa's store always gave her a good feeling. It was always full of so many things to eat; it didn't seem as though they could ever be all eaten up. It was nice to think that Papa owned everything in this place. The new cases and barrels smelled so clean, even the faint smell of over-ripe fruit was pleasant here.

It was fun to see the farmers who came in with loads of stuff—tubs of butter or boxes of eggs or loads of apples or potatoes—and waited for John to weigh them out so Joe could pay them. Sometimes Papa came out to talk to them. Jeanette could tell how much they liked him, and Papa always seemed to know them by their first names. Someway Papa seemed more important down here or on the trips than at home. You remembered that he was a big shipper and that hundreds and hundreds of those barrels would be shipped to Chicago. There was Papa's name printed right on the wood, Max Hauser, Produce.

Jeanette sucked her orange while a secret pleasure spread through her. The store was most exciting of all in the fall when ducks and quail and partridge hung up on the big hooks. Only their heads drooping made you feel kind of sad, and you wanted to touch their lovely glossy feathers and kind of not wanted to at the same time. It was fun to shake the great stalks of corn as big as the little trees by the house; they made such a terrible noise.

Suddenly Jeanette heard people running by outside. She decided to go and see about it when Chris came in breathless and hot. He went into Papa's office and then came running out again when he found Papa wasn't there.

"Chris!" Jeanette called from the barrel.

Chris came over to her. His face looked scared and excited at the same time, and queer, too. His mouth twitched the way Mr. Mathorn's did. Even though Mamma scolded about it when he got excited he forgot. He had run so fast he could hardly talk.

"Jeanette, Mr. Dorsett, he's . . . Somebody, they think Mr. Blackmore, you know in the stock company, shot him. Mrs. Golden heard the shot. They're bringing him home on the door, now. Come on quick if you want to see 'em." Chris brought out the word door, so it was more amazing than even shot.

Jeanette slid down from the barrel quickly and took

Louise by the hand. They went out to the doorway. Down the street came a queer little procession. There were two men carrying something between them. People were out all along the street. The children always came down to Papa's store to watch circus parades and political processions. It seemed natural enough to be there watching now. Only just as they came even with the store, Jeanette looked at the door. The long legs that stuck out from under the quilt were Mr. Dorsett's, and he was dead. Suddenly it wasn't natural to be standing there watching. It was different from any other time. She grabbed Chris by the sleeve. Her own legs felt queer.

"Come on, let's follow 'em. They're taking him up home."

Jeanette followed, keeping Louise close to her. The street was kind of funny and still. It was twice as hot after the cool store. There was a crowd now, mostly children following the procession.

"Why did he shoot him?" Jeanette whispered to Chris.

"Aw, you're too young to understand yet," Chris said, taking his agate out of his pocket and turning it over in his hand as he spoke.

But there were other ways of finding out things, Jeanette knew, when Chris and Anne put on that grown-up air. She kept still. They'd go past their house before they came to Dorsetts'. She could ask Mamma. Abruptly she wondered whether Mrs. Dorsett knew yet. The thought made her slow up.

"Come on," urged Chris impatiently. Louise began to whimper. "Let's make a chair; she'll make us lose 'em," said Chris, grasping one wrist with his other hand. Jeanette tried, but Louise was too heavy. "You walk slowly with her," decided Chris. "Mamma told you to take care of her."

"Aren't you big enough to carry her, Chris?" Jeanette asked with careful cunning.

Without a word Chris picked her up. "Come on then." They hurried after the procession.

It was fun the way people came to the door to watch. There was Mrs. Edwards whispering to Mrs. Rollins. And then Jeanette caught sight of the feet again. The shoes were shiny and looked as though the rest of him ought to be alive. The procession was turning the corner now. Some of the children were yelling.

Chris stopped to take Louise pick-a-back instead. It was easier. He'd been so excited at first. Now the excitement wasn't there. He began to think about Mrs. Dorsett. The men at the hotel said it served Dorsett right. Mr. Golden said he wasn't a-going to stop them if they drove past him on their way to the train. Chris looked at the quilt trailing on the road. They'd taken the door of the hotel room right off its hinges. He'd seen the empty doorway with his own eyes.

He thought of Miss Monteroy. It gave him a queer feeling to think she'd lived right in their house. She was bad. She must have been bad. Mrs. Golden said, "Anybody could have told what kind she was," and she wondered at the time when Mrs. Hauser took her in. Not but what Mrs. Hauser did it in all kindness. Chris had gotten red at that and gone upstairs to look at the room. Still Miss Monteroy was awful pretty. Then he thought of Mrs. Dorsett again. She was different; she was a lady like Mamma. He wished fiercely that he hadn't bought that bottle of perfume. He could have bought six new alleys instead, he thought bitterly.

They were up to their house. Jeanette was disappointed that Mamma wasn't out on the porch. Chris went in through the gate to drop Louise. Jeanette followed. Maybe

187

Mamma hadn't heard yet. Then Anne came to the door looking scared.

"Mamma's gone to Mrs. Dorsett's. You come right in here. I wouldn't be seen going up the street after . . ." she couldn't say his name. "You know Mrs. Dorsett is Mamma's best friend and my painting teacher." Anne burst into tears and went into the house. Jeanette and Chris were taken aback. Anne was crying!

"Aw, come on," whispered Chris. "Mamma won't care." Jeanette went. It seemed odd to both of them that Anne didn't come out to call them back. At the gate of the Dorsetts' the procession paused. The men talked among themselves.

"Well, he's her husband even if he is a . . ." The rest of his sentence was smothered.

"Here, sonny, you go call Mrs. Dorsett," one of the men said to Chris. Another demurred, but Chris was up the steps of the vine-covered porch in a flash, feeling important. On any other day he would have gone right in, but today he knocked. Mamma came to the door. He hadn't expected that; all his importance went out of him. Mamma looked so stern and queer.

"Why, Chris!" Her tone was shocked and disappointed. Chris's mouth twitched.

"Mamma, they've brought Mr. Dorsett you know."

Julia looked out with horror at the men holding the door between them with the figure of a man half covered by a quilt. Her mind flashed unaccountably to that time she had looked from the hotel window at the two men sitting in the carriage handcuffed, driving away to be hanged. She winced. Chris looking anxiously in her face saw it. Then she noticed the children, Jeanette bringing up the rear.

"Chris, take Jeanette and go straight home and stay

there." Chris had never seen her so cross. Her eyes flashed. He turned quickly and stumbled down the steps.

"Come on home, don't stand there," he said crossly to a bewildered Jeanette.

Julia stepped to the edge of the porch. "All of you, go on home. Bring Mr. Dorsett's body in here quietly." The children in the procession hesitated and then obeyed reluctantly. All the gentleness had gone from Julia. A harsh anger burned in her eyes and voice. The men felt her dignity and shuffled before it.

"We didn't know whether she'd want it in here," one of the men offered by way of excuse.

"Don't be stupid," said Julia Hauser, looking through the man.

On the porch the men laid their burden down gently. They lifted the body and carried it in through the narrow hall.

"In here," said Julia.

They placed the body down on the haircloth sofa and without a word went out again, not talking to each other until they were well down the block.

Julia arranged the quilt around the body. Even dead, James Dorsett had a kind of quickness about him. It unnerved her. Then she went quietly into the dining-room where Faith sat filling in a painted blossom on a china cup. A sudden panic had seized Faith when she heard the men. Reality seemed to be going from her. She rushed across to the table by the window and picked up the unfinished cup. The cold feeling of the china in her hands gave her a touch with reality again. Scarcely knowing that she did it she touched the delicate stem with green, keeping to the lines without effort. Something as slender as that stem lay between her and some unreal terror. She

189

dipped her brush again; she could feel Julia coming over to her without looking up.

"Faith!" Julia's voice was very tender. "Faith!" Julia put her arm under Faith's. "Come, dear."

Faith got up carrying the cup in her hand. She couldn't put it down. Her fingers tightened on it when Julia tried to take it. Together they went to the doorway of the sitting-room. Faith looked at once at the couch. Strangely her eyes began with the feet in their shiny shoes. James was always fussy about his shoes, keeping them polished even in the spring when everything was muddy and even now in the dust. He hadn't shined them just for that woman. Her eyes followed over the quilt and skipped his face to his hair. It was black with a little gray in it. Then she found his face.

Julia's arm around her urged her toward him until they stood by the couch. Faith reached out and touched his face with her empty hand. It was cool like the china. She knelt down beside him then and set the cup on the floor. With both hands she smoothed his hair and touched his closely shaven face again. She pulled the quilt up over his face. When she stood up her mouth trembled in a hideous uncertainty. She had given up so much; painting—really painting, that is—and now James. There was nothing ever to do about it. . . . Faith's mouth became firm again.

"Faith, dear, it was this awful heat; living way out here he . . ." Julia halted. "Oh, Faith, I'd give anything if I hadn't asked that woman . . ."

"It wasn't that," Faith broke in, "we never should have come here. He was never meant to live in a farming country, he missed the city so, and the long hot summers always made him irritable and nervous. . . ." So they told each other, knowing there was only a half truth in what they said.

"Come home with me, Faith, and I'll come back up to spend the night here," Julia urged.

Faith shook her head. It didn't seem right to go away and leave somebody . . . dead. It always irritated James so to be left alone in the evenings. Only she knew how to sit alone. She didn't mind it so much any more. Now it would be like that all the time. She turned to go into the other room. It was time to start supper. There was a brittle crunching sound.

"Oh, my teacup!" Faith said aloud. She bent to pick up the pieces with painstaking care. Julia stooped to help.

"Faith, dear, please come."

"No, Julia, not now. You go home and have supper and then come back if you don't mind."

There was a step on the porch and a knock. Dr. Chapman came in quietly. He didn't speak until he got way over to them. Then he said gently as though it were any day, "It's stifling this afternoon." He reached under the quilt and put his fingers around James Dorsett's wrist, then he pulled up the quilt again. The two women stood silently watching him.

"I'll be back, Faith," Julia said.

"Julia." Dr. Chapman caught up with her just as she was crossing over Second Street.

"Oh, Dr. Chapman, I'm to blame for this whole thing."

Dr. Chapman shook his head. "No, we're all to blame in a sense, Julia." They walked along the street silently. "Poor devils! I remember when they first came out here. James was in love with Faith then. He never should have come out here in the first place. . . . No, Julia, you can lay it up to his hankering for lobster!"

"They let the murderer get away as though this were

twenty years ago!" Julia burst out. "He and Lissa Monteroy went scot free!"

They walked toward Julia's gate in silence. Julia looked away across the street. "I'm not going to stay here any longer." She spoke the words quickly.

"I've wondered when you were going to make up your mind to that," answered Dr. Chapman. Then he added, "Max came for me. I've never seen him so upset."

He stood almost awkwardly beside her. Didn't she ever look at him as anybody but Dr. Chapman? He watched her in her light summer dress, her face so stirred by her own thoughts, she could never catch his love. He remembered how he had thought her like a gardenia that first time he saw her.

Julia said, "Good-by, Dr. Chapman," but the nearness had gone from her voice. She was removed into herself.

Dr. Chapman walked slowly down to his office to see if there were any calls. He took off his hat to Mrs. Grady. The woman was going to stop him.

"Oh, Doctor, I been having the worst dizzy spells lately."

"Is that so, Mrs. Grady; you drop up to the office sometime tomorrow." Not tonight; he couldn't listen tonight. He tried not to look quite at her. He still had Julia's delicately cut image before him. Mrs. Grady's broad silly face irritated him. He passed by. He was tired.

He remembered the time Dorsett and O'Connor and he went buffalo hunting beyond the North Loop; he felt better thinking of those days. He had come out in the first place for the adventure of the thing. Halstead was the Middle West now.

He looked down the street that had been one gray glare in the heat all day. Now there was a green edge to the

light. Two hours more and the green would have sub-
dued the sun entirely, like the green shade on his new
gas desk-light. Then dark!

"Pshaw!" muttered Dr. Chapman who could call things
by so many names, who could understand a woman like
Julia; here he was taking pleasure in the lights and shadows
on the street on the day when his friend was brought home
on the door of a hotel bedroom murdered. He was shocked
at himself. Then he shrugged. He was what he was under
the sun. What a nice Biblical ring that had, he thought
to himself. . . .

Julia went into her own front hall. It was hot and still.
She wondered where the children were. Mechanically
she took off her hat and pushed her hair back from her
forehead. She went directly to the kitchen.

"Supper's ready, Mis' Hauser," Lena said.

"Where are the children?"

"I give 'em supper in the backyard. I thought maybe
you wouldn't want to be bothered."

"Oh," said Julia, "thank you. I think I'll eat, Lena. I'm
going back to Mrs. Dorsett right away." She sat down at
the table in the dining-room and unfolded her napkin.
Max was late tonight.

But when Lena brought the soup, Julia still sat without
even taking up her spoon. She rested her elbows on the
table and looked out the window at the dull twilight.
One thing was finished along with James Dorsett's life.
There could be no more secret maneuvering. She was
leaving Halstead. She thought of Chris and Jeanette following James Dorsett's dead body up the street and winced
again at the sight. Then Max came in.

"Hello, Jule."

"Hello, Max."

She heard his chair, that was an armchair and heavier than the rest, as he pulled it out and sat down, hitching it up to the table, listening to it as though the sound of it must be different tonight, as though it would tell her something.

Max let his arms rest on the chair arms.

"I've just come from Dorsetts'." He shook his head. "Horrible thing."

"I should think they'd have caught the murderer, Max," Julia burst out.

"The town hasn't gotten over the early days yet when a man paid with his life for that sort of thing. . . ."

"It never will get over brutality and violence and . . . Oh, Max, I wish you could have seen the children following up through town in that procession! I tell you, Max, we're going to leave this place. I hate it. I won't have the children grow up here."

Max didn't answer. He slumped in his chair.

Julia, looking at him, thought of the night in the Lafayette House when he had gotten the telegram about his brother's death—only he looked much older now. Was he thinking that she was to blame bringing Lissa Monteroy home? She *was* to blame. Then he spoke.

"James and I boarded together for four months before they got the hotel built; he was seven or eight years younger than I am. He was in to see me Tuesday and he was joking. Said the town had quit growing. I told him he was wrong, that his corner lot on Eighth Street would be worth four times what it is today." To Max these words had taken on some deep significance. "And then I didn't see him till this afternoon."

"Max, drink some coffee."

"I don't believe I want any tonight, Jule. I'm going to take that corner lot off of Faith's hands at what it'll be worth a few years from now. . . . What did you say, Jule, about the children being in that procession?"

"Why, Max, when I came out on Faith's porch, Chris and Jeanette were there at the head of that mob. Of course Chris and Anne will hear all about it. . . . Oh, Max, don't you see, we can't have the children growing up here. You can't be proud of living here; I want the children to live where there's some . . ." Julia broke off. She couldn't get it into words. She looked down at her plate. She shouldn't talk about herself and the children now; she should be thinking of Faith and James, but it was this thing that had happened to them that made this place so intolerable.

Max was still thinking about the children . . . following in that procession.

He got up heavily and went out to sit on the porch in the long dusk. Louise came and climbed in his lap. Chris and Anne and Jeanette sat on the back porch and talked in lowered voices about "the murderer" until a shocked Lena sent them sharply to bed.

Julia went over to stay with Faith. All along the street she felt people looking at her from their porches. She knew what they were saying back of their vines.

Julia sat in the dining-room across from Faith. A dim light came through the door of the parlor, making a shadowy trellis on the carpet just under the knotted fringe of the portières. The gaslight above the dining-room table was turned on full. All the little bead fringes around the green shade sparkled heartlessly.

"I hate gloomy rooms," Faith burst out, and then sat silent again rocking in her chair. Julia looked at the dining-room table suddenly, trying to see Faith and James across from each other all those years as separate, perhaps, as she and Max.

On the plate-rail stood the hand-painted chocolate pitcher Faith had done. She used to pour from it when she had company. James always loved company and singing and acting. There was so little of that here.

"Oh, Julia." Faith crossed to Julia's chair with a kind of swoop as Anne or Jeanette might have done. She knelt on the floor and buried her face in Julia's lap before Julia could see it. How gray Faith's hair had grown. Julia put her arms around Faith's shoulders.

"Faith, dear," she whispered. What were the words people said to each other to comfort them? Words about religion—they seemed too far from James who had committed adultery. How much Faith had meant to James really—that was between them across their own table. How did she know? Those days when James had gone down to the hotel to see Lissa, striding through the lobby not caring who saw him. . . . He had paid for that. What could she say? She had introduced James to Lissa, but Faith knew . . . she could only hold Faith's shoulders more tightly. What if Chris had been James?

Out of the night dark that had shut down at last on the corn town and the cornfields beyond came the whistle of the midnight flyer, hurtling on toward the east away from this way-station where people wanted so much they never had, where a thirsty man could be murdered and the people let the murderer go. . . . Julia shuddered.

The whistle grew fainter, impersonal, not caring what happened here; that two women sat in the next room to a murdered man. It was far away now leaving loneliness behind.

23. 1892

THE corn stood in shocks again in the field beyond the town. The big calendar in Max's store was turned to October, 1892. Max had turned it himself, leaning over the desk that was littered with circulars, correspondence, samples of dried fruit, ledgers. His heavy gold watch charm dangled over the litter for a moment as he stretched to reach above the roll-top to the calendar, then it settled comfortably back against the wide vest as Max sat down again in his swivel chair and contemplated the calendar.

Wel-l, he told himself slowly, he had to go to Chicago sometime this fall; it might just as well be October. Introducing the first California fruits into Nebraska had enlarged the business so he needed Chicago contacts. Why, he was doing a South Water Street business of his own in four states. Let's see, it had been twelve, thirteen, yes, sir, sixteen years since he'd been on South Water Street. He'd take a trip down there next week, and he'd be there for the Fair dedication; that would please Julia. Julia even wanted him to look into business opportunities there.

Why, Julia was ready to take the whole family and camp on the spot. An indulgent smile showed beneath his mustache; his eyes crinkled at the corners slightly. But Julia was a mighty fine little woman. When he thought of her, the indulgent smile changed to a look not so far from reverence. Julia knew what was best for the children—he never questioned that, and she had her heart set on this Fair. He had again that feeling Julia always gave him when she set her mind on something like—like that drawing-room, for instance. He tugged at his mustache in embarrassment.

Well, she had put up with a lot out here. He didn't suppose she'd ever liked it the way he had. Liked wasn't

197

quite the word; he cared a lot for this place, he'd helped it grow you might almost say. Then there was the time she'd planned and planned on going home and her family went early. That had been hard; she hadn't made much fuss about it either.

Dorsett's death had upset her a good bit—upset everyone. Queer, though, the way a woman hitched things together when they didn't fit any more than a plow-horse to a victoria. Julia reasoned that the town or the country were to blame, and that it was bad for the children to grow up here. Well, he'd have a look around while he was in Chicago—Armour was crowding in here; not that he could do much damage, but it was a good idea to have two strings to your fiddle.

He'd send Julia and the children to the Fair for a week, maybe two. It'd be worth seeing. He hadn't forgotten that Fair in Philadelphia yet. That was where he'd seen the first refrigerator plant.

The door to the office banged open. Joe Michael appeared, pen behind his ear, his usual worried frown between his eyes. "Mr. Hauser, there's a farmer here to see you; he's got some corn. . . ."

Max rose quickly from his swivel chair, glad to be done thinking. "Be right there, Joe; here, you make a copy of this letter."

The week that Max was gone to Chicago an air of waiting filled the house. Julia said very little to the children about the trip. She wanted them to feel that they were all going to the World's Fair simply because there was a Fair. People everywhere, all the people that mattered, that is, were going.

Julia sat serenely at the table serving in Max's place.

"Chris, sit up straight in your chair."

"Not so fast, Louise."

"Anne, what did Mrs. Dorsett say about your cream pitcher?" It was all as ordered and calm as though they were going on here forever. After supper Julia sat by the sitting-room table with her embroidery. Anne curled in Max's big rocker with *Don Orsino*. Chris was frowning over the fine print on a folder that had come with Mule-team Borax. Jeanette and Louise sat on the couch dressing their dolls. Out in the kitchen they could hear Lena doing dishes. Sometimes the murmur of voices came through; Otto had gotten the habit of dropping in of an evening to talk when Lena was working.

It was cool now in October. Lena had made a little fire in the base-burner. The isinglass front showed red behind its elaborate framework as it had that first fall Julia had come to live in the house on Second Street.

If only Max would see, Julia thought, but surely he couldn't help it at the dedication. Julia suddenly dropped her embroidery on the top of her basket and picked up the copy of *Scribner's* that was lying on the table. A magnifying glass marked the place. It was an article on the Fair. Julia had read it already twice.

"Children, listen to this." Her voice had a queer note that vibrated in the room. Jeanette drew the draw-string of her doll's dress so tight it snapped. Even Anne looked up from the thrilling pages of *Don Orsino*. Julia read aloud:

" 'The Making of the White City

" 'He who goes to the lake-side desert a year from now will see, rising from a gracious and well-ordered garden, a white city of glass and iron, a system of structure, gigantic in plan and scope beyond anything that science has hitherto held feasible or desirable. . . .' Look here, children, at the pictures!"

"Mamma, are we really going to see it?" Chris was excited only by the things that were within his reach.

"Yes, Chris," Julia said, looking at him with eyes so glowing he stared back at her. Jeanette wished Mamma would talk some more, her voice was so exciting. She piled her doll in the candy box with her clothes on top of her. She didn't mind tonight stopping to go up to bed.

"And we'll see the place where you used to live, won't we, Mamma?" Anne asked.

The children went to meet Max's train Saturday morning. Julia paused in the kitchen to say to Lena, "We'll have those crullers Mr. Hauser likes so much," then she went out on the porch to watch Max come up the walk with Anne and Jeanette. Chris had gone down to Mr. Mathorn's. Max was carrying his alligator valise. He was talking to the children.

"Mamma, Mamma, look!" Jeanette ran ahead to show Julia the two silver Columbian half-dollars Max had given her.

"Hello, Jule." Max kissed her.

"Did you have a good trip, Max?" Julia tried to make her voice sound natural, not too excited.

"Mamma, Papa brought me a shirt-waist he bought at that big store!"

"And me a dress, Mamma!"

Max stopped in the hall to open his valise. It popped open the minute the clasps were released. "There you are, Anne, and Jeanette . . . let's see, I don't think I left it behind; no, there it is. Now what did I bring Mamma?

Max and his gifts! Julia fingered the net jabot at her neck in sudden impatience.

"There, Jule." He took out a white box.

"Oh, Max, dear, I wish you hadn't." Julia opened the

lid and felt in the tissue paper wrappings. Delicious feeling, both soft and cool. "Max!" Julia brought out a sealskin tippet.

"Oh, Mamma!" The girls left admiring their own gifts to see. "Put it on," Anne said.

Julia hooked it around her neck. "It's beautiful, Max."

Max smiled at her proudly.

"May I try it on, Mamma?" Anne asked. Julia gave it to her.

"Go look in my mirror upstairs, dear, and put on your shirt-waist." The girls went upstairs.

"And here's a dress for Louise." Max was bending over his open bag again.

Julia took it. "It's a lovely color." Then she broke off. "Max, tell me about the dedication. . . . Was it, did you . . . ?" What if he hadn't even gotten there, been busy seeing somebody about business? Oh, why didn't he burst out excitedly?

Max stood by his bag. "Julia, it was the most wonderful thing I've ever seen. Why, the Philadelphia Fair couldn't hold a candle to this one."

Julia relaxed. She laughed. "Oh, Max, tell me all about it. No, come into breakfast now." Max sat down with his overcoat still on. Julia made no pretense of eating.

"And you should see Chicago, Jule. It's changed so you'd hardly know it. I had dinner at the new Auditorium Hotel. . . ."

Julia's face was radiant. This was what she had wanted.

"And the Fair, Max?" she put in eagerly.

"I brought you a newspaper to read about it. It's in my bag. I never saw such crowds, Julia, in all my life, and the buildings . . . Course they aren't finished yet, but that Manufacturers' Building—I guess it could hold the whole town of Halstead. The exercises were wonderful. . . . You couldn't hear the speakers, but you should have heard the orchestra and the singing."

It was like hearing Max talk boom talk again. Only this time her own imagination went with him, even ahead of his words, seeing everything as he talked. A deeper pink glowed in her cheeks.

"And, Max, weren't you ready to sell out and move to Chicago? Did you talk to anyone about the opportunities there?"

Max was slow in answering. He tugged at his mustache. "Yes, in a way, Julia." His voice had lost its animation and become careful. "South Water Street, that's where the commission houses are, is a sight busier than when I was there last. I guess there are plenty of opportunities if a man wanted to take a chance and had the capital to invest. . . . I'd have to take time to study it out first; but, you know, Jule, I was thinking as I came in on the train I like being here. I like getting around in Kansas and Iowa, seeing the farmers. . . . Well, I better get down to the store. Joe'll have the place all upset."

Julia sat still at the table after he left her. Max would never want to sell out. Not even the dedication had made him want to. But then he had said there were plenty of opportunities.

"Mamma, look how it fits!" Anne and Jeanette came excitedly downstairs: Anne in her dark blue silk shirt-waist. It made her look older. How grown-up she was. It would mean so much to her if they moved now.

"Yes, Anne, it fits perfectly; now put it away carefully," Julia said in a quiet voice. She went in to get the newspapers from Max's valise. She must get him to talk more about South Water Street and the prospects in the produce business.

24

MAX sent Chris to tell Julia he was staying down at the store late tonight. He had gone through the snow over to Golden's and had some coffee and fried eggs and bacon. Now he was back in his office with a fire in the round-bellied stove. The gaslight over the desk gave a brave glare on the big ledgers, the litter of papers, a bunch of winter parsnips that Couzac had brought in proudly from his root house.

Max lighted a cigar and tipped far back in his chair. He ran his fingers through his curly hair and stared thoughtfully at the picture of the Holstein cow on the calendar over his desk. He puffed in silence for fifteen minutes, then his chair came down with a protesting squeak. Max fumbled through the litter for a certain letter. Then he brought it out. He had read it a dozen times before. His eye found the sentence he wanted without reading to it.

"I shall be in Halstead the week of December the tenth to talk over the final terms with you, relative to taking over the Max Hauser Produce Co."

Max shoved the letter from him. Tomorrow Robinson would be here. Why had he ever written him? He would tell Robinson tomorrow that he took his word back. He wouldn't sell. This place; this office, every bit of it was his. Joe Michael and John Sorenson wouldn't know how to get on with anybody else, neither would the farmers. He thought back to the time he got his first carload of oranges from California . . . the time he rigged up his first cold-storage room before he had the refrigerator plant. . . . He'd done well.

Of course the price Robinson agreed on wasn't bad. It wasn't often you could get a deal like that. Then his satisfaction became tasteless. He'd sold out, given his word anyway. He wondered suddenly how he'd come to do it.

There were greater opportunities in the city. With that amount of ready capital he could go in for himself, right on South Water Street. Chicago was the natural marketplace of the world. Maybe Jule was right; maybe ten years from now . . . He could see his name printed on the side of one of those warehouses across the river from the street.

Max pulled down the top of the roll-top desk, checked the stove and turned out the light. He knew his way in the dark through the outer store to the door. He turned the big key in the lock. His business wasn't just here down at the end of Omaha Street; it was in Iowa and Kansas and Illinois. He'd advanced money to farmers fifteen hundred miles away. He'd believed in the country and made other folks believe in it. It was a pretty big thing to turn the key on!

Max turned up his coat collar against the snow. Winters in Nebraska hadn't changed any. This was going to be a cold one, he thought, falling back on the safe subject of the weather.

25

IT was early for spring house-cleaning in Halstead. The frost wasn't out of the ground. The sky's warmth was only for the eyes, color deep. Mrs. Polkas, driving into town on her husband's big green farm wagon, looked at the unmistakable signs around the green house in silent disapproval. What could they be thinking of, those women folks, throwing up the windows before winter was even over, leaving chairs on the front porch? You could see in easy; the curtains were down in the upper story. Mrs.

Polkas let her hands lie loosely on her aproned knees as she drove by, forgetting the eggs she had been sorting into two baskets in the wagon behind her.

Eight years she had been jogging into town past the houses of the town, and she had never even known who lived in them. Her mind was always on the eggs or fowls or fresh truck in the back of the green wagon, not on houses. The sod-house still did for her. But this morning she broke the silence to make a click of disapproval to Stanislas.

"That's Max Hauser's place. He's going away," Stanislas said.

Then Marthe Polkas' brown weathered face expressed an emotion; dismay, suspicion as to the future showed in her slackly opened mouth, in her eyes. Marthe Polkas had no natural trust in people or fate. Only eight years of taking farm-stuff in to Max Hauser's store, getting solid silver dollars for it, made the universe secure. Now he was going away. That was where he lived. She stared from under her black wool shawl. Her small black eyes looked at the amazing size and elaborateness of the house—all those windows, the two chimneys—and then took in again those signs of disturbance in the established way of things.

What did people move for when they had a house like that and a store? It was queer country! The green wagon jogged around the corner of Omaha Street, Stanislas Polkas and his wife on the front seat, two peasant figures against the wide blue sky and the flat land.

Upstairs in the front room Julia was looking at the black walnut bedroom furniture. She had known it so well; the wide mirror above the marble top reflected Julia's full length from the towel tied around her head to the hem of her many-gored skirt. It reflected, too, a new look in the delicately colored face bound around by the dust cap. In all the years that Julia Hauser had looked in that mirror, it had always reflected back a look of sureness around the mouth, of directness in the eyes. Today, just for a moment, there was uncertainty, misgiving. She had finished polishing the furniture for the last time. Ned and Alice Jenks were buying it for their new spare bedroom. More than anything else this brought home to her the knowledge that she was going, that she had brought it about finally, even to persuading Max.

In the top drawer of the dresser still lay the letter to Senator Withers from Harlow M. Higinbotham in Chicago, taken up mostly with expressions of gratification at being able to render the Senator, "so old and esteemed a friend, a service. . . ." It stated in a handwriting that was as perfect as a copper plate that the Senator might be assured that "Mrs. Julia Hauser will be given an appointment in an honorary capacity that will make her a part of the great Fair. The post of hostess of the Children's Building seems to the writer ideal for a lady of such vision and such qualities. It is a pleasure, believe me . . ."

It had been a triumph. Her way was clear now. Even Max was agreed. While he was getting established, she and the children could revel in the Fair and its glories for its whole duration. The stipend attached to the position gave her a secret sense of importance. Yet just for a minute as she looked at the tall carved bed, the brackets on either side of the mirror, each piece so familiar in its place that it seemed to have been built there, a terrifying qualm possessed her. What if it weren't wise? Then she tossed the doubt aside contemptuously, and raising the window shook out her cleaning cloth just as the green wagon of the Polkas' creaked past the Jenks' house.

"So you're going to the city for good, Chris?" Mr. Mathorn leaned on the marble soda-fountain that was Chris's pride. Chris polished a glass.

"Yep," he said tersely.

"Well, Chicago's a great place. You're liable to have your money taken right out of your pants pockets and your tie pulled off your neck!"

Chris eyed Mr. Mathorn solemnly.

"Yes, sir, Chicago's about as wicked a place as you'll ever find. I'd a good sight rather be wandering around the cabarets of Paree than down the midway at the Fair!" Mr. Mathorn's mouth twitched.

Watching him, Chris's lips twitched likewise. Then he was conscious of it, and that Mamma had said he could stop it if he put his mind on it. He caught his lip between his teeth to make sure of it.

"Mr. Mathorn, I don't know's I'll ever find as good a job as this," Chris said wistfully. "I've liked it a lot." In embarrassment he ducked down behind the corner to get the polish cloth.

"Well, say, Chris," said Mr. Mathorn soberly, "I don't know where I'll ever get another druggist like you." It was his little joke to call Chris a druggist. He was teaching him how to put up prescriptions. "But you know what, Chris, I wouldn't be a whole lot surprised if you was to come back out here to settle when you get growed up. You might even take over your pa's business some time, you know, come back here with a lot of money and buy this Mr. Robinson out."

Mr. Mathorn disappeared behind the half-door to the office behind. "I don't know what's wrong with your father anyway, selling out! What if he has made enough money. Halstead needs him a big sight more than Chicago." He adjusted his glasses on his nose. "Guess I'll put up the cough syrup first."

Behind the soda-fountain counter Chris Hauser polished the nickel faucets thoughtfully, pridefully.

Course it was going to be great to see the Fair. He wanted to do that. There wasn't a boy in Halstead that didn't envy him, but after that, gee! he wished they could come back here. He was fifteen; it wouldn't be long before he was grown-up. Then he could do as he pleased. He'd be too old then to help in a drug store. Mr. Mathorn wasn't so far off about what he'd like to be. Chris squinted through the window. He wondered if Chicago were as wicked as Mr. Mathorn said.

Anne was packing the things she would take with her. Jeanette sat on the bed watching her, feeling a little queer. It was queer for one thing not to be in school. They had all stopped last Friday because they were leaving Thursday.

"Mamma says I can give my blue muslin and last winter's petticoats to Lena for her girl," said Anne with obvious satisfaction. "Just think, Jeanette, we'll go shopping for new clothes in Chicago in really big stores where they have all the latest things." Anticipation quivered and thrilled along Anne's words. "I'm going to have a new skirt to wear with the shirt-waist Papa brought me and a new sailor hat."

Jeanette looked down at the pattern on the bedspread. "Anne, do you suppose we'll have bicycles?"

"I wouldn't wonder," Anne answered mildly. She was trying to decide whether to take her yellow hair ribbons.

It was queer, too, how excited and yet sad you could feel at the same time. It wasn't exactly comfortable. Jeanette knew wordlessly that Papa wasn't as excited about it as Mamma. Mamma was busy every minute; she managed everything. Papa was down at the store most of the time. The house was upside down. People were always coming in to see about buying things. When Mr. Mathorn bought her bed and dresser for Sadie, Jeanette had hated going.

Of course it was nice to have everybody stop and ask you questions and envy you. Other children were always asking what it would be like. First Jeanette didn't quite know herself, and then all of a sudden sitting on the desk at recess with Sadie and Mary and Thelma Byres around she had known just as clearly: it would be like a circus all the time, in a park ten times as big as Burns Park, with great, big, beautiful buildings like Solomon's temple in the Bible. Nobody else in Halstead was going to stay for the whole Fair or move away for good, and most of all nobody else's mother was going to be a hostess. But there was an uncomfortable unhappy place in her mind. Papa hadn't said anything, but she could tell how he felt.

"I don't suppose I'll ever go on trips with Papa any more, do you, Anne?"

"Well, we're all going on a trip four times as long as any you ever took with Papa."

"Oh!" Jeanette hugged her knees in anticipation.

Anne started to sing:

"'After the Ball is over
After the break of day . . .'"

She was going from her drawers to the trunk, and she took little dance steps as she went.

"Anne!" Louise pushed the door open. "Mamma says I'm to stay up here with you 'cause I get in Lena's way." She climbed upon the bed with Jeanette, hugging her doll. She liked to be with the big girls.

"'Many a heart will be broken . . .'" Anne sang softly.

Suddenly the sadness rose higher than the excitement in Jeanette's soul. She couldn't even talk about it to Anne.

"Play this is a train, Jeanette, and you and me and the doll are going to Chicago, shall we, Net?" Louise urged.

Louise was only five and too young to know about feeling bad, Jeanette thought in the sad wisdom of her ten years.

26

MAX went on to Chicago a week ahead of the family to find suitable living quarters. He had an early supper in the dining-room that already had an air of unrest with the empty china cupboards and the window that seemed so naked without any plants there. Julia sat down with him.

"Max, be sure you find a place near the Fair grounds so the children can go alone, a furnished flat or one of those new ones with dining-service provided," Julia admonished for the third time. "And don't be in a hurry to invest, Max."

Max nodded briefly.

"You don't think you could wait and go with us? It wouldn't take long to find a place."

"No, it ought to be ready for you," Max answered. "I want to see that man at Swift's this week, too, and Robinson is here. There isn't any point in being around at the store." Max wasn't eating much. He gulped his coffee.

Lena came in to say good-by. Max saw her red-rimmed eyes and was more brusque than he meant to be.

"Don't you want me to drive you down, Max?" Julia asked.

"No, I'll walk; I'd kind of like to. Well, good-by, children, help Mamma and be good. I'll meet you at the station Friday." He kissed them all standing in the hallway. Julia came out with him to the steps.

"Max, have you a clean handkerchief?" Then swiftly she was beside him on the second step. "Max," she murmured in a low voice, "don't be too sorry, please." Something about his figure standing reluctant on the step forced it out of her.

Max kissed her again quickly. "Of course not, Jule, little hard to leave, that's all." Then he walked down the path from the house that he had built and clicked the gate behind him. He hadn't told folks just when he was going. They all supposed he was leaving with the family. Max Hauser who loved celebrations and company was suddenly shy about saying good-by.

He slipped in at the store on his way, pretending to himself that he had forgotten to leave the key. It was after store time. He looked around at the little office, at the desk, so strangely clear of litter, with the new typewriter standing beside it. He walked down toward the cold-storage room. He looked quickly without turning up the tiny gas flame, knowing even in the half-light what was in those big barrels back in the corner, the sacks next to them, the cases. Instinctively he drew a deep breath, drawing in the smell of new wood, grain, moist straw, faint decay and something more, some tincture of plenty. Then he turned and walked slowly out.

On his way past the barrel-backed chairs he remembered a poker game played there one hot night that had been the start of—a lot of things in Halstead: the grain elevator, the new Opera House; perhaps it had even saved Halstead. He remembered so many things here. He thought of the night he had left to go to Chicago that time to be married. Then he shut the door behind him and turned down toward the station, carrying his alligator bag and umbrella.

211

"Yes, sir, say what you would, it was a mighty good town."

On the way to the station Ned Jenks caught up with him. "Max, we're planning a kind of demonstration, and Julia tells me you're leaving early!"

"Yes," said Max; "got some things to tend to 'fore the family come."

"Well, I'll see you off, anyway, Max." The two men walked along in silence.

"You know, Max," Ned Jenks hesitated, "it won't seem like the same place with Regan gone out West and Dorsett dead and now you going to Chicago."

"Well, Ned, I wouldn't like to think of the bank going to any other hands."

Oscar Holtz made out his ticket and stamped it. "Sure hate to see you go, Max," he said.

Ned Jenks and Max stood on the platform waiting for the train.

"Keeps raw, don't it?" Ned asked.

"It's going to be a late spring," agreed Max. "That won't be good for the Fair."

Then the train came charging through the early dusk. Max shook Ned Jenks's hand.

"G'-by, Ned."

" 'By, Max. Remember to give that letter I wrote you to the President of the Chemical National. That'll introduce you to a good banker. Pshaw! Alice 'n' I are coming down to see the Fair in July unless things get too bad at the bank; we'll see you then."

The conductor touched his cap to Max. All the trainmen knew him. The brakeman waved his lantern. Max stepped up on the platform. It might almost have been any business trip. He stood on the little back platform waving to Ned Jenks, watching the line of buildings on Omaha

Street, the tall roof of the hospital, the new home for the poor, the Opera House, his warehouse. He did not see consciously the wide graying sky, or the softening darker fringe of trees that marked the town, or the last vestiges of snow on the bare cornfields beyond the town, but some swift sadness made him open the door into the lighted train.

Inside the car he found a shipper out from Omaha and sat down by him to talk. He would rather have sat alone watching the gray country slide into darkness, but he was a man of sociable habits, and habit was easy. The shipper got off at Lincoln, and Max went into the smoker to find more talk, but in spite of the talk he could not keep from his mind the fact that this wasn't just another little business trip.

When Julia and the children left, half of Halstead crowded the station platform. They brought candy for the children, flowers for Julia. A reporter from the *Halstead Courier* was there. It was an occasion.

"Julia, I'll see you in August," Faith Dorsett murmured. "I can't say good-by."

Mrs. Withers cried over them. The Senator had a dollar for each of the children. Dr. Chapman was there to help them on.

"We'll see you at the Fair, won't we, Dr. Chapman?" Julia asked.

"Perhaps, Julia. I'm glad to see you go. I've seen you wanting to go for so long." He pressed both her gray-gloved hands so tightly her ring tore through the glove, and looked down at her with an expression that was all sternness. "Here," he put a green paper bundle in her hands, then he bowed abruptly and left.

"God bless you, ma'am," Lena called out for the hundredth time. Then she kissed Chris on the face and embarrassed him so he blushed red to his ears and escaped into the train. Anne and Jeanette stood close to Julia. The trainman waved his lantern. Everybody called at once. The Hospital Board presented a bouquet, having to omit the speech that was to have gone with it.

"See you at the Fair, Mrs. Hauser," someone called above the others. Julia stood on the platform like a prima donna taking leave of her audience. Then she guided the children into the train. She was still glowing and triumphant.

"Here, Anne, you and Jeanette have a berth together, Chris the upper, and I'll take Louise in with me. Anne, where's your bag?"

Jeanette was already in her seat pressing her nose against the pane. Julia stopped in the middle of unhooking Louise's coat to look, too.

"There's Bittersweet Creek," Chris called from his window. Julia watched the gray border of trees along the winding bank. That was where . . . She turned back to Louise. They were going. Her fingers shook as she undid the last hook. But now she was tired. She sat back, shut into a world of her own, letting the children talk excitedly to each other. She kept seeing the faces of people she knew in Halstead. The triumph was a little dulled. Then she thought of Dr. Chapman's package and unwrapped it. A single gardenia already turning brown along the edges lay on wet cotton. He must have sent to Omaha for it. Julia smelled it. Dr. Chapman had always understood how she felt. She bent over and kissed Louise's head gently.

Julia lay quietly beside Louise, but she could not sleep. In the strange stuffy dark, things lost their proportion. Now they were on the train. They were started. The house was sold. The furniture brought more than she had expected. She was sure it was the wise thing not to move it. It hadn't been so bad getting off.

How queer and nice of Dr. Chapman. Did he mean by that . . . Don't be ridiculous, Julia. How sad Faith Dorsett looked. Would Max be wise about the flat? Tomorrow, right away, she would call on Mrs. Potter-Palmer or Mr. Higinbotham. Her letter was in her pocketbook. She hadn't had time to think of the Fair for weeks, it seemed. She wondered if Chicago would be as changed as Max said. Round and round . . . she couldn't sleep.

She raised her shade so she could see the dark moving country. It was unfamiliar, eerie, lonely. She heard Jeanette cough. What if she should have croup and be sick. She would miss Dr. Chapman.

Anyway they were going East, away from . . . queerly it came to her, away from home. Sixteen years had made it that in spite of her. It was familiar. Chicago would be strange after all these years. She had never thought of it before. They were going to the Fair just as she had planned it. The children would see everything; they would be part of it. But a restless qualm persisted, eating into her feeling of achievement. The gardenia she had laid close to the window. Its sweetish smell was too strong in the curtained berth. It was a shame to throw it away; she thrust it under her pillow, but the fragrance lingered in the berth.

Would Max be wise in his investments? . . . He was shrewd; they would never need to worry, she thought comfortably. The house and the business had brought in enough for Max to retire on if he wanted to. . . . Her appointment made her part of the Fair even if Max did chuckle at the stipend.

The train slowed down perceptibly. Julia leaned against the window. There were lights at regular intervals, a black railing close to the train. Over the railing the lights twinkled back out of the darkness, wavering. They were crossing an endless bridge. Julia slipped out of her berth into the dark aisle. She reached up to Chris's berth and pulled the curtains.

"Chris, Chris, wake up!" Her voice was excited. "It's the Mississippi River; we're crossing it!" She went across to Anne's. Two heads were buried in the pillows.

"Girls, Anne, Jeanette; it's the Mississippi!" Then she went back to Louise, not caring whether the other passengers heard her or not.

"See, Louise! look, we're crossing the Mississippi River." Halstead was far behind. She was suddenly confident; sure of herself, of the future.

PART THREE THE WINTER GARMENT

T HERE was Max!
The children waved. Max was beaming. He looked
already as though he belonged to the city. He had even
bought a new hat. The train had stopped.

Julia kissed Max, scarcely thinking of it, her eyes on the
station, the gloom of the dirty-paned roof over the tracks,
the crowds of people. Noise, station-porters shouting, hurry
. . . Julia caught her breath in a sudden sharp ecstasy.
The noise was good; it rushed around her filling her ears
after the heavy silences of Halstead.

They were walking down the steps out into the street
now, Jeanette and Louise holding on to Papa, chattering,
Chris squinting a little, trying like Anne to be grown-up
and unimpressed.

The street burst upon them all at once: the horse-cars,
the crash of the cable-cars, the gigantic drays borne along

by monster horses, clattering over the cobble-stones, the buildings, twice as tall as the Golden House or the hospital or even the new stone block.

"Papa!" Jeanette squealed as Max dashed straight out into the maelstrom of that busy street. She was terrified and delighted at the same time, clinging to his arm. How wonderful Papa was! He even looked unafraid. Anne and Chris were amazed, too, at the calm way Mamma lifted her skirts and followed Papa across, right in front of a shiny black horse-cab with a coachman sitting way up on top. The children felt a little proud. Papa and Mamma were used to this; all the noise and confusion didn't scare them . . . then they wouldn't be afraid either. They followed bravely.

"We'll eat at Kohlsaat's, Jule," Max said.

What a tremendous place, all white and shining. There was cocoa in great cups with whipped cream on top and big baskets of rolls, all different shapes. Jeanette wondered if she should have taken a crescent roll like Chris had instead of the fat round bun.

"Does it seem good, Jule?" Max asked. Julia smiled back across at him. Jeanette biting into the hard sweet crust of her roll saw Mamma. Mamma was so quiet and awfully pleased about something. How pretty Mamma was when she looked so happy! The whipped cream had made a line all around Chris's mouth just like a mustache. Jeanette laughed, stepping back into her own world out of Mamma's.

"Where are we going to live, Papa?" Anne asked. Anne had worn her new silk shirt-waist and looked very grown-up.

"The Maybelle Apartment," Max answered more to Julia than to Anne. "It's just new, Jule, hardly finished. We'll go right over."

"Will we live in a hotel, Papa?" Louise asked.

"Of course, people in the city all live in hotels; this isn't Halstead," Chris answered.

Max and Julia smiled, but the words "this isn't Halstead" hung in Julia's mind like a happy charm. How silly of her to have felt anxious last night about the move. This morning, sitting in Kohlsaat's, everything was full-savored, as fragrant as the coffee that ran steaming from the shining little faucet at the bottom of the big nickel tank.

The entrance of the Maybelle was impressive. Two lions crouched on either side of the double glass doors. Max swung the door open for them ceremoniously. What a big family they were, really, it occurred to Julia. It was a little clammy in the big hall. The interior was clearly less impressive than the exterior.

"Our flat is right here on the first floor." Max led the way to a door at the foot of the stairs. He unlocked it and flung it back. The children entered silently, curiously. This was their first close experience with an apartment house.

Julia looked around at the lace curtains, a little dingy along the scalloped edges, the red tufted seats of the rockers, the lamp; the shade was a full yellow moon. She walked on into the dining-room, then to the kitchen.

"I thought I'd let you engage a maid, Jule." Max was happy rushing ahead, arranging everything. After the uncomfortable business of leaving Halstead, of selling their things, it pleased him to feel instated again. He could see himself living here, sitting in that morris chair by the window after dinner.

Julia came back from her survey of the three bedrooms. She said nothing.

"Jule, the Maybelle's new, put up for the World's Fair

219

visitors. The owner was telling me he'd invested fifty thousand dollars in this place."

One bedroom opened on the court; the other had an inner window. They'd have to use the couch in here, Julia was thinking.

"Look, Mamma, they've got cut glass in the cupboards!"

"What's the odor, Max?"

"That's nothing but damp plaster," asserted Max.

That meant it was damp then. Max couldn't be expected to notice a thing like that. She mustn't spoil anything for him or let the children feel his judgment poor, but this place just wouldn't do. They would have friends here, people from Halstead, the first friends they made in Chicago. . . . Where they lived was so important. She unsnapped her bag as a sign of partial permanence. "We had quite a time getting off, Max," Julia said.

"Oh, Papa, everybody in town was at the station to see us off," Chris began with gusto. "You should have seen all the flowers! We wanted to bring them, but we hurried so fast this morning we left 'em on the train."

"And, Papa, even Dr. Chapman brought flowers, only it was only one little bit of one, sorta wilted," Louise told him, climbing on his knee.

Julia could see that Max was content again to have his family. She would wait until tonight to ask him about business. She went in to lay out her best satin dress on the bed. She would go to see Mrs. Potter-Palmer this afternoon.

"When can we go to see the Fair Grounds?" Jeanette asked. "Is it pretty, Papa?"

"Well, I haven't gotten around to see it yet, this trip. I thought it was about the prettiest thing I'd ever seen in October."

Julia went out to the kitchen and found the bags of

provisions Max had brought in. There were anchovies and caviar and a special brand of expensive crackers, great unreal-looking clusters of grapes out of season, an Edam cheese, some coffee, a big loaf of Vienna bread, some summer sausage—thank goodness! two quarts of milk. Max had bought all the things he had always wanted to import for the grocery stores of Halstead. She opened the window and arranged the perishables along the sill.

"Well, Jule, I guess I'll go on downtown," Max announced. Leisure rested heavily on his hands. He had taken a desk in the establishment of a former customer where he carried on a free lance commission business. He was studying South Water Street while he made plans for a permanent location.

An eager impatience fell upon Julia—to see about her appointment, to look at the city and realize that she was here. The children would be safe with Anne. Tomorrow, she herself would take them to the Fair Grounds, to her building. How appropriate it was that she would be hostess of the Children's Building. Everything was working out so well.

Mrs. Potter-Palmer's residence was on the north side. Julia walked to the corner. The air had the moist smell of the lake. It was easier to breathe here. How unbelievable to be back. She signaled a hansom cab. She felt a faint tinge of guilt at the joy of being out alone, free to take a cab and drive along city streets. Coming in at the station. with the children hadn't been quite the same.

"Mrs. Potter-Palmer's residence on the north side," she told the driver. The driver touched his hat, impressed.

She sat back against the cushions. She must keep her eye out for a suitable place for them to live. Of course that apartment would never do. It wasn't well built or planned. It had been thrown up to catch the Fair guests. It hadn't the right air for the children, and it was too far from the Fair Grounds. Julia had planned everything out so long ago it was almost as though she had a picture in her mind that she must carry out. Serenity settled upon her.

As they drove under the porte-cochère of the Potter-Palmer residence, Julia looked at the palatial stone building unawed. She only smoothed a wrinkle out of one finger of her glove.

"You may wait," she told the coachman. Perhaps she should have written; Mrs. Potter-Palmer might be out. A footman opened the door and took Julia's card. "Please tell her I have a letter from Mr. Higinbotham."

The house was hushed as though time itself were withheld by net and velvet draperies. Far off in some upper room a silvery chime as tinkling as a Venetian music-box told the hour; then, belatedly, in the room where Julia waited a white marble clock struck the hour in a deep full tone. Julia sat very straight on a white satin chair.

This room had that richness. . . . Perhaps it was a little too ornate; still it had some of the lovely things she had craved for her own drawing-room in Halstead. Her eyes dwelt lovingly on the mahogany doorway beyond with the glimpse of the Art Gallery through it, the soft carpets, the silken portières—this was the sort of background she wanted her children to be acquainted with. The tinkling chime above sounded the quarter; the marble clock in the drawing-room kept silence until the half-hour. The footman reappeared.

"Mrs. Potter-Palmer will see you, Mrs. Hauser."

Julia followed him over a purple velvet carpet into a room at the left. At the end of the room sitting behind a heavily carved black table was a woman Julia recognized as the much-pictured Mrs. Potter-Palmer. She made no sign until Julia was standing by the table. Julia smiled confidently.

"How do you do, Mrs. Palmer?"

Mrs. Potter-Palmer bowed distantly and looked at the card in front of her. "Mrs. Hauser?" she questioned. She was a figure of sufficient dignity to match these rooms.

Julia opened her bag. "I presume Mr. Higinbotham has spoken to you, but this was his letter to me." Julia proffered the paper she had treasured so many weeks in her top bureau drawer. Even now a faint scent of verbena water clung to the sheet.

Mrs. Potter-Palmer raised her lorgnette to read the letter. Julia waited, still standing.

Mrs. Potter-Palmer moistened her lips with her tongue and dried them with a fragment of lace. Then she laid the letter on the table in front of her and rested the lorgnette on it with slow deliberate movements. With a smile that was scarcely more than the relaxation of the tiny muscles at the corners of her mouth she turned to Julia.

"Of course, Mrs. Hauser, the gentlemen's board has no power over the decisions of the board of Lady-Managers. Mr. Higinbotham, who is my very dear friend and whom I respect greatly, was unwise in leading you to expect something that was not in his hands to bestow." Mrs. Potter-Palmer paused, looking back at the letter. "I have no doubt of your capacity and worth, but you can readily understand how I am besieged constantly by persons of the highest merit whom I myself know for these positions. I am very sorry." Mrs. Potter-Palmer ran the two words together and lowered her eyelids as she said them. "This highly desirable position has already been given to a Chicago woman."

"Oh, I'm sorry. I thought, of course . . ." Then with the

same voice with which she might have accepted the position she said, "Please let me have Mr. Higinbotham's letter."

Mrs. Potter-Palmer picked up the paper so that the lorgnette rattled on the tabletop. She half rose in her chair to hold it out to Julia.

"Thank you," said Julia and walked quickly out of the room. Julia looked past the footman at the Potter-Palmer monogram worked in the net curtains of the door. The door opened and she stepped out into the spring air that was still moist with the smell of the lake. The hansom cab was waiting. She had forgotten it completely. The coachman opened the door of the cab.

"Where to, ma'am?"

"Drive"—Julia hesitated. She couldn't go back to the Maybelle yet—"south toward the Fair Grounds," she said firmly and leaned back in the shelter of the cab out of sight of the forbidding elegance of the Potter-Palmer castle.

She had been so sure after the letter from Mr. Higinbotham. Senator Withers had been sure as well. She had even let it be known in Halstead, and Halstead had been proud of her. That was why they had presented her with flowers when she left. The Withers, Alice Jenks, all of them who would visit the Fair, expected to see her there at the Children's Building. And the children would be so disappointed now that she had no part at all in the Fair.

She mustn't think of Mrs. Potter-Palmer. Her name meant nothing to Mrs. Palmer. She must never tell Max about this visit. "Given to a Chicago woman"—she had thought of herself all these years as a Chicago woman, belonging here. After all, she was just some woman from Nebraska.

There was the lake again, blue and so blessedly big.

After the narrow twistings of Bittersweet Creek this was magnificence, bigger even than all the cornfields that stretched beyond Halstead. Cornfields—there she was again, seeing things in terms of Nebraska.

"The Fair Grounds starts here, ma'am." The coachman's voice came through the tube. He was knocking on the window with his whipstock.

Julia leaned forward to look. Pillars, smooth and beautiful as quietness, and the blue lake! How tremendous the buildings were—the only way they could be against that lake—and so white! All of them harmonizing, perfectly proportioned. They dwarfed the Centennial buildings completely. . . . She couldn't wait for the children to see them. She wanted more than ever to be a part of this Fair.

The coachman started slowly on.

"Oh, wait!" Still, there was plenty to see—a whole city spread out along the lake.

She picked up the speaking tube: "Mr. Harlow Higinbotham's residence."

It was getting late, but she couldn't wait until tomorrow. She watched the World's Fair buildings as she passed, the disappointment replaced by excitement—sheer joyful, childlike excitement. Her thoughts jumped around; she couldn't think connectedly. If the cab only went faster, she wouldn't have to think at all. She wished she were driving January. Some sudden queer sense of familiarity settled upon her. Driving, thinking, driving, wanting, sitting in a public cab, the same smell of the livery-stable robe; oh, why didn't he drive faster? . . . It wasn't so long ago since the last Fair really.

"Wait, stop the carriage a minute!" she called through the tube. There was the old house! She had known she would go past it, and yet, suddenly, it was in front of her, unexpectedly—the gate, the familiar curve in the front path, the white stone, the porch. People were living there. Mamma had written that they sold it advantageously. Oh, why had the family left? If only she could have brought the children here. She hadn't seen it since the night she was married. She had gone down those steps laughing, clinging to Max's arm, in her green traveling dress. That was . . . seventeen years ago this October! She had thought there would be so many people to look up in Chicago—all the girls she used to know—but seventeen years made so much difference. She wasn't sure there were any still here. Like her, they had married and moved away. She felt a little strange now that she was back again.

Mr. Higinbotham had just returned from his office.

Julia told her story simply. "Perhaps there is nothing available. I understand how this has happened, but if there is some opening I—" she hesitated and then looked at Mr. Higinbotham with a smile—"I would be so glad," she ended simply.

Mr. Higinbotham nodded. "I understand." How eager she was. He excused himself to telephone. Julia waited.

It was close to five. The children would wonder where she was. Max would be worried. What could she tell them if Mr. Higinbotham could do nothing for her? Perhaps he couldn't understand why she wanted the appointment. It wasn't the stipend attached, it was just that she wanted the children to feel—she wanted to feel herself—that they had a part in all this.

Mr. Higinbotham, as he came back along the hall, saw a small woman sitting quietly in a chair by the window; no trace of her inner confusion showed in her face. She seemed so intense. How much importance women put on positions. . . . This whole business of appointments was a nuisance!

"Mrs. Hauser, I can assure you this time of the position of head of the Hostess House." He paused. "It is not as—" the pride of the figure in front of him made him choose his words carefully—"as interesting as the Children's Building, but it carries a certain degree of responsibility, too. It will, of course, carry an official rating for yourself and a share in what we who are associated with it feel is the greatest exposition of the age."

Max met her at the door. His coat was off. "Jule, where have you been all day? It's six o'clock. Jeanette's got a high fever. Shall I send for a doctor? If only Chapman were here. . . ."

Julia threw off her hat and the sealskin tippet and her long broadcloth coat. Max always was upset when the children were sick, she reflected calmly.

"I'll see to her. Have the children had any supper, Max?" It did not occur to her that she had not eaten since breakfast.

"No; I'll go out and get something. Maybe I better take them out to eat."

Julia went into the narrow little bedroom. Even Anne looked worried. Jeanette's face on the pillow was flushed.

"Mamma?"

"Yes, Jeanette," Julia answered calmly. She was equal to anything today.

2. MAY IST

JULIA sat in the last row of the tiers of reserved seats back of the presidential platform. She could just see the back of President Cleveland's head, the plume of Mrs. Potter-Palmer's hat and the end of a waxed black mustache belonging to one of the Spanish nobles. The chorus was singing the Columbian hymn. The music spread around and enclosed her. If she leaned very far forward between the two in front of her, she could see the thousands— there must be millions down there—pushing like a crowd in a fire. She wondered if the children were safely out of it. Max would be with them, and that nice young man who had charge of some of the electrical equipment had offered them a seat where they could see everything, even if they couldn't hear, in the Manufacturers' Building. It was amazing how many friends the children had made those first weeks before the Fair was officially opened. Except for Jeanette they had been there every day watching the exhibits unpacked, following the workmen, going in and out of every building on the grounds. Already they knew their way.

The sun was coming out after the awful weather they had had all month. It was clearing just in time. Everything looked so much more beautiful under the sun, and the lake beyond the peristyle was bright blue. Julia leaned forward watching the milling crowd disinterestedly, her mind on the occasion.

Only half noticing, she saw the minister rise to make a prayer. That little man, General Davis, spoke a few words. Even on the reserved seat she couldn't hear what he said. President Cleveland stood up. Now she could hear. His words came out with a mighty roll to them, but even hearing she scarcely listened. Like the music, the ponderous oratory surrounded her, flowed around her and beyond down on the crowds below the platform. The sun was warm on her face, on her hands clasped tightly together in her lap. Now it was beginning! All the unsettled days of March and April, that mix-up—already Julia's nimble mind called it that a little generously—about the appointment, Jeanette's being sick so they had to stay in the Maybelle, were unimportant now. You had to expect a few hitches.

". . . proud national destiny . . ." President Cleveland turned to the right and brought the words out thunderously upon Julia Hauser. Julia's face glowed. She was listening now. She had known it would be like this: a triumphant spectacle that they couldn't miss. Why, it would be as good for the children as going to Europe, and they would see it all, and then, afterwards, they wouldn't have to go back to Nebraska. They were part of this city. Julia's hands tightened.

"Let us hold fast to the meaning that underlies this ceremony. . . ." That was what she wanted. Life in Halstead had had so little meaning. "As by a touch the machinery that gives life to this vast Exposition is now set in motion. . . ." President Cleveland reached his square hand toward the key on the purple plush casket.

Julia caught her breath, hoping, fearing disappointment. It must be as tremendous as she had fancied it, a spectacle to fill her. . . . She had gotten so tired of looking at the wide empty prairie. Flags unfurled everywhere, catching the sun, flying before the wind as proudly as the flags of that other Fair. Suddenly water poured liquid crystal from the MacMonnies fountain. The two smaller fountains on either side repeated the miracle. A great statue of the Republic, only a little too large for beauty emerged from its covering, was transfigured for a second in the sun. Guns boomed out on the lake. The World's Fair had begun.

Julia's eyes turned from the brilliance of the gilt statue to the crowd that had stood still an instant and now burst into shouts, the Spanish nobles who were shaking hands

with President Cleveland. Unaccountably she thought of
Dr. Chapman; what he would say to all this. "Lobster's
as good a symbol as any," with his rueful smile. Julia
stood up as though to push something from her lap. She
must get to the Hostess House. She didn't have to be
there all the time, just to direct it; but today people would
be flocking in to eat their lunches on the big tables provided, to wash their hands and bring their tired-out children. The children and Max would meet her there.

She straightened the official badge on the lapel of her
coat. The honored guests of the front rows on the platform were leaving now. The steps were thronged. The
crowds were moving. Julia stood still to see it all: bright
colors, flags, the world in its glory. Dr. Chapman was
wrong.

3. MAY 9TH. IN THE MORNING

IT was only nine o'clock. Julia had come over early this
morning with the children. This first week she wanted
to see that the attendants of the Hostess House understood
how it must look: the floors polished, the windows shining,
the morning papers on the stand with the candy, souvenirs,
magazines, guide books. The rotunda of Julia's building, as
Chris said, looked just like a station. In the restroom for
women a colored maid in black and white dusted the
chairs and laid out fresh towels and refilled the drinking-
cup machine.

"Here, Simon," Julia said to the colored man in uniform
who pushed the dust mop over the tiled floor. "You must
change the calendar every day; people are always looking
up at it when they write their picture post-cards and letters." Simon flashed his white teeth and shook his head.

"Yes, ma'am, you do think of more things. Anybody'd think this here building was your own house." He lifted himself on the magazine counter to tear off yesterday's date, leaving May 9, 1893, supreme on the calendar pad.

Julia went into her tiny office out of the main restroom. There was a small desk there, a rocking-chair and a swivel chair. A window by the desk looked toward the Court of Honor and the lake. Even now after weeks of looking through that window she could not get used to the crowds surging past nor the great white buildings. The Episcopal church of Halstead should be out there, and the Jenks' house and, way over to the west, cornfields and empty sky.

There was scarcely enough business to transact to justify the tiny office. Still it was a place in the Fair set aside just for her, a place for Jeanette and Louise to come to. Max had looked around with a smile, almost of amusement, the first day when he had met her there.

"Well, Jule, it's you who has the going concern these days."

"You must get established soon yourself, Max," she had answered.

"No hurry, no hurry; things are still pretty unsettled. After the Fair starts pouring money in the city and the spring crops are sure, I'll buy in to what looks like a good proposition."

Julia straightened the pile of *Official Guides* on her desk and laid the pens straight with the ink well. Things were all working out so well. Chris had a position at Victoria House, the official building of the British Government. He ran errands and helped with the exhibits. It was a wonderful thing for him to be there with Sir Arthur Wood. And Anne had been asked to take an appointment in the

Italian section explaining jewelry to visitors. Jeanette and Louise roamed the grounds all day, playing where they wanted to. Julia didn't worry about them. Most of the attendants had gotten to know them; they were a part of the place.

Julia went back into the waiting-room and arranged the iris more loosely in the big bowl on one of the tables. She had bought them herself on her way over this morning, from a flower-seller on the corner. The morning air was cool and fresh with the lake breeze moving in it. The building had a certain spaciousness about it, early, before too many people had filled it.

There were half a dozen now in the room. A young woman in a dove-gray suit held Julia's eyes. She looked like a bride on her wedding trip. Julia touched the flowers gently without disturbing them, watching the girl in the stylish suit. A bunch of violets was pinned to her coat. She wondered if the girl were happy. Did she feel that this World's Fair was partly to celebrate her wedding? Would she look back to it next winter and many winters after as the high peak of her life? It was a dangerous thing to go to a World's Fair on your wedding trip; it started life out too well, with flags and music and that feeling that life must be . . . The girl in the gray traveling suit went toward a young man standing by the magazine counter. He took off his hat and smiled at her. She laid her fingers on his coat sleeve as though it were still a conscious gesture. They came towards Julia. There was no mistaking Julia's official capacity in her black satin dress, the white collar and cuffs of real lace, the badge, but more, Julia's dignity of manner.

"Could you tell us," the young man began, "the way to that Spanish Convent?"

Julia directed them.

"Thank you." The girl smiled at Julia a little patronizingly because nobody could be having quite so good a time as she. They went out of the building. Julia watched. The young man lifted his cane. He was pointing with it. A flicker of amusement, almost ironic, darted across the line of Julia's smile. Something in the gesture made the young man so like Max. Perhaps she had been like the girl.

"Mamma!" Jeanette came up behind her with Louise. "Oh, Mamma, please go and see the chair in the Idaho Building. It's all made of horns and skins of animals."

"Really horns, Mamma, from bulls and deers and—and stuck on. You can feel them," Louise added excitedly.

"Mamma, can we go in the Baker's Chocolate Building and have cocoa twice? We came back to ask."

Julia laughed. "You ask the people in charge, Jeanette."

Julia watched them go, crossing the bright band of sun on the white stone steps, sliding on the sloping stone curbing, then disappearing into the streaming crowd.

Max demurred about giving them so much freedom, but Julia gave them full permission to go any place but the Midway. It was a whole world, and she meant them to absorb it all.

She turned to tell a harassed mother with four children where she could buy a twenty-five-cent lunch. Then she took her mail into her own desk, enjoying it all, the letters, the address: "Mrs. Julia Hauser, Head, Hostess House, World's Fair." How nice! She was asked to pour at a tea at the Nebraska Building. One letter contained a reserved seat for a concert in Music Hall. She thought of the "musical evenings," the Philomathean Literary Club in Halstead. That curator of precious pictures she had met yesterday was so interesting. Each day was different.

233

Julia pinned on her hat and went out of the building. The Columbian guard at the end of the walk touched his cap to her.

"Biggest crowd yet, ma'am." His voice implied that it was a reason for personal congratulation. It was their Fair, his and hers, and something of that was in the carriage of Julia's head and shoulders and in her step.

How beautiful the gold door of the Transportation Building was! It dazzled your eyes. She must see that new horseless carriage Chris and Max were talking about. What a funny idea!

That woman looked a little like her sister, Polly. How dreadful, Polly wouldn't get to the Fair. And she, Julia, had lived farthest away and had gotten to both Fairs. She couldn't have missed them. Things happened the way you wanted them to if you knew what you wanted. Even Max was glad that they had come.

Julia looked at the lake; each small blue ripple as hard and regular as the waved hair of the golden statue there. The very firmness of the waves, the undiluted blue, matched the sureness in her own mind.

"How do you do; yes, isn't it? The weather seems just made for the Fair." He was head of the French exhibit. How queer to be knowing these people from the ends of the earth . . . how delightful! Sometime this week when Max was here they must go to that lovely square that Mr. Obermann had said might really be in Vienna and have dinner together; perhaps even champagne again as they had in Philadelphia. Max would like that. Just to celebrate being here!

IN THE EVENING

JULIA stood by the window in the flat. The heavy green shade of the maple trees seemed to crowd the street, dulling the May twilight, blotting up the light. She had lived in Halstead so long she was unused to a green gloom of shade. At home across the open cornfields there was always a stretch of whitish sky. The lights came on in the building across the street. She was aware again of the nearness of human living; so many buildings that shut out the reaches of prairie sky; their lighted windows brightening the green gloom of the leaves gave her a sense of warmth. She was meant to live in a city, she reminded herself.

Dinner was late tonight. Chris and Anne were staying for the illumination. Jeanette and Louise had come home with her and were playing out in front on the steps. Julia had just been showing Flora, the maid who came in by the day, how to mold potatoes Lena's way. She thought regretfully of Lena who had needed no showing. And they paid this girl twice what they paid Lena. Help was exorbitant because of the Fair. Everything was high. The merchants were out to make profit while they could, but who cared? It was the Fair year!

Perhaps Max would go over to the Fair tonight with her. He hadn't seen it illuminated with the searchlights, and the Electric Building . . . Then Julia saw Max turning the corner. She went out to the kitchen door.

"Flora, Mr. Hauser is here. We won't wait any longer."

"Papa!" Jeanette saw him at the same moment and ran down the street to meet him. "Hello, Papa."

"Hello, dear." Papa put his hand out on her head heavily, half over her eyes as though he weren't paying any attention. His voice was lower than usual, queer. . . .

It stopped you. Jeanette pulled back from Papa's hand and looked at him, wondering.

"Is Mamma home?" Papa asked in the same queer voice.

"Yes, Papa." Jeanette wondered about going in too, but Papa went in and shut the door as though he didn't expect her to come. Jeanette sat down on the lion's back.

"Let's go in, Net," said Louise.

"No, let's play one more game of hopscotch," answered Jeanette in her most grown-up voice.

"Jule!" Max sat down heavily in the big red morris chair by the window. He took his hat off and let it lie on his knee. "Jule?"

"Yes, Max." Julia came in from the dining-room. "Why, Max, don't you feel well?"

"Jule!" His voice broke strangely. Julia's fingers flew to the brooch at her collar. Something warned her. But nothing could happen now; one of the children . . . but Max always got so excited. . . .

"What is it, Max?"

"Jule!" Max looked at the crease in his hat. He smoothed the binding of the brim with careful fingers that yet shook a little. "Jule, the Chemical National failed today." He spoke haltingly as though the words hurt him. Then his voice broke again into a half groan. "Oh, Jule!" He buried his face in the crown of his hat. "Everything's gone, Jule."

A thick silence enveloped them. Julia heard the clink of china in the dining-room, sounds of the city outside the window, Max's breathing. Her face matched the whiteness of her collar.

"Max, it—it can't be as bad as that." Now that she had said something, that her voice had stayed calm, she could move across the room to Max. She leaned over him. "Max, dear."

He reached around to his coat pocket for the evening paper and handed it to her as though he could not bear the sight of it. She unfolded it. Black headlines leaped from the page:

"Chemical National fails . . . Crowds storm doors!"

"Why, Ned Jenks sent you to that bank." It helped to have Ned Jenks' judgment at fault instead of Max's.

Max shook off the remark. "It's conditions." Max Hauser put the blame on no man. "But I'm—I'm wiped out, Jule." He went back to the specific.

"Oh, Max . . ." she broke off, "how awful!" But she had a feeling that she wasn't taking it in yet. Later when she was by herself she could think it out. Now she must say something to cheer him. The heavy silence was on them again. "Wiped out," Max had said. The sound of his words as he had said them hung in the room. All those years in Halstead. . . .

"Jule, why did we ever leave Halstead?" The words were wrung out of Max. He said them more to himself than to her.

A shiver ran over Julia. The shock of the words pulled her up straight. If they had never left Halstead this would never have happened. Max would still be in business. They would still have their home. . . . She had gotten Max to leave. She had contrived and planned it all.

"Oh, Max, it was my fault." She said the words, but she pushed the knowledge of them off behind other things, that the children should be here, that dinner was waiting, that it couldn't be as bad as Max said.

The first note of naturalness crept into Max's voice. "I didn't have to come, Jule. I did my own thinking."

There was another silence. It thinned out the naturalness again from Max's voice. When he spoke again it was heavy and low.

"I had a notion I'd like to have a business on South Water Street myself," he added. Max was honest. There was nothing shoddy in him. Heavy, slow, but as clear as truth, she felt him.

"Max—" Julia bent swiftly and pressed her face against his head—"but it was my fault in the beginning." She wanted to have him deny it again. Instead there was silence in this strange room that accused her. It would have been easier in their own sitting-room. But if they were still there, all this . . .

"I'll have to look for work," Max said after a pause. "I'll tell Armstrong tomorrow I haven't any capital. He's been waiting for me to decide about buying him out. I'd almost made up my mind to. . . . Then I'll . . ." His voice trailed off.

If it only wouldn't do that! Why couldn't he talk naturally without those long pauses between? That tone in his voice made her weak. She couldn't think when he talked that way.

"I suppose I could go back to being a salesman," Max said.

"But, Max, you aren't sure yet that everything's gone."

Max looked up at her solemnly. "As sure as death, Jule." The words sounded oddly dramatic, grotesque on Max's tongue, more dreadful because of that. Julia heard the door click.

Jeanette had opened the door very quietly. She stood still looking at Max's bowed head, at Mamma standing by him. She tightened her grasp on Louise's hand. Louise peered around her to see why Jeanette was so quiet.

"Get ready for dinner, Jeanette, and then help Louise. Papa's tired." Julia strove to make her voice natural.

A tightness in Jeanette's throat loosened as she heard it.

238

Nothing dreadful had happened. Papa was just tired. "Come on, Louise," Jeanette said happily.

Then Chris and Anne were there, excited and in a hurry.

"Oh, Mamma, it was wonderful! We're going to stay every night, can we?"

"Mamma, did you see the sentence they write in the air with electricity?"

Max didn't seem to hear. He sat slumped in the big chair. Julia looked at him hopelessly a second.

"Yes, it's lovelier at night than in the daytime. We'll have dinner as soon as you children are ready," Julia heard herself saying.

"Max," she said as soon as the children were out of the room, "the children mustn't know about it. It would spoil everything." Julia spoke to him almost sternly, trying to get that one fact through to Max. That was important and she clung to it. Then her voice softened. "Max, dear, would you rather lie down until dinner is over? I'll bring in a cup of coffee."

"I don't want anything," Max said. "I think I'll go out for a while." But his voice sounded undecided. The room that he had come home to as a refuge from the crowd around the bank, the desperate faces, the newsboys, was suddenly close. He wanted to get away from it again, but where did a man go when he had no office? For a moment he thought of the store. . . .

"Max, dear, you lie down; you're so tired. Things will look different when you're rested." Silly words she knew them to be even as she spoke them, but they were words to fight off that silence, to keep Max from sinking his face in his hands again.

Max got up slowly from his chair. He hesitated a minute.

"Come on, Max." Julia went with him into the bedroom. His acquiescence frightened her. She lighted the gas. Max

239

looked old and drawn. "You don't want the light, do you, Max?" Max only shook his head. Julia laid her hands on his eyes a second to give them sleep. She pulled the spread down. "I'll go eat dinner with the children, then I'll be back."

Max lay down on the bed, turning his face into the pillow as Chris or Anne might. Julia stood by the foot of the bed. Her fingers twisted around the bedpost as though, unconsciously, they were feeling for the oak leaf carved into the foot of the walnut bed at home. Max looked so tired. Now that he had done as she urged she wanted to get him up again, to see him brusque and hearty and occupied with business. There was something so final in his lying down that way. Max never lay down except to go to bed.

"Mamma." Anne hesitated at the door. "Dinner's ready."

"Yes, Anne, just a moment." Max turned on the bed; the springs creaked under his weight.

Julia stood between them, between the children and Max, in here in the dark unfamiliarity of this rented bedroom. He must come out and eat dinner and act as if everything were all right. Then it would be! Lying down, burying his face . . . "Max?"

Julia hesitated. "I'll be back, Max." Then she went out to eat dinner, to hear about the day's excitements.

She had been gloating in the way the children had so much to see and talk about. Tonight it made her impatient. But she must listen; she must seem interested; it was because of the children that they had come. That was why she had urged Max to sell out.

"Mamma, one of the Columbian guards picked Louise up and carried her a whole block 'cause she got tired," Jeanette said.

"Mamma, Mr. Biondi said to tell you he was greatly pleased with the way I explained the jewelry," Anne was saying with pride in her voice. "A woman said to the woman who was with her that she never knew Italians had light hair. She thought I was really an Italian!"

The children laughed at the idea.

"Some Italian!" Chris mocked. "Say, Mamma, there was a man in my building today that was the worst rube. He kept saying, 'I s'pose that's the English of it!'" Chris was developing a certain feeling of superiority for the English ways. It amused Julia usually.

She set her cup down and looked at them. They were fast dropping off the ways of Halstead, taking the city and the whole World's Fair as their own. . . . That was why they had come. . . .

"It is too called the Farmers' Bridge cause it goes over to the Agricultural Building," Chris asserted. Then he interrupted his own wrangling, "That bull out there in the Statue of Plenty looks just like the one out on Mr. Hetzel's farm. I've seen lots taller corn than that stalk the woman's holding, though."

"Oh, Chris, it's an art statue. You aren't supposed to notice all those things. It's artistic." Anne corrected him scornfully.

Julia got up abruptly. "You finish, children; I'm going to take some coffee in to Papa; he has a headache." It smote her suddenly that they weren't more concerned about Max. She wondered if the excited sound of their voices came in to him.

She and Max in the dark bedroom were separate from the children, shut in together by a kind of desperate fear. The silence was broken now by the children's talk, or did that make it deeper? She wanted to go back to the dining-room, to the children around the table under the light talking about the Fair. Max lying so silent on the bed was still apart from her as he had always been. Then Max reached out his hand, patting her arm heavily, awkwardly.

"Jule, I . . ."

"Don't worry, Max, we'll move out of here, somewhere less expensive. The children will be happy all day at the Fair. You'll find an opening; we'll work it out." She talked at random with a heartiness she didn't feel. "Here, Max, drink your coffee."

Max sat on the edge of the bed and took the cup. His hair was tousled, his vest wrinkled. He looked unkempt, pathetic, as he bent his head to drink.

Julia could feel her eyes burning as though with tears. An immense tenderness came over her. She wanted to smooth his hair, straighten the stick-pin in his tie, help him on with his coat, to say, "There, you're just the same, Max. You're not hurt." She thought of him as he was when he bought that refrigerator plant. She kept the picture in front of her eyes, torturing herself with it, keeping back the hideous knowledge that she had . . . No, don't think of that now. She took the cup from Max's hand.

"Let's go out and walk a bit, Max. It's close in here." Again he acquiesced too easily. If only he would fly out at her angrily with something of the impetuous Max about him, tell her to leave him alone. She helped him on with his coat. "Brush your hair, Max." They mustn't alarm the children. She followed him through into the sitting-room.

"Children, I'm going out with Papa. Louise and Jeanette, you must go to bed in a half-hour; Anne, you and Chris go by nine." She made her voice sound as though it were any evening. "Good night, we shan't be gone long." She kissed Louise, comforting herself a little with the sight of them all.

The air was fresh and cool after the stuffy bedroom.

They went past the impersonal stone fronts of other apartment hotels, under the regularly placed street-lamps that each illumined Max's face and the tired droop of his shoulders.

It was so long ago since morning.

They had walked ten blocks.

"Let's turn around, Max." Max obeyed with the same terrifying childlikeness he had shown before. Now that the silence was broken, she must say something else while her lips were still wet from speaking.

"When did it—did you know it, Max? Where were you?" She held her breath to see if Max heard her, if he would answer, he seemed so deep in his own thoughts.

"I was down on South Water Street. There was an extra out. When I went over, there was a long line in front of the bank." Max saw it all again. He shook his head. Suddenly he flopped his arms uselessly against his sides in a grotesque movement of hopelessness.

It seemed to Julia that she would never forget this place in the street. The iron grating on the basement window of the house they were passing—five bars going one way and a curved one out and then in—would always be impressed on her mind. She wondered if the people in the row of windows above the grating were talking about the Fair. Then she came back again to herself and Max.

"What time is it, Max?" Why on earth did she want to know? What did it matter? Still it was somehow important to mark this feeling of desolation.

Max, out of long habit, stopped under the lamp, took out his big gold watch, pressed the spring of the case. "Quarter after nine, Jule."

"Oh," said Julia, "I thought it was later."

They went up the steps of the Maybelle between the crouching lions. The faint odor of damp plaster came to

Julia. She would have to look for some place tomorrow where it would be less expensive. She should have told Flora not to come in the morning. She would have to manage herself, now.

Anne had left the table light on. The flat was still. Julia could feel the children sleeping by the warm full sense that came to her from the stillness. She might have been back in Halstead, coming home from the Withers'. The room would have felt like this. For a second this thing that had happened seemed not to have happened. Nothing could have touched her safety, her children's.

"I'm going to bed. I've been walking all day, since ten this morning," Max said.

"Why, Max, we needn't have gone out tonight."

"I couldn't sit still, Jule; now I'm tired enough, maybe I'll sleep."

Julia saw him walking along in the crowds, despairing, bewildered, flopping his arms at his sides that way, while she was walking in the Fair Grounds, feeling so excited and proud. She fastened the windows and turned out the light, busying herself. She went out to see how Flora had left the kitchen, as though she cared, then she went into their bedroom.

Max had sat down on the edge of the bed, going over it all again. When Julia came he got up, walked over to the dresser and took out his watch to wind it. The little metallic clicks sounded so familiarly, so reasonably in the room. Max laid the watch on the dresser and Julia knew beforehand how the links of the watch chain would rattle into a nest beside it. But the sound on the wooden top of the dresser was different, less clear, less decisive, than on the marble top of the dresser at home.

Julia undressed quickly. Then she went into the children's rooms, pretending to herself that it had turned cooler. In their rooms she felt a sense of relief. They were free from worry: Anne, lying with her face on the crook of her arm looked strangely woman-like without her hair ribbons, Jeanette hunched warmly under the covers, back to back with Louise. Chris flat on his stomach; they had all had a good time. She felt better as she went back to Max.

Max was asleep. She turned out the light and got softly into bed, lying rigid so as not to move the bedclothes.

She was wide awake. Now she would face it, that knowledge she had been keeping back from herself and yet known all day, no, all night; it was only since dinner-time she had known. She had brought Max here. She had gotten him to sell out. He had never wanted to. Max had said . . . but she knew he never would have done it if it hadn't been for her. He would still be safely in business in Halstead, one of Halstead's wealthiest men. It was her fault. Julia looked at the streak of light from the street-lamp that came in under the shade disturbing the darkness. The room was cramped after their big front bedroom at home. She could hear the cable cars jarring past two blocks away. Julia pressed her hand against her mouth. The room oppressed her, frightened her.

They had lost everything. . . . She was to blame. There was no getting away from it, lying stiffly in bed beside Max so he could sleep for a little and forget what had happened. If the room were only dark; but the street-lamp glared in mercilessly, showing Max's clothes thrown over the chair arm, one shoulder of the coat was outlined, wrinkled and drooping. His clothes were more pitiful than Max. His white waistcoat gleamed out from the darkness of the heap. Julia looked away.

Her neck cramped from its tense position. She must move. Just to sit up for a minute to see that the room was only a room, Max's clothes, nothing to torture herself with;

but Max might wake up. He would fall back into his troubles; his voice would break. The cramp would go, better to endure it. No, she couldn't. She would turn ever so slightly, shift her weight . . . that wouldn't wake him. But she lay rigid.

She had done it for the children. But had she? The light under the shade was brutal; it insisted on truth. The cramp in her neck ran up into the nerves at the back of her head. She had wanted to come for her own sake, too. There, she had faced the truth! She had admitted it.

But it was better for the children even with nothing, she told herself. She had never thought of life without money; they might even be poor; they were poor. Still, Max would find a way. He would build up a business again, but Max was older now. There were his clothes holding the beaten curves of his body in their creases. He had seemed old tonight. It wouldn't be easy for him. She twisted her head, the cramp lasted so long.

Suddenly she knew that Max was awake, had been awake long minutes, staring into the same close room, lying rigid so as not to disturb her. Now she could move. She shifted her shoulder; the exquisite relief as the cramp disappeared blotted out every other feeling for the instant; she could move her head.

"Jule?" Max had heard her. He was glad she was awake. The stark silence of the room was broken. Julia reached out her arm without speaking. She held his head against her shoulder.

4. JUNE

THE children had set off for the Fair. Max had gone, too, but not to the Fair. Max had a position as buyer for

246

one of the big commission houses on South Water Street. He had to be down early.

Julia was alone in the housekeeping rooms they had taken on the top floor of Mrs. Daggerty's house. She wasn't going to the Fair today. She was staying home to get ready for the Withers and Faith Dorsett. There was dinner to get and the rooms to tidy and extra beds to set up and make just in case they stayed here, but Julia stood idle by the table. Some part of her saw the things to do: she must go out to the market, the far one that was cheaper, and buy some meat, and buy flowers at the corner. . . . The other part of her looked down at the tomatoes Max had brought from "the Street." They lay blood-red on the white board table. There was a knot in the white board top. Flour had gotten in around the knot and made a pattern. Julia looked at these things, wanting to be drawn out of herself by them. There was dinner to get and the rooms to tidy and some things to press for the girls.

The Withers were coming, and they must not know how . . . but how could they help it? There it was written on the rooms. It was written in her own face; it must. be. Julia touched her face with her fingers. The skin was soft under her fingers just as it always felt. She moved her fingers up and touched her hair, brushing it back from her forehead, reassured by the familiar feeling of the wave.

But now she was alone. She need hide nothing. It was a relief, like unlacing the tight laces of her best stays, but the release brought an ache, too, like the ache in her back when there was no support for it. When she was busy and the children and Max were there, the stays were laced tight.

It wasn't good to be idle; that made the ache twist a little. Still, the children had the Fair. But she was like a woman who had paid too much for some silk and could not forget the price even when the dress was made up.

Be busy, Julia, peel the tomatoes, think of the Withers' coming; that would make eight of them. She would have to put two tablecloths together. Make it all a joke. . . . "We're camping out during the Fair." Say it with a deprecatory wave of the hand; don't notice that Max was a little silent, talk a little more, laugh. It would be good to see Senator Withers again. But the ache was not bemused nor taken in. She felt it while she peeled the tomatoes.

Julia wrapped the tomatoes in a damp cloth and laid them in the little ice-box on the fire-escape outside the window. Its dinkiness hurt her; the contrived look of it out there on the grating. The ice was dwindling. They would need more today. She put the card up in the front window: ICE; and even though she didn't have to look up from the street and see it there, the knowledge of it hurt her. At home Louie came in through the alley. All she knew of his coming was the sound of the ice-wagon and the heavy jar on the back porch, then the sound of the tongs clattering on the floor; but this was only temporary.

Julia closed the little ice-box door and looked beyond the railing of the fire escape at the city. She had never thought of it before in terms of rooming-houses, hotels put up with false, grandiose fronts and smelling of damp plaster inside, of people managing in "rooms." Yet even now, looking out over the fire escape in the middle of the morning, there was something about it that was hers. The sounds from the street, the up and down line of the roofs of the buildings so tall you had to count the windows —that one was eight stories tall!—looking out of your window across at a dozen other windows without any least idea of the people behind them—all pleased her.

248

She had always been part of the city; that was why she couldn't be satisfied with Halstead.

It would be as well to slice the potatoes, too, and have them ready. They fried crisper if they were cold. She bent to look for a kettle under the shelf on which the gas-plate stood. There were only tin kettles. If she were home . . . The fat couldn't get as hot without an iron one. She could see the iron kettle Lena always used. It hung in the cellar-way on the third hook from the door. You could reach it without going down a step. The handle always hung out a little, separate from the bulge of the kettle, but you never took it by the handle; it was too heavy. It was a solid black; it never looked discolored like the cheap tin ones. Renting rooms with cooking dishes provided was a poverty of soul. She needn't have. She might have been still in Halstead . . . quick! think of the children, the lack of advantages in Halstead, how Anne and Chris needed to get away. It was coming to be a formula, a kind of ladder; each thought was a rung by means of which she could climb to a bearable ground. The top rung was always the same; it had all been worth it. She was glad.

She dumped the wedge-shaped slices of potatoes into the tin kettle and covered it with a cracked plate. The meat could wait. She went out of the kitchen into the bedroom.

Julia threw back the sheets on Anne's bed. A book fell out on the floor; a book bound in limp leather with gold letters on it. Anne must have taken it to bed with her. Julia picked it up curiously.

THE RUBÁIYÁT

Julia liked the sound even though the word itself was meaningless. On the fly-leaf was written,

To Anne Hauser
from
Ruggero Ricci

Julia was startled. That must be the young Italian in Anne's exhibit. Anne wasn't old enough to receive presents. Anne had kept it secret, taken it to bed with her. Now the parts of Julia's mind slipped docilely together under a new worry. Perhaps Jeanette and Chris and Louise did most of the talking when they came back from the Fair. She hadn't really noticed. Perhaps Anne was quieter. How separate they were in these four rented rooms: Max, herself, now Anne. Julia sat down on the bed, turning the pages:

VIII

> Come, fill the Cup, and in the fire of Spring
> Your Winter-garment of Repentance fling:
> The Bird of Time has but a little way
> To flutter—and the Bird is on the Wing.

How lovely, and how it fitted her! Would it be wicked to give over repenting and regretting? She mustn't let repentance spoil everything. How a string of words could pick you up! But this wasn't the thing for a young man to give a girl.

Then she came on two lines made like the rest of little curled letters. The capital S was illumined, swirling down to a tail. Julia would always see it just as it was on the page.

> Some for the Glories of this World; and some
> Sigh for the Prophet's Paradise to come; . . .

There it was; what she wanted was some of the glory of this world now. If she could just keep this feeling; it was better than the ladder she had already made.

These rented rooms that the Withers would see tonight didn't matter. The Fair was within reach even if she were here getting meals ready. And after the Fair they would still be here at the center of things.

Julia put the book over on the dresser. She wouldn't

take it away; she would talk to Anne about this young man. Maybe it wasn't safe for Anne to be there; there was that to think of . . . There was so much to think of that this room with its ugly brown wallpaper was unimportant and the limp pillow that couldn't be plumped into shape.

The Withers could only stay three days. She must take them out tonight after dinner to see the searchlights.

5.

ANNE arranged the filagree enamel brooch on the black velvet cloth. It was the loveliest of them all; the little vine of greenish gold that twisted itself in and out ended in a cluster of emerald grapes, the top grape hidden by a fine-veined leaf. And the earrings that matched the brooch . . . Anne held them up to her ears for a second and looked at her image in the glass top of the velvet-lined case. She leaned her head a little to one side so one earring dangled free.

She glanced up suddenly, guiltily, to see Signor Ricci watching her. She blushed and put the earrings back on the velvet cloth.

"But you are lovely, Miss Hauser, even perhaps lovelier when you blush."

Anne could not look up. Signor Ricci would think her vain. He had been out of the Italian section and must have come back when she was talking to the visitors.

"Miss Hauser, please look at me. Don't feel shy. I was only admiring you." His voice was different; it was a man's voice and yet so . . . like the low notes in her violin, the ones that sounded of the polished wood where the light shone on it.

251

Two women and a man wandered in through the Italian entrance. They came toward the jewelry case. Anne felt at ease again. Signor Ricci went back to the bibelots and examples of Italian bindings. His skin was rather like the parchment pages, Anne had thought secretly. He wore fine brown gloves that made her think of the leather bindings. Even his hat distinguished him. It was softer with a gayer roll to the brim than Papa's.

Another group of people drifted in. More people came in if they saw others already there. An elderly woman looked through her lorgnette at the contents of the jewelry case. A man was discussing the enamel picture frames.

"To what period does this belong?"

Anne smiled graciously, a smile that held in it a marked resemblance to Julia's. "This is the jewelry of the Renaissance." The word Renaissance was a lovely word, so rich and elegant; it made her think of Signor Ricci. Anne paused; then judging that her audience was interested, she added in the conversational tone that the head of the Italian exhibit had suggested, " 'While the designs of antiquity excel in abstract beauty of form and color and those of the Medieval craftsman possess a peculiarly naïve and ingenuous charm . . .' " Her voice went on with the carefully learned words. The woman in the blue hat was smiling at her. People were apt to smile at Anne Hauser and the seriousness of her manner.

" 'It is not so much the intrinsic value . . . When the Countess of Chateaubriand was requested to return to Francis I the precious ornaments that were desired by her successor to the royal favor, she sent them first to the melting pot, thus making the gift trivial instead of magnificent.' " Anne liked it when people laughed at this little story. She had found it herself in the encyclopedia.

"The foremost name among the sixteenth-century Italian

Renaissance goldsmiths is that of Ruggero Cellini. . . ."
She stopped in confusion. Had she said Ruggero? She
had meant to say Benvenuto Cellini, or had she just
imagined it? She stole a glance toward the book-bindings.
If Signor Ricci had heard, he gave no sign. He was turning the pages of a book. Anne recovered herself swiftly.

She stopped to let the crowd drift on and another took
its place. So far it had never grown tedious to Anne. It
was still exciting to have a part, a speaking part, in the
most magnificent building of all.

"Yes, that is enamel; a mosaic of tiny pieces. . . ."
Julia Hauser was on her way through the Manufacturers'
Building. She was always drawn irresistibly toward the
Italian corner where Anne was. Now she saw her. Julia
stood by the "marble" pillar to watch her. Anne was bending her head over the glass case. Julia had a swift painful
feeling of strangeness. Anne was so grown-up, already half
her age. She seemed so sure of herself—the way she answered questions, the way she smiled. Where had she
learned that superior little manner? Last night after the
Withers had gone out to their hotel and the children and
Max were asleep, Julia had gone in to Anne and asked her
about the book.

"He's just a friend, Mamma, at the exhibit. He's with
the Italian books. He wrote you a note; I've been meaning to give it to you all evening. It's about going to dinner
with him. Oh, please do, Mamma."

It was a very nicely written note. Perhaps if she had
said no, there might have been an end to it. Instead, she
had said, "Thank him, Anne, and tell him we will be
pleased to go this once." And then this morning she had
even written a note herself for Anne to give him.

Julia had meant to say something about the poetry, but
there would be time for that later. Anne had kissed her

good night, but the way she did it seemed to brush her aside.

Julia pressed through the crowds toward the display of bibelots. She stood still a minute with the group looking at the examples of early Italian bindings. She was just in front of the slender dark young man who fingered one page and said:

"This is sheepskin, of course, dating from the fourteenth century. Here you see the watermark." He held the page to the light with tapering fingers.

He had a mustache as black as his hair. Julia caught his glance for an instant. He hesitated on the word ex-ex-quisite, er, exquisite, he repeated and went on. He had dark eyes; a handsome young man, Julia told herself fearfully.

She left the group, knowing that the young man's glance followed her. She went on to the main corridor without even speaking to Anne. This wasn't the time. She must be careful. Anne was a sensitive child; all children were sensitive sometimes, but Anne . . . For the time it took her to walk between the Spanish façade and the lacework exhibit of Brussels, Halstead seemed such a safe place for Anne. Then Julia went out of the tremendous building into the bright sun.

But Anne had disliked Halstead. Anne was pretty. A book—after all, a book was a proper gift; it was just a souvenir. Only a poetry book was a little different. Well, the Fair would only last until November. And then what for Anne? Anne must meet the right people.

Julia went by the Agricultural Building without looking at it. Her face was sober under the flowered hat. She must find some way. Anne was at the wrong age for uncertainty. Julia tried to think of some of the girls she had known in Chicago. They were married now. Who had Sally Bates married? Was it Youmans? Somebody Youmans. She would write Sally a note; ask her to have lunch with her at the Fair. Julia rested her eyes a second with the sight of the lagoon.

How had Max seemed last night? She had laid the question away in her mind like tucking a bill in her writing desk to face later. It popped out now when she was after something else, and she had to stop and see it.

When Max was gone, down on South Water Street, she could see him as he was in Halstead—brisk, hearty, equal to building up another business; but when he came home to dinner, it was different. He didn't listen to the children's reports of the Fair very closely. He hadn't even gone to the Fair again, not since May.

He sat down on the porch of Mrs. Daggerty's house after dinner smoking his cigar, talking with the other roomers. They talked alike, aimlessly complaining about the Government, about the city, like spectators outside of things. Last night she had hesitated on her way downstairs. She could see the back of Max's head through Mrs. Daggerty's front parlor window, his hat tipped back a little. Then his voice had come in to her.

"When I was in business for myself, I used to get over to . . ." and something in the tone, the emphasis, chilled her, held her there in the hallway, kept her from asking Max to go out to the Fair. "When I was in business. . . ." It had a final sound as though—as though he were contented to let it be that way.

Then she had gone back upstairs, taking off her hat and unfastening her black silk gloves as she went. Max wouldn't want to go out to the Fair. He was tired. He worked all day, that was all it was; Max had done well to find employment at a time like this. By this fall, perhaps . . . But the note in his voice stayed with her. "When I was in business for myself . . ."

"Can you manage on ten dollars a week, Jule?" Max had asked her at breakfast, and she had answered:

"Yes, Max," suddenly embarrassed, ashamed of taking money when it was so little.

"I'll take care of the rent, and then if you can manage the meals and clothes . . ."

"Oh, yes, Max." She had used to pay Lena five dollars a week. She had taken the crumpled bill, folding it in her hand, covering it up. "Oh, yes, Max," she had kept repeating, "that will do nicely." He mustn't look that way; it wasn't his fault, it was hers that there were only ten dollars for everything.

Whatever was done now, she would have to do for the children on ten dollars a week. It was as though Max had said, "Don't count on me for anything more; I'll take care of the rent; but the rest, the children's future, can you manage on ten dollars a week, Jule?"

Oh, yes, she could manage for the children, but for Max? What could she do for him? Max didn't need anything. He was content to sit on the porch and talk of the past. Some sense of resignation seemed settled in the brim of his hat, his shoulders that had always drooped, the loose knot of his cravat—though she had pressed that tie just yesterday when she was pressing Anne's blue shirt-waist, the one that Max had brought back from Chicago that time. . . . Julia looked at the Art Palace across the blue lagoon. The pillars wavered. The crowds going up and down the steps in their different colored clothes blurred. Oh, yes, the Art Museum was much more beautiful than the old Memorial Hall at the Centennial.

Anne put on her hat, one of the new sailor hats Mamma had taken her to Field's to buy. She drew on her gloves. Back in Halstead young girls wore gloves to church, never to dinner in the evening.

"You are very quick." Signor Ricci was smiling. He held his soft brown hat in his hand. He offered her his arm. Should she take it? Why hadn't she noticed what ladies did? She let the very tips of her gloved fingers touch the cloth of his coat sleeve.

It was still light across the lagoon. The searchlights weren't on yet. The fountains were still white water, not liquid flame—turquoise, amber, emerald like the jewels in her case. Out on the promenade Signor Ricci took her gloved hand, small. like Mamma's, and pulled it through his arm. Anne blushed and pulled away a little. She looked down at the walk, at people's feet moving in dizzy succession ahead of her own, heels, toes, ten-button, fifteen button, two-strap slippers.

Signor Ricci laughed his wonderful low laugh. "I had heard American girls ·were so bold. You are very shy."

Anne wished she could think of something to say, just easily, but she couldn't. She wished for a moment that they were going alone to dinner; but that would be improper. What if Mamma had refused! But she hadn't. Still, it was delicious to walk over for Mamma, to have Signor Ricci draw her hand through his arm. They looked almost like lovers; people might even think they were. Heels, toes, high-laced shoes—elegant brown kid ones—her own black boots moving miraculously beside Signor Ricci's.

"Anne," said Signor Ricci; "it's a beautiful name. Anne Hauser." He stopped as though he were a little shy, too. Anne wished it were a farther distance to Mamma's building.

"In Padua . . ." Signor Ricci was saying. Padua! It seemed unbelievable that she was Anne Hauser from Halstead. She wished Bessie Hetzel could see her, but that was childish. She dismissed Halstead and Bessie Hetzel. The lights would come on just as they were eating. Lovely, lovely . . .

"Did you read the poem all through?"

He had asked before, and she had said, "Just part," although she had, of course, read all of it.

"Yes, I loved it."

" 'Yet Ah, that Spring should vanish with the Rose!
    That Youth's sweet-scented manuscript should close!
    The Nightingale that in the branches sang,
    Ah whence, and whither flown again, who knows!' "

Signor Ricci quoted in a slow low tone.

Anne was suddenly, miraculously, alone. Jeanette, Chris, Louise, even Mamma and Papa had dropped out of her world. Signor Ricci was asking her a question as though she were very wise and knew the answer. He looked into her eyes as though he could find the answer there.

" 'Ah Love! could you and I with Him conspire
    To grasp this sorry Scheme of Things entire,
    Would not we shatter it to bits—and then
    Re-mould it nearer to the Heart's desire!' "

How could the flag on the Horticultural Building ripple so bravely when the world was a sorry scheme of things? There was sadness in all of this, in all the people walking together from building to building, in the late June light that would soon disappear into dark, in the waiting for dark and the lights to come on. Only she and Signor Ricci together could stand it. The very knowledge of the sadness drew them together. They could remold things to the Heart's desire. Anne Hauser could find no words. She looked down from the flag to the steps leading to the

258

lagoon. They were almost to Mamma's building. What if Mamma had expected her to come over alone and have Signor Ricci meet them both there?

There was Mamma. Should she say, Mamma, will you meet Signor Ricci, or was it the other way round? Signor Ricci . . . She felt hot and confused. Mamma was coming toward them smiling. She was pretty in her black silk dress.

"Mamma, Signor Ricci," Anne muttered the words. Would Mamma guess how she loved him? She did love him. "Ah Love! could you and I with Him conspire . . ."

"How do you do?" Did Mamma hear that tone in his voice, like the low tone of her violin that sounded of the wood?

"I'll only be a moment," Mamma said, and they were left alone again.

"Your mother is a beautiful woman; how unusual for her to be in charge here. I mean—" he examined the seams of his gloves and then looked up smiling—"of course, America is so different a place from Italy." He chose his words carefully, paying attention to each little syllable.

Anne could say It-a-ly the way he did, between her tongue and teeth, softly to herself. Ah Love!

"May we take wheelchairs down to the Midway, Mrs. Hauser?"

"Yes, I should like to," Mamma said. For a second Anne felt as she used to when Mamma let them go down to Mathorn's for a soda. Signor Ricci stepped up on the curb and beckoned. He was so lordly! The three wheelchairs had to separate because of the crowds.

"Your mother is a beautiful woman," Signor Ricci had said. She had never really thought of that before. "How old is Signor Ricci?" Mamma had asked. She didn't know. He had been through the University at Padua, older than she was. . . . Twenty; no, perhaps he was twenty-two, but a man should be older than a girl. A girl was so dreadfully mature at seventeen. Why, Mamma had been married then!

There was the Ferris wheel. It would be fun to go up in it after dinner; maybe she could suggest it, offhand, with a little laugh. It was gay down here. . . . That was the Persian Theatre where the dancing was terrible. The Board of Lady Managers made them change it. There were so many places. . . . There were the streets of Cairo. She remembered the improper song Chris had told her:

"She had never seen the Streets of Cairo,
On the Midway she had never strayed;
She had never seen a Hootchie Koochie.
Poor little innocent Maid. . . ."

Signor Ricci's chair passed hers. It pulled up by Mamma's. Mamma was nodding her head. Signor Ricci was waiting for her. People had to go around them.

"We are going to eat in Old Vienna."

Anne smiled and nodded. They were getting out of their chairs now. She slid her hand under Mamma's arm in an ecstasy of excitement. Signor Ricci joined them.

"The old Rathaus is good, don't you think?"

"Yes, they've gotten the effect of age wonderfully," Julia said.

"Oh, I like the music. Can we eat outdoors?" Anne asked.

The lights were on around the village square and behind the small-paned windows of the buildings. The awning under the lamplight was very bright. A tinkle of music came from some place, and the waiters clinked their dishes as they passed.

"Champagne?" Signor Ricci was asking.

"Yes, thank you." Mamma smiled almost like a girl. Signor Ricci consulted with Mamma over the menu.

The music was starting again. It was a violin. Anne wished she could get that piece. She stretched her hands out on the table. "Oh, it's lovely! I'd like to go to Vienna, really!" Signor Ricci laughed. Then he stooped to pick up his napkin.

"Perhaps you shall some day," he whispered.

Anne dipped her spoon in the soup and looked across at Mamma. The clock in the main tower of the Rathaus chimed slowly, but she hadn't begun to count in time.

"I can see it." There was still light enough on the clock face. It was seven o'clock.

A girl came by the table with a tray of flowers. Signor Ricci stopped her. He picked out a nosegay of mignonette for Mamma. He chose violets for her.

"Smell, Mamma. They smell like the violets at home."

"Your home isn't Chicago?"

"No; I mean it is now. We used to live in Halstead," Anne explained.

"Halstead?"

"Nebraska," she laughed. "Way west of here. But we're always going to live in Chicago now, aren't we, Mamma?"

"Yes. How long are you staying in America, Signor Ricci?" Julia asked.

"For the Fair. I do not believe any longer, unless—" he paused and lifted his shoulders ever so slightly—"unless I cannot bear to leave."

Did Mamma know what he meant? The violets felt cool when she smelled them. Mamma hadn't noticed.

"You are through with your education then?"

"I finished the University in time to come for the exposition, but I am going to read the law."

"Isn't it a shame there aren't people living in all those

261

buildings?" Anne burst out. She must say something. Signor Ricci would think her a child to be so silent.

Now the waiter was changing their plates. She hoped they would have chicken like Sunday dinners at the Golden House. But this wasn't even the least little bit like that. The waiter was filling their glasses. How bubbly it was. Mamma raised a finger at the waiter, and he lifted the neck of the bottle above Anne's glass. "That's plenty," Mamma said. She wished Mamma wouldn't, but Signor Ricci was smiling at her, not as though he thought her a child. Anne thought of the poem:
"Ah Love! could you and I . . ." Mamma didn't understand at all.

The waiter filled Signor Ricci's glass.

"I don't believe Anne's ever had champagne before, have you?"

Oh, why did Mamma have to go on like that?

"Of course," she murmured, but neither Mamma nor Signor Ricci believed her.

"There is a champagne for the throat and a champagne for the heart," Signor Ricci said. There was nobody like him.

The music ended. A clatter of clapping fell unevenly across the sudden silence. Signor Ricci tapped his spoon against his glass for applause. Then a single violinist in a velvet jacket appeared across the square. He tucked his violin under his chin. With the first note a deeper silence drifted over the people at the tables until it covered them. The waiters hushed the noise of their crockery.

"Ah, *The Blue Danube*," Signor Ricci whispered.

The turquoise sky was darkening. There were stars, tiny ones, pale beside the bright striped awnings and the lights. The music flowed on like a river; no, like a fountain. The world was sad again:

". . . this sorry Scheme of Things . . .

The Nightingale that in the branches sang,

Ah whence, and whither flown again, who knows!"
Anne closed her eyes.

Then she opened them and saw Mamma. Mamma was sitting straight in her chair. Her face above the high neck of her black silk seemed so pale. Her eyes . . . how awful! Mamma was touching her handkerchief to her eyes. Anne's throat contracted. She took a sip from her glass, but the champagne burned. Signor Ricci was looking down at his menu. Why didn't the music stop? Then it did. Mamma turned and looked at her. Anne couldn't look away. People clapped, but stillness covered their table. Then Mamma laughed.

"They played *The Blue Danube* at the Centennial in 1876. That was a long time ago."

"Ah," said Signor Ricci politely.

"I was a bride then," said Mamma; then she ate her ice. Signor Ricci was paying the waiter; how handsomely he waved the waiter away with his tray full of coins.

"You would like to go home, Mrs. Hauser?" he asked gently. "May I take you home?"

Anne was seized with a sudden fear. Signor Ricci would see Mrs. Daggerty's boarding house with the sign "Rooms" in the front window. The letters were small and dignified; still it was a sign. He mustn't see them home, oh, please . . . She looked at Mamma pleadingly.

Mamma understood.

"Thank you; that isn't necessary. We have a regular arrangement; if you will take us back to my building. . . ."

But it was different going back. It was even a little cold now. Mamma had understood, but had she been hurt?

Well, they were awful rooms. Mamma said they were so convenient, but they looked rented.

"Good night, Signor Ricci."

"Good night, Miss Hauser." He bowed. She couldn't tell. Did his eyes say things? "Ah Love . . ." Why hadn't she given him her flowers? It was too late now. Oh, dear, she could cry. And now they would have to go home all the way on the street car. She couldn't look at Mamma yet. What had Signor Ricci thought?

6. JULY

NOW! Around this corner with a kind of swaying as though the car were breaking away from the conductor, the reckless discordant screeching and then a feeling of gathering speed. You could look ahead and see the straight tracks reaching to the Fifty-seventh Street terminal. It was more fun to take the open car so you could lean out a little ways. Jeanette always knew when the conductor would turn and call in that triumphant way, "All out! World's Fair Grounds!"

The people grabbed for their things: umbrellas, lunchbaskets, small children. Some of them stood up. . . . They needn't; the car stopped; there was plenty of time. Jeanette always sat still with that queer swelling feeling rising in her heart and head.

"Wait, Louise!" Even watching out for Louise didn't hurt the feeling, even hoping Louise wouldn't get tired so soon today, trying to decide where they'd go first, smiling at the conductor because they were old friends, fingering her pocket to be sure she had her official pass—the feeling always lasted. There was so much to see that they hadn't ever seen before. It was all hers. It was like having every day Saturday and Saturday a circus day. . . . No, it was more than that.

Nobody guessed, seeing her, the quick rush of feelings within her. She was a fat little girl, serious-eyed. Her brown curls reached to her straight plaid-covered shoulders. She was a trifle heavy beside Louise's picture prettiness.

"Are you coming out here all by yourselves?" The woman in the seat behind leaned over to ask. Strangers were always talking to them at the Fair.

Jeanette stared solemnly at the young woman with the plume in her hat.

"Yes; we know our way," she answered gravely.

"My! and is this your little sister? Look, Ralph, isn't she a dream?"

Jeanette was used to that. "Yes, she's five." That was bound to be the next question.

"I'd like to steal her. Shall we steal you, honey?"

Louise was also used to this. She smiled a dazzling smile. Dimples appeared, blue eyes sparkled through black lashes.

"Here, you kids, buy something." The young man gave them each a quarter.

Jeanette hesitated. "It's yours," the young man said. Jeanette knew it was wrong to take it.

"What do you say, L'uise?" She nudged her gently, fighting with her own conscience.

"Oh, the adorable thing!" The couple were getting off the car now. They had almost disappeared in the crowds. She couldn't give it back to them.

They came to the turnstile. Jeanette unfastened the safety pin that secured the pass. The old man knew her. He smiled as he detached the coupon.

"You're here bright and early!"

"Yes," said Jeanette, unsmiling. She drew Louise out of

265

the stream of people to get her pass fastened again. It was valuable. It made her special, not just any little girl, but Jeanette Hauser whose Mamma had an official appointment. It made her feel at home anywhere inside the grounds.

"Let's go and see the babies," Louise urged.

"No, that's over in the Children's Building. We'll do that on our way back. Let's go . . . Oh, look, L'uise; that's a Hindu man; see his funny turban!" They stared, blue eyes and brown eyes acquiring cosmopolitanism as they stared. "I'll tell you, let's do all the state buildings we can before lunch and then we'll go over to Mamma's building."

One thing got in her way in the state buildings, that was her feeling of loyalty for the Nebraska Building. Still, they lived in Illinois now, and they always would. It was confusing, like finding some things in the French pavilion or the German Government Building that really truly were more beautiful than things in the American Building.

"Look, Net, at the oranges; it's like Papa's store." They were in the California Building now. They stood in front of the tremendous globe of oranges mounted on a platform of oranges.

"Want one?" a man asked Louise, and then gave one to Jeanette, too. Jeanette frowned a little, remembering John Sorenson, but she nudged Louise automatically.

"Thank you," Louise said, smiling back at the man.

Papa's store seemed far away and the dark room where John sorted the fruit, but the smell of the ripeness was the same. They finished sucking their oranges in front of the Miners' Statue.

"His finger's pointing right at us, Net."

"It's supposed to be pointing at the rock where he's

going to get gold," corrected Jeanette precisely. "That one's prettier." They wandered on to the statue of California. Always California would conjure up for both of them the figure of a beautiful woman with long waving hair.

"Look how big her toes are," Louise said.

"Oh, Mamma, there's too much to see!" Louise sat down on the chair by Julia's desk.

Julia smiled. That was the way the world should seem to her children.

"Mamma, this is Saturday, isn't it?" Jeanette asked abruptly. It was hard to keep track of the time here.

"Yes, Jeanette." Julia tidied her desk.

"Oh, dear! then tomorrow's Sunday and most everything's closed up. You know it's all here to see, but you can't get at it." Jeanette always took great care to make her meaning plain.

"I know," Julia answered, her eyes quickened with understanding. After all, wasn't that the feeling she had had in Halstead for many years?

Now Jeanette walked briskly along. This was her time. Louise was asleep in the little office at Mamma's building. Jeanette was free to go where she wanted to, to run a little or walk slowly or sit still. There was the Agricultural Building; Agricultural, Horticultural, Colonnade, lagoon. . . . Words she had never even heard of two months ago. She said them aloud in a sing-song, liking the sound of them. There were the Spanish ships; that was the *Santa Maria*. . . . How little it must have looked out on the ocean! That was what discovered America, the one with Columbus in, only Chris said Leif Ericsson really saw America first in a ship like the Viking ship. Pooh! Leif

Ericsson hadn't gotten out with his flags and knelt down on the sand and claimed it in the name of a queen.

The sun made the monolith shine on all its edges. The peristyle was the prettiest part, the white pillars with the blue lake spaces in between. Jeanette sat down on the ledge against one of the pillars. It was shadowy under the peristyle. It was like sitting under the lilac bush at home, looking out at the bright sun on everything.

Maybe she'd been gone longer than she said she would. She hurried up to one of the Columbian guards.

"What time is it, please?"

"Quarter to four," the man answered, smiling.

"Thank you." She'd have to go back to get Louise. Then she felt the two quarters in her pocket; the hard thin feeling decided her. She'd get Louise, and they'd have really paid tea in that East India room. Jeanette ran now.

Louise was awake. Mamma had had to go home early to do the marketing.

"Come on, L'uise. Oh, my gracious! you need your hands and face washed, child." Jeanette felt very grown-up. She took Louise in and washed her hands and face. "There, you'll do. Now, Louise, we're going to have tea, and you must do just what I tell you." Louise's light curls bobbed. She was in the shining goodness of mood that comes just after a nap.

"Here, L'uise." Jeanette chose a carved and inlaid table in a corner near one of the big hangings. She felt very important; surely no one could guess that she was only ten! Most of the tables were filled, but the conversation of the occupants of the tables seemed hushed.

Jeanette ordered gravely. "And some of those spice wafers; will that be under fifty cents?"

"Forty cents," the turbaned waiter assured her.

"Then I want ten cents' worth of something."

"Candied ginger?"

"Yes, please." Then remembering, "That will do nicely." The two little girls sat back in their chairs. Jeanette picked up a palm-leaf fan and waved it slowly back and forth. Louise watched the people. This was better than playing tea in the backyard at home.

The joy of having paid tea! The steam coming out of the narrow brass spout was exciting. The little cakes were delicious, only too thin. But the candied ginger wasn't like candy and made your throat burn. Louise coughed so hard Jeanette had to pound her on the back. A woman came by with a child Jeanette's age. Jeanette sat straighter. Then she saw someone. At least it looked like . . . it was . . . Mrs. Jenks. Jeanette pushed back her chair and made her way in and out between the tables.

"Hello, Mrs. Jenks." Jeanette was so excited she had to call out. "Hello, Alice!"

"Why, Jeanette Hauser!"

"We were having tea," Jeanette explained, "and I saw you. There's Louise." It was so good to see people she knew.

"We only got here today. We tried to get your mamma, but they said you'd moved so we decided to look you up later."

"Yes, we did move so we'd be nearer to the Fair. Mamma's home now, so why don't you come home with us?" Mamma would want them to. "Anne's here and Chris; they have appointments here at the Fair, too." There was so much these people didn't know; why, they'd been home all this time, and the Fair was half over.

They met Mr. Jenks on the steps of the Nebraska Building. Jeanette was proud leading the way. Mr. Jenks looked just the same as ever.

"Well, well, well, look who's here! Louise, you're a sight

for sore eyes. Jeanette, there hasn't been any first-rate reciting done in Halstead since you left." It embarrassed Jeanette to be kissed out in public, but she flushed with pleasure when he mentioned her reciting.

Anne and Chris were surprised. Anne was just a little funny at first, Jeanette thought, and wondered why.

"Well, this is an occasion; we'll get one of those tallyhos and all ride down together," Mr. Jenks announced.

The children sat on top. They were higher up even than the street cars. If they went close enough to the side, they could even touch the branches of the trees. The buckles on the horses' harnesses shone as bright as January's used to. People stopped to look at them as they went by.

Alice was Anne's age. She and Anne were talking together so low nobody could hear them. Chris had sat with Mr. and Mrs. Jenks. He was feeling grown-up, too. Louise was a little scared. She held Jeanette's hand tightly.

When they turned down their street, it seemed too narrow for the tallyho. How surprised Mamma would be! Jeanette climbed down first. Mr. and Mrs. Jenks were hesitating again. It bothered Jeanette. Then they got out.

"It makes me feel just awfully, Ned," Jeanette heard Mrs. Jenks say.

"We're on the top floor. I'll go up and tell Mamma you're here," Anne said all in a rush. Jeanette led them into the parlor downstairs. It didn't seem right to leave them there alone so Jeanette and Louise stayed, answering questions.

"So you're having a good time at the Fair, Jeanette!"

"Yes, thank you."

"Certainly is plenty to see! How's Max; your father, I mean?"

"He's very well, thank you." The Jenks, why, they had

always known the Jenks. What made her feel so different with them? She tried to puzzle it out while she was answering politely. Then she heard Mamma coming down the stairs.

"Alice, Ned." Mamma's voice made everything all right again. She was smiling, and her face looked really glad. "Come right up; we're camping out, but we have plenty of room," Mamma said. Then Jeanette saw Anne. Anne was watching Mamma. There was a look on Anne's face just for a second as if she didn't believe Mamma.

"We're so glad to see you . . ." Mamma was saying.

"I didn't know whether you would be or not, Julia, after—after the Chemical National affair." Even Mr. Jenks with his glasses and brown mustache looked embarrassed. Mamma made a little movement with her hands; the Chemical National . . . whatever it was, fell through her opened fingers onto the carpet.

"My dear, we've worried so about you. . . ." The queerness was in Mrs. Jenks's voice. Mamma felt it. She glanced briefly at the children; Jeanette felt her glance.

"Don't mention it; nobody could help it. Now!" There was gayety in Julia's voice that swept the room. "Max will be so happy to have you here. He should be home any minute."

"You must go out to dinner with us tonight, Julia; the whole family."

"Oh, thank you, Ned; I don't know about the children."

Mamma must let them, just this time. . . . Jeanette squeezed Louise's hand behind her back.

"Oh, yes, Julia."

"Well . . ." Mamma laughed. She would, Jeanette could tell. "Come upstairs, now, away from this public parlor."

Jeanette ran ahead with Louise. On the last bend of the second flight she looked back down. The stairs seemed crowded with them all streaming behind. Jeanette threw the door of their rooms open. They had been here almost three months; the rooms began to seem like home.

"My dear!" Mrs. Jenks drew in her breath on a little sigh. "Jessie Withers said you were in a flat, but I never . . ."

Jeanette turned in time to see Mamma raise her finger to her lips.

"It's like a telescope. It grows large or small according to the number of guests," Mamma said.

Mr. Jenks took out a cigar and sat down by the front window. Alice and Anne went into the middle room. What did they have to talk so much about? Jeanette walked along the hall. She had to change her dress; and if she wanted to walk quietly and not make a lot of noise, why, it wasn't sneaking on them.

"And sometime we're going gondola-riding together."

"Oh, Anne!"

Pooh, she had been gondola-riding already; that was nothing. Jeanette changed into her red silk dress. She took the ribbon in for Mamma to tie.

"The Jeffreys bought the O'Connor place," Mrs. Jenks was saying. "Ned says I shall have to have them to dinner."

Mr. Jenks put down his paper. "Alice, shall we tell them or wait to surprise them?"

"Let's tell Julia."

"The O'Connors are coming to the Fair; yes, sir, way from Wyoming. They're going to be here tonight."

Julia's face lit up. "Oh, what a surprise for Max."

It was more exciting than Christmas. Jeanette felt she must talk to someone. Louise had to have too many things explained. She would hunt up Chris. "Mamma, where is Chris?"

Mr. Jenks laughed. "He asked me if he could ride downtown a ways in the tallyho. He's going to get his money's worth. He's developed, Julia!"

Developed; what had Chris done to develop? Chris wasn't much bigger, Jeanette thought.

"Yes, being in the Victoria House has taught him a sort of poise."

"Your children will all have that, Julia. You'll never need to worry."

Mamma smiled a pleased smile.

Poise; what was it they would all have? It was something nice anyway. She would ask Chris what poise was. Jeanette decided to go downstairs and watch for him. She perched at the top of the porch steps.

There was Papa getting off the street car. Jeanette jumped off the coping and ran to meet him.

"Hello, Jeanette." Jeanette took little hop steps to keep from telling. Together they went up the two flights of stairs. Mamma and the Jenks must have heard Papa coming and were keeping still. The hallway along the stairs was narrow. Jeanette squeezed ahead. She had to see him when he knew.

"Hello, Jule."

"Hello, Max."

Papa went straight along the hall to the front where the sitting-room was. He stopped in the doorway, and his face lighted up almost as much as Mamma's.

"Why, Ned Jenks!" Papa was wringing Mr. Jenks' hand. He kissed Mrs. Jenks. "You're the best surprise I can think of! How's everything, Ned? Halstead still there?"

Jeanette sat down on the corner of the couch bed. This was what she liked best, grown-up talk. Chris came upstairs. What if he had ridden a ways in the tallyho. Chris had missed seeing Papa be surprised.

273

"Well, we better go. Max, you're going downtown to dinner with us."

Papa looked over at Mamma. "Hadn't we better keep them with us, Jule? I'll go out and get some things. . . ."

"Not this time, Max; it's all been decided, and the children are going along with us."

"Ned, do you remember the time you invited me to dinner when we got to the first town on the South Loop River, and when we got there . . ." They both laughed so hard they couldn't talk. Mamma and Mrs. Jenks laughed, too.

Mamma slipped out to dress Louise in her white muslin with blue ribbon in the beading. It was all so exciting. Then Papa went downstairs to phone for a hansom cab, two of them.

When the hansom cabs drew up before the Palmer House a fat man with braid across his coat and wearing white gloves opened the door of the cab. How pretty Mamma looked. She had worn her beautiful coral earrings and the big brooch. Jeanette took hold of Louise. Mamma hadn't told them to be good. She just expected it. They all went up the thick carpeted steps and sat down in big upholstered chairs. "Don't keep looking all around, L'uise," Jeanette whispered.

"Why, Anne Hauser!" Jeanette burst out. That was what Anne and Alice were giggling about! They had both pinned up their hair, and they were sitting over there together waiting for Mamma and Mrs. Jenks to notice. Then Mamma did look over. She laughed instead of being cross.

"Now you're all grown-up," Mrs. Jenks said. Mamma looked at Anne again, not laughing.

"Well, shan't we go in to dinner, Ned?" Papa asked.

"Oh, wait a bit, Max; you always were hungry."

Then a big man, taller than Papa with black hair and a big mustache, came toward them. The woman with him was tall, too. She had a homely face. She must be the Mrs. O'Connor who used to live in Halstead.

"Regan O'Connor!" Papa had jumped up from the sofa. She had never seen him so excited; he was almost hugging Mr. O'Connor. Mamma and Mrs. O'Connor were kissing each other.

"And these are the children! The only way I can ever think of you, Julia, is as a bride."

It was the most wonderful dinner Jeanette had ever had. It wasn't just the magnificence of the dining-room, the ferns and palms and roses, nor the things to eat; it was watching Mamma and Papa. Papa was talking or laughing every minute. He remembered things that made them all laugh. Mr. Jenks had invited them, but the waiter kept coming to Papa and showing him things, to see if they were just right.

"Do you remember that poker game, Max?"

"Will I ever forget it?" chuckled Mr. O'Connor. "I'll tell you; you and Ned had better come West. If you believed in Nebraska, you'd be carried away with Wyoming."

Max shook his head. "I moved once, that's enough." Sudden silence fell on them. Jeanette had left off listening to the grown-up talk trying to catch up with Chris.

"Max, I would like to hear you sing again." Mrs. O'Connor leaned forward. "I always wondered if you sang when you were courting Julia."

It seemed so short a time ago that she had sat on the sofa at Mrs. Withers' beside Mrs. O'Connor listening to Max sing, Julia thought. It was good to see him like this again. She felt as though a weight had been lifted from her.

"And to think you have an official appointment at the Fair, Julia!" Mrs. O'Connor exclaimed. "You're wonderful. Halstead must be proud of you."

"I thought we all ought to take in the Midway tonight," Ned Jenks suggested.

"Not the children," Julia said. "They've had enough excitement for today." Anne and Alice Jenks pouted a little. Chris looked indifferent. Jeanette didn't care tonight. There was enough to think over after she got in bed.

"Remember when you and Dorsett and I . . ." Regan O'Connor began, then he broke off suddenly.

"Faith was here last month. She's left Halstead for good. I think she'll try teaching china-painting in some school," Julia filled in.

"I believe James' death was what finally persuaded me to leave," Max commented soberly.

"Well, Max, Armour's have cut your successor's business badly," Ned Jenks told him.

"They wouldn't have cut Max's business, though," Regan objected. "Did you ever see him lose business?" They all laughed again. Max pulled at his mustache in a pleased way.

Jeanette put the cherry of her dessert out on the side of her plate to save. She looked over at Chris. He had eaten his. Anne and Alice didn't count; they had put their hair up. Louise was so sleepy she sat holding her spoon, forgetting to eat. Jeanette ate her cherry Melba slowly. She wondered whether drug stores made this.

Papa lit his cigar gayly. "On to the Midway," he said. Jeanette had never thought of grown people having so much fun. She followed Mamma out of the dining-room. There was still the drive home in the hansom cab left. It was exciting to ride home with nobody older than Anne.

Jeanette sat quietly in the hansom cab. She didn't want

to talk. She watched the houses again along the streets. The lighted windows looked as though they had secrets. She had discovered a secret, too. Even after you grew up you had fun, maybe even more fun than now.

The horses stood still. They were back home again.

7

CHRIS hung his hat in the little closet off the tiled vestibule in the Victoria House. It was his home. It took the place of Mathorn's and their own house. He felt a sense of ownership about it.

The morning's mail was on the little tray on the table by the door. He sorted it—Mr. Shirley-Smythe, Mr. Lawler, Sir Arthur Wood. Then he carried it into the library that served as a perfect example of an English library and a registration office for English visitors to the Fair. He glanced around the book-lined walls, the mullioned windows. The rich bindings of Dickens's works, Carlyle's, Thackeray's, never tempted him inside; still he felt the air they gave to the place.

"Good morning, sir."

"Oh, good morning, Christopher; thank you."

Chris straightened a chair, pushed in a book that was uneven with the rest. Mr. Shirley-Smythe looked up smiling.

"Well, how do the new glasses go?"

"Fine, sir." Chris fingered the black string that ran from his glasses to the button in his coat lapel very much the way Mr. Shirley-Smythe did.

"Sit down, won't you?"

Chris sat down in one of the heavy Tudor chairs. He let

his arms lie along the arms of the chair, his fingers resting on the square nail studs.

"Christopher, what are you going to do after the Fair is over?"

"I mean to go into business, sir."

Mr. Shirley-Smythe frowned and drew his sandy brows together as he looked over at Christopher.

"How old are you?"

"I'll be sixteen next July."

"And twenty-five ten Julys from now."

"Yes, sir." Chris wondered if he were ragging him, but his face was serious.

"What kind of business have you chosen, Christopher?"

"Well, I'd like to sell something; not in a store, you know, but . . ."

"What is it your father does?"

"He's in the wholesale produce business, sir."

"Have you thought of that?"

"Yes, sir." Chris looked back stolidly. His face showed no expression. It was such a square face, more stolid now with the glasses. Not one of your quick, modern, young men; that was what drew Mr. Shirley-Smythe toward him. "Still water runs deep . . ." all that sort of thing.

"I kind of thought maybe I'd go back to Halstead some day."

"Halstead?"

"That's the place where we used to live. It's west of here."

"Oh, yes, I remember." Mr. Shirley-Smythe nodded. Curious—one of the most curious stories he'd ever heard. The boy's family had come to Chicago to live, apparently, because the Fair was here. It was as though he should give up his bank in Exeter to be at St. John's Woods for the cricket matches. Well, almost as bad. He hadn't heard much else about the family. The boy didn't say much. That was another thing he liked about him.

"I'd like to talk with your mother some time, Christopher. I wonder if she would come to tea tomorrow?"

"I think so," said Christopher, "but I don't think she likes tea. She likes coffee."

"Perhaps she would drink tea for local color, though, don't you know?"

Christopher looked dubious. Mr. Shirley-Smythe laughed.

The next afternoon Chris was sitting on the long oak settle on the square stair-landing, thinking. The big window had a coat of arms of Queen Victoria made in colored glass. It was fun to look out through the amber panes and then over at the side through the red ones and watch how the people changed. The water looked pretty all red.

Chris was thinking about England. Mr. Shirley-Smythe and Sir Arthur Wood and Mr. Lawler had told him about it; and this house, why, Mr. Lawler said it might really be an old house on some London street instead of here. Chris wondered what the difference was between this and their own house back in Halstead. People were always coming in here, women especially, and saying, "How English, don't you love it?" They were silly, that's what! Chris decided gravely. This house was bigger and had a lot of wood instead of wallpaper, that was all.

He could hear the tea things. Bridges must be bringing it in now. He'd better go and help. Then he saw Mamma. Mamma always looked so cool and . . . nice. Chris went down the stairs to meet her.

"How do you do, Mamma." The occasion seemed to demand something more than hello.

"How do you do, Chris." Julia's eyes twinkled proudly. Chris had improved. She was grateful to Mr. Shirley-Smythe for noticing that he needed glasses. Next year in school he would do better. Perhaps he would be quicker. His way of staring solemnly before answering had bothered her a little.

"They serve the tea in here," Chris explained with a touch of ownership. He took his mother's elbow, a little too high up for comfort, and guided her through the people into the library. Mr. Shirley-Smythe saw them and came across to the door.

"Mamma, this is Mr. Shirley-Smythe." Chris was so eager to have them know each other he forgot to be embarrassed. He wanted Mamma to notice how Mr. Shirley-Smythe bowed. Chris could do that now, but not so well.

"Christopher, you get the tea for us, will you?" Mr. Shirley-Smythe drew Julia over to the window-seat between the books.

It was quite perfect, Julia thought; the tempered light through the mullioned windows, the tall carved mantel, this friend of Chris's. Julia smiled to herself ever so slightly.

"Mrs. Hauser, I have become very fond of your son in these two months."

"I am glad. He has enjoyed it here," Julia said.

"He is not like many lads his age. He seems older."

"Yes," agreed Julia, and almost without thinking, she added, "He is a great deal like his father."

Mrs. Hauser was not as he had imagined she would be. She might have been visiting her son's school, talking to his instructors. He felt a little like a head-master. He hesitated to broach the subject. He stole a look at Julia and fingered his watch fob almost awkwardly.

"I think," he began, "that your son has more than an ordinary inclination toward business."

Julia smiled. Still Mr. Shirley-Smythe could not shake off the annoying simile. He might have been a tutor saying, your son has more than an ordinary inclination toward mathematics. They both watched Chris coming through the crowd carrying a tray, very carefully, very seriously. The sun from the long window flashed for a second on his glasses. He looked up, beaming a little, proudly. He had never been in a place before where he felt so competent.

"I told Mr. Shirley-Smythe that you didn't like tea, Mamma, but you don't mind drinking it, do you?"

Julia looked at Mr. Smythe and laughed gently. How young Chris's mother was, Mr. Shirley-Smythe thought.

"Have you ever been in England?"

"No." Julia looked up eagerly. "I hope to go some-time."

"I was, ah, wondering . . ." Dammit, how awkward he felt. He might have been Chris's age. Julia was looking at him, eyes widened a trifle. What clear eyes they were! "Ah, as I said, I have grown very fond of your son. I wondered if you might permit him to go back to England with me. You see, I am in a position to place him in the bank at Exeter. He could learn the business. . . . I have no son of my own." He had been stirring his tea as he talked. He never took sugar, how foolish! Now he looked up to see if Mrs. Hauser were interested.

"How very kind." Julia hesitated. "There would be a good many things to consider, of course . . ." The gravity of her face broke into a smile that excused his own awkwardness. "What does Chris say?"

"He says he wants to go into business. I haven't mentioned England."

"I will want to talk with Mr. Hauser and think about it. I do appreciate your interest in Chris. The closing of the Chemical National has embarrassed us somewhat. . . ." She broke off as Chris came back.

"May I speak to Christopher about it?" Mr. Shirley-Smythe asked.

"Yes, indeed."

"Christopher, I have just told your mother that I should like to take you back to England with me, to Exeter, where you would learn the banking business."

Chris listened without any expression. "I thought I would go into business with Papa," he said slowly.

"But, Chris, Mr. Smythe is offering to take you to England. We will go home and talk it all over, Mr. Smythe. Thank you. Chris is a little bewildered, I think." She smiled and stood up.

Chris rode home with Julia on the street car. They sat quietly; there was enough noise to preclude talking. Julia looked at Chris, but Chris's profile told her nothing; the glasses made him look older. The string of his hat fastened to his coat lapel crossed the boyish line of his cheek; his lips were full and soft, a little stubborn-looking. He seemed to be looking at the waving straps of the car. Could she let him go way off across the ocean? But that wasn't it; it was the opportunity for Chris she must think of. Max wouldn't be able to give him an opening.

It was their corner. They crossed to Mrs. Daggerty's side of the street.

"Mamma, I was too far away to offer my seat to that woman way down in front of the car, wasn't I?"

Chris had looked as though he were thinking of Mr. Shirley-Smythe's invitation. Instead he was busy with the present. He was like Max. Julia laughed. "Chris, I never even saw her."

"She looked pretty strong," Chris said seriously, "but I would have if she'd been nearer to me. Mr. Shirley-Smythe says he is shocked at the carelessness of American men on the street cars."

At the top of the third flight of stairs Julia was met as always by the improvised kitchen. If she thought of what they would have for dinner quickly, it wasn't so bad. Tonight she spread the table in the front sitting-room. It was too hot in the little back kitchen. Outside the front bow window the city was softening, blurring in the six o'clock light. Soon there would be a breeze. It was time to make the coffee.

"Hello, Jule; it ought to be good corn weather!" Max wasn't so tired as usual. His tone was hearty.

"We're ready, Chris, Max. Anne you put up the chairs." It was a good evening. The children were back in time. Julia relaxed.

"Well, Jeanette, where did you and Louise go today?" Max asked.

"We spent all afternoon in the Fisheries Building again."

"I'd like to see the ocean, Mamma," Louise said suddenly, shaking back her curls, emphasizing her words in the pretty confidence that her wish was important.

Chris would go across the ocean, Julia thought. Better not mention Mr. Shirley-Smythe till later, when she and Max were alone.

Anne buttered her bread. Her eyes followed the knife along the crust. If she should go to Italy with Signor Ricci, she would cross the ocean. Her neck above the stiff collar of her shirt-waist warmed in color.

Max pulled one of Louise's curls. "Why would you like to see the ocean, Louise?"

"So I could see the fish in the ocean."

Chris laughed out in a way that was getting more rare with him, that quick outburst at anyone who knew less than he. Max frowned at him.

"What's the dessert, Jule? I have a surprise for dessert."

"Ice cream, Papa?" Louise called out.

Max got up and went out to the hall. He came back with a bag. His face crinkled mysteriously. He flourished his hand and brought out a pear that he twirled on its stem.

"Pears; it's pears!" Jeanette shouted, reaching for one.

"How nice, Max."

"Look like pretty good ones. A whole carload came in today. They'll never get rid of them before they spoil."

"Papa, Mr. Shirley-Smythe wants me to go back to England with him."

Julia caught her breath. She hadn't meant to bring it up now.

"To England!" Anne echoed. "Why would he want you to go to England?"

Max looked up startled. Jeanette bit into her pear. Always the rush of pear juice through her teeth, the mild sweet taste, the sight of a yellow-speckled skin with one soft brown place on it, would bring back to her a warm July night, a tingle of excitement, a feeling of suspense, something from far off touching them—England.

"It's good," Louise said. "I like pears."

"Chris, did he really ask you to go to England?" Anne persisted.

" 'Course he did; he wants me to go into his business."

"What is his business?" Max asked, still frowning.

Chris shouldn't have brought it up this way. Julia picked the dishes up from her own place. She would tell Max alone so he would see.

"Banking," Chris answered as though he had associated himself already with Mr. Shirley-Smythe's banking house.

"It would be an opportunity," Julia said, coming back from the kitchen. Max got up from the table and went down to the front porch with his cigar. He would wait to talk it over later with Julia.

"Jeanette, you and Louise can go out and play. Anne will help me," Julia said. Sometimes the rooms were too full of her children. Tonight she needed to concentrate on Chris.

Anne carried the dishes into the little kitchen. Julia stood by the sink rinsing them. Chris came over to the chair by the sink. He sat down holding a dishcloth in his hand. Julia glanced up at his pondering expression. For a second the water spattering into the dishpan and the clink of the dishes were the only sounds in the kitchen. Chris had come to help so he could talk.

"Of course, Chris, we'd have to know more about Mr. Shirley-Smythe; I'll stop in and talk to Sir Arthur Wood tomorrow, but if he can do all he says for you, it might be a bigger opportunity for you than here. After all, England isn't so far." As she said it she felt the falseness of it. England was across the ocean from here. But that was the way Chris should feel.

"Signor Ricci says Italy seems so far away to people here, but really . . ."

The plate clattered out of Julia's soapy fingers into the dishpan. Signor Ricci had talked to Anne about Italy. Julia standing by her dishpan could feel the currents pulling. A sudden fear made her stop to dry her hands nervously on the towel by the window, as though her hands must be free. Then without thinking she took the silverware and plunged it into the dishpan. The fear turned to excitement in her.

"Chris, you're a help!" Anne jibed at Chris as she flapped the dish towel at him.

"Give me something to wipe then."

"I will not. You don't have to sit down to wipe even if you are going to England."

Chris dried the handle of a coffee cup meticulously. "I'm

not going to England," he muttered; "not if you'd promise me I could be president of the bank some day."

"Why, Chris!" Anne said. Julia's eyes were on him.

"I wouldn't like being in a bank, in a cage. I'm going to do something like Papa."

"But, Chris, you aren't sure. You must look ahead. It's so important to decide wisely," Julia said almost as if she had read the words somewhere. She felt a little lost.

Chris's face set stubbornly.

"And I'm going to start in this fall, too, after the Fair closes." He slung his damp towel over the back of the chair and went out of the kitchen. Julia heard him going downstairs. The front sceen door banged.

"Chris is foolish, isn't he, Mamma?" Anne began. There was an accent of superiority in her voice that grated on Julia just then.

"I don't know, Anne," Julia murmured. "I haven't been to the Fair at night all this week; I think I'll go. Perhaps Papa will go with us."

But Max didn't want to go to the Fair. He sat on the front porch talking the future of the canning industry with a man from the next porch. Chris sat on the rail listening.

"We won't be gone long, Max," Julia called back.

"Well, sir, there's no mistaking the tendency toward concentration. Reid-Murdoch have experts in South America buying up coffee, I hear. . . ."

Chris leaned back against the post. He liked the talk. Papa's voice had a kind of sound to it that made you feel he knew what he was talking about.

"Sprague-Warners about control the canneries now, I guess," Mr. Lewis put in.

Chris liked names like that. He liked to look at them on the smoky buildings along South Water Street. Sprague-

Warner, Armour's—he'd like to work for one of them. It gave him a kind of satisfaction just to think about it. It was nice at the Victoria House, Mr. Shirley-Smythe and Sir Arthur Wood; but they weren't, why, they were tame alongside of his father.

The cigar smoke floated out to Chris. He wondered if it would make him sick now if he tried smoking again. He hadn't tried since last summer. Mr. Mathorn had given him some medicine and told him to wait awhile. He was older now, though; besides, deciding to go into business made him feel older.

"Well, good night." The man from the next porch got up and went down the steps.

"Good night, Lewis," Max said as he might have to Ned Jenks or Hetzel back home.

The chair Mr. Lewis had left was still rocking when Chris moved over and sat down in it. He sat down heavily like his father. He pulled a little closer to the front so he could put his feet on the railing.

Max didn't speak for a few minutes. It was pleasant out here on the porch. He scowled over his cigar. There was something he was thinking about when Lewis came over. . . .

"Papa, d'you suppose I could get something to do down where you are after the Fair stops?"

"Why—" Now he remembered; it was about this Englishman's offering to take Chris back to England with him. "Why, Chris, I thought you were thinking of going to England to learn the banking business."

"Oh, that was just talk. Mr. Smythe asked Mamma if I could. I don't want to. I'd like to go into the produce business." He hesitated shyly. "I sort of thought maybe sometime I'd go back to Halstead, later on. D'you think you could find a job for me, Papa?"

Max puffed at his cigar contentedly. "I think maybe, Chris."

8

MAX was at home in Salter's Commission House on South Water Street. It was his own store, but on a larger scale; the same sounds, smells, talk, the same kind of people, but more of them. It was mid-morning, but only a gloomy light came through the dingy windows. A gas-light burned over the bookkeeper's ledger. Max sat at a littered desk listening to two men across from him who had come to sell a boatload of Michigan grapes before the season began. As always the talk had drifted to conditions.

"It used to be so a man could make up in one line what he lost in another; wasn't that so, Hauser? You old-timers must have had things pretty much your own way!"

It came to Max that these men liked to stop in to talk to him because he had been in the game so long. Max's tone took on a note of firmness. He tipped back in his chair and talked as he did in the evening on Mrs. Daggerty's front porch. He could tell them a few things about the produce business.

Abruptly he leaned forward, took his cigar from between his lips, and pounded on the desk with such vehemence that his detachable cuffs standing along the edge fell to the floor.

" 'S the ruination of the commission house if Packers Incorporated's going to ship in direct. Look at the prices on butter and eggs we got this morning!" Max fumbled in his pocket and brought up a torn envelope covered with figures.

The two men stared back gloomily. There was a curious similarity about all the men on South Water Street; about these three—in their vests, suspenders plainly visible, hats on the back of their heads, black sleeve protectors like badges on their arms. As they talked there was the usual procession of drivers with receipts, messenger boys with telegrams, the loud jangle of the telephone.

"Hauser, Hauser!" Salter came in shouting before he was wholly in the room. "Max, see if you can find some-one to handle that cartload of greenstuff. We'll have to dump it if it don't move today. Where's that bill of lading? Say, Wheatly, wait a minute. . . ."

Max shoved his hat forward on his head, rammed the envelope and the stubby pencil he had been figuring with down into his pocket and went out onto the Street. He liked it on the Street. It had a small town air about it for all its frantic jumble; men you knew called you by name. He climbed heavily over skids, dodged the barrels sliding down some planks that straddled the sidewalk, and threaded his way between the boxes and high-piled crates. A great dray-horse thrust his head suddenly in front of Max, pursuing the cabbage in a half-open crate. Max pushed the horse's head back to pass. A teamster cursed at his horses, trying to back his dray closer to the curb and force the horses of the next wagon to move over. The other driver swore back, but the voices were lost in the bang and rattle and roar of the whole Street.

Max ducked suddenly into Russo's banana cellar, following behind a wheelbarrow of green bananas.

"Seen any tarantulas today, Tony?" Max was in good spirits.

The swarthy little man unloading bananas laughed. "Sure!" It was that Mister Hauser from Salter's.

Max looked around for Russo himself and went on again, scarcely smelling the rank odor of rotting vegetables, horses, sweating laborers, wet straw and the foul stink of the river back of the two- and three-story buildings. It was the Street.

"Max!" Joe Little standing in an open doorway watching the crates of peaches unloaded saw him and jumped down to the walk to draw him aside.

Silently he offered Max a peach.

Max bit into the peach, nodded his head.

"Give you the load, Max, at . . ." He held up his hand to whisper the price, as though anything could be heard above the racket.

Out came the envelope, the stub of a pencil. Max leaned against the door jamb to figure. Then he shook his head.

"Salter isn't taking any more peaches."

"Take 'em yourself, Max. You ought to be on your own. Armstrong was tellin' me the first of the summer you was just waiting till you saw the lay of the land awhile."

"Nope." Max shook his head again. He threw his pit through the spokes of the wheel. Joe Little was already watching the flow of the Street, looking for someone else. Max went on, still figuring in his head. If he had his own capital now, even half of it, something back of him to draw on, he could turn over that load by three o'clock. Suppose he only got two hundred and fifty; he'd make half again what he got in salary from Salter. The way he'd planned before the bank failed . . .

He had to step around two women quarreling over the rotting vegetables in a scavenger's wagon, but his thoughts were scarcely disturbed. It was a common enough sight on South Water Street, as common as the ever-present rats in the dark cellars.

"H'lo, Max!"

"H'lo, Sam!"

"C'mon in here and look at these Wisconsin cheddars." Max followed Sam Bloom into the cave-like store of a cheese dealer. They each helped themselves to samples from the big yellow rings.

"D'you hear what prints are selling at, Max?"

Max nodded.

"You ought to be on your own, Max."

Max nodded. The cheese in his mouth lost its flavor.

"Say, Sam, what you got in eggs? Salter's looking for refrigerator extras. You could sell him some dirties and checks. If prices ease, he'll take anything offered in carloads." Salter's looking for . . . that was safer. He wasn't the power he had planned to be on the Street; he was in for Salter now and lucky to have the job. Max talked prices, but without his usual relish. Listening to Sam Bloom talk about the government he went far back in his mind.

When he'd first started to handle produce, Omaha was nothing but a clay bank at the end of the railroad. You could start in with almost nothing in the old days. He wished, suddenly, that he could tell Sam how he'd gone to Halstead as soon as they could get through shipment, and by '73 he'd . . . Well, he was able to go way to Philadelphia for that Fair. He and Julia had been able to do things in style, no scrimping then. Standing in the dark little office shaving himself another sliver of cheese, he could see Julia sitting by him in the train on that trip. She wasn't any older than Anne when he married her, and Anne, why, she was still a child. It made him feel protective for an instant. He'd promised to give Julia everything she wanted. . . . 'Course he'd meant to stay in Halstead in those days.

A man blocked the doorway. "H'lo, Sam; Hauser. I thought I saw you go in here. Come an' tell me what you think of this butter."

Max followed Fletcher into another cave a few doors

down. He'd known Fletcher in the old days; shipped into him. . . . A. L. Fletcher, Dairy Products. The two men waited while the salesman thrust a sampler into the heart of one of the butter tubs and passed it to Max.

Max tasted the morsel of butter gravely. For a second there was silence in the narrow store.

"Well, sir, I think you're out on this lot; poor stuff, below standard. Better send it out to the yards for oleo."

"Thanks, Hauser! I'll turn it down then; there's no call for it in the yards. Packers aren't taking any; shipping in their own stuff from Nebraska. Now if you were out there in Nebraska, we'd know where we could write to, but I guess even you couldn't buck Packers Incorporated."

Max stepped back out on the Street, trying to pick up his thoughts. If he were out on his own the way he'd meant to be, it would be a gamble, but so was anything. Plenty of men had come down on the Street and made a sizable fortune . . . not worth a cent one day, several thousand another. You had to know a thing or two, that was all. Still, Salter had taken a loss of a thousand dollars on that load the other day, and Salter knew the ropes. You had to have capital to play the Street on your own and come out on top. Even if he could raise the money, borrow it back in Nebraska, it was too uncertain. There were Julia and the children. Julia was a good manager, but she had to be able to count on something coming in steady.

At first after the bank failed he'd been pretty well licked. Then Salter had got wind of the fact he wasn't going in for himself and made him a proposition. He remembered how Jule had looked when he told her. "See, Max, I knew it would work out; now we know what we have to do with." He still felt queer about getting paid by the month, the way he used to pay the boys, but Jule was right; you had to know what you could count on. Max's face settled into the lines it took at poker, sometimes, when the cards were running against him.

He came to Klemper's and turned in, aware suddenly of the heat. Klemper was receiving a cartload of apples. Laborers were sorting and repacking them. The big dark store smelled like an orchard.

"H'lo, Max; have an apple?"

Max selected an apple carefully, discarding a couple first. Klemper took one, too. Both men took out their pocket knives and cut themselves sections while they talked.

"We've got a car of mixed green vegetables over in the Northwestern yards; got 'em in yesterday, late. If you can handle 'em, you can have 'em for what they cost to get here," Max offered impressively.

"Graded?" A quarter of an apple disappeared beneath Klemper's white mustache. He was old to be active on the Street. The risks on the Street were hard on a man; burned him up young, Salter used to say to Max, sometimes delighting in the ominous sound of his words. But Klemper didn't take big chances so much any more; that was why he was interested in an extra load like this without much risk to it. There was even talk on the Street of Klemper selling out.

"All graded; they're from a fellow in South Dakota; he's all right," Max answered, but he was wondering whether Klemper was any older than himself. Klemper got up heavily and took a sheet of quotations from a hook over his desk.

"If there's enough cucumbers and cauliflowers I can allow something," Klemper muttered, as though he weren't glad for the chance. "I'll remit through the Union National; give me the bill of lading."

Max turned back up the Street. He walked slowly, not bothering to size up the contents of the drays, not even looking in at the open doors. When the odor of fresh roasting coffee came from a wholesale grocery house across the river, covering over the stench of the sewer-filled water for a minute, he was unconscious of it. He was vaguely depressed. Heat was bad today. It was just like being back in Halstead, down here, he told himself again; adding hastily, on a bigger scale of course. But it wasn't. He was in for Salter. Salter gave him a free hand, but it wasn't the same. He couldn't take the risks nor the gains. Why, if he'd started out on his way to Klemper's with a few hundred dollars in his own name . . . The roar and flow and mad jumble of the Street went on around him. He was too busy figuring to know what a small figure he was, walking between the barrels and wholesale offices, borne along by the current.

Salter was out when he got back. The office was empty. Max hitched up his chair and pulled out the envelope, turning it impatiently on the other side. Suppose he had started out with five hundred dollars, say, and five hundred dollars wasn't much on the Street. On that peach deal alone . . . or suppose he were back in Halstead shipping stuff in, he could build up a business again. There were plenty of farmers all through there that would rather sell to him.

Max glanced up from his figures, dazzled a little by his own daring. An enormous lithograph of a golden horn of plenty from which tumbled bright green and red fruits stared back at him from the opposite wall. Beneath the fruits was printed in bold letters:

The Fruits of the Earth
Packers Incorporated

294

Unlimited capital, those words meant, all the new facilities. Salter was telling him how Packers Inc. and some of the big houses operated on a credit system that was way beyond the credit of the old days. Take the new refrigerator cars now; he had thought he was pretty up to date, but conditions were so different now; seemed as though you had to have everything to begin with or the big houses could crowd you right out. That fellow said this morning, "You old-timers must have had things pretty much your own way." The words sounded in his head now with a hollow sound. They made him feel out of the running; an old-timer he was to the folks around here; to Salter, too, maybe.

Max shoved the envelope from him. The stub of a pencil rolled across the desk and rattled on the floor. He took out his handkerchief and mopped his neck. The heat sure took the starch out of a man.

9

"YOU know," said Signor Ricci in his low voice, "I hate to think of the Fair ending just because I shall miss you, Miss Hauser." Anne blushed. She examined a little thread on the finger of one glove.

They were finishing dinner together. Anne felt only the least little bit guilty. After all she had stayed late to help Miss Simms as she told Mamma, and Mamma couldn't come to the Fair tonight as she had told Signor Ricci. Anyway she was practically a woman now. . . . Still, it wasn't exactly proper.

"I think we should go," she managed in a half-frightened voice. "I mean, don't you think it would be nice to walk?" She wouldn't look at him until the feeling of color in her face stopped. He pulled back the iron chair for her. She couldn't think what to say next. She watched the other couples passing by. This was being grown-up. They walked along, stopping by the railing to look at the lagoon. The pillars of the Fisheries Building were mirrored in it. "Isn't it lovely tonight?"

"Your mother is an understanding woman. She understands what it is to be young," Signor Ricci said, trailing his cane against the balustrades. It made a brittle whacking sound. "In my country this would be impossible, and yet how natural it is!"

Anne was silent. How natural it was. The light was changing a little; the lagoon was green, obscuring in its shadows the image of the pillars. Then a gondola came by slowly, quietly.

Signor Ricci looked at her. "You said the other day that you hadn't been in one of the gondolas."

Anne laughed lightly. She heard her own laugh and was almost shocked by it.

The gondola came alongside the low steps. The gondolier wore a wide red sash. He was romantic. Signor Ricci helped her in. The boat floated away from the sidewalk and the people, on water that was a dark mirror. They went under the arched bridge. It was funny sitting so low in the boat, almost like sitting on the floor. A whole chain of water-ways opened beyond the bridge. You couldn't tell in the beginning where you were going. Anne felt Signor Ricci looking at her.

"It's like Venice, Miss Anne."

"How nice." The frilled jabot on her shirt-waist trembled idiotically. She hoped he didn't notice. It wasn't what he said exactly; it was the tone of his voice.

The gondola was moving toward the wooded island. The

gondolier began to sing huskily behind them. Signor Ricci leaned his head back and said something in Italian.

"Si, Signor," the boatman answered eagerly, in a deep rumbly voice; then he began to sing:

"Ogni sera di sotto al mio balcone"

"The title is *Forbidden Music*," said Signor Ricci. "It is exquisite, I think."

Something within her vibrated. She was no more Anne Hauser. She was made just to answer the yearning in the song. Her hand was in Signor Ricci's between them on the cushioned seat; his hand was warm on her own cold one. It helped to stand the wistful sadness of the song. She had learned some Italian words; now she understood, "Your lips, your eyes . . ." The song ended. The water splashed against the pole. As they slid close to the bank of the wooded island there was a dank smell, strangely sharp, unpleasant; it pricked her nostrils. Then the boat slid away again from reality. It left behind the bank of the wooded island, the dank smell of water on half-rotted wood. Everything was unreal. It was so quiet underneath the hood of the boat after the gondolier's song.

"You are strangely young and yet strangely old, Miss Anne; is it a gift in your family?"

She hated even to swallow for fear he might stop. Not meaning to, her fingers tightened a second on his. His fingers closed tighter. Uneasiness spoiled her delight.

"Anne, I have written my father about you, about your mother. Of course in my country it would be different. Oh, Anne, you are lovely. . . ." He put his arm around her abruptly. His face was so close to hers in the dark of the boat's hood she could feel his breath. She pulled back against the low seat. Panic seized her.

"Oh, Signor Ricci, please, please don't." She turned her head away. What if he should kiss her!

The boatman began to sing again, the same words over. The strange syllables cut deep grooves in her mind. Her frightened fingers played with the frill of the jabot.

"I—I want to go right home. Tell him, please!"

"Why, Anne, don't be frightened; you're just shy." His voice didn't make her think of her violin. She was afraid; no, angry. She sat up as straight as she could on the low seat.

"Please, tell him . . ."

Signor Ricci leaned out and spoke to the boatman. Anne watched the tall curved prow of the boat cutting across the water toward the white steps. She couldn't tell where it was. They came alongside; there was that smell of damp wood pricking at her nostrils. The boat grazed against the step. Signor Ricci got out and took her hand.

Maybe she had been silly. "Please, I have to go," she said reluctantly. "I didn't tell Mamma. . . . If you'll just put me in a hansom cab. . . ." Her voice trailed off in confusion.

"I couldn't do that. I'll take you to your home."

"No, I want to go alone." There was a sharpness in her voice.

He shrugged ever so slightly. "As you will, believe me, I . . ."

"Oh, please, don't let's talk." Perhaps he was hurt. . . . They had seemed so far away out there. Why, there was Cottage Grove Avenue! The cable cars reassured her.

When she reached home the front door was open. The little light on the stair-landing showed through the screen. It was safe in there. She wondered why she had been so frightened. She ran up the stairs. She was mortified now. . . . Signor Ricci would think . . . She could never go back to the Italian exhibit. She squirmed a little, thinking of it.

"Mamma!" They were all in the front room. Then she stopped in the doorway. There was a stranger.

"Anne," Mamma was saying, "this is a nephew of your Aunt Polly's, Joseph Foley."

"How do you do?" Anne nodded. The young man was not so tall as Signor Ricci, nor so slim. He must be older, though. He was smiling at her, but he looked embarrassed. His embarrassment put her suddenly at her ease.

"Joseph is going to be in Chicago, and your Aunt Polly sent him to us," Papa was saying.

"Cousin Joe, you wait till you see the Fair!" Louise told him.

"Cousin" . . . he was really a kind of cousin, then.

"I hear you have an appointment at the Fair," he said to Anne. She felt he was too embarrassed to call her by her name.

"Oh, yes, you must come in and let me show you the Italian jewelry," she answered, smiling back at him.

10. OCTOBER

"HERE, Jeanette!" Julia signaled the conductor. It was impressive, Jeanette thought, getting off in the dead silence while the conductor held the bell cord and all the passengers on the street car sat silent watching you. Mamma looked as though she were thinking about things. She waited a minute on the corner looking at the street sign. It said "Larchwood Street." Mamma looked up and down. Then Jeanette knew: they were looking to see where they'd live when the Fair was over. Jeanette looked up and down the street now too, seeing the maple trees, each in its wire cage. The leaves were yellow and some were caught inside the cage and rustled a little. The houses were large and comfortable-looking, built of wood, set far back from the street in wide yards, surrounded by fences. It was quiet on the street away from the street cars.

"Oh, Mamma, what cunning balconies!"

Julia was looking in her bag for a card. "2316," she murmured aloud. "Look, Jeanette, for . . . That's 2308 over there. . . . It will be on that side."

They came to it almost at the end of the street and went up the steps of the porch. Sunk in the porch post was a brass plate that was polished to a gleaming luster. It read, "The Harrington."

Jeanette felt the letters cut into the brass with her finger-tips as they went past the post. Perhaps they would live here! Mamma rang the bell. Jeanette could hear the ringing far back in the house. It made the house seem deep. A maid opened the door. It was like being back home.

"I came to see the flat that is vacant," Julia began.

"Yessum. I'll get the key. Mrs. Harrington left word."

They crossed the vestibule. Jeanette saw the red tile under her feet. Blue diamonds made a pattern in the center. It felt under her feet like the floor in Mr. Jenks' bank at home. The hall was dim and cool after the sun outside. A big hatrack faced the door. It had lion heads on the arms. There were Mamma and herself looking back at them from the great square mirror. Jeanette smiled at herself.

"You jus' go right upstairs an' see it fo' yourself, ma'am."

They went up the oak stairs. The carved balustrades made little windows on the second landing. The wall along the stairs was dark red and rough, kind of pebbly, like a real wall instead of wallpaper. There was a stained-glass window on the landing that made purple and green and red squares on the stairs.

Mamma unlocked the door at the head of the stairs. This must be theirs, Jeanette thought.

"This would be the sitting-room," Mamma was saying.

"Look, Mamma, there's a fireplace with a make-believe log in it."

"A gas-log," Mamma said. Mamma stood by the big front window looking out at the street. Jeanette went over to look, too. You could look right into the tops of the maple trees. There was a little handle on each side of the window. If you turned it this way the blind moved toward the window. It was fun.

"Don't, Jeanette, don't touch things," Mamma said in a voice that showed she really didn't mind.

The built-in sideboard in the dining-room was nice. Then there was a pantry and a kitchen, not just a gas-plate.

"Oh, Mamma! this must be Louise's and my room. Look at the window-seat." It would be like home again. She could hear Mamma walking across to the next room. Her feet on the bare floor made a loud noise. Jeanette went on to the bathroom. There was a bathtub with claw feet and a marble washbasin. They must live here. Then a sudden doubt sent her to find Mamma.

"But, Mamma, we sold our furniture, didn't we?" The rooms yawned before her, large, empty, echoing.

Mamma nodded.

"Will we buy new furniture? Can I have a real dresser all my own?"

"We'll have to manage, just at first. It won't be convenient for a while, Jeanette, to furnish the rooms permanently."

"Oh." Just for a while, but afterwards . . . Jeanette went back to the bedroom with the window-seat. She knelt on the seat and looked out again across a strip of careful green

301

lawn to another wooden wall, cut into by heavily curtained windows. She wouldn't really mind if the Fair ended next week, then they could begin living here. A man came out of the house and raked the yellow leaves off the grass. Maybe when he got a pile he would make a fire, and it would smell like fall at home.

Julia walked back to the sitting-room and stood in the bow window. This was the sort of place she had been looking for. All the rest of the houses on this block were private homes; and the Harringtons, themselves, lived on the first floor here.

She would buy furniture at the second-hand stores, just the necessary things at first. Anne could go to the Art Institute; Jeanette could start in at Armour Institute; perhaps next year she could take dramatics. Louise must go to the fashionable convent school from the beginning.

Julia looked around the empty room. She remembered how she had planned her drawing-room. It was to have a malachite mantel and portières. She could still see it as clearly as though she had lived in it. When you were younger you were so sure things must be a certain way. Then they were different, and after a while you even stopped being surprised.

If they could just manage this for the children; they would be so safe here. What would Max say to thirty-five dollars for rent? Still, considering the location . . .

"Mamma, are we going to live here?"

"Yes, Jeanette." Julia's voice had no doubt in it. Doubts were for herself, not the children.

Jeanette went down to the porch to wait while Mamma took the key back. The porch was hers now; the stone urns of flowers, the rustling trees with the leaves turning yellow. Across the street two houses down, a little girl her age sat on the wide step reading.

They stood on the corner waiting for the street car. There was none in sight. Julia lifted her big gold watch out of her belt and opened the case.

"It's five o'clock," she told Jeanette. Jeanette was tracing the intricacies of the iron fence with her fingers. The iron was blistered and a little rusty under her fingers. It had a crackly feeling. She had been so excited about the Harrington and the room with the window-seat and the stairway with the really stained-glass window. Then she remembered in Anne's room, when they were packing, Anne had told how it would be in Chicago, how Papa would buy a new house, bigger than the one in Halstead, and they would be very fashionable and have parties and go to parties. It made her uncomfortable. This house on Larchwood Street was nice, and it was bigger than their house in Halstead, but of course they were only having a flat in it. They wouldn't really own the porch and the flower urns. What if something were wrong?

"Here's the street car," Mamma said. Jeanette watched it coming, bobbing just as it always did, behind the two horses. She looked at Mamma. Mamma was stepping down from the curb toward the tracks. Jeanette followed. She wanted to take Mamma's hand the way Louise did, but Louise was only five. Something sure and safe and firm that had always been around her had slipped away.

"Look, Jeanette, you can see a little ways down Larchwood; how quiet it looks, like Halstead."

"Mamma? Mamma, are we just as—as rich as we used to be?" The car swerved.

"Why, Jeanette, what an idea. How silly!" Mamma laughed. Her eyes were very bright in the sun.

"Well, I just wondered about . . . Anne said we'd buy

a big house after the Fair, and we aren't going to." She spoke very close to Mamma's ear.

"In the city it is different, Jeanette; many people prefer to rent," Mamma explained.

"Oh!" Jeanette sat back. She slid along a little on the straw seat, nearer the outside where it was grandly terrifying, her eyes speculative, dancing. "Mamma, the room with the window-seat will be my room, won't it?"

Julia nodded, but her eyes had taken on Jeanette's worried expression. She sat very straight in the seat. The sun made a streak down the car along the outside edge. Jeanette's hat, her rounded chin, the folds of her skirt, were glinted with the light. Only Julia was over too far for the streak of bright sun.

11. OCTOBER 28

"MAX, you must get to the Fair tonight; you've only been three times this whole summer." Julia looked across the supper table at him. The children had finished. Their empty dishes marked their places. Jeanette and Louise had gone out in front to play jacks on the pavement. Chris was down on the porch talking business with Mr. Lewis. Joseph Foley had been here for supper, and he and Anne had gone for a walk. . . . "Just eight blocks, Mamma; we'll be back before dark."

It was only seven, but the October dusk came earlier now. The yellow leaves of a spindly maple tree, just visible through the balcony, were one color with the dusk, fluttering languidly like sluggish bats. While they sat there, the gray dusk took on a bluish cast. Smoke and soot were part of it, giving it depth. Julia put off lighting the gas; the shadows of the room closed in around the window and the table in front of it, bringing a kind of intimacy. Max was silent so long Julia poured a third cup of coffee and added the cream and two lumps of sugar.

"Here, Max."

"Seems like home, Jule."

The remark twisted across Julia's mind leaving a little sting after it, like a whip. But then she knew Max missed Halstead.

"Max, we'll be settled over on Larchwood soon. That will seem more like home. I wish you'd go over and see it. The neighborhood really is the right sort for the children."

Max wiped his mustache carefully, then he crumpled the napkin and tossed it over on the table. He looked tired again tonight. If he would only answer her more quickly. . . .

"That's nice, Jule."

"Of course, Max, the rent is higher than I like."

"Rents are bound to be high here in Chicago, though," Max said judiciously, not objecting, accepting things as they were. She almost wished he would protest or have some new scheme so he would talk with the old excitement. She knew now without looking above her coffee cup that he was taking out his cigar, biting the end so that his teeth showed beneath his mustache.

"But you can't make a fuss," Max said; "the Fair's sent prices sky-high, but it's saved the city. I was talking to a man that sells to Marshall Field just yesterday; he says . . ."

Amazing that Max could feel interest in the town's upturn when all his own money was gone. Max pushed his chair back, the slumped, easy angle of his body looked so —so settled.

"And Salter was telling me . . ."

305

Max had owned his own business all the years they had been married. Now he was working for this man named Salter. Bitterness rose in Julia's throat. Things didn't come out even.

Max broke off as though he felt Julia wasn't listening to him. "I don't believe I want to go to the Fair tonight, Jule; would you be disappointed?"

"Max, the Fair will be closed in a couple of days. This is the twenty-eighth. You'll forget you're tired once you get there."

Max shifted in his chair. "All right, Jule; I thought maybe you'd had enough of the Fair. I don't care so much about it, you know."

Julia got up and carried out the dishes. She had had enough of the Fair today. She was tired, too, but she wanted to go some place with Max again. Max mustn't act so old.

She changed into her best china silk shirt-waist and the alpaca skirt and put on the hat with the blue velvet knot on it. Now she felt better.

"Max, do you need a clean handkerchief?" Her tone was blithe, like the old days.

"I have one, Jule."

The stairs were dark with only the gaslight on the stair landings. Max took her arm. For a second it gave her a feeling of security. She had gone everywhere alone or with the children since they had come to Chicago.

"Shall we take a hansom cab, Jule?"

"Of course not, Max." But Julia was grateful. . . . Max would never learn the ways or the words of petty economy. "The cars aren't crowded at this time of night."

And then they were sitting in the summer car that was open at both sides. The summer cars would be all taken off next week when the Fair ended. Julia dreaded every

306

sign of the end. If she could only be sure how things would turn out after the Fair. It was a good feeling to have rented that flat in the Harrington. But anyway there was no going back to Halstead and all of its tight smug little ways. Julia lifted her head as though to feel the fresh air blowing through the open car. She glanced at Max.

He was drowsing. His chin rested on his tie. His hat was down over his forehead a little. He really had been too tired to come. He had only come for her. There was the sag in his shoulders. Why did she have to keep noticing it? She looked at his hands resting loosely on his knee. It came to her that she hadn't looked at his hands in years, really. You grew so used to people, she to Max, you forgot to see anything but their faces. The skin on his hands was wrinkled under the hairs. There were brown spots on the skin. Did they used to be there? She couldn't remember. Strange not to know Max's hands. Strange not to know Max better. Back in Halstead, though, it had been the same way; Max was so busy. There had been so much to do, so much to think of, that Max wouldn't be interested in.

The car lurched around the corner. Julia took hold of the seat in front of her to steady herself. Max woke.

"Forty winks," he said loudly above the car's noise. He rubbed his eyes, twisted the ends of his mustache, adjusted his hat, making sure of himself.

"Pretty?" Julia called back and nodded her head at the lights of the Fair, calmly in spite of her delight; some part of her always leaped when she saw those lights.

Now she and Max were following toward the entrance with the rest of the crowd. The crowd surrounded them, gave out a kind of warmth and made her feel snug.

"Let's just look in at my building, Max, to see . . ." Her voice trailed away apologetically.

Max stopped to light his cigar. The glow showed the debonair line of his mustache, the dark flash of his eyes. Julia watched. He threw his match away, and they set off briskly. She began to feel exhilarated. Max wasn't tired after he got here; she had been right to get him to come.

There weren't many people in the Hostess House to-night. Only a couple of more days of the Fair. Most of the world had been here and was back home now talking about it. Julia went into her little office. Max followed. She turned on the droplight over her desk.

"Why, Max, look; Dr. Chapman's been here. Here's his card."

Max read the card: "Tried to find you here first. Jenks gave me your address. I'll call there tonight. Chapman."

"We must go right back, Jule. He might be there now. I wondered if he wouldn't get around to coming to the Fair." Max was excited; anyone from Halstead excited him.

"But, Max, we've just come. We can't go yet!" Why couldn't Dr. Chapman have come last month? There was enough to plan for and think about now without Dr. Chapman's being here. "He'll wait there, Max; probably he won't go over till late. The children will entertain him." An uncomfortable nervousness possessed her. She pushed the locket up and down on her watch chain.

"I'd rather see someone from Halstead than all the build-ings of the Fair, Jule."

They were walking out of the Hostess House now. Max was not like her, Julia thought; he was more genuine. He didn't care if Dr. Chapman saw them in those rooms. Probably the Jenks had told him all about them, anyway. Perhaps he had come out of pity. . . . No, that wasn't so; Dr. Chapman wasn't like that. . . .

"I remember, Jule, when I first met Chapman. He sat

in on a game at the Golden House. I couldn't believe he was the doctor, he looked so young."

Even Max's tone of voice was excited. She was excited, too. She was glad she had worn her blue hat and silk shirt-waist.

"Max, let's just walk through the Manufacturers' Building, then we'll go."

Max wasn't looking, though. People were all that mattered to Max. Things didn't interest him. But it was the things that people saw that made them different; even Dr. Chapman said so.

"Look, Max, did you ever see anything lovelier than the fairy lamps?" Why did she try to put off going? Max stood still on the step looking across the bridge at the Electricity Building.

"I wonder if Chapman saw that. Too bad we missed him out here."

Just at the Italian façade, Julia thought, she saw Signor Ricci. Anne hadn't mentioned him for weeks. Max had never known about him. He didn't approve of Anne's position, anyway. Joseph had come along just at the right time. Joseph was . . . safe. He would never give her poetry. Yes, it was Signor Ricci. She bowed. Max bowed, too, unseeingly.

"You've enjoyed meeting folks here at the Fair, haven't you, Jule?"

"Yes, indeed, Max," Julia answered, suddenly humbled at Max's reaching over into her world.

"Well, I've met some fine fellows on the Street. Say, Jule, if we get off at Thirty-ninth Street we can stop in somewhere and buy some delicatessen. Chapman loves a celebration."

"All right, Max." There was that time when Lissa Monteroy was in Halstead. She had invited the Jenks and

Withers and Dorsetts over, and served wine and little cakes. Dr. Chapman had left early, stamping out in the rain with his talk about lobster. Julia's mouth twitched. "Max, see if you can get a lobster. Dr. Chapman loves it."

"And some cheese, Jule; maybe an Edam."

By the time they reached home Julia was as eager as Max to see Dr. Chapman. She picked up her skirt and ran up the stairs as Anne might have done.

"Oh, Mamma, we couldn't go to bed cause Dr. Chapman's here." Jeanette came running out to the stairs. Dr. Chapman followed her.

"How do you do, Julia."

"How do you do, Dr. Chapman." It was just the way it had always been.

"Well, well!" Max stopped to cough. It made him cough to come upstairs so fast. "We hustled back from the Fair to find you."

"Mamma, please can we go with Dr. Chapman to the Fair tomorrow?" Louise begged.

"Did he invite you?" Julia looked down at her to laugh gently.

"Yes, he did, Mamma, truly." Julia met Dr. Chapman's eye over Louise's head.

"Come, children, you should all be in bed."

"Oh, Mamma, not tonight."

"Never mind, chickens, we'll celebrate tomorrow." Dr. Chapman winked at them. Anne looked at Joseph. Chris looked uneasy, not sure that his age gave him exemption.

Julia shook her head at Anne. Anne was old enough, but not tonight. Tonight just she and Max and Dr. Chapman. She felt suddenly gay, irresponsible.

"Oh, Mamma, you're going to have a party," Louise moaned, poking into Max's packages.

"We'll save some for you, Louise." Julia's voice was firm.

Joseph bowed. "Good night, Mrs. Hauser. Good night, sir; pleased to have met you."

Joseph did have good manners. But Anne was so young. Julia wondered if Max noticed how much he was there. She brushed it aside to think of later.

The children disappeared into their rooms. Dr. Chapman must notice how cramped they were here. No matter, it was good to see him.

"You're looking well, Julia, in spite of the summer."

"Oh, it's been a wonderful summer, Dr. Chapman."

"It must have been," Dr. Chapman answered, looking steadily at her. There was his old bitter way of saying things. He always cut below the surface. Other people talked about things on the top as though they were afraid to go any deeper.

"We stopped on the way home to get some lobster for you, Dr. Chapman," Julia said aloud.

He put back his head and laughed. It was good to hear him laugh again.

Julia picked up the packages and hurried out to the kitchen corner. Max was out there pouring wine into the little glasses. They were only cheap ones, not like the real cut-glass ones in the sideboard in Halstead . . . no matter.

It would take all the butter for breakfast to make the sauce for the lobster. She shouldn't have told Max to get lobster; it must have been expensive. She dropped the scallops of butter into the pan.

"This is like old times, Max," she heard Dr. Chapman say.

"Can we help, Julia?" Dr. Chapman called.

"No, I'll only be a few minutes." Let them talk a bit.

It would do Max so much good. She would ask Dr. Chapman how he thought Max was; about that bad cough of his. It worried her; he seemed so short of breath sometimes. There, the water was boiling. Dear, if she'd only thought to say a lemon, too.

She had a rich sense of pleasure. What it actually was escaped her for the minute as she stirred the butter gently. Then it came to her: Dr. Chapman knew how hard it must have been here. He didn't blame her for bringing them all here; he even . . . There was admiration in his eyes. Julia moved across a stage of her own setting to put the heated platter on a tray.

"Max, if that had happened to me, I'd have given up. Why, Ned Jenks came back and told us that in a week's time you were down on South Water Street behind a desk. . . ." He whistled.

Julia stepped into the wings and saw Max now, taking his steady way across the stage. Max hadn't complained. He had scarcely mentioned it after that first night. She had had so much to think of; sometimes she had felt Max might take more responsibility; still, Max had been brave. People in Halstead weren't pitying them. . . . She got out her best cloth from the trunk.

"Oh, Julia, I'll tell you a funny one; the Literary Club had a banquet at Mrs. Kauf's. Here, let me carry those things in for you. My, it smells good!" Max came out, too. He was beaming.

They made a procession along the dark hall. The children weren't asleep yet. She could hear Louise and Jeanette talking.

"Oh, Max, I forgot the cream for the coffee. There!" Julia placed the lobster on the table with a flourish.

"This is a feast, Julia. To tell you the truth, I was so disappointed to miss you I didn't bother to eat much supper. I wandered around and gaped at a few things and then decided that what I had come for was to see you."

Julia was suddenly shy. She couldn't lift her eyes to Dr. Chapman. She straightened the cloth under the wine bottle.

"Well!" Max came back with the cream. "This beats sightseeing at the Fair. Say, we had a fine time with Regan and Ned and their wives. Regan's just the same; hasn't changed a bit."

Julia poured the coffee for the second time that night.

"Are you still eating your meals at the Golden House, Dr. Chapman?"

"Yes, but Golden sold out this summer. It's still under the same name, but a young man from St. Louis runs it now. He's turned the place topsy-turvy trying to make it like St. Louis. He has shell oysters on the menu now; next thing he'll be putting on lobster dinners."

"Pretty difficult proposition shipping lobster out that far!" Max remarked. "It'll come, though."

"I haven't eaten any yet in Halstead," Dr. Chapman murmured dryly. "You have to go a long way to get lobster, don't you, Julia?"

It was his old silly way of talking. What he meant was . . . Julia sipped her wine.

"I had a great time with the children. They've surely gotten plenty from the Fair," Dr. Chapman chuckled.

"Yes." Julia turned to him glowing.

"Did Chris tell you he wants to go into business?" Max asked. "Here, Chapman, give me your glass."

"N'EXTRA . . . ALL ABOUT THE MURDER . . ." came shrilly up to them from the street. Julia's hand flew to her throat. Max went to the window still carrying the bottle of wine. Dr. Chapman followed.

"MAYOR HARRISON ASSASSINATED . . . READ ALL ABOUT THE MURDER," voices of other newsboys took it up farther away.

Max leaned over the false balcony and whistled. "I'll go get a paper." Mrs. Daggerty's boarding-house seemed full of people running along the hall and down the stairs. Julia and Dr. Chapman looked at each other, but not seeing, only listening to the newsboys' cries.

Max came back, reading the paper as he came. He spread it out before them, shaking his head.

"Mayor Harrison shot tonight at his home by disappointed office-seeker." The type stared up at them.

"What do you think of that?" Max said heavily. "There was a lot said against him, but he had the city back of him all the same. Never could have been a Fair like this without him!"

"What a pity to be killed just now!" Julia said softly.

"Confounded crank!" Dr. Chapman muttered. "The world's full of such half-crazy people running at large."

They were no longer in a quiet sitting-room. The full current of the city itself flowed through it. They sat oddly silent.

"He'll be a big loss to the city. We needed him to get us through the winter," Max murmured.

Julia caught the "we." Max's saying it about Chicago touched her. She looked up to catch Dr. Chapman's eyes.

"You can't get away from murders," he said to her in a low voice. She knew he was thinking of James Dorsett.

"Mamma, what happened?" The children were standing out in the hall.

"Who killed him, Papa?" Chris called in.

"And you can't keep children from knowing about them either," Dr. Chapman said to her while Max was talking to the children.

"Papa, did he die cause the Fair's going to stop?" Louise came running in in her nightgown. She was almost crying.

Max picked her up to take her back to bed. The newsboys were farther down the street now, but the distance added to the frightening quality of the night. Only a garbled echo came back to them.

Julia looked up to find Dr. Chapman looking at her as though he were studying her.

"But this is entirely different," she said, going back to what he had said. She thought of the children following James Dorsett's body up the street. "Everybody will honor Mayor Harrison. He was a figure. . . . She hesitated.

"Well, Dorsett was a figure, too, in a way, but he was a victim of the sort of thing you were taking the children from."

Julia looked away from the table out the window. Sometimes Dr. Chapman irritated her.

Blocks away another newsboy called faintly, "All about the murder!" The strident call gave the dark outside the window an ominous quality. Lights from the house across the street scratched the darkness. Other sounds, of late hansom cabs, and the periodic cable cars, came up through the window. That other night, at Faith Dorsett's, there had been only a heavy stillness.

"I did take them away," Julia said, feeling Dr. Chapman still looking at her.

"And yourself, too, Julia."

Julia was glad that Max came back then.

"Carter Harrison must have felt satisfied about the Fair, anyway," Max said; "it's put Chicago on its feet."

"I must be going." Dr. Chapman got up in his old quick way. "I'll be back early in the morning to pick up the children. That's enough melodrama for tonight."

There was that old flatness in his voice. Julia heard it,

but without feeling it herself. She picked up the glasses to carry them back to the kitchen.

12. JULY—1894

"THIS Debs ought to be tarred and feathered! If we had him in Nebraska in the old days, Jule, we could fix him!" Max thumped his newspaper on his knee so emphatically Jeanette and Louise both looked up from their paper-dolls. "Why, if this business of bombarding trains and rioting keeps up, the whole country'll be living on vege-tables. I was talking to a man today; he says the stock-yards look as though cattle had stopped breeding."

Julia sat mending on the other side of the table. The windows on the balcony stood open to the soft July night. Up here the strikes and fantastic industrial warfare of the city seemed only some of Max's talk. But it was good to see Max so excited. He was more like he used to be. Per-haps his heart was better.

Max turned the page with an impatient rattle, then he laid it down again. "I think a lot more of Cleveland for the stand he's taken. Yes, sir, he sent the troops out here in a hurry."

"Say, Pop, Bundy Williamson said today that he wouldn't be surprised to hear some of these radicals had shot Cleve-land!" Chris sat on the edge of the couch. He was eager to talk with Max about politics or business. Sometimes Julia smiled over him and the new importance that work-ing had given him in his own eyes.

"If anyone could have told last summer what the sum-mer of '94 would be like . . ." Max began.

Last summer! Ever since May Julia had been measur-ing back to last summer and the Fair. When she passed the white buildings standing empty along the lake-front, she wished she could bring the Fair back, even with the uncertainties and worries. The children felt that way, too.

"Do you remember last summer, Mamma, when . . ." Jeanette would say.

Once Anne had said, "I wonder if Signor Ricci is back in Italy?" And the story of the gondola ride had come out. "Oh, Mamma, I did . . . admire him so. I don't know why I was scared that night," she had said wistfully.

Julia looked over at her now. Anne was sitting across from Max, listening but not listening, withdrawn a little into herself. She was embroidering a pillow-case. She was so slender; her eyes were a soft blue that looked easily scornful, easily hurt. Even sitting there she was intense; her mouth twisted a little as she worked. Whatever she had it must be the loveliest or she felt a kind of anguish.

Anne was engaged to marry Joseph in the fall. Joseph was in California now. He was making money. Anne would be able to live well, to have time to go on with her art work.

"Look, Mamma! I didn't get it even." Anne looked up in dismay.

"Here, Anne, let me take it." Julia took the embroidery. "See, Anne, keep your cloth taut between the hoops."

"I don't agree with the Governor at all; the men ought to be starved till they're ready to work," Max burst out with sudden irritation.

"All the strikers couldn't be anarchists, though, could they, Pop?" Chris asked, but more as his own opinion than as a question.

Julia's needle flashed in and out. How hopeless it must be in those homes with nothing coming in; men sitting around, not daring to go to work because of the Union.

She glanced up to see Jeanette and Louise listening spellbound to Max.

"Papa, we saw where the horse was shot in the fight!" Louise announced proudly.

"We did, really, on Grand Boulevard, where the cannon exploded," Jeanette broke in. Her eyes were round with excitement. The children were living in the excitement and unrest of the city as they had lived the Fair. Julia had a moment of satisfaction in them. Well, why not exult in them, in their aliveness? Even Chris seemed less slow. When Anne came back from the Thomas concerts, or Jeanette practiced hours by herself for the dramatic art class, Julia thought proudly, they would have had none of this in Halstead. The children mentioned Halstead less and less. She wondered, sometimes, if they missed it at all. Of course with Max it was different; he would never get over missing Halstead and his business. Julia checked her own thoughts; she had grown so into the habit of sewing and thinking, justifying herself, trying to make things come out even all through this hard year. She who had meant to enjoy the city—concerts, new friends—had been here at home trying to cover up their "reduced circumstances" from the children—

"Jeanette, Louise, it's time for . . ."

The shriek of a siren drowned her voice.

"It's the fire alarm! It must be a 4-11!" Chris ran to the balcony. The other children crowded after him. Max was out of his chair. The warm summer night was suddenly filled with the clatter of vehicles drawn by galloping horses, of whistles shrieking terror into the sky.

"Max, what could it be?"

"You can see more on the back porch." Chris was already halfway there. "Papa, look at the smoke! It must be the Fair buildings!"

318

"I'm going out on the street," Max said. Chris went after him.

"Can we go, Mamma?"

"No, you stay here." Julia could hear herself speaking quietly. It might be a second Chicago fire. She couldn't take her eyes from the gusts of black smoke across the lake.

"Do you think it could be the Administration Building?" Anne asked almost in a whisper.

"Look, Mamma, the sky looks as if it were an illumination night!" Jeanette exclaimed, her face thrilled as though seeing it again just as it had been.

The weird light creeping up above the smoke illumined the back porch, making the ice-chest stand out, showing Louise's hair bright yellow. All the trees on the streets were a queer yellow-green. People were crowding by as though it were Chicago Day again at the Fair.

Jeanette caught her breath as a tower stood out a moment against the red glow and then toppled into darkness. Suddenly Anne burst into wild sobbing.

"Oh, Mamma, it's all going!" She buried her head in her lap. Louise whimpered half in fright, half in sympathy with Anne. Jeanette stood close to the railing, her hand clenched into a fist against her mouth, her eyes fixed across the lake.

"There'll never, never be anything like it again, I know," Anne wailed.

Julia stood by Jeanette watching. A sense of calamity chilled through her. The Fair had ended a year ago, but the empty white buildings along the lake had been there. Now they were going while she watched.

"Anne, children," Julia was aware again of her own voice speaking quietly, "you can't ever forget it; you saw all of it!"

Strange exaltation surged through her. She forgot Louise clinging to her, Anne, Jeanette standing so tensely silent. Her life of making over dresses, counting pennies, doubting and worrying no longer oppressed her. This was the feeling she had had before, at that other, lesser Fair years ago, the feeling that exciting things were around her, ahead of her, but anyway and whatever happened, she was equal to them. It was a feeling of strength.

But the black smoke was gathering volume now, wiping out all the color. Even the dark sky was light above it. The blotting out of the flames made the warm summer night seem cold to Julia standing there on the porch. The weird clamor of the engines and fire alarms and thin human voices passing by on the street broke into her mood of exaltation. Julia shivered and turned away.

"Will it be all out tonight, Mamma?" Louise asked.

"Not tonight. It will smolder for a long time," Julia said.

PART FOUR THE BIRD OF TIME – 1933

IN THE center of a wide stone-paved court that served for dining a large magnolia tree had been inveigled into growth. Now the sky-lights above it were opened and noon-day sun poured directly down on the twisted branches and the pink-white petals. The long oval-shaped blossoms cast shadows on the neighboring tables. A few petals lay care-lessly on the paving, one already had been bruised into yellowing shreds by the waiters' feet. The curiously heavy fragrance of the blossoms lay upon the court, keeping its identity apart from the savory smells of broiled steak, fresh mushrooms, chicken à la Magnolia Court and the hearty aroma of coffee that lifted into the air from the passing trays. It was not affected by the varied perfumes of the women at the tables nor by the smoke of the cig-arettes.

"Nice; it really is, Stanton." Louise Ryder looked at

the petaled shadows on the paving and the green awnings above the tables. "But it would have kept, wouldn't it? I didn't need to see it this particular day."

"Perhaps, but I had to see you here on this particular day," Stanton Blair answered gravely.

"But, Stanton, I was to have lunch at the Fair with my mother. She's going to fly to California; she's leaving this very afternoon. At seventy-four that is something! All of us are to be there, sort of a family occasion. I explained it all to you."

"I'm sorry," Blair answered; "I'm unmoved, though. Tomorrow there would have been something else. You've made rather a point of not seeing me all week."

A waiter wheeled a cart of hors d'œuvres to the table.

"These are excellent. Spécialité de la maison, n'est-ce pas?" Blair smiled at the waiter. "Here, Louise, let me choose them for you. I've tried them all."

Louise let him do it. She leaned back and studied the gray-green colors of the court. As an interior decorator she looked at all effects with a calculating eye.

"Imagine finding a place that depends neither on mirrors nor fountains for its decoration but on sunshine and a single magnolia tree! But it can't be paying very well."

"Why do you say that? Its clientele is the best in Chicago. Besides not wishing to be indelicate, the prices are, shall we say, fitting?" He put the menu in her hands. "Consider if you must be hard-headed."

"Yes, but in the long run it isn't the select clientele, it's the popularity of a place that makes it a success. I am hard-headed, that's my virtue."

Stanton Blair watched her, delighting in her.

Louise Ryder felt that delight.

Then he said, "This is the perfect background for you. This and Rome."

"How unfortunate to need a background, though."

"You know what I mean, Louise; don't be brittle."

"I'm not. I'm getting mellow, I'm afraid. One does at forty-five."

He looked at her. "Nor flippant."

"I won't be. Middle-aged women who are flippant are impossible."

"Perhaps we better not talk at all," he suggested with the whimsical smile that made him look younger than he was.

"Seriously, I must eat and run. I told my sister I would meet her at twelve-thirty in front of the Belgium Village at the Fair. I can't make that now, but I can be there as they finish."

"Seriously, I must talk to you, Louise. I'm going to Rome next week. It will be bad in July, but we could take a long time getting there. I want you to go with me."

"But, Mr. Blair!" Louise made a face of shocked surprise.

"Louise, I thought you weren't going to be flippant."

"Oh, you mean as Mrs. Blair!"

Stanton Blair made a wry face and lighted a fresh cigarette. "Now you are being flippant. You know my situation."

"I'm sorry; I'm touched, really."

"Touched isn't really the word."

"Oh, Stanton, I shouldn't have come to lunch with you in the first place. I should be at the Fair. I can't talk now. It's twelve-thirty already."

"It's too late to meet them there then. I'll drive you out to the aviation field. When does the plane go, do you know?"

"Two-forty-five, I think."

The waiter changed the plates and poured a demi-tasse

of coffee. People straggled over the paved court, disturbing the shadows of the magnolia blossoms. The sun passed under a cloud and the courtyard was more gray than green.

"Of course there is Colton; he might not care about having his mother involved in a scandal," Louise said, as one considering.

"He's in college. I mean, it seems scarcely sensible to consider him. It's your own life after all."

"And why Rome?"

"I'm going to look into a painting there, but that's a story in itself. I rather want it."

"And you want me. A profitable trip if you secure both."

"You're in a charming mood!"

"That's because I shouldn't have come at all."

"I think marriages at fifty are always a trifle odd, don't you?" Stanton said dryly.

Stanton Blair was married for the second time. Louise thought of that, looking over at him, and yet, it didn't really matter. Even today when he insisted she come to lunch with him she had phoned Anne that she couldn't get to the Fair. She had gone about all morning with a tremulous excitement within her. Stanton Blair was the son of Mrs. C. Walton Blair of that idiotic old brownstone pile on the north side.

Stanton was watching her. When the light breeze moved the branch of the magnolia tree, a shadow fell across her face. It was a lovely face, he thought, so fair, and yet with a sense of vitality that was rare in so large a woman. Stanton Blair had been educated as a connoisseur.

Louise Ryder reached over and picked up a petal that had fallen on an iron bench. The skin of the petal was strangely tough, unpleasant in her fingers, like the white of an egg. There had been a magnolia tree in the garden in Germantown where she had lived before Colton died, where little Colton was born, before she had become a successful business woman. She had used to break a few branches where it wouldn't spoil the tree and put them in a mulberry-colored jug in the hall. Life wasn't so simple now. After all, at forty-five it was something to have Stanton Blair wanting her.

And her son was a modern young man. Perhaps he had his own ideas about life. Certainly he didn't want her to think of him. Children didn't ever thank you for what you did, or didn't do.

She looked at her watch. It was one-thirty.

She pushed back her chair and stood up out of the shadows of the magnolia branch.

"Stanton, I've got to go. Do you think you can get me there in time? Mamma would feel dreadfully if I weren't there to see her off."

"Certainly," Stanton said courteously.

They walked across the gray-paved court. She thought of Mamma who had dragged them all out of Nebraska so they could see the whole Fair, and live in Chicago afterwards. She always acted as though that Fair were priceless, something you couldn't do without. Louise could remember some of it: tagging along with Jeanette, the feeling of excitement. And then, afterwards, Mamma had scrimped to put her in the best schools. . . . Children didn't ever thank you for what you did.

She had never thanked Mamma. She couldn't even get there in time to see her off on a trip. Well, at least she wouldn't go to Rome.

"I remember your mother," Stanton Blair said casually, as someone who could follow the change of a mood. "I thought she was a jolly old lady."

"Oh, Stanton, I really have to see her off. Why, she'll be seeing Colton tomorrow night." That fact rushed over her suddenly.

Stanton's cigarette case closed with a snap. He glanced at his watch.

"We'll try to make it, anyway."

2

"SHE'LL be all tired out, Jeanette, before she goes and then with the excitement of flying, I think it's dangerous." Anne Foley spoke emphatically, turning her car off the boulevard into Larchwood Street.

"I always remember how wide I used to think this street when we first moved here," Jeanette Stone said irrelevantly.

"Furthermore," Anne went on, undiverted, "her keeping the old flat with all that absurd furniture in it is idiotic. She ought to be with one of us or in a hotel."

"Anne, you're way out from the curb."

Anne backed the car impatiently and drove closer. She dropped her keys in her black suède bag and got out of the car gracefully for a woman of her figure. She shifted her fur on her shoulder while she waited for Jeanette to come around.

"After I haven't been here for some time, I always remember the first day Mamma and I came to see it." Jeanette glanced up at the old-fashioned houses. "They've kept their dignity well. There's Mamma watching for us." They both waved, like children again.

"I'm so glad Mamma's going to get out of the city in this heat. She's just beginning to enjoy herself after being tied down so all those years when Papa was sick," Anne said.

"It's a pity she hasn't more grandchildren. She adores Therese and Colton so," Jeanette said.

Anne opened the front door and they went in. Jeanette saw the red and blue tiled vestibule. The hall was dim and cool after the sun outside. The big hatrack faced the door. She noticed, as always, the lion heads on the arms. There were Anne and herself looking back at them from the great square mirror.

Anne was a handsome woman, that just described her, Jeanette thought as she had before with secret amusement. Anne had rather a genius for clothes; that black cloche, that new dress fitted her perfectly. She looked exactly Mrs. Joseph Foley of the North Shore Drive. Her sensitiveness showed in her face; she still had that way of acting a little that matched her way of exaggerating when she talked. Mamma gave us all a sort of pride in each other, even in Chris, it came to Jeanette. Then she glanced at herself. Turbans did look best on her, and sheers. She wasn't nearly so large as Anne, but a little shorter. She was more like Mamma in build, other ways, too. Instinctively she smiled at herself.

They went upstairs. The carved balustrades made little windows on the second landing. The wall along the stairs was a faded red and rough, that dreadful stucco effect they used in the 'nineties. There was a stained-glass window on the landing that made horrible purple and green and red squares on the stairs. The purple light fell across Anne's face and the gray scallop of hair under her black cloche. It made her look older. Anne was harassed about Joseph's health. She was proud of Therese but a little worried, too. A daughter who was a concert-singer wasn't restful.

Mamma unlocked the door at the head of the stairs. They must still be living here, Jeanette felt.

"Hello, Anne, Jeanette!" Mamma's voice was so quietly animated. She looked well. Always there was the same aliveness about her. Jeanette kissed her cheek. It was unbelievably soft and fresh. Only around the eyes the skin was like finely wrinkled tissue paper. Those round bright eyes that were so like her own. . . . She hoped she would look like Mamma at seventy-four.

Anne was walking around the room restlessly.

"Why, Mamma, you've left the table still set up!"

"I decided to lend the apartment to Faith Dorsett. She's so tired of that Old Ladies' Home." Mamma still had that way of stating a decision as completely made, as though they were all still children.

"But, Mamma," Anne began.

Mamma went across the hall and knocked at the bedroom door. She never walked like an old lady, always with grace.

"Faith, the children are here."

Who was Faith? The name was vaguely familiar. Jeanette puzzled.

"I'm so glad to have her here," Mamma said happily.

When the door opened an old lady came out, an angular old woman with dark sullen eyes in a wrinkled face. Her thin white hair was curled in a kind of frizz.

"How do you do, Mrs. Dorsett." Anne must remember her then. She must be somebody from Nebraska, of course.

"It's a long time since I taught you china-painting." The woman's voice made complaint by its tone.

"Jeanette, you wouldn't remember Faith. She went back to Nebraska right after the Fair and lived there for a good many years."

"How do you do." Jeanette could feel herself smiling at

her with the smile she had for the women at the clinic, and just as it always did with them it did now with Mrs. Dorsett. It must be like Mamma's smile.

"I remember you, Jeanette. James was always fondest of you. My, I've heard of your wonderful work at the Child Guidance Clinic."

She was rather a pleasant person, really. Wasn't there something, some tragedy about her?

"And, Faith, you invite people over all you want to. And remember, the Art Palace is no distance from here at all." To Mamma, the Field Museum was still the Art Palace at the Fair.

Jeanette could see Anne growing impatient, anxious to be off. She herself had a feeling of giving the day to Mamma. It made the day take on a timeless quality. Going to this Fair with Mamma gave her a feeling of age, and age was incredible for herself; it would evoke too many memories. The Fair, itself, didn't interest her. Mamma had been going out there, though, ever since it had opened.

"Good-by, Faith." Mamma kissed her.

"Julia, you're so good to me! I believe that's why I came back to Chicago."

Suddenly Jeanette remembered. James Dorsett had been shot and brought home on a door; she and Chris had followed the procession home and Mamma had been so cross. What a nine days' scandal it must have been in the town! Jeanette looked at this thin plaintive woman. Her eyes were the only thing about her that might have lived through such a thing.

They followed Mamma downstairs.

"Mamma, when you come back you must move. That flat is so big for you and no elevator!"

"We'll see; I rather think I'll ask Faith to live with me,"

Mamma answered independently. "Wasn't Louise coming down with you?"

"Oh, Louise is going to meet us there. She's far too busy to drive down with us."

There was an injured note in Anne's voice, Jeanette noticed. It was amusing the way Anne couldn't stand Louise's making so much money, particularly now with Joseph's income probably cut down to around ten thousand a year. Yet she boasted of Louise's success to other people. But it was fantastic, Louise's making so much money.

There was the corner by that iron fence where they used to wait for the horse-car.

"I really should be taking Louise with me to the Fair," Jeanette said aloud, trying to get the gently reminiscent note for this expedition. Mamma loved all the undertones of an occasion. This must be perfect for her. If only they would all play up to Mamma this time, Chris too.

Chris was growing so immersed in business, so completely in a rut. How amusing to have Chris a sales-distributor for drug supplies over some tremendous extent of territory through the West. He dropped in to see Mamma more often than they knew, probably. When he came back from Nebraska, he always had news for her of people she used to know. It was funny that Mamma was still interested after all those years. Chris's wife was a nice enough person. Their lives must be a trifle stuffy, though, like their apartment. Mamma was the only link between Chris and his wife and the rest of them.

"I never can get over having the Fair Grounds out here where the lake always was." Mamma was enjoying it, sitting up straight in the back seat, watching everything. "This certainly ought to help Chicago out of the depression. I was down in Field's last week, and it was crowded."

"Just looking, though," Anne said scornfully over her shoulder.

"I remember Max used to say the Fair saved Chicago in '93," Mamma added.

"It's a pity it didn't save some of Papa's fortune," Anne said bitterly. Anne after all these years still dramatized to herself their loss, half enjoying doing it, insisting that she had suffered at the time. It was a little childish of her; Papa's capital had grown in her mind until it was a Fortune, in just that tone of voice, Jeanette thought to herself.

Maybe Mamma hadn't heard Anne. She was watching the traffic intently. Did Mamma remember riding out on the old cable cars? That swelling, triumphant feeling when the conductor called, "World's Fair Grounds, all out!" came back to her even now.

"We might as well park here. It costs more closer down." Anne and her petty economies. They were growing on her.

They walked toward the entrance, Mamma between them. How impossible to make it seem like the other Fair. The people even were different, that girl in slacks, for instance!

"Really, I don't think I'll come out again. It's so commercialized. It doesn't have any of that really international atmosphere that the other Fair had," Anne burst out.

"Anne, you must go through some of those modern houses before you do over your sunroom," Mamma said.

How alert Mamma was. It always surprised her.

"We're to meet Louise and Chris for lunch at the Belgian Village at twelve-thirty," Anne said with that air of getting on with the day. "Here, Mamma, we'll take rickshaws through the Court of Honor and have them drop us at the Belgian Village."

How Anne hated to be overwhelmed by things. Even today she must have a plan, to know the way to do it.

That came from years with Joseph. Joseph always knew head-waiters, "a man on the railroad," "someone in the firm." Anne had led a life of inner tracks. Jeanette stopped herself. Mamma seemed a little quiet. Perhaps she was getting nervous about flying.

How agile Mamma was as she helped her into the rickshaw. Mamma was smiling at the college boy with the lean brown limbs and Cornell on his jersey.

"Don't tip me out," Mamma joked. Already the boy liked Mamma, had seen the gayety in her. Mamma had a distinguished air about her in that close-fitting hat and her black dress. Anne had helped her buy it.

"They've had to renew these flags once already!" her rickshaw boy told her, taking up his duty of explainer. "The weather's hard on them." Jeanette nodded. It gave you a feeling of being in some foreign city, being pulled along under the flags.

It was not being part of this Fair that made it so different from the other Fair. These queer modern buildings meant nothing to her. A sense of nostalgia for the White City of Grecian buildings, so unified, so pure in line, rose in her. This Fair was all confusion of people and colors and angles. . . . Perhaps it was characteristic of the age. . . . It made you feel how long ago the other was. The crowds surging past, the noise, the rickshaw boy shouting, "Rickshaw, Rickshaw, make way . . . rickshaw," merged into a kind of impersonal wall. Jeanette Stone settled back in her seat.

Should she give up the directorship of the clinic; could she give up being in public life? Would she ever be happy out of Chicago? Being the wife of a professor in Chicago was one thing, but to be the wife of a college professor in a small North Dakota town . . .

Still, it was an opportunity for Harrison. He would be

head of the department there. And perhaps Harrison might be a little tired of having a wife who was so prominent in civic affairs: Mrs. Jeanette Stone, Director of the Child Guidance Clinic, author of important contributions to . . . member of the Hoover committee . . . Harrison would never urge her.

"It's for you to decide, Jeanette." And then afterwards, very quietly, "You could help me so much with the book." His book that had interested her in him in the first place, years ago. It was still in the making. It was brilliant, accurate, unhurried. Harrison had seemed so unusual to her after the many slap-dash sociologists she knew who were always rushing into print.

· They had been married suddenly, after a symphony concert, before tea. She loved the way Harrison did things. They had found an apartment high up above the city looking over the lake, a place to come to week-ends. She had gone on with her work in the clinic as usual, keeping her old apartment there.

The year of his sabbatical leave she had had a leave of absence from the clinic. Oh, she had always managed things very well. She had known such quiet, such contentment, living simply out of Paris, working with Harrison, waiting for her baby to be born. Then the nightmare of birth and death on Christmas Eve, lying in the silence out of reach even of Harrison, watching the black gowns of the sisters passing by in the hall, those chimes to prayer somewhere in the hospital, feeling only coldness and injustice around her, knowing herself a woman who should have children denied them. She had had no intention of returning to the clinic, but some instinctive caution had made her ask for a leave of absence; and she had been glad to go back after all.

They had come back from that cold spring in the south

of France, and she had taken up her work again. No one knew what had happened except Mamma. She had been sorry she told Mamma; her trying to comfort, her affection, irritated her. Mamma had had four children. Only Harrison understood completely.

"Jeanette, the Hall of Science is lovely from here." Mamma's rickshaw came alongside.

Jeanette nodded. Mamma was enjoying it. Didn't these buildings and crowds confuse her, make her feel old? What was Mamma thinking?

"Jeanette, this boy is from Omaha, Nebraska. He knows Halstead."

"Oh, yes, I've been up there to play on their golf course. They've got a keen one." The boy was pulling the rickshaw backward, talking to Mamma. Mamma was always making friends.

Mamma looked a little foreign today. Her face had an old-world look from the side. How really charming she was!

Anne came up beside them. Anne was paying the boys, tipping them, Jeanette judged, from the broad smile on their faces. Anne liked doing things magnificently. She had gotten that from Joseph; no, perhaps it was from Papa.

Joseph had given Anne security at the time when she needed it. Perhaps that was how she had come to marry so young. Joseph had a big open-handed way about him, some quality of the old West like Papa had had. But he was an odd one for Anne to marry. Anne was so much more sensitive. But Papa; how had Mamma come to marry Papa? Papa had adored Mamma, of course.

"Even these foreign villages are commercialized. Jeanette, do you remember the Bedouin Village?" Anne asked, no need to add "at our Fair."

"Chris and Louise were going to meet us outside here, weren't they?" Mamma asked.

"Yes, but let's not wait; let's go on inside. I'll leave word here."

"Will the steps be too much for you, Mamma? Take them slowly." Anne walked up them more heavily than Mamma.

"This is nice," Mamma said with obvious pleasure in the costumes, the twisting steps, the Cathedral wall. It was well done, rather.

"Mamma, do you still want to fly with Therese?" Anne asked. "Therese didn't just talk you into it?"

"Indeed not! I wouldn't miss it. . . . Of course I hate to be away from the Fair all summer."

"Oh, Mamma, it isn't like our Fair; and it's hot and crowded here. It'll do you worlds of good to be away, and you'll see Colton at Stanford, and think how you'll enjoy visiting that Mrs. O'Connor in Pasadena."

"Yes, I do want to see Nell. She must be lonely without Regan," Mamma said thoughtfully.

Jeanette wondered if Mamma were lonely without Papa. Of course in those last years he was so dependent.

"Don't forget to wire Colton that I'm flying." Mamma's eyes sparkled like a girl's.

"We won't. I'll go out and look for Chris and Louise; maybe that boy at the entrance didn't tell them we're inside," Jeanette said.

"Mamma"—even to Anne Foley who had so nice an ear for oddities, the name didn't sound incongruous on her lips—"I'm worried about Therese. She's going to sing with the Chicago Symphony this year, you know, and she has all kinds of invitations, but she's thirty. And what is there ahead of her? She'd be better off married if it were the right person."

Julia Hauser watched the heads of the village dancers bobbing up and down above the low wall at the top of the stairs. Her mind went back to that time in old Vienna with Anne and that young Signor Ricci. . . .

"Clark Ashton, you know, the Forbes-Ashtons, is mad about her, but she doesn't seem to care anything about him."

It was hard to see in this distinguished gray-haired woman across the table from her anything of the Anne who had been so shy that night at dinner with that young Italian. He was the one who gave her a book of poetry. . . . There was a poem in it. . . . But Anne was a fine-looking woman. Julia looked at her proudly.

"I wouldn't worry, Anne; let her enjoy her fame. Those things work out; I remember how I used to worry about you girls."

Anne laid one white glove exactly on top of the other. Then she flung her head back dramatically. "Mamma, Joe has grown so irascible lately. You know business isn't picking up very fast; I don't know, sometimes, I feel that we're so far apart nothing could ever pull us together. If we were younger, there might be a solution of course; at our ages there's nothing for it but to go on. . . ."

Julia watched her. After all, it wasn't hard to see the old Anne, always making herself unhappy, always acting a little. Of course Joseph didn't understand her. . . .

"I know, Anne, but Joseph is so fond of you. I don't believe he could get along without you. Papa was like that, too."

"They weren't there," Jeanette announced. "Let's order lunch. You have to be at the flying-field at quarter of three, don't you, Mamma?"

How calm Mamma was about flying.

A waiter came up to them with a wire. "Mrs. Hauser?"

"Yes," Julia said quietly. "Chris can't get here. He'll meet us at the flying-field. He's been detained by some business."

"Business comes first with Chris, always," Jeanette said and then stopped.

"Yes, he's a good deal like his father that way," Julia said. "Faith tells me people think the world of him in Halstead. When he goes through there he usually stops a day or two." Mamma seemed pleased, or was it amused, Jeanette couldn't quite tell.

"Joe says in a business way Chris is considered pretty highly," Anne said. "Joe thinks he must have a nice block of stock in the business that he isn't telling anyone about."

"I've often wondered how things would have worked out if he'd gone to England with that Mr.— What was his name, Anne? I wanted him to go so much."

Jeanette looked at Mamma. She had probably had plans for all of them. Had any of them turned out the way she would have them, Jeanette wondered.

A little silence grew between them. Jeanette could feel them each thinking back, remembering.

Anne pushed back her chair just as their orders came. "I'm going to look for Louise again."

"Louise is a busy person," Julia said. "I'm proud of the success she's made, only I always hate to think of her giving up that lovely home in Germantown. Colton has to go to her hotel instead of having a home when he comes back from school."

"But he's away at school most of the time, and a house would be so lonely," Jeanette said.

"Oh, yes," Julia agreed, "but a woman's home means so much to her, more than she knows sometimes."

"Mamma, Harrison wants to take a position as head of the Sociology Department in a town in North Dakota, a small college, you know. Of course he won't do it unless I'm willing to go. It would mean giving up a good deal. Mamma, do you think I'd go crazy in a town way off out there? You hated it in Nebraska, didn't you?"

"Yes," Julia answered, "I hated it—all that flat country with cornfields coming way up to the town, and people thinking of nothing but getting ahead. . . ." Julia clasped her hands in a gesture of intensity. "Even that year after the Fair I was never sorry we'd left Halstead, but it would be different now, of course. People in small towns aren't the same. Distances don't matter so much. And you've already lived the other kind of life. If it matters to Harrison, I'd—" She broke off, then she said, "Some things you can't make up to your husband, Jeanette, ever."

"Really, Louise does try me!" Anne said, coming back. "Now imagine not getting here!"

"Of course she doesn't feel the same way we do about the Fair; she probably doesn't even remember how I dragged her all over." Jeanette felt suddenly tolerant.

"Well, the Fair doesn't mean much to the rest of us, but this is an occasion for Mamma."

Anne was so tactless, putting everything into words. Jeanette drank her coffee silently.

"I wish now I'd let Joe come. I told him that we wanted to be alone with Mamma."

Jeanette thought of Harrison listening to the talk as he always did, keenly interested, a little amused, a little baffled when faced by the whole family. "You baffle me when you're together, Jeanette," he had said the last time; "you seem so different from the rest of them, and yet when you're together I see how alike you all are." She had been nettled over the remark at first. She never thought of herself as like anyone but Mamma.

"Joe wouldn't make very good company, anyway. He's

338

so gloomy over things. And, really, I don't see what we're coming to." Anne was talking again. She flung out her hands in a hopeless gesture. She sounded like any woman talking from what she had heard her husband say, but Anne did keep up, even if she read *Time* in the bathtub, the *Wallstreet Journal* just before bed, and the *Tribune* while she was having her hair done. That was a habit they had from Mamma, that interest in affairs.

"Roosevelt is growing more high-handed every day," Anne went on.

"I remember how drastic Cleveland was that year after the Fair. Do you remember the Pullman strike, girls? Why, Chicago was under martial law. Papa used to read aloud from the paper and get so excited I thought you children would have nightmares when you went to bed."

Jeanette remembered: the yellow light of the gas lamp on the table in the sitting-room that made a tiny sound as it burned, the feeling that tremendous things were going to happen and they would all be part of them.

"Even then I used to be glad we were here in Chicago," Julia said.

"For Therese, everything is excitement all the time. She didn't come home until four this morning. Now she's flying to California this afternoon. She said, 'Oh, I can sleep in the plane.'" Anne smiled with just a touch of pride. "If we ride back to the entrance now we can just make it easily."

"I wish I could wait to see the Fair light up again from that star," Julia said. "It's almost as lovely as the World's Fair was at night."

"I must try to get out here some evening," Anne said. "I don't know, living right here you keep putting it off; there's always something more interesting to do."

They were in the car again, threading through the traffic out towards the flying-field.

"I hate to leave without seeing Louise. You tell her, girls."

"She ought to have enough sense to come on down to the field. She knows when you leave," Anne said disgustedly.

"Look at the lake," Mamma interrupted. "Do you remember how it used to look through the peristyle?"

"The lake was lovely when we were having breakfast this morning out on our porch. Oh, Mamma, I meant to have you come out before you left, to see the tulips. They're wonderful this year. Joe thinks I ought to exhibit some in the flower show."

"You know it seems foolish to leave just now," Julia began wistfully.

"Now, Mamma, the city is no place for you in summer, and you haven't had a good trip since Papa died—that's fifteen years ago this spring." Anne insisted.

"I know, but the Fair . . ."

"But, Mamma, you've seen the Fair."

Were they pushing Mamma off because their own lives were so full just now, when she really didn't want to go? Jeanette wondered. It was too late now; all the arrangements were made. It had been Mamma's own idea to fly with Therese. When she came back next fall, they'd see more of Mamma. . . . But if she and Harrison were out in North Dakota—Jeanette stopped short in her own mind. Still, maybe Mamma would enjoy visiting them there.

"Are you scared, Mamma?" she leaned over to ask gently.

"No." Julia shook her head, smiling stoutly. "There's Therese!"

Nobody could help seeing Therese, surrounded by luggage and flowers, a young man with her, another young man there with a pad of paper, probably a reporter. Therese, herself, slim to the point of emaciation, vividly dark, sleek with the bright round eyes that gave that air of charming innocence to her sophisticated young face. Her clothes . . .

"Grandma!" She came halfway across the station with her arms out. Jeanette watched.

"Hello, Anne, Jeanette; you know Clark Ashton?" This was always the way; Jeanette thought, so casual and artificial, but later when you were with her a bit it only seemed natural that Therese was just as she was.

"You didn't let me down, Grandma! Oh, this is Mr. Hodges; Mr. Hodges, this is Mrs. Julia Hauser, my grandmother. Darling, we're going out and have our picture taken by the plane. The Sunday rotogravure wants it; you don't mind, do you; it's good publicity."

She would clip the picture and send it to Mamma; Jeanette started to follow with Anne.

"Oh, Chris, good; you got here!" When she first saw him it was always a little shock to her. He had grown so heavy; there was nothing distinguished-looking about him, not even the air of joviality Papa always had.

"Say, Jeanette, I don't like this business of Mamma's going in a plane." He looked troubled.

"But she wants to do it, Chris." Maybe they shouldn't have let her do it. Jeanette was suddenly unsure.

It was windy out on the field. There was a plane just landing from the East. Mamma looked so small, fragile, standing with Therese by the plane. She was smiling.

"See, Chris, she's excited about it."

"Where's Louise?"

"I don't know. She's so bound up with her own affairs. . . ."

"Good-by, Mamma," they were all shouting to her at once.

"Good-by, dear, you keep an eye on Therese!"

"Mamma; you're braver than I would be," Chris said. "The luggage is in; there you go!"

"Good-by, you landlubbers, don't you envy us?" Therese grinned down at them. There was a glitter about her, it seemed to Jeanette, of youth and success and an air of competence. She looked just a little like Mamma, standing there. Anne was throwing kisses. Anne did adore her. She was too much wrapped up in her. Why couldn't she remember how free Mamma had always left them? What was Mamma thinking? She looked just as she could remember her so often, serene, quiet, in that way that showed the excitement through.

The plane was flying higher. Surely it was safe. People took them every day, and Mamma had wanted to go!

3

THERESE reached over and patted Julia's shoulder.

"Fun, darling? Aren't you amazed at yourself?"

But Julia Hauser sitting in the third seat from the end of the plane was not amazed. She would never be quite amazed. Her soft brown eyes surveyed the flying world with tranquil expectancy. There was a gentle poise about her head and shoulders borne of her spirit rather than of all the experiences of her seventy-four years.

She sat quietly, sorting things in her mind. There hadn't been time at the Fair. The children, Anne and Jeanette had been so full of their problems. Louise would feel so guilty if she had forgotten to come; she would write her right away and tell her it didn't matter.

The children had thought they were doing such a nice thing to plan this summer in California; she couldn't seem ungrateful, only there was so much that she hadn't seen. They had forgotten how hard she had struggled to get to the last Fair. Of course the children didn't think much of the Fair. People didn't need Fairs now, they had radios and moving-pictures; they weren't isolated, that was it.

Going away now wasn't like leaving that first Fair in Philadelphia when she had felt she was leaving everything, going into a kind of exile. Max had seemed almost like a stranger; everything ahead was unknown. And then they had gotten there and Halstead was worse than she had feared, not even dangerous nor rough, just cramped, already set in a narrow rut. She had tried to live there. But she couldn't have the children grow up there. Max never wanted to leave. Even now she was sorry because of Max; even taking care of him all those years when he was sick hadn't made up to him, but Max hadn't blamed her. Maybe Max understood. . . . They had never talked about it. Everything she had done had been for the children. . . . Or was it for herself, after all, that she had been so eager for the children to get where . . . where they were now?

Julia looked out the window of the plane into the hazy sky. The edges of the land below were blurred a little. She leaned her head back against the chair wearily, contentedly.

It was something to have seen three Fairs. Max had said that time, that going to two Fairs makes you feel old, but it didn't, not even three Fairs did.

"Asleep?" Therese leaned over and touched her arm.

Julia shook her head.

"See, we're crossing the Mississippi; that's Nebraska down there!"

343